My Rose in Paradise

Richard Scott

About the Author

Richard Scott began writing stories at a young age and is the author of multiple award-winning screenplays. He has lived in several states in all regions of the country and finally ended up in California. With a passion for books, films and engaging stories, he enjoys entertaining people and hopes to help his readers escape the pressures of the world, if only for a short time.

Table of Contents

A Chance Meeting

On a beautiful and almost perfect Spring morning in 1991, a gleaming black Cadillac DeVille purred to a stop in front of the sprawling department store that anchored the southern end of the mall. Garrett Sinclair cut the engine and sat for a moment, adjusting his rearview mirror to check the damage. The red wine stain on his silk tie looked even worse in the afternoon sunlight streaming through his windshield. He shook his head; this was becoming a habit he couldn't afford, especially not with the Morrison account meeting in two hours.

The automatic doors whooshed open as he approached, and the cool blast of air conditioning carried the familiar scent of expensive perfume and new fabric. The marble floors gleamed under the department store's crystal chandeliers, and soft jazz played from hidden speakers, creating an atmosphere of refined elegance that usually felt comfortable to him. His eyes swept the store's layout, searching for the men's section, when, near the suit displays, he spotted her.

She was arranging ties on a rotating rack, her movements graceful and deliberate. Even from across the store, something about her drew his attention—maybe it was the way she tilted her head slightly as she worked, or the genuine smile she offered to a passing customer. There was an ease about her that he rarely saw in his world of calculated interactions and strategic conversations. *She* looks... content, he thought, surprised by the observation. *When was the last time I felt that way about anything?*

Garrett found himself walking toward her before he'd consciously decided to do so, his usual business-focused mindset dissolving into something he couldn't quite name. Curiosity, perhaps. Or maybe it was simpler than that—maybe he was just tired of being surrounded by people who wanted something from him.

"Excuse me, Miss." He stopped a respectable distance away, close enough to read the small gold nameplate pinned to her blazer. "…Rose. What a beautiful name."

She looked up, and he was struck by the warmth in her eyes. There was something refreshing about her—no practiced sales smile, just natural friendliness. The kind of genuine expression he'd almost forgotten existed.

"Thank you, Sir. My great-grandmother's name." Her voice had a slight Southern lilt that made even the formal greeting sound welcoming. "So, what can I assist you with today?"

Garrett gestured ruefully at his stained tie. "I seem to need a new tie. I had a mishap at lunch, and it really doesn't go with the suit."

Rose's eyebrows rose as she took in the extent of the damage. "Wow—not sure if the cleaners could get that out or not. Hope it wasn't a gift from your wife."

"No, actually, it was a quick purchase to cover up my last lunch disaster." The admission surprised him; he wasn't usually so forthcoming with strangers. *There's something about her that makes me want to be honest,* he realized. *When did I start measuring every word I say?*

Rose laughed—a genuine, musical sound that made him smile in return. There was no judgment in it, just shared amusement at life's small absurdities. The sound seemed to lighten something in his chest that he hadn't realized was tight.

"It sounds like you are rough on neckties."

"Guilty as charged." He found himself relaxing despite the time pressure. "Do you think you could help me match up a new one to this suit before I go back to work? I have an important meeting this afternoon."

"I'm sure we can come up with something." Rose moved toward the tie display with the confidence of someone who knew her business. "Did you want a solid or a thin stripe perhaps?"

Garrett watched her fingers trace along the silk patterns, noting how she seemed to instinctively know which colors would complement his charcoal suit. Her hands were graceful but practical—no elaborate manicure, just neat, capable fingers that moved with purpose. *She takes pride in her work,* he thought. *There's something attractive about competence.*

"What would you suggest?"

"Well, if I was buying this as a gift, I would probably go with something like this." She held up a deep burgundy tie with a subtle geometric pattern—sophisticated but not flashy.

"That looks nice." He could already picture it at the conference table. "Is this guaranteed to wow everyone at my meeting?"

Rose tilted her head, considering. The gesture was unconsciously charming, and Garrett found himself studying the way the store's lighting caught the auburn highlights in her hair. "Well, I don't know if I can promise that, but it does look nice with your suit."

Something in her modest response emboldened him. Here was someone who didn't oversell, didn't make grand promises she couldn't keep. *How long has it been since someone told me the simple truth?* "Does it wow you?"

A faint blush colored her cheeks, but she maintained eye contact.

Rose felt her heart skip slightly—this wasn't the kind of question customers usually asked. There was something different about this man, something that made her want to answer honestly rather than deflect with professional courtesy. *He seems genuinely interested in what I think,* she realized, not *just what I can do for him.*

"Well, from a strictly professional view, I think you look pretty wow."

The compliment hit him harder than it should have. When was the last time someone had complimented him without wanting something in return? Without an agenda hidden behind the words? "I'll take it." He paused, knowing he was about to cross a line he rarely crossed. "So, do you offer your professional opinions in other areas also?"

Confusion flickered across her features. "I'm not sure what you mean."

"There's a new restaurant open downtown that I really want to try and see how their food is. I hate to eat alone and thought you could possibly give me your 'professional opinion' of the place."

Rose's posture straightened slightly—not defensive, but cautious. She'd been asked out before, but usually by men who seemed to think her friendliness was an invitation. This felt different somehow, but she'd learned to be careful. *He seems sincere,* she thought, *but then again, they usually do at first.* "Well, that is very kind of you, sir, but I don't even know your name. Right now, you are just the guy with the stained necktie."

Her directness charmed him. No games, no coy pretense. Just honest boundaries stated with a smile. "It's Garrett... Sinclair. I'm president of Southtrust Bank downtown in Macon." He felt oddly nervous, like a teenager asking someone to prom. "I don't usually do things like this, but you have the most amazing smile and personality. I would really like to take you to dinner and thank you for rescuing me in my time of need. I'm horrible at matching things up."

"And get my professional opinion of the new place?" There was a teasing note in her voice now. "As you can see, I mainly manage men's accessories. I'm not sure how much of a restaurant critic I am."

"But you do know good food, right?"

"I know what I like."

"So do I." The words came out with more meaning than he'd intended, and he saw her catch it—a flicker of understanding in her eyes that made his pulse quicken.

Rose studied his face for a long moment, weighing her options. *Lucy's always telling me I'm too careful,* she thought. *Maybe it's time to take a chance.* There was something about his nervousness that seemed genuine, something that made her want to trust him despite her usual caution. Besides, it's just dinner. What's the worst thing that could happen?

"Well, you don't seem that boring. Okay. Why not? I get off work at six. I can run home and change..."

"That isn't necessary unless you just want to. You look lovely the way you are."

A genuine smile spread across her face—the first time in months that a compliment had felt completely sincere. "Well, you certainly know how to give compliments. Let me ring this up for you before my boss thinks I'm harassing the customers."

As Rose processed the sale, Garrett watched her efficient movements—the way she carefully folded his stained tie into the shopping bag, the professional smile she maintained even as something more personal flickered in her eyes. When she handed him his credit card, their fingers brushed briefly, and he felt a spark of possibility he hadn't experienced in years. *This is what I've been missing*, he thought. *This feeling of connection with someone real.*

"Thank you for the help with the tie, and I look forward to dinner. See you at six."

"See you then." Rose's smile was warm but professional as other customers began to mill around the department.

Garrett walked toward the exit with a lighter step than he'd had in months, completely missing the red wine stain that had started his afternoon crisis. Behind him, he didn't notice the young woman who'd been watching the entire exchange from behind a nearby rack of dress shirts.

Lucy Butler had worked alongside Rose for over a year, and she'd never seen her friend look quite so flustered after helping a customer. The moment Garrett disappeared through the automatic doors, Lucy practically bounced over to Rose's station.

"So, who was that? He looked like he really had his eyes on you." Lucy's dark eyes sparkled with curiosity as she glanced toward the exit where Garrett's Cadillac was pulling away.

Rose busied herself straightening the tie display, but couldn't hide the slight flush still coloring her cheeks. "That was Garrett Sinclair, president of Southtrust Bank. He asked me out to dinner tonight."

"I hope you said yes." Lucy's voice rose with excitement, causing a nearby customer to glance their way.

"I did. He needed a new tie, and he seemed quite charming." Rose's tone was measured, but Lucy caught the small smile tugging at the corners of her mouth.

"And rich. Girl, he's a banker. You need to hold on to him." Lucy was practically vibrating with vicarious excitement.

Rose shook her head, though she was still smiling. *Lucy always jumps to conclusions*, she thought with affection. *But maybe this time...* "Well, let's see how charming he is at dinner first. Let's not start planning a future yet. Besides, we need to get back to work before we both get fired."

Lucy grabbed Rose's arm as she started to walk away. "Notes! I want detailed notes of your date, and don't you leave anything out!"

"Go back to work. We'll talk tomorrow." Rose laughed and gently extracted herself from Lucy's grip, but there was an anticipation in her step that hadn't been there an hour ago. Six o'clock couldn't come fast enough.

Dining with Mr. Right

Rose pushed through the department store's glass doors just as the black Cadillac DeVille glided to a stop at the curb. The evening air was warm against her skin, carrying the familiar scents of summer in Georgia—magnolia blossoms and the faint hint of barbecue from somewhere nearby. She'd changed into a simple navy dress that she hoped struck the right balance between casual and elegant, though her nerves were making her second-guess everything.

Maybe I should have worn the blue one instead, she thought, smoothing the fabric with suddenly damp palms. *Or maybe I shouldn't have said yes at all.* But even as the doubt crept in, she felt a flutter of excitement. When was the last time she'd been on a real date? When was the last time someone had looked at her the way Garrett had this afternoon—like she was the most fascinating person in the room?

Garrett stepped out of the car with the same confident stride she'd noticed earlier, but now there was something more relaxed about him. He'd changed ties—this time wearing the burgundy one she'd helped him select—and the wine stain crisis seemed like ancient history. The sight of him in the expensive suit, moving with that easy assurance, made her acutely aware of the differences between them. *He belongs to a world I've only seen from the outside,* she realized.

"I was going to come in and get you. Am I late?" His voice carried just a hint of concern, as if keeping her waiting would be an unforgivable offense.

"No. I actually got off a few minutes early." Rose tucked a strand of hair behind her ear, a nervous habit she'd never quite shaken. *He was going to come in and get me like a real gentleman.* The thought warmed her more than it should have.

"Good. It's more time I get to spend with you. Shall we go?"

Garrett moved to the passenger side of the Cadillac and opened the door with old-fashioned courtesy that surprised her. In her experience, most men her age considered such gestures outdated—if they even thought about them at all. *Lucy would die if she could see this*, Rose thought, remembering her friend's excitement about the date.

"You look absolutely beautiful."

Rose felt heat rise in her cheeks. The compliment sounded so natural, so genuine, that it caught her off guard. "Well, you are just full of compliments today, aren't you? Besides, I look about the same as I did when you saw me at lunch, if not a little worse for wear."

"I think you look perfect." The sincerity in his voice made her stomach flutter as she slipped into the leather seat. The car's interior smelled of expensive cologne and new leather, and she ran her fingers along the smooth dashboard while Garrett walked around to the driver's side. *This is definitely not my usual Friday night*, she thought, taking in the luxury surrounding her. Her own car—when it was working—smelled like fast food and had a crack in the windshield she couldn't afford to fix.

The drive through downtown Macon felt like entering a different world. Garrett navigated the streets with easy familiarity, pointing out landmarks and sharing stories about the city's history. Rose found herself relaxing despite her nervousness, drawn in by his obvious affection for their hometown and his genuine interest in her reactions to everything he showed her.

"I drive through this area all the time for work," she said, watching the elegant storefronts pass by, "but I've never really seen it like this."

"Sometimes we need a different perspective to see what's been there all along," Garrett replied, glancing at her with a smile that made her pulse quicken.

The restaurant was everything Rose had imagined when she'd driven past it but never dreamed of entering. Soft jazz music drifted through the dining room, where candlelight flickered across white tablecloths and fresh flower arrangements. Crystal glasses caught the light, and the murmur of conversation created an intimate atmosphere that felt both romantic and intimidating. The maître d' had greeted Garrett by name, leading them to a corner table with a view of the city lights beginning to twinkle in the growing dusk.

This is not new to him, He's a regular here, Rose realized, noting the way the staff moved around him with practiced deference. Of course he is. *This is probably just another Friday night for him.*

Rose smoothed her napkin across her lap and tried not to gawk at the other diners, many of whom looked like they belonged in the society pages of the Macon Telegraph. The women wore jewelry that probably cost more than Rose made in a year, and the men had that polished look that came from generations of privilege. "This certainly seems like a nice place."

"I guess we'll see after they bring us our food." Garrett was studying her face rather than the menu, as if memorizing every detail. The intensity of his attention was both flattering and slightly unnerving.

"I'm honestly not used to eating at elegant places like this much." The admission slipped out before she could stop it, and she immediately felt self-conscious about revealing too much about her circumstances. *Great, Rose. Make it obvious you don't belong here.*

But Garrett's expression didn't change, didn't show any of the judgment she'd half expected. Instead, his eyes softened with something that looked almost like protectiveness. "That's too bad. You deserve only the best and someone to treat you as such."

Rose set down her water glass and met his gaze directly. There was something about the way he said it—with such conviction, such certainty—that made her both grateful and cautious. "You probably need to get to know me better before making a statement such as that."

"Let's get to know each other better then. I want to know everything about you. Where you grew up, your parents, where you went to school, things you love." The intensity in his voice was both thrilling and slightly overwhelming.

Everything? she thought. *That's a lot to ask on a first date.*

"This had better be a long dinner then."

"You and I are both in agreement on that one."

Rose took a sip of wine—something French and expensive that Garrett had ordered without consulting the price—and felt herself beginning to relax. The alcohol warmed her from the inside, and the elegant atmosphere began to feel less intimidating and more magical. *When will I ever get another chance like this?* she asked herself. *Just enjoy it.*

"Well, I grew up in Milledgeville, but after my father passed, my mother and I moved here to Macon."

Something shifted in Garrett's expression, a gentleness replacing his earlier eagerness. She could see him processing the information, filing it away with the care of someone who genuinely wanted to understand her story. "How did he pass?"

"He had a heart attack. It was sudden. He hung on for a few days, but..." The familiar tightness in her chest made her pause. Even after all these years, talking about her father's death felt like pressing on a bruise that never quite healed. *Why did I bring this up?* She wondered. *This is supposed to be a happy evening.*

"I'm sorry to hear that. That had to be hard. How old were you?"

The gentle concern in his voice made her throat tighten with unexpected emotion. Most people, when faced with her loss, either changed the subject quickly or offered meaningless platitudes. Garrett seemed genuinely interested in understanding her experience. "Eleven. It was tough. I loved him very, very much." Rose traced the rim of her wine glass with her finger, gathering herself. "After he passed, we moved to Macon, my mother got a job, and I finished school here. I consider this my home. It's where most of my life has been. I never really had the means to travel or anything, so basically it's been here, just me and my mom."

Just me and my mom. The words sounded so small, so limited, in this elegant restaurant surrounded by people who probably summered in

Europe and wintered in Florida. But Garrett didn't seem to judge her for the simplicity of her life—if anything, he leaned in closer, as if her story was the most important thing he'd ever heard.

"You live at home?"

"No. I have my own place. I like my space. I like to paint." She was grateful for the change of subject, away from the sadness that always accompanied thoughts of her father. The mention of her art brightened her mood—it was one of the few things in her life that was purely hers, purely joyful.

"I'll remember that the next time I want to change the color of my walls."

Rose laughed despite herself, some of the tension leaving her shoulders. "Very funny. I can do that type of painting as well. What about you? Tell me something about yourself. This isn't all about me. Have you ever been married?"

The question seemed to catch Garrett off guard, and for a moment, his polished composure slipped. A shadow crossed his face, and Rose saw something darker flicker in his eyes—pain, perhaps, or anger. "No. I came close once. I tried to give her everything a person could want, but she betrayed me and left me. It was a bad parting of ways."

Betrayed. The word hung in the air between them, loaded with implications. Rose felt a stab of sympathy for him, mixed with curiosity about what had happened. "I'm sorry. She must have been crazy. Who wouldn't want a man to give her his full attention?"

The moment the words left her mouth, she saw something change in Garrett's expression. His eyes fixed on hers with sudden intensity, and Rose felt as if she'd inadvertently revealed something important. A slight smile played at the corners of his mouth, but there was something almost predatory about his focus that made her skin prickle with unease.

"What's wrong?" she asked, suddenly uncomfortable under his stare.

"Nothing. Did you mean that? Would you like that in a man? Someone who devotes himself to you fully?"

The question seemed loaded with more significance than casual dinner conversation warranted. There was a hunger in his voice that made Rose's instincts flare with warning. Full attention and devotion sounded romantic in theory, but something about the way he said it made her think of possession rather than love.

Still, she found herself answering honestly. "Well, I can't speak for all women, but I would personally love it. Most men I meet treat me like an afterthought. They're too wrapped up in their own stuff to pay me much attention."

"I would never treat you as an afterthought, Rose. I would always make sure you were treated like the lady you are."

The promise felt both wonderful and overwhelming. There was something absolute about the way he said it, as if he were making a vow rather than a casual statement. Rose set down her fork and studied his face, trying to read the emotions playing across his features. "You say a lot for such a short acquaintance. You hardly know me, Garrett. I think you'll have to know much more about me to make promises like that."

"I want to know it all. I've never met anyone like you, Rose. I want to know the whole story of who you are."

The intensity of his gaze made her pulse quicken, but something warned her to slow things down. This felt like standing at the edge of a cliff, exhilarated by the view but aware of the drop. *He seems so sure, so certain*, she thought. *But how can anyone be that certain after one afternoon?*

"Well, how about we start with enjoying our dinner and deciding what would be absolutely sinful for dessert? Then we can decide what comes next."

Garrett's smile returned to something more relaxed, more charming. The predatory edge faded, replaced by the warmth that had first drawn her to him. "Anything you say, ma'am. I just want to make you happy."

Rose picked up her wine glass and took another sip, studying him over the rim. The candlelight flickered across his face, highlighting the strong jaw and the eyes that seemed to see everything. He was handsome, successful, attentive, everything she'd dreamed of in a partner. So why did she feel this nagging sense of unease?

"You, sir, seem too good to be true." But even as she said it, she couldn't shake the feeling that there might be more truth to those words than she intended.

Maybe I'm just not used to being treated well, she told herself. *Maybe I'm looking for problems where there aren't any.* But as Garrett reached across the table to touch her hand, his fingers warm and possessive against her skin, Rose couldn't quite silence the small voice in her head that whispered: Be careful.

Mother Knows Best

Rose settled into the familiar comfort of her mother's living room, where afternoon sunlight streamed through sheer curtains and highlighted the collection of family photographs that chronicled their life together. The small apartment was immaculate as always. Eileen Nichols had never lost the habit of keeping a house as if company might arrive at any moment, a holdover from her days as a young wife in Milledgeville.

Eileen emerged from the kitchen carrying two glasses of sweet tea, her movements graceful despite the years of hard work that had left their mark in the lines around her eyes. At fifty-three, she was still an attractive woman, with the same delicate bone structure Rose had inherited, though her auburn hair now showed silver at the temples.

"I haven't seen much of you this week," Eileen said, settling into her favorite armchair and studying her daughter with the keen perception that only mothers possess. "Where have you been hiding? Or shall I ask who you've been hiding out with?"

Rose felt heat rise in her cheeks, a dead giveaway that her mother had hit the mark. "Oh, Mom. I met this wonderful man. He's not like any man I've ever been out with."

Eileen's eyebrows rose with interest, and she leaned forward slightly. "Really? Do tell. Who is this wonderful man?"

"His name is Garrett Sinclair. He's president of Southtrust Bank downtown." Rose could hear the dreamy quality in her own voice and didn't care. "He's handsome and sophisticated and a perfect gentleman."

"A bank president, huh?" Eileen's tone was carefully neutral, but Rose caught the calculating look that crossed her mother's face. "He sounds like he might also be wealthy too."

Rose set down her teacup with more force than necessary. "Well, he is, but the money really doesn't matt—Don't look at me like that." She recognized that expression—the same one her mother had worn when Rose had announced she was dropping out of community college to work full-time. "He's special. He really treats me like a lady, and he listens to me. My day, stuff I do, things that I enjoy. He's actually attentive to me. He makes me feel special."

The defensive edge in Rose's voice made Eileen soften her expression. She'd raised her daughter alone for over a decade, watching her struggle through the awkwardness of adolescence without a father's guidance, seeing her settle for boys who barely deserved her attention. If someone was finally treating Rose the way she deserved to be treated, Eileen wasn't going to discourage it—but she wasn't going to stop being a mother, either.

"Wow. He sounds like a dream. How did you meet this dreamy guy?"

"He came into work one day at lunch and I sold him a tie. We started chatting and he asked me out, and we've been going out all week." Rose's face lit up as she relived the memory. "Every single day, Mom. He takes me to lunch, or dinner, or we go for drives. Yesterday he brought me flowers just because it was Tuesday."

"Every single day?" Eileen's voice carried a note of surprise she couldn't quite hide. "That's... well, that's very attentive of him."

"It is, isn't it?" Rose beamed, missing the subtle concern in her mother's tone. "He says he can't stand to go a day without seeing me. He calls me three or four times a day just to hear my voice."

Eileen felt a small chill run down her spine, but she kept her expression neutral. "Three or four times a day? When does he find time to run a bank?"

"Oh, he's very efficient," Rose said quickly, her defensive instincts kicking in again. "He just... he says I'm always on his mind. He likes to know what I'm doing, how my day is going. It's sweet."

"And what about your days off? Does he give you time to yourself? Time with your friends?"

Rose shifted uncomfortably on the sofa. "Well, Lucy's been so busy with her job at the store, and I... I mean, why would I want time away from him? We're getting to know each other."

"Honey," Eileen said gently, choosing her words carefully, "it's wonderful that he's so taken with you. But healthy relationships need a little breathing room too. You don't want to lose yourself in—"

"I'm not losing myself," Rose interrupted, her voice rising slightly. "I'm finding myself. For the first time in my life, someone sees me as more than just a shop girl. He sees potential in me, Mama. He talks about all the places he wants to take me; the things he wants to show me."

"It sounds like you're very taken with this Mr. Sinclair."

"I am. He's so different. I really do like him." Rose tucked her legs under her on the sofa, settling in like she had as a child when she'd had something important to share. "When I'm with him, I feel like... like I'm the only person in the world who matters to him. He remembers everything I tell him—little things, like how I take my coffee or that I've always dreamed of having a rose garden. And he looks at me like I'm something precious."

"The only person in the world..." Eileen repeated quietly, something in that phrase unsettling her. "What about his friends? His family? Surely, he has other people in his life?"

Rose's brow furrowed slightly. "He... well, he says he's been alone for a long time. He doesn't talk much about his past. He says he wants to focus on our future together."

"Your future together? Rose, sweetheart, you've known him for a week."

"Sometimes you just know, Mama," Rose said, her voice taking on that dreamy quality again. "He says some things don't need time to understand. Some things are just meant to be."

Eileen watched her daughter's animated face and felt the familiar tug between happiness and worry that came with loving someone so deeply. Rose was glowing in a way she hadn't seen since her daughter was very young, but there was something almost fevered about her enthusiasm. The phrases Rose was using—they sounded rehearsed, as if she were repeating someone else's words.

"Well, I'm very happy for you, but just remember not to rush into anything. Give it time. If it's true love, it will just grow deeper with time. If it's not, you'll find out."

"But why wait when something feels so right?" Rose's voice carried a conviction that made Eileen's maternal instincts prickle with concern. "He makes me feel like I'm the most important person in the world. Like I'm perfect just the way I am."

"No one is perfect, honey," Eileen said softly. "And anyone who expects you to be—"

"He doesn't expect me to be perfect," Rose said quickly. "He just... he appreciates me. He notices things. Like how I always tuck my hair behind my right ear when I'm nervous, or how I hum when I'm happy. He says I have the most beautiful smile he's ever seen."

"I can honestly say I've never heard you talk like this about any other guy you've dated."

"That's because he's not like any other guy I've dated. Oh, Mama." Rose's eyes were bright with an almost childlike excitement. "I can't wait for you to meet him. He's already asking about you, wanting to know all about our family. He says family is everything to him."

"Is he close to his own family?"

Rose's expression flickered for just a moment. "He... he lost his parents when he was young. He says that's why he values family so much now. Why he wants to be part of ours."

The way Rose said it made Eileen's chest tighten with unease. "Part of ours? Rose, you've been dating for a week."

"I know how it sounds," Rose said, leaning forward earnestly. "But when you meet him, you'll understand. He's just... he's everything I've been waiting for. He's going to take care of me, Mama. Really take care of me."

"Honey, you don't need someone to take care of you. You're a strong, independent woman—"

"But I want to be taken care of," Rose interrupted, her voice soft but fervent. "I'm tired of being strong all the time. I'm tired of worrying about money, working retail, and wondering if I'll ever amount to anything. With Garrett, I feel like I could be something more."

Eileen reached over and squeezed her daughter's hand, noting how Rose's fingers trembled slightly with nervous energy. "You already are something more, sweetheart. You don't need a man to make you valuable."

"I know that," Rose said, but her voice betrayed uncertainty. "It's just... he makes me feel valuable in a way I've never felt before."

"Well, I can hardly wait to meet this special man who treats my daughter like a lady. When do I get to place my stamp of approval on him?"

"Soon. I want you to meet him soon." Rose's smile was radiant, but something in her eagerness reminded Eileen of the way Rose had talked about her father in the months before his death—as if he were larger than life, as if loving him completely would somehow protect them from disappointment.

"Maybe we could have him over for dinner this weekend?" Rose continued, her words tumbling out in a rush. "I could cook that pot roast you taught me to make. He's always talking about how much he misses home-cooked meals."

"Always talking about it? How many times has this come up?"

"Oh, you know, just... in conversation. He says he's been eating in restaurants for years. He's lonely, Mama. He just needs someone to care for him."

As Rose continued chattering about Garrett's virtues, Eileen sipped her tea and listened with the practiced ear of a woman who had learned that sometimes the most dangerous situations were the ones that felt like fairy tales. Every instinct she'd developed as a single mother was screaming warnings, but she knew pushing too hard would only drive Rose further into this man's arms.

"Rose," she said finally, when her daughter paused for breath, "I want you to promise me something."

"What?"

"Promise me you won't make any big decisions without talking to me first. And promise me you'll keep spending time with your friends, keep some part of your life that's just yours."

Rose's expression clouded slightly. "Mama, you're worrying about nothing. Garrett would never try to keep me from my friends or anything like that. He just wants to make me happy."

"I know, sweetheart. I just... I love you. And when you love someone, you worry. It's what mothers do."

"Well, stop worrying," Rose said, rising from the sofa and smoothing her skirt. "Everything is perfect. For the first time in my life, everything is absolutely perfect."

As Eileen watched her daughter gather her purse and prepare to leave, she felt a chill that had nothing to do with the air conditioning. Perfect was a dangerous word. In her experience, nothing in life was perfect—and the things that seemed perfect usually carried the highest price.

Starting to Fall

Two days later, the evening air was thick with the scent of magnolias and the promise of rain as Garrett's Cadillac pulled up to the curb outside Rose's apartment building. The soft jazz playing on the radio seemed to wrap around them like velvet, and Rose found herself reluctant to break the spell of their perfect evening. They had spent hours at Le Bernardin, the most exclusive restaurant in Macon, where Garrett had ordered wine that cost more than Rose made in a week and spoke knowledgeably about each course as if fine dining were as natural to him as breathing.

Her mother's words from their afternoon visit still echoed faintly in her mind—warnings about rushing, about keeping some part of her life that was just hers—but sitting here beside Garrett, those concerns seemed foolish and small.

"I had a wonderful time tonight," Rose said, turning to face him in the leather seat that still smelled faintly of his cologne—something expensive and masculine that made her feel dizzy in the best possible way.

Garrett's smile was warm and genuine as he reached over to tuck a strand of her hair behind her ear, his fingers lingering against her cheek. "The evening doesn't have to end yet. We could go for a drive, maybe park somewhere, and talk under the stars."

Rose felt her pulse quicken at the suggestion, but her mother's voice echoed in her mind— *don't rush into anything too fast, keep some part of your life that's just yours*. "I should probably get inside. It's getting late, and I have to work tomorrow."

If Garrett was disappointed, he didn't show it. Instead, he lifted her hand to his lips and pressed a soft kiss to her knuckles, a gesture so old-fashioned and romantic that Rose felt her knees go weak. "Of course. I wouldn't want to keep you from your rest. You're far too precious to me."

The word *precious* sent a thrill through her that she tried to suppress. It was still so early, just their fifth date, but the way he looked at her made her feel like she was the center of the universe. No one had ever looked at her that way before—not Jimmy from high school, not any of the boys she'd dated in her early twenties. Garrett saw something in her that she wasn't even sure existed.

"Thank you for dinner," she said, her voice barely above a whisper. "It was incredible."

"You're incredible," he replied, his thumb tracing circles on the back of her hand. "I keep waiting to wake up from this dream. A woman like you, choosing to spend time with someone like me."

Rose laughed softly, the sound musical in the quiet car. "Someone like you? Garrett, you're the most amazing man I've ever met. You're successful, you're handsome, you're kind—"

"I'm also twelve years older than you," he interrupted, his voice carrying a note of vulnerability that made her heart ache. "I've been alone for so long, Rose. I'd almost given up on finding someone who could make me feel alive again."

The raw honesty in his voice made her chest tight with emotion. She could see the loneliness in his eyes, the same loneliness that had haunted her own reflection for years. "Age is just a number," she said firmly. "What matters is how you make me feel."

"And how do I make you feel?" His voice was low, intimate, as if they were the only two people in the world.

Rose looked into his eyes and felt herself falling into their depths. "Like I'm finally exactly where I'm supposed to be."

Garrett's expression intensified, and for a moment she thought he might kiss her. Instead, he brought her hand to his chest, pressing it against his heart. "Do you feel that? It's been beating like this since the moment I saw you in that store. I've never felt anything like this before, Rose. Never."

The declaration should have thrilled her, but something about the fierce intensity in his voice made her stomach flutter with nerves. It was exactly what her mother had been worried about, the way he talked about them as if they were already destined to be together forever. "Garrett..."

"I know it's fast," he said quickly, as if sensing her hesitation. "I know we barely know each other. But some things don't need time to understand. Some things are just... meant to be."

Rose felt caught between the romance of his words and that small voice in her head that sounded suspiciously like her mother's warnings. "I should go in," she said finally, though she made no move to open the car door.

"Of course." Garrett released her hand immediately, but his eyes never left her face. "May I see you tomorrow? I could take you to lunch, or we could go for a drive to the lake. There's a place I'd like to show you."

The eagerness in his voice was endearing, and Rose found herself nodding before she could think better of it. "I'd like that."

"Perfect," he said. "I'll call you first thing in the morning. What time do you wake up?"

"Oh, you don't need to call that early—"

"I want to hear your voice," he said simply. "I want to be the first thing you think about when you wake up, and the last thing you think about before you sleep."

Rose's breath caught at the romantic declaration, but something about it made her feel slightly claustrophobic. "Garrett, you don't have to—"

"I want to," he said, his voice firm with conviction. "I want to give you everything you deserve, Rose. I want to show you what it feels like to be truly cherished."

Before she could respond, he was out of the car and walking around to her door, opening it with the same courtly gesture he'd shown her all evening. As she stepped out onto the sidewalk, he caught her hand again, his fingers intertwining with hers.

"Walk me to the door?" she asked, though she already knew he would. He'd insisted on escorting her to the door after every date, waiting until she was safely inside before leaving.

They walked slowly up the path to her building, their joined hands swinging gently between them. At the door, Garrett turned to face her, his free hand coming up to cup her cheek.

"Thank you for tonight," he said softly. "For every night. You've given me something I thought I'd lost forever."

"What's that?"

"Hope." The words hovered in the air between them for a moment, heavy with meaning. Rose felt her heart swell with emotion, but underneath it was that same flutter of unease she couldn't quite identify. "Garrett..."

"I know," he said, his thumb stroking her cheekbone. "I know this is overwhelming. I know I'm coming on strong. But I can't help it, Rose. You've awakened something in me that I thought was dead."

Before she could respond, he leaned down and kissed her forehead, a gesture so tender and reverent that tears welled up in her eyes. "Sleep well, my darling. Dream of me."

Rose watched him walk back to his car, her heart pounding in her chest. As his taillights disappeared around the corner, she stood in the doorway for a long moment, trying to sort through the tangle of emotions in her chest.

She was falling in love—she could feel it happening, like stepping off a cliff into thin air. But love wasn't supposed to feel this intense this quickly, was it? Love wasn't supposed to make you feel like you were drowning in attention and affection.

Stop it, she told herself firmly as she climbed the stairs to her apartment. *You're overthinking this. He's wonderful. He treats you like a queen. Most women would kill to have a man look at them the way he looks at you.*

But as she closed the door and stepped into her quiet apartment, Rose couldn't shake the feeling that she was walking into something much bigger than she understood. Something that might be too big for her to handle.

Tomorrow, she told herself. She'd think about all of this tomorrow. Tonight, she just wanted to hold onto the fairy tale feeling a little longer, before the questions in her mind grew too loud to ignore.

An Elaborate Gesture

The afternoon shift at the department store had settled into its usual rhythm when Lucy and Rose found themselves at the tie display, straightening merchandise and catching up on the kind of gossip that made retail work bearable. The lunch rush was over, and the store had that peaceful lull that usually lasted until the evening shoppers arrived.

"Okay, so I'll come over tomorrow about two," Lucy said, expertly refolding a silk tie that a customer had left wrinkled. "That should give us plenty of time to make you look like a princess going to the ball. I am so jealous. A good-looking, wealthy man taking you to the event of the year here in Macon. Why don't I ever find the Prince? All that seems to be in my pond are frogs—with warts."

Both women dissolved into laughter, the kind that drew disapproving looks from the more serious shoppers but made the workday infinitely more enjoyable.

"Oh, Lucy. I do feel like a princess when I'm with him." Rose's voice took on that dreamy quality that had become familiar over the past weeks. "It's always like I'm the most important person in the world. I can't believe this is happening to me. I want to make this work. I mean, really work."

Lucy studied her friend's glowing face and felt a mixture of happiness and concern. She'd never seen Rose this invested in a relationship this quickly. "The way you two are going, I'd say it's working out pretty well.

I wouldn't be surprised if you came in to work one day with a ring on your finger."

"We're not quite to that point, but we are getting closer." Rose's cheeks flushed pink, and she busied herself arranging the tie rack with unusual intensity.

"Rose Nichols?"

Both women looked up to see a deliveryman in a brown uniform standing at the edge of their department, clipboard in hand.

"I'm Rose Nichols," Rose said, her voice uncertain.

"Okay, guys. These are for you, ma'am." What happened next would be talked about in the break room for weeks. Three delivery men appeared as if from nowhere, each carrying enormous arrangements of roses in every color imaginable—deep red, soft pink, pristine white, sunny yellow, and delicate peach. The flowers seemed to multiply as they were set down throughout the menswear department, transforming the corporate space into something that belonged in a fairy tale.

"Oh my God!" Lucy's voice was barely a whisper. Rose stood frozen, her hand pressed to her mouth in shock. "I can't believe this!"

Around them, the department store seemed to pause. Other employees had begun to drift over from their stations—Janet from cosmetics, Mike from suits, even Mrs. Henderson from customer service had abandoned her post to witness the spectacle. Customers stopped mid-stride, some staring and trying to capture the moment. Rose felt dozens of eyes on her, and heat crept up her neck.

"Rose, honey, who died?" Janet whispered, though her tone suggested she was more impressed than concerned.

"Nobody died," Lucy said, still staring at the floral display in amazement. "Somebody fell in love."

"There's a card," Lucy managed, though her voice sounded strangled with amazement. "As if we had to guess who these are from. How are you going to get all of these home?"

Rose laughed, a sound caught between joy and overwhelm. The laughter felt a bit forced, even to her own ears. "I hope my best friend will at least help me carry them to my car after work."

"You know I will. What does the card say?"

Rose's fingers trembled slightly as she opened the small envelope attached to the largest arrangement. She was acutely aware of the audience that had gathered, of the way conversations had died down throughout the store. "'Though nothing compares to your beauty, maybe these will bring a smile to your face and compliment my beautiful Rose.'

A collective sigh went up from the small crowd that had gathered. Someone—Rose thought it might have been Janet—actually applauded.

"Wow." Lucy shook her head in disbelief. "Does he have a brother? Cousin? Anything? This guy is truly a catch. 'His beautiful Rose.' Sounds like love to me."

Their moment of romantic reverie was interrupted by the appearance of Mr. Patterson, the store supervisor, whose expression suggested he was less charmed by the floral display than the growing crowd of curious customers and employees. The audience scattered like startled birds, suddenly remembering they had work to do.

"Ms. Nichols, this isn't a flower shop. We can barely even see the checkout counter anymore, and the whole place smells like a perfume factory," he yelled as he threw his arms around, gesturing toward the overwhelming amounts of flowers in the shop.

Rose's face went crimson. "I'm sorry, sir. I had no idea these were arriving. I'll take them to the stockroom."

The other workers giggled, but Mr. Patterson shot them a look, and they continued busying themselves while still remaining within earshot.

Mr. Patterson's gaze shifted to Lucy, who was trying to look invisible behind a particularly large arrangement of pink roses.

"The banker, I would guess?"

"Yes, sir," Lucy replied quietly, keeping her eyes down so that she would not burst into laughter.

Patterson surveyed the sea of flowers that had transformed his orderly department into something resembling a wedding venue. "The way that romance is heading, I'd say there's going to be an opening in menswear before long."

As the supervisor walked away, Rose emerged from behind an arrangement of white roses, her arms full of vases. "Was he mad?"

"No. He was being his normal, cheerful self," Lucy said with heavy sarcasm. "Let me help you with those. I have an idea. We're both off tomorrow, and since I need to help you get ready for the gala anyway, why don't we make it a girls' night? Just us. We'll eat and talk and watch romantic movies, and then I'll already be there to help you get ready. Besides, you need someone to help you unload all of these when you get home."

Rose's face lit up with genuine pleasure. "I think that sounds wonderful. Take these to the stockroom for me. I want to call Garrett right quick and thank him before Attila comes back."

"I've got these." Lucy gathered up several arrangements, shaking her head at the sheer extravagance of the gesture. As she walked toward the stockroom, she noticed how the other employees were still stealing glances at Rose, whispering behind their hands. It was sweet, but Lucy couldn't shake the feeling that it was also a bit much. Who sends that many flowers to someone's workplace?

Rose hurried to the employee break room, where the ancient phone hung on the wall next to motivational posters about customer service. Her hands were still shaking slightly as she dialed the number she'd already memorized. As she waited for him to answer, she found herself thinking about all those stares, all those whispers. Part of her had loved the attention, the way everyone had looked at her like she was the heroine of a romance novel. But another part of her felt exposed, like she was on display in a way that made her slightly uncomfortable.

"Garrett Sinclair, may I help you?"

Even his professional phone voice made her pulse quicken, and all her doubts evaporated. "Yes, you may, sir. The flowers are beautiful... and extravagant. You shouldn't have."

"I'm glad you like them, and it's not too extravagant. Nothing is too good for you, Rose."

The sincerity in his voice made her knees weak. "You treat me just like a princess. I can honestly say no one has ever done that before."

"You are a princess. My princess, and I can't wait to show you off to everyone at the gala."

Something in the possessive way he said "my princess" sent a little thrill through her that she didn't want to examine too closely. *Show her off like a prize.* The thought flitted through her mind and was immediately pushed away by the warmth in his voice.

"You should be careful about spoiling me, Garrett. I might get used to it."

"I want you to get used to it. You should be spoiled, and I want to be the one to spoil you... forever."

The word 'forever' hung in the air for a moment, loaded with more promise than their brief relationship should reasonably carry. Rose felt her breath catch. Forever. It was what every girl dreamed of hearing, wasn't it?

"I'll talk to you tomorrow night. Seven still?"

"Yes, seven. Until tomorrow."

As Rose hung up the phone, she leaned against the break room wall for a moment, trying to process what had just happened. The gesture was incredibly romantic, but it was also overwhelming in its scope. How many dozens of roses had he sent? And to her workplace, where everyone could see them, where her supervisor had to comment on them, where she'd become the center of attention whether she wanted to be or not.

A small voice in the back of her mind whispered that maybe it was a little too much, too soon. That maybe sending flowers to someone's workplace was more about making a statement than making her happy. But then she thought about his voice on the phone, the way he'd called her "my princess," the way he'd said "forever" like he meant it with every fiber of his being.

She pressed her hand to her chest, feeling her heart race. This was what love felt like, wasn't it? This overwhelming, breathless feeling that made everything else seem small and insignificant? Lucy was right, this really did sound like love.

And if that little voice in her head was trying to tell her something else, well, she wasn't ready to listen to it yet.

What she didn't know was that, three blocks away, Garrett was standing at his office window, checking his watch and calculating how long it would take for the flowers to be delivered. He'd spent his lunch hour at three different florists, buying out their entire stock of roses because he couldn't decide which color would make Rose happiest. In the end, he'd decided she deserved them all.

But it wasn't just about making her happy. He'd wanted everyone at that store to see how much he cared about her, wanted them to know that Rose Nichols belonged to someone who could give her everything she'd ever dreamed of. He'd wanted to unequivocally mark his territory, though he wouldn't have put it in such crude terms.

The word 'forever' had slipped out before he could stop it, but as he replayed the conversation in his mind, he realized he meant it completely. Rose was different from all the others. She was special. She was his, and he was going to make sure she knew it. He'd make sure everyone knew it.

Past Memories

The break room at Southtrust Bank was a study in corporate functionality—fluorescent lights humming overhead, a coffee maker that had seen better days, and motivational posters that no one really read anymore. Garrett pushed through the door, loosening his tie slightly, when he nearly collided with Jack Morrison, who was refilling his coffee mug.

Jack was one of the few people at the bank who remembered Garrett from before his promotion to president, back when they were both junior loan officers trying to prove themselves. At thirty-eight, Jack had the easy confidence of someone who worked out religiously and never seemed to doubt himself—qualities that had made him both a successful banker and Garrett's closest friend.

"Mr. Sinclair, will we all be seeing you at the company gala next weekend?" Jack's tone was formally professional, but there was a hint of amusement in his eyes.

"Jack, you don't have to call me Mr. Sinclair in the break room." Garrett moved to the coffee maker, grateful for something to occupy his hands.

"I do work for you, and you are my supervisor." Jack's grin widened as he leaned against the counter.

"You're also my best friend."

"So, as your best friend, am I going to see you at the company gala, and are you going to finally let us all see this mystery woman you're so smitten with?" Jack took a sip of his coffee and studied Garrett's face. "You've been like a ghost around here lately. Always rushing off somewhere, always with that look."

"What look?"

"The look of a man who's got it bad."

Garrett felt heat rise in his neck. "First, I'm the bank president, so it would be rude not to attend our company event of the year. And second, yes. I plan to ask Rose to let me escort her to the event."

"Rose," Jack repeated the name thoughtfully. "She must be pretty special. You've been out with her several times lately. I've hardly seen you at the health club. That is, unless you're getting your workouts in some other way."

The casual innuendo hit Garrett like a physical blow. His coffee mug clattered against the counter as he set it down hard. "NO! It's not like that! Rose is special. She's a lady. She's not some roll in the hay!"

Jack's eyebrows shot up at the vehemence in Garrett's voice. The reaction was so swift, so disproportionate, that Jack felt his stomach drop. He'd seen this before—this protective fury that seemed to come from nowhere. "Relax, buddy. I was just kidding."

"Don't joke around like that. Not about Rose." Garrett's hands were clenched at his sides, his jaw tight with an anger that seemed disproportionate to Jack's harmless teasing.

Jack studied his friend's face with growing concern. In all the years he'd known Garrett, he'd rarely seen him lose his composure so completely over something so trivial. But it wasn't trivial to Garrett, was it? Nothing about this woman was trivial to him. "Geez. I didn't realize just how caught up in this lady you really were. You seem like you might be falling for her."

The observation seemed to deflate Garrett's anger, replacing it with something that looked almost vulnerable. "She's special, Jack. She's someone I really want to make things work with. She's beautiful and exciting, and I love every moment I'm with her. I am falling for her." There was something in Garrett's tone—an intensity that made Jack's chest tighten with recognition. The way his friend's eyes had gone distant, almost dreamy, while his voice took on that fevered quality. Jack had heard this before, had watched Garrett spiral into something that wasn't quite love but wasn't quite sane either.

"I haven't heard you talk like this in quite some time. Not since—"

"Don't!" Garrett's voice cracked like a whip. "Do not even compare the two. This is not at all the same. It's not."

Jack held up his hands in a placating gesture. The last thing he wanted was to trigger memories of that dark period in Garrett's life, when his friend had nearly lost everything because he couldn't understand the difference between love and obsession. "Well, I can honestly say I'm glad to hear that. I wouldn't want to see a repeat of those times, and I know you wouldn't want that either."

"This is different. Okay? It is. I don't want to talk about 'her' anymore, ever. Let's drop it." Garrett's voice was strained, as if he were forcing the words through gritted teeth.

"Of course, man. You know I have your back. I'm here for you in whatever." Jack's voice was gentle now, the way it had been during those long nights when everything had fallen apart. But even as he offered support, Jack was studying his friend's face, cataloging the signs he'd missed before.

The defensive anger. The immediate denial. The refusal to even acknowledge that there might be similarities. And underneath it all, that same obsessive gleam in Garrett's eyes that Jack remembered too well.

"I know. Just be happy for me."

"I am. I really am." But even as Jack said the words, he watched his friend's retreating figure with growing unease.

After Garrett left, Jack remained in the break room, staring at the door and remembering another time when Garrett had spoken about a woman with that same fevered intensity. The similarities were undeniable now that Jack was looking for them: the way Garrett had been disappearing from work early, declining invitations, and becoming increasingly isolated except for his time with this Rose.

But there were differences too, and they worried Jack more than the similarities. Seven years ago, Garrett had at least been willing to talk about his feelings, to share details about the relationship. This time, he was secretive, protective in a way that suggested he knew his behavior wouldn't stand up to scrutiny.

Jack picked up his coffee mug with hands that weren't quite steady. He'd promised himself he'd never let Garrett go down that path again, but watching his friend's reaction just now—the explosive anger, the defensive denials, the refusal to even acknowledge the pattern—Jack couldn't shake the feeling that history might be preparing to repeat itself.

Only this time, Garrett was older, more established, more capable of controlling his environment. This time, he had resources and influence that he hadn't possessed before. And this time, he seemed to be going into it with his eyes wide open, as if he'd learned from his mistakes but drawn all the wrong lessons.

Jack thought about the woman—Rose—who had no idea what kind of storm she was walking into. He thought about Garrett's explosive reaction to even the mildest teasing about her. He thought about the way his friend's voice had gone soft and possessive when he'd said her name.

This time, though, he was going to pay closer attention. This time, he wasn't going to let things go as far as they had before.

Even if it meant losing his best friend in the process.

A Night to Remember

The soft glow of vanity lights cast a warm amber hue across Rose's small apartment bedroom, transforming the modest space into something that felt almost magical. Lucy stood behind her best friend, hands resting gently on Rose's shoulders as they both gazed into the mirror's reflection. The evening gown—a deep sapphire blue that complemented Rose's eyes—seemed to shimmer with each breath she took.

"You look absolutely gorgeous!" Lucy's voice carried that mixture of pride and wonder that only a true friend could possess, as if she were witnessing something miraculous unfold before her eyes.

Rose's fingers trembled slightly as she adjusted a strand of hair that had escaped Lucy's careful styling. "Thanks, but it was with the help of my best friend. Thanks for everything." Her voice was soft, almost reverent, as if speaking too loudly might break whatever spell had transformed her from the everyday Rose into this vision of elegance.

Lucy's smile faltered for just a moment, a shadow passing across her features like a cloud drifting over sunlight. "I had a blast! I needed a girls' night. We haven't had one in quite a while. I've missed them." She paused, her hands sliding away from Rose's shoulders as she moved toward the window. "It kind of makes me sad though."

"Sad? Why?" Rose turned in her chair, the silk of her gown whispering against itself with the movement. The concern in her voice was immediate and genuine—Lucy had been her anchor through so many storms, and the thought of her friend being unhappy was almost unbearable.

Lucy's back was turned now, her silhouette framed against the curtained window. When she spoke, her words carried the weight of inevitable change, of seasons shifting and friendships transforming. "Well, the way this romance is heading, I feel like you're going to be Mrs. Garrett Sinclair before long."

The words came floating into the air between them like a bridge—connecting the present moment to an uncertain but glittering future. Rose felt her heart flutter, not just at the possibility Lucy had voiced, but at the way saying it aloud made it feel suddenly, thrillingly real.

"Do you really? Oh, Lucy, that would be like a dream come true." Rose's voice grew stronger, infused with a happiness so pure it seemed to light up the room. "He is the most wonderful man and treats me like I'm the most important thing in his entire life. Nobody—and I mean nobody—has ever made me feel like that. It truly is a fairytale".

Lucy turned back from the window, and despite the melancholy that had touched her moments before, her smile was genuine. "As much as I would miss you, I would be happy for you. Garrett really is a great catch. I'm just surprised nobody has swept him up before now."

A flicker of something—protective instinct, perhaps, or simply the desire to understand the man who had so completely captured her heart—crossed Rose's features. "Well, there was the one woman he loved. He doesn't like to talk about her much, but I think she hurt him so badly that it's taken him time to put himself out there again."

Lucy walked back to the window, her movement restless, almost prowling. She pushed aside the sheer curtain with one finger, peering down at the street below. "What was her problem, I wonder. Who couldn't want a man who makes her the center of the universe, showers her with flowers and gifts, who's good-looking, wealthy, and puts her needs first? I guess her loss was your gain."

Rose stood from the vanity chair, the full skirt of her gown settling around her like petals falling into place. "I want to make him happy too. I want him to know that I really appreciate having someone who makes me feel special, and it's not about the money. It's him."

The sincerity in her voice was absolute, the kind of truth that could only come from someone who had known what it felt like to be overlooked, undervalued, invisible. Garrett hadn't just given her gifts and attention—he had given her worth.

Lucy's posture suddenly changed, her spine straightening as she pressed closer to the window. "Well, you have your chance. A sparkling clean black Cadillac just pulled up. I guess it's time for Cinderella to go to the ball."

The doorbell's chime seemed to reverberate through both women, though for entirely different reasons. For Rose, it was the herald of magic about to begin. For Lucy, it was the sound of change arriving at their door, dressed in an expensive suit and carrying promises she wasn't sure she was ready for her best friend to accept.

Lucy moved through the small apartment with familiar ease, her hand already reaching for the door handle as Rose disappeared back into the bedroom for one final check of her appearance. When the door swung open, Garrett Sinclair stood framed in the hallway light like a figure from a romance novel—tall, impeccably dressed, holding himself with that particular combination of confidence and nervous anticipation that marked a man deeply in love.

"Hi Lucy. I didn't know you would be here. Is Rose ready?"

His voice carried that warm politeness that Lucy had come to associate with him—genuinely kind, but always with an undertone that suggested his real attention was focused elsewhere, waiting for Rose to appear.

"She is, and I think you're going to have the most beautiful date there tonight." Lucy stepped aside, raising her voice just enough to carry through the apartment. "Rose! Garrett's here."

The moments that followed seemed to unfold in slow motion, as if the universe itself wanted to savor what was about to happen. Rose emerged from the bedroom, and Lucy watched Garrett's face transform. It wasn't just attraction or appreciation—it was something deeper, more profound. His eyes seemed to actually glow, as if Rose's presence had lit something inside him that couldn't be contained.

"I have never seen anyone look more beautiful."

His words were quiet, almost reverent, but they filled the small space with such warmth that Lucy felt like an intruder witnessing something sacred. From behind his back, Garrett produced a single red rose—perfect, just beginning to open, its petals the same deep red as blood or wine or the kind of love that changes everything.

Rose moved toward him with unconscious grace, her gown flowing around her like water made of starlight. "Thank you. It's beautiful."

Garrett's smile was soft, his eyes never leaving her face. "Yes, she is."

Lucy felt her throat tighten with an emotion she couldn't quite name—happiness for her friend, certainly, but also something that felt suspiciously like grief. "You two look fantastic. I know you're going to have a blast."

Rose turned back toward her, and Lucy saw in her friend's face the kind of radiant joy that poets spent lifetimes trying to capture in words. "Thanks for your help with everything."

"What are best friends for?" Lucy managed, her voice steady despite the tightness in her chest. She leaned forward to press a gentle kiss to Rose's cheek, breathing in the scent of the expensive perfume they had chosen together—something floral and sophisticated that seemed to transform Rose into someone from a different world entirely.

Garrett offered Rose his arm with old-fashioned gallantry, and Lucy watched as her best friend was transformed once again—not just by the dress or the makeup or the setting, but by the way Garrett looked at her, as if she were the most precious thing in existence.

As they moved toward the door, Garrett lifted his free hand in a polite wave. "Goodbye, Lucy."

Lucy stood in her doorway, watching them walk toward the elevator, and called after them with forced lightness, "Don't do anything I wouldn't do!"

The words were meant to be playful, the kind of teasing farewell friends had been exchanging for generations. But as the elevator doors closed and took Rose away into her magical evening, Lucy couldn't shake the feeling that she had just said goodbye for more than just a night—she had said goodbye to the way things used to be, when it was just the two of them against the world.

***

The grand ballroom of the Macon Country Club had been transformed into something straight out of a dream. Crystal chandeliers cast dancing shadows across marble floors polished to mirror perfection, while towering arrangements of white roses and baby's breath stood sentinel at every corner. The soft murmur of conversation mixed with the gentle strains of a string quartet, creating an atmosphere of refined elegance that spoke of old money and older traditions.

When Garrett and Rose appeared at the top of the sweeping staircase, it was as if someone had dimmed the lights on everyone else in the room. Conversations faltered mid-sentence as heads turned toward them, drawn by something magnetic about the couple descending the stairs. Rose's sapphire gown caught the light with each step, but it was the way Garrett looked at her—as if she were the only person in the world who mattered—that truly captured attention.

Garrett's hand rested protectively on Rose's elbow as he guided her through the crowd, his chest swelling with obvious pride. Rose felt the weight of every gaze, but instead of making her nervous, it filled her with a strange confidence. She was Cinderella at the ball, and this was her moment.

"Well, at long last, we get to meet this beautiful woman." A man with an easy smile and laugh lines around his eyes approached them, extending his hand toward Rose. "I wasn't sure you actually existed since Garrett has been keeping you all to himself. Hi, I'm Jack."

Rose accepted his handshake, immediately charmed by his warm, genuine manner. "Hello, Jack. Very nice to meet you."

Garrett's expression softened as he looked at his friend, the tension in his shoulders easing slightly. "The one thing we can always count on is Jack's witty personality."

"Nice to know there's something constant in this uncertain world," Jack replied with a theatrical sigh that made Rose smile despite herself.

"From what I hear, you're a good friend to Garrett and very good at your job," Rose said, and she watched Jack's face light up with pleasure at the compliment.

Garrett groaned dramatically. "Don't tell him that. You'll make his head swell even bigger than it already is."

Jack pressed a hand to his chest in mock offense. "That's okay. I think I have a little room left in my hat for my head to swell."

Their shared laughter felt easy and natural, and Rose found herself relaxing further into the evening. This was what she had hoped for—acceptance, warmth, the feeling of belonging in Garrett's world.

"How about I get you some wine, Rose?" Jack offered, already scanning the room for a server.

"Thank you, Jack. I would love that."

"Anything for you, Garrett?"

Garrett shook his head, his arm tightening almost imperceptibly around Rose's waist. "No thanks. I need to keep my wits about me tonight."

Jack raised an eyebrow at the comment but said nothing more than, "Okay. I'll be back in a minute with your wine, Rose... and see if you can get him to loosen up a little."

As Jack disappeared into the crowd, Garrett began what felt like a royal procession around the ballroom. He introduced Rose to colleagues, clients, and business associates with the pride of a man showing off a priceless work of art. His hand never left her back, his attention never wavered from her comfort and happiness. Rose found herself charmed by his colleagues and impressed by the obvious respect they held for Garrett.

But as the evening progressed, Garrett was inevitably drawn into a heated discussion about quarterly projections with several board members. Rose assured him she would be fine mingling on her own, though she could see the reluctance in his eyes as he released her hand.

She had been chatting with a group of wives about the upcoming charity auction when a man approached her with confident strides. He was of average height with graying temples and the kind of smile that suggested he was used to getting what he wanted.

"Hi. I don't believe we've met. I'm Daniel Lockhardt. And you are?"

"Rose Nichols," she replied politely, accepting his offered handshake.

"What department are you in? I don't know how I could have missed someone as beautiful as you around. Are you in a branch office?"

Rose felt a flutter of uncomfortable awareness at the way his eyes lingered on her. "Well, actually, I'm here with Garrett. We're dating."

Daniel's smile widened, but something in his expression shifted—became more calculating, perhaps more dangerous. "Well, wouldn't you know it. He has the top position in the bank, and now he shows us he has the most attractive lady friend. So sad."

"Why is that sad? Shouldn't you be happy for him?" Rose asked, genuinely puzzled by his response.

"I guess I should be, but that only means my heart is broken because I can't have you for myself."

The words were delivered with practiced charm, but Rose could hear the underlying presumption in them. Still, she laughed politely—the kind of laugh women had been perfecting for generations to deflect unwanted attention without causing a scene.

What Rose didn't notice was the way conversations across the room had begun to fade as people became aware of a sudden shift in the atmosphere. Garrett had frozen midsentence in his discussion of market projections, his attention laser-focused on the scene unfolding near the bar. His colleague continued talking, but Garrett heard nothing except the sound of Rose's polite laughter mixing with Daniel's more aggressive one.

When Daniel placed his hand on Rose's shoulder—a gesture that lasted perhaps three seconds—something primal and possessive ignited in Garrett's chest. The rational part of his mind recognized that Rose was simply being polite, that this was nothing more than cocktail party small talk. But the rational part was quickly drowned out by a roaring in his ears that sounded suspiciously like the word "mine."

Garrett moved through the crowd like a shark cutting through water, his usual social grace abandoned in favor of direct, purposeful movement. People stepped aside without quite knowing why, responding to something dangerous in his expression that they couldn't name but instinctively recognized.

Jack, who had been watching the interaction with growing concern, began moving toward the same destination from across the room.

"Rose." Garrett's voice cut through the ambient noise with surgical precision. "I want to introduce you to some people you need to meet. Let's go."

The words were polite enough, but the undertone was unmistakably territorial. Rose looked up, surprised by the sudden intensity in Garrett's voice and the rigid set of his shoulders.

Daniel, either oblivious to or deliberately ignoring the warning signs, smiled up at Garrett with infuriating casualness. "Garrett, I'm not finished admiring your beautiful date. She is quite the stunner tonight."

The silence that followed was thick enough to cut. Rose felt her cheeks flush, not with pleasure but with embarrassment at being discussed like an object rather than a person. Around them, conversations died as people sensed drama brewing.

"Yes. You are through admiring her, and she IS my date. Please find someone else to harass."

Garrett's words fell like stones into still water, creating ripples of shock throughout their immediate vicinity. Rose stared at him, stunned by the barely controlled anger in his voice.

Jack appeared at Garrett's shoulder, his expression tight with concern.

Daniel raised his hands in exaggerated surrender, but his smile suggested he was more amused than intimidated. "Message received," he said, and walked away with the satisfied air of someone who had accomplished exactly what he'd set out to do.

Rose felt heat creep up her neck—not the pleasant warmth of attraction, but the uncomfortable burn of public embarrassment. "Garrett, what was that all about? We were just talking."

Garrett's jaw was still tight, his eyes still tracking Daniel's movement through the crowd. "He wasn't just talking. He was flirting."

Rose felt a flutter of confusion. Daniel had been forward, certainly, but Garrett's reaction seemed so intense. Then again, maybe she was being naive. Maybe this was what it meant to be cherished, protected. Maybe this was how a man acted when he truly loved a woman—when he couldn't bear the thought of losing her.

"Come on. Let's go out on the terrace," Rose said quietly, placing a gentle hand on Garrett's arm. She needed air, space to think, and most importantly, privacy to sort through the conflicting emotions churning in her chest.

They walked toward the French doors that led to the moonlit terrace, and Jack followed at a discreet distance—close enough to intervene, if necessary, far enough to maintain the illusion of privacy.

The cool night air was a relief after the stifling atmosphere of the ballroom. Rose could see the tension in every line of Garrett's body, the way his hands clenched and unclenched at his sides.

"Now, do you want to tell me what that was really about?" she asked, keeping her voice calm and nonconfrontational.

"I just didn't like the way he was coming on to you. He's a player, and he had to know you were my date."

Rose studied his profile, the sharp line of his jaw, the way his eyes kept darting back toward the ballroom as if expecting Daniel to materialize at any moment. "He didn't know at first, but he did after I told him. It's a party. People are drinking and having a good time and sometimes they have some innocent flirting."

"With him, it's never innocent. I know him. He was trying to make a move."

Rose found herself remembering small moments from earlier in their relationship, how he'd seemed to have strong opinions about other couples' actions, how he'd rearranged his schedule to make things work on her time schedule. At the time, she'd thought it was sweet, caring. Now she wasn't quite sure what to think.

"Well, even if he was, it wouldn't matter. I'm with you. I love you." Rose moved closer, placing her hand on his chest where she could feel his heart racing beneath the expensive fabric of his tuxedo. "Besides, why would Cinderella go after the frog when she has a prince?"

The tension in Garrett's shoulders began to ease, and when he looked down at her, Rose saw not anger but fear—the kind of bone-deep terror that came from losing something precious once and living in constant dread of losing it again.

"I'm sorry. I just care for you so much and the thought of anyone coming on to you or trying to take you away from me... well, I can't even fathom that."

His arms came around her with desperate intensity, and Rose felt herself enveloped not just in his embrace but in the weight of his need for her. It was overwhelming, yes, but also intoxicating. No one had ever wanted her this much, needed her this completely. Maybe this was what real love felt like—all-consuming, desperate, fierce.

"Nothing and no one is going to take me away from you, Garrett. I do love you. I do."

She meant the words when she said them, and saying them felt like stepping deeper into the fairy tale. Yes, his intensity could be overwhelming sometimes, but wasn't that better than being ignored? Wasn't it better than dating men who didn't care enough to fight for her?

"Are you two lovebirds trying to sneak out of the party already?" Jack's voice cut through the tension with deliberate lightness as he stepped onto the terrace.

Garrett straightened, immediately regaining his composure and his successful businessman persona. "No, we were just talking."

Jack's expression suggested he had heard enough of their conversation to understand exactly what kind of "talking" had been necessary. "I just want to tell you, buddy, that every guy has been envious of you tonight.

Not only did you arrive with the most beautiful woman, but she has told everyone how much she adores you. Hearts are broken all over Macon. You are a lucky man."

Garrett's arm tightened around Rose's waist, and she could feel some of the tension leave his body at Jack's words. "That's something I already know, Jack. Let's go back in. I want to dance with Rose."

They began walking back toward the ballroom, but Jack's voice stopped them. "I don't suppose you would allow your best bud just one dance?"

Rose felt Garrett's entire body stiffen beside her, and for a moment she thought he might refuse. The pause stretched just long enough to become uncomfortable, and Rose felt a little flutter of something she couldn't quite name.

"Okay, but just one," Garrett finally replied, and Rose was relieved to hear him sound almost normal again.

The music was soft and romantic as Jack led Rose onto the dance floor, a classic waltz that allowed for conversation while they moved. Rose was acutely aware of Garrett watching them from the edge of the dance floor, his eyes never leaving them for a second. She found herself hoping her smile looked natural, that she appeared to be having a pleasant but not too wonderful time.

"I think you're really going to be good for Garrett," Jack said quietly, his voice pitched low enough that only she could hear. "He hasn't had anyone in his life for quite some time, and I've seen a lot of positive changes in him lately. He's really taken with you."

Rose smiled, feeling some of her earlier tension ease. "Thanks for saying that, Jack. I'm quite taken with him too. I've never had a guy make me the center of his world like Garrett does. I really love him."

Jack's expression grew more serious, and Rose caught a glimpse of something that looked like concern in his eyes. "I'm glad to hear that. Just always do me one favor and make sure he always knows that. He has some... well, let's call them trust issues. From before."

"Trust issues?" Rose asked, though she kept her voice light, her smile in place for Garrett's benefit.

"The woman before you—she really did a number on him. Left him pretty broken, actually.

I've never seen him as happy as he's been lately while seeing you, but sometimes I worry..." Jack trailed off, then seemed to choose his words carefully. "Sometimes I worry he might love too much, if you know what I mean. Hold on too tight."

Rose felt a little chill run down her spine. "What do you mean, exactly?"

"Just that he's been hurt before, and when someone's been hurt like that, sometimes they get a little... protective. Maybe more than they should be. Tonight, with that Daniel situation—that's not really about Daniel, you know?"

Rose nodded, though she wasn't entirely sure she understood. "What happened with her? The woman before me?"

Jack's eyes flicked toward Garrett, who was still watching them intently. "I probably shouldn't say. But she left him, Rose. Just up and left one day. No explanation, no goodbye. He came home, and she was just... gone. Really messed him up."

Rose felt her heart clench with sympathy. "That's terrible. I can't imagine doing that to someone."

"I know you can't. That's why I think you're good for him. Just remember that when he gets a little intense sometimes, it's coming from a place of fear, not anger. He's terrified of losing you."

"I know about 'her,'" Rose said quietly.

Jack's eyebrows rose in genuine surprise. "Really? I'm surprised he told you that story. That must mean he really does love and trust you, then." His smile returned, but there was relief in it now. "Well, I really do wish you the best. Garrett is a good guy. If he loves you, he'll do anything in the world for you."

Anything in the world. The words should have sounded romantic, but paired with Jack's warnings about holding on too tight, they felt more like a promise that might become a threat.

"I know he thinks the world of you, too," Rose managed.

They continued dancing, Jack skillfully steering the conversation to lighter topics, college stories, funny memories, the kind of easy chatter that should have put Rose at ease. But she found herself thinking about the woman who had left Garrett, wondering what had driven her to disappear without a word. Had she felt suffocated? Had she tried to explain and been unable to make him understand? Or had she really been as heartless as the story suggested?

When the song ended, Jack escorted her back to Garrett with old-fashioned courtesy. "Thank you for allowing me one dance with your lovely date, Garrett."

Garrett's possessive arm immediately encircled Rose's waist, and she noticed how his hand settled at the exact spot where Jack's had been during the dance, as if he was reclaiming territory.

"Notice you're the only one I trusted with that request," Garrett said, and Rose heard the emphasis on the word trusted.

Jack's smile was knowing. "I certainly did. Thank you again for the dance, Rose."

"My pleasure, Jack."

Garrett's hand was already guiding Rose toward the exit as he spoke. "How about we get out of here and go somewhere we can be alone? I've had enough rubbing elbows for one night. I want to spend some time alone with you. Maybe the riverfront?"

Rose looked around the beautiful ballroom, the elegant crowd, the perfect setting, the enchanting evening she had dreamed of. Part of her wanted to stay, to dance and laugh and feel like Cinderella for just a little longer. She wanted to prove to herself that she could enjoy the party without Garrett's constant supervision, that she could be trusted to socialize without igniting the flicker of jealousy she had begun to notice in him.

But the need in Garrett's voice, the way his fingers pressed against her back with just a little too much pressure, the way his eyes had never left her during her dance with Jack—it all made it clear that this wasn't really a request. This was a test, and if she failed it, if she chose the party over him, there would be consequences.

"That sounds nice," she heard herself say, hating how easily she capitulated, how quickly she was learning to read his moods and adjust her behavior accordingly.

As they made their rounds, saying goodbye, shaking hands, and accepting compliments on what a lovely couple they made, Rose felt like she was performing in a play she hadn't auditioned for. Everyone commented on how devoted Garrett was, how lucky she was to have found such a romantic man. If only they knew how exhausting it was to be the center of someone's universe, how conscious she felt to be loved with such desperate intensity.

She caught sight of Daniel across the room just as they were heading toward the door. He raised his wine glass to her in a small, private toast, and she saw something in his expression that made her stomach tighten with unease. It wasn't attraction or even mild flirtation—it was the satisfied look of someone who had learned exactly what he wanted to know. Someone who had conducted an experiment and gotten the results he'd expected. Had he been testing Garrett deliberately? Had he wanted to see just how possessive, how volatile, how controlling the perfect gentleman could become?

Garrett's hand pressed more firmly against her back, urging her toward the door, and Rose pushed the uncomfortable thought aside. This was her fairy tale evening, and she wasn't going to let Daniel Lockhardt or her own paranoid imagination ruin it.

But as they walked to the car, Rose couldn't shake the feeling that the real fairy tale was over, and what was about to begin was something else entirely.

The drive was mostly quiet, except for the symphonic sounds playing softly over the radio of the car. It only seemed an instant before Garrett was parked in a deserted lot by the river.

As Rose emerged from the car, she noticed the riverfront at night was transformed into something magical. Moonlight painted silver paths across the water's surface, while the distant lights of downtown Macon twinkled like fallen stars along the opposite shore. The gentle sound of water lapping against the stone retaining wall provided a romantic soundtrack that seemed designed specifically for moments like this.

The air itself seemed to shimmer with possibility. Spanish moss draped from the ancient oak trees like nature's own bridal veils, swaying gently in the warm breeze that carried the sweet scent of magnolias and jasmine. Rose could hear the distant strains of jazz music drifting from a riverboat somewhere downstream, adding to the enchanted atmosphere that made everything feel like a scene from a movie.

Rose leaned against the wrought-iron railing, her sapphire gown pooling around her feet like liquid starlight. The fabric caught the moonlight, making her feel as though she were wearing the night sky itself. The cool night air felt refreshing after the warmth of the ballroom, and she closed her eyes for a moment, savoring the peaceful solitude. When she opened them, she found Garrett watching her with an intensity that made her pulse quicken.

"You know it's rude to stare, right?" she said, but her tone was playful, inviting.

Garrett's smile was soft, almost reverent. "I couldn't wait to be alone with you."

Something in his voice—a hunger that went beyond simple desire—made Rose turn to face him fully. "Didn't you enjoy the party?"

"It was okay. I did enjoy dancing with you and showing you off. Letting everyone see how lucky I am and how much luckier I hope I will be."

The words sent a thrill through Rose, but also a flutter of something she couldn't quite name. "Luckier? In what sense?"

Garrett moved closer, his footsteps silent on the stone walkway. In the moonlight, his features seemed carved from marble—beautiful, perfect, but somehow unyielding. He reached out to touch her cheek, his fingers trailing down to lift her chin, so their eyes met.

"Rose, do you remember the first time we met?" he asked softly.

"Of course. You came into the store looking for a tie."

"I did need a tie," he said with a gentle smile, his thumb tracing her jawline. "But the moment I saw you, I knew I'd found something I needed much more. You were so graceful, so beautiful, and when you smiled at me... I couldn't stop thinking about you. Even now, after time has passed, I still can't believe you're real. That you're here with me."

Rose's breath caught. "You make me feel like I'm living in a dream."

"Are you?" His voice carried a vulnerability that made her heart ache. "Sometimes I watch you, and I can see something in your eyes, like you can't quite believe this is all real. Like you think it might all disappear."

"Sometimes I do worry about that," she admitted. "I've never had anything this wonderful in my life. It scares me a little."

"I know I can be... intense. But Rose, if you don't know how much I love you, then I want to make it clear. You are the most important thing in my life. I can't wait to be with you, to talk to you, touch you, and just be in your presence. I hope that you feel the same way about me."

The words should have filled her with joy—they were everything a woman in love wanted to hear. But there was something in the way Garrett said them, an undertone of desperate need that made Rose feel both cherished and somehow trapped.

"I do feel the same way about you. I have never met anyone who makes me feel more special than you do. I feel like I'm the most important person in the world with you. It's almost like a dream sometimes, where I wait to wake up, and this isn't real. I think, how can this guy be so great and so in love with me?"

"Tell me about that dream," Garrett said, his hands moving to frame her face. "Tell me what you see when you imagine our future."

Rose felt her cheeks warm. "I see... us. Happy. Maybe a house with a garden where I can grow roses. Children, someday. Sunday mornings in bed with coffee and the newspaper. Simple things, but perfect because they're with you."

"What about traveling? Paris, Rome, anywhere in the world you want to go?"

"That sounds wonderful, but honestly? I'd be happy anywhere as long as you're there."

Garrett's eyes darkened with emotion. "And if I told you I wanted to give you everything? Not just the simple things, but the world itself?"

"I'd say you already have. You've given me love, Garrett. Real love. After growing up the way I did, with so little... I never thought I deserved something like this. Someone like you."

Even as she spoke the words, Rose realized they were truer than she'd intended. It did feel like a dream—the kind that was so perfect you knew it couldn't last, the kind that left you wondering what price you'd have to pay when you finally woke up.

"It's not a dream. You are the most important person in my world, and that's why..." Garrett's voice trailed off, and Rose watched in stunned silence as he slowly sank to one knee before her.

The moonlight caught the facets of the diamond ring in his hand, sending sparkles of light dancing across the water like scattered diamonds. The ring box was small and elegant, covered in midnight blue velvet that seemed to absorb the light around it.

"Oh my God," Rose breathed, her hand flying to her mouth.

Time seemed to stop. Rose could hear her own heartbeat thundering in her ears, could feel tears pricking at her eyes before her mind had even fully processed what was happening. This was it—the moment every girl dreamed of, the culmination of every fairy tale she'd ever read. The riverfront had become a cathedral, the moonlight a spotlight, and she was the star of her own romantic movie.

"Rose," Garrett began, his voice strong and clear despite the emotion she could see in his eyes. "From the moment I first saw you, I knew my life would never be the same. You've brought light into corners of my heart

I didn't even know existed. You've made me want to be a better man, a man worthy of your love."

The ring trembled slightly in his hand—the only sign of his nervousness.

"I hope that I can have the honor of making you Mrs. Garrett Sinclair. I love you, Rose. Will you do me the great honor of becoming my wife?"

The ring was exquisite—a perfect solitaire that must have cost more than Rose made in a year. The diamond was flawless, catching every ray of moonlight and throwing it back in brilliant sparkles. The platinum band was delicate yet substantial, clearly chosen with care and an unlimited budget. But it wasn't the diamond that took her breath away; it was the look in Garrett's eyes as he gazed up at her. It was devotion so complete, so consuming, that it felt like standing too close to a fire.

"Garrett, I..." Rose felt tears streaming down her cheeks, her voice breaking with emotion. "I can't believe this is happening. I can't believe you're really asking me to—"

"Say yes," he whispered, his free hand reaching up to take hers. "Please, Rose. Make me the happiest man alive and say yes."

"Oh yes. Yes! Yes! Yes. I love you and I would love to be your wife."

The words tumbled out of her before rational thought could intervene, carried on a wave of emotion and moonlight and the sheer impossibility of saying no to such perfect love.

Garrett sprang to his feet with athletic grace, sliding the ring onto her finger with hands that shook slightly. The diamond fit perfectly, as if it had been made specifically for her hand. Then suddenly Rose was in his arms, spinning in a circle as tears of joy streamed down her cheeks.

"It's beautiful," she gasped, holding her hand up to watch the diamond catch the light. "Garrett, it's the most beautiful thing I've ever seen."

"Not as beautiful as you," he murmured, setting her down but keeping his arms wrapped tightly around her. "God, Rose, I was so nervous. I've been carrying that ring for weeks, waiting for the perfect moment."

"This is perfect," Rose said, meaning it completely. "The river, the moonlight, after such a magical evening... It's like something out of a fairy tale."

"You deserve a fairy tale," Garrett said fiercely. "You deserve everything beautiful this world has to offer, and I'm going to spend the rest of my life making sure you get it."

This was her moment. This was her dream coming true. Prince Charming had found her, chosen her, and now he was making her his princess forever.

"You have made me the happiest man on earth, Rose," Garrett whispered against her hair, his arms tightening around her with fierce possessiveness. "And nothing will ever separate us... ever."

The words were meant to be romantic, Rose knew that. They were the kind of vow that romance novels were built on, the promise of undying devotion that every woman wanted to hear. But as Garrett held her against him with an intensity that bordered on desperation, as his words echoed across the water with the weight of an unbreakable contract, Rose felt a tiny shiver that had nothing to do with the cool night air.

Nothing will ever separate us... ever.

The phrase repeated in her mind as she clung to her new fiancé, watching the diamond on her finger catch the moonlight. It was a promise, yes. But promises, Rose was beginning to realize, could sometimes sound better in thought than reality.

She pushed the thought away as quickly as it had come. This was her moment of triumph, her Cinderella story come to life. She was engaged to the most wonderful man she'd ever met, wearing a ring that proved his love beyond any doubt, standing in the most romantic setting imaginable. So why, in the midst of all this perfect happiness, did she feel as though she'd just signed her name to a contract she hadn't been allowed to read?

"When?" she asked, pulling back to look into his eyes. "When do you want to get married?"

"Tomorrow," he said immediately, then laughed at her expression. "I know, I know. You want a real wedding. Your mother will want to plan something special. But Rose, I don't want to wait. I've waited my whole life to find you, and now that I have... every day we're not married feels like a day wasted."

"Soon," she promised, touching his face tenderly. "But not tomorrow. I want to do this right. I want the dress, the flowers, the whole beautiful ceremony. I want to remember every detail of the day I become Mrs. Garrett Sinclair."

The way he smiled at hearing his name paired with hers made her heart skip. This was love, she told herself firmly. This was the kind of love that poets wrote about, the kind that would last forever.

And if a small voice in the back of her mind whispered that forever was a very long time, well... she was getting very good at not listening to that voice at all.

An Exciting Tale of Love

Three weeks later, Rose's small apartment had been transformed into a wedding planning headquarters. Fabric samples were draped over every available surface, like silken waterfalls—ivory silk, champagne satin, and pearl-white organza cascading from chairbacks and doorframes. Bridal magazines formed towering stacks on the coffee table, their glossy covers promising "The Perfect Wedding" and "Your Dream Day." Post-it notes covered the walls like colorful confetti, each one marking a decision made or a detail to remember.

The dining table had disappeared beneath layers of venue brochures, catering menus, and endless lists written in Rose's careful handwriting. Flower catalogs lay open to pages of elaborate arrangements, while fabric swatches were organized by color and texture in neat little piles. The entire space hummed with the energy of a dream taking shape.

Lucy and Eileen sat squeezed together on the large sofa, tissues in hand and tears of joy streaming down their faces as Rose finished recounting the proposal story for what had to be the dozenth time. Despite having heard it before, they hung on every word as if it were a beloved bedtime story—the moonlight, the riverfront, the perfect diamond that caught the light like captured starlight.

"That has to be the most romantic story ever," Lucy declared, dabbing at her eyes with a crumpled tissue. "As a matter of fact, I'm checking all my fairy tales to see if you stole that story."

Their laughter filled the small space, bright and infectious. Rose felt a warm glow spread through her chest- this was what she had missed during all those quiet evenings with Garrett, this easy camaraderie with her friends, the simple joy of being silly and happy without having to worry about being perfect.

"Sometimes I think it is all a fantasy, and I'm going to wake up and find out this isn't real. It has all been a dream that was too good to be true." Rose twisted the engagement ring around her finger, a gesture that had become unconscious over the past few weeks. The diamond caught the afternoon light streaming through her windows, sending tiny rainbows dancing across the walls. "I mean, who does this actually happen to? Garrett is good-looking, has a great job, is very wealthy, and treats me like I'm a storybook princess."

"Girl, you better pinch yourself because this is real," Lucy said, reaching over to give Rose's arm a playful squeeze. "And we have the credit card bills to prove it!"

Eileen reached over to squeeze Rose's hand, her expression fierce with protective love.

"Enjoy it, baby. You've earned it from all the not-so-great guys you've dated in the past."

"Remember that guy who took you to Burger King for your birthday?" Lucy added with a snort. "And then asked you to pay for your own meal?"

"Don't remind me," Rose laughed, covering her face with her hands. "Or the one who brought his mother on our first date."

"And his mother paid!" Eileen chimed in, sending all three women into fresh peals of laughter.

Lucy bounced slightly on the sofa cushions, her excitement bubbling over. "I am very happy for you... and as your maid of honor, I am obligated to throw you the most fantastic bachelorette party the state of Georgia has ever seen."

"Oh no," Rose said, though she was grinning. "What are you planning?"

"That's for me to know and you to find out. But I'm thinking... Atlanta? Savannah? Somewhere fabulous where we can celebrate you properly."

Rose felt her heart flutter with excitement. "I had no doubts you would go all out. There's so much to do."

Eileen picked up one of the venue brochures, her eyebrows rising as she took in the elaborate details. The Macon Country Club brochure was opened to a photograph of their grand ballroom, with its crystal chandeliers and marble floors. "I can't believe you're doing this in three months. Most people plan for a year."

"Garrett said he didn't want to wait, but he wouldn't deny me the largest wedding Macon has ever seen because he wanted to show me off anyway." Rose's voice carried a note of pride, but underneath it was something else, a breathless quality that suggested she was still trying to catch up with the speed of her own life.

"Show you off," Lucy repeated with a dreamy sigh. "God, Rose, he's so romantic. What did he say when you showed him the venue prices?"

Rose's smile was radiant, untouched by any shadow of doubt. "He said he didn't want money to be an issue. He said to make it the day I always dreamed of and not to worry about the cost."

"Are you kidding me?" Eileen nearly dropped the brochure. "Do you know how much the country club charges for a wedding?"

"I have some idea," Rose said, her cheeks flushing slightly. "But Garrett just said to book whatever I wanted. He's taking care of everything—the venue, the flowers, the reception, everything."

Lucy shook her head in amazement. "That was incredible of him to say if you would pay for the rehearsal dinner, he would pay for the wedding."

"Actually," Rose said, her voice dropping to an almost whisper, "he's paying for that too. He said he wanted to handle everything so I could just focus on being happy."

The silence that followed was filled with awe. Lucy and Eileen exchanged glances, both clearly struggling to process this level of generosity.

"Rose," Lucy said carefully, "honey, that's... that's a lot of money. Are you sure—"

"I'm sure," Rose said quickly, her smile never wavering. "He said I deserve the perfect day, and he wants to give it to me. I've never had anyone care about me like this before."

"We need to see the dress again," Eileen said, clearly deciding to move past the topic of money. "I still can't believe you found it so quickly."

Rose's eyes lit up as she practically bounced to her bedroom, returning with a garment bag that seemed to glow with promise. She unzipped it carefully, revealing layers of ivory silk and French lace that seemed to shimmer in the afternoon light.

"Oh my God," Lucy breathed, reaching out to touch the delicate beadwork. "Rose, this is... this is like something a real princess would wear."

"The moment I put it on, I knew," Rose said, her voice filled with wonder. "It was like it was made for me. The seamstress said she'd never seen a dress fit someone so perfectly right off the rack."

"How much did—" Eileen started, then stopped herself. "Never mind. I don't think I can handle any more sticker shock today."

"Let's just say Garrett was very generous," Rose said, carefully hanging the dress on the back of her bedroom door where they could all admire it. "He said he wanted me to feel like a princess on our wedding day."

"Mission accomplished," Lucy said softly. "Rose, you're going to look absolutely stunning."

They spent the next hour poring over details with the enthusiasm of generals planning a campaign. The flowers would be white roses and baby's breath, with touches of silver and crystal. The cake would be four tiers of vanilla and chocolate, decorated with sugar flowers that looked real enough to fool a bee. The photographer had shot weddings for three governors and a senator.

"What about the music?" Eileen asked, flipping through a vendor catalog. "Please tell me you're not having some boring string quartet."

"Actually, Garrett hired a full orchestra," Rose said, almost apologetically. "He said he wanted our first dance to be perfect, like something out of a movie."

"An orchestra?" Lucy's voice cracked. "Rose, this isn't a wedding, it's a coronation."

"It does feel a bit like that sometimes," Rose admitted, twisting her ring again. "But Garrett says I deserve to be treated like royalty. He says, after the way I grew up, with so little, I should have everything I ever dreamed of."

"And what's your first dance song going to be?" Eileen asked, leaning forward with interest.

"'Nobody Loves Me Like You Do,'" Rose said, her voice soft with emotion. "It's perfect, because that's exactly how I feel. Like I've been waiting my whole life for this moment, for him."

"Oh, and Lucy," Rose added, turning to her best friend with sparkling eyes, "I have something to ask you. I know you're already my maid of honor, but would you also sing at the wedding? Maybe during the ceremony, and at the reception?"

Lucy's mouth dropped open. "Are you serious? Rose, I would be honored! What song were you thinking? The one you just mentioned?"

"We haven't decided yet, but something beautiful and romantic. You have such a gorgeous voice, and I've always dreamed of having you sing at my wedding."

"Stop it, you're going to make me cry again," Lucy said, reaching for another tissue. "This is seriously the most romantic thing I've ever heard, and now I get to be part of it too."

"I know," Rose said, her smile so bright it seemed to light up the room. "Sometimes I have to pinch myself to make sure it's real. In three months, I'll be Mrs. Garrett Sinclair. I'll have a beautiful home, a husband who adores me, and a life I never even dared to dream about."

"What about after the honeymoon?" Eileen asked. "Are you going to keep working?"

Rose shook her head. "Garrett says he wants to take care of me. He says I won't need to work anymore unless I want to. He wants me to be able to focus on making our home beautiful and maybe taking up some hobbies. We'll see."

"That sounds amazing," Lucy said wistfully. "What kind of hobbies?"

"Maybe gardening? He mentioned wanting to have beautiful gardens around our house. And maybe some charity work, like the other wives at the country club." Rose's eyes were bright with possibility. "I've never had time for hobbies before. I've always been working just to pay the bills."

"Look at you," Eileen said, her voice thick with emotion. "Our little Rose is going to be a lady of leisure."

"I still can't believe it," Rose said, looking around at all the wedding preparations. "In three months, all of this will be real. I'll be married to the most wonderful man in the world, and this will all be a beautiful memory."

"So, let's get to work," Lucy said, clapping her hands together with renewed energy. "We have a fairy tale to plan."

The three women dove back into their planning with renewed enthusiasm, their voices overlapping as they debated flower arrangements and discussed guest lists. The apartment filled with the sound of their laughter and the rustle of turning pages, the excitement of a dream wedding taking shape before their very eyes.

***

Miles away in another town, in a tastefully appointed living room decorated in muted earth tones and expensive antiques, another woman sat in contemplative silence. The morning light filtered through heavy curtains, casting everything in a golden hue that should have been peaceful but somehow felt ominous. The room was immaculate—every surface polished to perfection, every object placed with deliberate precision, as if the very air had been arranged.

The Macon Telegraph lay spread across her lap, opened to the society section where engagement announcements shared space with charity event photos and country club news. Her manicured fingers traced the edge of the paper with the careful precision of someone who had learned to control every gesture, every expression, every breath.

At the center of the page, a professional photograph smiled back at her—Rose in her sapphire gown from the gala, radiant with happiness, leaning into Garrett's protective embrace. The girl's smile was incandescent, her eyes bright with the kind of joy that came from believing in happy endings.

"Mr. Garrett Sinclair, President of Southtrust Bank of Macon, announces his engagement to Miss Rose Nichols. The couple plans to wed at the Macon Country Club. Miss Nichols is employed by Macy's Department Stores. Mr. Sinclair graduated summa cum laude from the University of Georgia and..."

The words blurred together as the woman's hands began to tremble. The newspaper shook slightly, the cheerful photograph wavering like a mirage in the desert heat. Her knuckles had gone white as her grip tightened on the paper, her carefully manicured nails creating small crescent-shaped indentations in the newsprint.

She had known this day would come eventually. Had told herself she was prepared for it, that she had moved on, that the past was safely buried beneath years of carefully constructed indifference. But seeing it there in black and white—his face, his name, his happiness with someone else— felt like a physical blow, like someone had reached into her chest and squeezed her heart until she couldn't breathe.

The girl in the photograph was so young, so obviously naive. She gazed up at Garrett with complete trust, her body language screaming of total surrender to the enchantment he was weaving around her. The woman studying the photo recognized that look—had worn it herself once, had believed in those same promises, had felt that same intoxicating certainty that she was the chosen one, the special one, the one who would finally be enough.

Rose Nichols had no idea what she was walking into. She couldn't see past the expensive gifts and romantic gestures to the man underneath, the man who required complete and total devotion, who needed to own rather than love, who would slowly, systematically, strip away everything that made her who she was until there was nothing left but his reflection staring back at him.

The newspaper crumpled slightly in her grasp as her hands continued their involuntary trembling. Rose Nichols. The name echoed in her mind like a challenge, like a declaration of war she hadn't known was being waged. The girl looked so confident, so secure in her happiness. She had no idea how fragile that happiness truly was, how easily it could be shattered.

Miss Rose Nichols doesn't know what she's getting herself into, the woman thought, her lips curving into a smile that held no warmth whatsoever. *But she's about to find out.*

The telephone sat on the antique side table beside her chair, its black surface gleaming in the filtered light. She stared at it for a long moment, remembering other phone calls, other warnings that had gone unheeded by her in the past. Her fingers itched to pick up the receiver; to dial the number she could still recite from memory, to hear his voice one more time.

But what would be the point? He had made his choice, just as he had made it before. And Rose Nichols would learn, just as she had learned, that Garrett Sinclair's love was a beautiful prison, and by the time you realized you were trapped, it was far too late to escape.

The newspaper fell to the floor with a soft whisper, landing open to that smiling photograph. In the quiet of the expensive living room, with its heavy curtains and careful silence, the sound seemed to echo like a promise—or perhaps a threat.

The woman leaned back in her chair, her breathing slow and controlled, her hands finally still. She had learned from bitter experience what kind of man Garrett Sinclair truly was, had paid the price for loving him with everything she had. This time, she would wait. She would watch. And when Rose Nichols finally realized what kind of man she had married, when the dream crumbled and the girl came looking for answers, she would be ready. Some lessons, after all, could only be learned the hard way.

A Visit from the Past

The morning sun streamed through the stained-glass windows of First Baptist Church, casting jeweled patterns of light across the sanctuary that had been transformed into something from a fairy tale. Toile and lace draped every surface like delicate cobwebs, while cascades of fresh-cut roses and baby's breath created fragrant clouds of white and pink throughout the space. The main aisle had been adorned with lace swags connecting each pew, creating an ethereal pathway that seemed to float above the rich burgundy carpet. Green ferns and trailing ivy provided a lush backdrop to the altar, where a white baby grand piano sat like a pearl, its gentle melodies drifting through the air as early guests began to arrive.

Crystal chandeliers had been brought in especially for the occasion, their prisms catching the colored light from the windows and scattering rainbows across the cream-colored walls. White silk ribbons cascaded from the ceiling like gentle waterfalls, creating an intimate canopy over the altar. The scent was intoxicating, roses and baby's breath mingling with the lingering traces of lemon oil from the wooden pews and the faint vanilla of burning candles positioned throughout the sanctuary in tall, elegant candelabras that cast a warm, golden glow over everything.

It was exactly what Rose had dreamed of, every detail meticulously planned during those frantic weeks of preparation. Now, hidden away in the small bridal suite behind the sanctuary, she stood before a full-length mirror while her mother and Lucy fussed over the final touches.

"I'm going to see how things are going out there," Lucy announced, smoothing down her rose-colored bridesmaid dress. "I'll be back in a few minutes."

As Lucy slipped out, Eileen stepped back to admire her daughter, her hands clasped together in front of her heart. "I can't tell you how beautiful you look, baby. You look like you just stepped out of a magazine."

Rose turned from the mirror, the hand-sewn beads on her fitted gown catching the light and sending tiny sparkles dancing across the walls. The dress was everything she had imagined—elegant, timeless, with a train that pooled behind her like spilled cream. French lace adorned the bodice in intricate patterns that seemed to tell their own romantic story, while tiny seed pearls created constellations across the silk that shimmered with every breath she took. "Oh, Mama, thank you. You are beautiful too. You and Lucy have made this day just perfect."

But even as she spoke, Rose noticed the shadows under her mother's eyes, the way Eileen seemed to lean against the chair for support. "The most important thing is that you are truly happy," Eileen said, her voice carrying a weight that seemed too heavy for such a joyous day.

"I am, Mama. I love Garrett, and I know he loves me. We are going to be very happy together." Rose reached for her mother's hand, squeezing gently. "I just wish you felt better."

Eileen waved away her daughter's concern with a tired smile. "I'm just tired. It has been a busy few months. I will rest while you are on your honeymoon. But don't worry about me. This is your day. Enjoy it. You will remember it for the rest of your life."

A sharp knock at the door interrupted them, and Eileen moved to answer it. Rose watched in the mirror as her mother opened the door to reveal a woman she didn't recognize—attractive, somewhere in her thirties, with an urgency in her posture that seemed at odds with the peaceful atmosphere of the church.

"Hi, can I help you?" Eileen asked, her voice polite but cautious.

"Hi, I was curious if I could speak to Rose for a moment, please?"

Rose turned from the mirror, her train rustling against the floor like whispered secrets. "I'm Rose. What can I do for you?"

The woman's eyes were intense, almost desperate. "It's not me. It's what I hope I can do for you. Please. Can we speak for a moment in private?"

Something in the woman's tone made Rose's stomach flutter with unease, but she nodded.

"It's okay, Mama."

Eileen hesitated, clearly uncomfortable, but stepped outside and closed the door behind her, leaving Rose alone with the stranger.

"What did you need to speak to me ab—" Rose began, but the woman interrupted.

"My name is Bonnie. Have you heard that name before?"

Rose frowned, searching her memory. "Should I have?"

"I used to be involved... with Garrett."

The words hit Rose like a physical blow. The room seemed to tilt slightly, the scent of roses suddenly overwhelming. "You are the woman he was in love with that ran out on him, aren't you? I never knew your name. He didn't like to talk about you."

Bonnie's laugh was bitter, devoid of any humor. "I'm not surprised. I can understand why he wouldn't want you to know about our nightmare of a relationship."

Rose felt her carefully constructed composure beginning to crack. "Listen, this is my wedding day, and if you have come here to try and—"

"I'm here to try and save your life! I risked a lot coming here today just to warn you."

The words were so unexpected, so dramatic, that Rose almost laughed. "Save my life? Warn me? From Garrett? This takes sticking it to an ex to a whole new level, lady."

But Bonnie stepped closer, her eyes burning with an intensity that made Rose's laughter die in her throat. "I know you think right now that he is the man of your dreams, that you are the center of his world. I know.

So did I, but it will turn into the greatest nightmare you have ever lived because I lived it."

 Rose's hands were shaking now, and she gripped her bouquet tighter to stop the trembling.

"You need to leave."

"No! Not until I warn you before you walk down that aisle and it's too late! I had to run away, far away to escape his crazy, insane jealousy."

"Right now, I think the one who is crazy and insane is you!"

"Please! You have got to listen to me!"

The door burst open, and Eileen and Lucy rushed in, their faces tight with concern.

"What's going on? I could hear you two outside," Lucy demanded, immediately positioning herself protectively near Rose.

"This woman was just leaving," Rose said, her voice steadier than she felt.

"You heard Rose. I think you need to leave," Lucy added, her tone brooking no argument.

Bonnie looked between them, her desperation palpable. "Fine. I'll leave, but at least I tried. If you two really care about her, you will not let her walk down that aisle today."

"I don't know who you are, but this is my daughter's wedding, and you are not a guest. You need to go," Eileen said firmly, though Rose could hear the tremor in her mother's voice.

Bonnie dropped her head in defeat and walked toward the door, but paused at the threshold. When she looked back, her eyes met Rose's one last time, filled with a sorrow so deep it made Rose's chest ache. Then she was gone, leaving only the lingering scent of her perfume and a silence that felt heavier than lead.

"What was that all about? What happened? You are crying," Eileen said, reaching for her daughter.

Lucy immediately sprang into action, pulling makeup from her small purse. "Here, let me touch up your makeup."

Rose touched her cheek, surprised to find it wet with tears she hadn't realized she'd shed. "That was Garrett's ex, here to save me from making a huge mistake," she said.

"Oh wow. Are you serious? Today of all days. What a—" Lucy caught herself, glancing around the small church room. "Sorry, but that is one of the cruelest things a person can do. On your wedding day. What did she think she would do? Convince you Garrett wasn't the guy of your dreams?"

"That is exactly what she was trying to do. She said he wasn't the man I thought he was and how I would regret it."

Eileen took her daughter's hands in both of hers, her grip firm and grounding. "Rose, listen to me. That woman is a cruel and sick person. Do not let her ruin your day. You and Garrett love each other more than any two people I know. Put her out of your mind. Remember how you felt a few minutes ago? This is your special day. You are marrying the man of your dreams, and he does love you. You know that."

Rose nodded, trying to push Bonnie's desperate words from her mind. "I know. Just give me a moment. Lucy, thanks for helping with my makeup."

Lucy's voice was soft as she carefully applied powder under Rose's eyes. "Hey, you may be running off to get married, but you will always be my best friend, and I will always be there for you."

The first strains of the processional music drifted through the door, and Lucy straightened. "That's my cue. Got to go. See you up front."

As Lucy left, Rose took one final look in the mirror. The woman staring back at her was beautiful, radiant even, but there was something in her eyes now that hadn't been there an hour ago—a shadow of doubt that no amount of makeup could conceal.

The Ceremony

The sanctuary had filled completely while Rose was hidden away, every pew packed with friends, family, and colleagues who had come to witness this union. The very air seemed to shimmer with anticipation, as if the church itself was holding its breath in wonder at the spectacle before it.

Garrett stood at the altar looking impossibly handsome in his black tuxedo, the fabric so perfectly tailored it seemed to have been crafted by angels. His bow tie was made of the finest silk, and a single white rose adorned his lapel. Jack beside him as best man, along with four other groomsmen, each one looking distinguished in their matching attire, but none able to compete with the radiant joy emanating from the groom.

The wedding party was a vision of coordinated elegance. Each bridesmaid carried a bouquet of garden roses in varying shades of blush and cream, tied with silk ribbons that trailed like poetry in motion. Their rose-colored dresses, made of the softest chiffon, seemed to float around them like captured sunset clouds. Lucy's dress, as maid of honor, was adorned with delicate beadwork that caught the light with every movement.

When the ushers cut the ribbon blocking the main aisle and unfurled the white satin runner like a river of silk, a collective sigh of appreciation rose from the guests. The runner seemed to glow in the colored light from the windows, creating a pathway that looked as though it led straight to heaven itself.

A string quartet, positioned discretely in the balcony, began to play, their music floating down like invisible butterflies to dance around the assembled guests. The melody was hauntingly beautiful, a piece Garrett had specially commissioned for this moment—a love song written just for Rose, though she didn't know it yet.

Eileen was escorted down the aisle first by Garrett's eldest groomsman, taking her place in the front pew with a dignity that belied her exhaustion. She wore a dress of soft lavender silk that complemented her auburn hair, and around her neck was a strand of pearls that had belonged to Rose's grandmother. Despite her illness, she looked regal, every inch the mother of the bride.

One by one, the bridesmaids followed, each carrying bouquets of roses that matched the abundant arrangements throughout the sanctuary. They moved with practiced grace, their steps timed perfectly to the music, creating a procession that looked like something from a Renaissance painting. The guests murmured their appreciation, their eyes discreetly capturing the beauty of the moment.

Finally, Lucy appeared, her bouquet slightly larger than the others, her face glowing with joy for her best friend despite the earlier disruption. She had composed herself completely, becoming once again the picture of the perfect maid of honor, her love for Rose evident in every graceful step.

When Lucy reached the front, the pastor—a distinguished man with silver hair and kind eyes—motioned for everyone to rise. The sanctuary filled with the rustle of silk and the gentle murmur of three hundred guests getting to their feet in unison.

The music swelled, building to the crescendo of the wedding march, and both doors to the sanctuary opened wide as if moved by invisible hands.

Rose appeared like a vision from another world, every eye in the church drawn to her radiant beauty. The hand-sewn beads on her gown caught the colored light from the stained-glass windows, creating the illusion that she was wrapped in stars. Her train flowed behind her like a river of dreams, carried by two young flower girls who had been carefully chosen for their angelic faces and golden curls.

The dress itself was a masterpiece of craftsmanship—French lace that had been handsewn by artisans in Paris, silk that seemed to flow like water, and a bodice that fit her like it had been sculpted by Michelangelo himself. The neckline was modest yet elegant, framing her collarbones with intricate lacework that shimmered with every breath.

Her veil was a work of art in itself—cathedral length, made of the finest tulle and edged with the same French lace as her dress. It seemed to float behind her like a cloud, held in place by a tiara that had been in Garrett's family for generations, its diamonds dispersing the light and sending tiny rainbows dancing across the walls.

But it was the bouquet that truly took everyone's breath away. Garrett had commissioned it from the finest florist in Atlanta—a cascade of white roses from the finest garden, interwoven with baby's breath and delicate greenery, bound with ribbons of silk and lace. Hidden within the flowers were tiny crystals that reflected light like dewdrops, making the entire bouquet seem to glow with inner fire.

But it was Garrett's reaction that made the guests catch their breath collectively. His face transformed the moment he saw her, every emotion written clearly across his features—love, wonder, possession, and something deeper that bordered on reverence. Tears gathered in his eyes as he watched her approach, and he had to grip Jack's arm to steady himself.

The love radiating from his expression was so intense, so pure, that it seemed to fill the entire sanctuary. Several guests dabbed at their eyes, moved by the obvious depth of his devotion. This was a man who had found his soulmate, his other half, his reason for existing.

Rose felt that familiar flutter in her chest as their eyes met, the same sensation she'd experienced that first night at the gala, but magnified a thousandfold. Whatever doubts Bonnie had tried to plant withered in the face of Garrett's obvious devotion. This man loved her completely, utterly, and she could see it written in every line of his face, in the way his hands trembled slightly as he waited for her, in the tears that threatened to spill from his eyes.

The walk down the aisle seemed to take both forever and no time at all. Rose felt as though she were floating, carried by the music and the love that seemed to emanate from every person in the church. Friends and family smiled through their tears, reaching out to touch her dress or simply to be part of this magical moment.

When she reached the altar, Garrett stepped forward to meet her, and for a moment, the rest of the world disappeared. He reached out to lift her veil, his hands shaking slightly with emotion, to kiss her. But then their eyes met, and time seemed to stop.

"You're so beautiful," he whispered, just for her ears, his voice thick with emotion. "I can't believe you're really going to be my wife."

He took her hand with the reverence of a man handling something precious and irreplaceable, and Rose felt the last of her doubts melt away like morning mist.

"Who giveth this woman today?" the pastor asked, his voice carrying across the hushed sanctuary.

"Her mother," Eileen replied, her voice carrying across the hushed sanctuary despite its fragile quality.

"You may all be seated. We have gathered here today to join two people who have declared their love for one another and ask to be joined together in the bonds of matrimony before these witnesses."

The pastor's voice was warm and resonant, filling the sanctuary with a sense of sacred purpose. "Marriage is a commitment that should not be entered into lightly. It is a joining of two hearts, two souls, two lives into one. Rose and Garrett have come here today to make that commitment and declare their love for one another before God and this congregation." The pastor's words washed over Rose like a benediction, and she found herself focusing on Garrett's face, the way his eyes never left hers, the way his thumb traced gentle circles on her hand. In this moment, surrounded by love and beauty and the promise of forever, she felt more certain than she ever had about anything in her life.

"Marriage," the pastor continued, "is both a gift and a responsibility. It is the promise to love not just in the easy times, but in the difficult ones.

Not just when the other person is at their best, but when they are at their most vulnerable. Rose and Garrett, you have chosen each other out of all the people in this world, and that choice is both precious and sacred."

Garrett squeezed her hand gently, and Rose felt tears forming in her eyes at the intensity of love she saw in his gaze.

"Garrett Jackson Sinclair," the pastor said, turning to face the groom, "do you take Rose Marie Nichols to be your lawfully wedded wife, to love and to cherish, in sickness and in health, for richer or poorer, in joy and in sorrow, forsaking all others and keeping yourself only unto her for all the days of your life?"

"I do." His voice was strong, certain, carrying to every corner of the church with the conviction of a man who had never been more sure of anything in his life.

"And do you, Rose Marie Nichols," the pastor turned to her, "take Garrett Jackson Sinclair to be your lawfully wedded husband, to love and to cherish, in sickness and in health, for richer or poorer, in joy and in sorrow, forsaking all others and keeping yourself only unto him for all the days of your life?"

For just a moment, Bonnie's words echoed in her mind—save your life... warn you...

nightmare—but then she looked into Garrett's eyes and saw only love, only devotion, only the promise of the fairy tale life she had always dreamed of.

"I do." Her voice was clear and strong, carrying across the sanctuary with the certainty of a woman who had found her destiny.

"The commitment of marriage is sacred and special. Rose and Garrett have made their commitment to each other with their hearts and their words. Now they will give a token of that love with the exchange of rings."

Jack stepped forward, presenting the rings on a small velvet pillow. The wedding bands were works of art—platinum bands that had been specially crafted by a master jeweler, each one inscribed with words of love in flowing script that only the couple would know. "Garrett," the pastor said, "take Rose's ring and place it on her finger, repeating after me:

'With this ring I thee wed, as a symbol of my love and commitment to you for all eternity.'"

Garrett's hands were steady now, his voice strong and clear as he slipped the band onto her finger. "With this ring I thee wed, as a symbol of my love and commitment to you for all eternity."

The ring settled next to her engagement ring like it had always belonged there, the diamonds catching the light and sending tiny sparkles across the altar.

Rose's hands trembled slightly as she took Garrett's ring from the pillow. The weight of it surprised her—solid, substantial, a circle of precious metal that would bind him to her forever. "Rose," the pastor said gently, "place the ring on Garrett's finger and repeat after me: 'With this ring I thee wed, as a symbol of my love and commitment to you for all eternity.'"

When she spoke, her voice carried just the faintest shake, but it was from emotion, not doubt. "With this ring I thee wed, as a symbol of my love and commitment to you for all eternity."

As the ring slid onto Garrett's finger, Lucy stepped forward and gathered the bridal bouquet, passing it to the other bridesmaids before moving to stand near the piano. The opening notes of a song filled the sanctuary as Lucy's clear, sweet voice rose above the gentle accompaniment.

But this wasn't just any song; it was the piece that Garrett had secretly commissioned, the love song written just for Rose. As the lyrics began to flow, Rose's eyes widened in surprise and wonder. The words spoke of a love so deep it could move mountains, of a devotion so pure it could light up the darkest night. Each verse seemed to capture perfectly everything she felt for the man standing beside her, everything she had ever dreamed of hearing.

"In your eyes I see tomorrow, in your smile I see the sun, in your heart I find my harbor, two souls dancing, now as one. Every dream I've ever whispered, every prayer I've ever said, led me to this perfect moment, where my heart and yours are wed."

Rose felt tears tugging at her eyes as the lyrics washed over them, and when she glanced at Garrett, she saw that his eyes had filled with tears as well. Without thinking, she reached up to gently wipe one away with her gloved hand. The gesture was so tender, so intimate, that a collective sigh rose from the congregation.

Lucy's voice soared through the sanctuary, filling every corner with the beauty of the melody. The song spoke of eternal love, of two hearts becoming one, of a bond that would last through all the trials and joys that life could bring. It was everything Rose had ever wanted to hear, everything she had ever dreamed of feeling.

"When the world grows dark around us, when the storms of life appear, I will be your strength and shelter, I will hold you ever near. For you are my heart's true treasure, you're the reason that I live, and until my final heartbeat, all my love to you I'll give."

The love between them was so palpable, so real, that it seemed to fill every corner of the sanctuary. Guests dabbed at their eyes with tissues, moved by the obvious depth of feeling between the couple and the beauty of Lucy's performance. Even the hardest hearts in the congregation felt softened by the magic of the moment.

As the final notes faded and Lucy returned to her place, wiping away her own tears, the pastor smiled at the couple before him. The sanctuary was filled with such peace, such joy, that it felt like heaven itself had descended to bless this union.

"Rose and Garrett," he said, his voice warm with emotion, "you have shown the symbols of your love through the commitment of your vows and the exchanging of rings. You have declared before God and these witnesses that you choose each other, now and always. May your love be strong and last forever, growing deeper with each passing day."

He raised his hands in blessing over the couple. "By the power vested in me by this church and this state, I now pronounce you husband and wife. Garrett, you may kiss your bride."

Garrett lifted Rose's veil with hands that shook slightly with emotion, and for a moment they simply looked at each other—husband and wife, bound together for life. The sanctuary held its breath, three hundred people witnessing this most sacred moment.

When he kissed her, it was with the reverence of a man who knew he was holding his entire world in his arms. The kiss was soft, gentle, filled with all the love and promises they had just made to each other. Rose felt as though she were floating, carried away on a cloud of pure joy and love.

The congregation erupted in applause, the sound washing over them in a wave of celebration and joy.

"I would like to present to you for the first time," the pastor announced, his voice carrying over the applause, "Mr. and Mrs. Garrett Jackson Sinclair!"

The wedding march filled the sanctuary as Garrett offered Rose his arm and they began their first walk together as husband and wife. Rose felt as though she were floating, the train of her dress trailing behind her like a white river as they moved down the aisle toward their new life together.

The recessional was a celebration of joy and love. Rose petals fell like snow from the balcony as they passed, scattered by the flower girls who had been waiting with baskets full of roses from Garrett's garden. The guests rose to their feet, applauding and cheering, their faces glowing with happiness for the couple.

Jack offered his arm to Lucy, and she took it with a radiant smile, her own eyes bright with tears of joy for her best friend. The rest of the wedding party followed, but Rose was aware of none of it. There was only Garrett, only the feeling of his strong arm beneath her hand, only the radiant joy on his face as he looked down at her.

As they reached the front of the church, Garrett paused for just a moment, turning to look at his bride in the golden light streaming through the windows. "I love you, Mrs. Sinclair," he whispered, and Rose felt her heart swell with such happiness she thought it might burst.

"I love you too, Mr. Sinclair," she whispered back, and in that moment, surrounded by love and light and the promise of forever, she knew that this was exactly where she was meant to be.

Whatever shadows Bonnie had tried to cast over this day had been burned away in the light of this perfect moment. She was Mrs. Garrett Jackson Sinclair now, and she had never been happier in her entire life.

The fairy tale was complete, the dream had come true, and as they stepped out into the warm Georgia sunshine, Rose felt as though she was stepping into a future filled with nothing but love, happiness, and endless possibilities.

Behind them, the church bells began to ring, their joyful peals echoing across the city of Macon, announcing to the world that love had triumphed, that two hearts had become one, and that the most beautiful wedding the town had ever seen was complete.

The real test was still to come, but for now, in this perfect moment, there was only love, only joy, only the promise of forever that gleamed as bright as the diamonds on Rose's finger and the tears of happiness in Garrett's eyes.

The Reception

The grand ballroom of the Macon Country Club had been transformed into an elegant wonderland that rivaled the church's fairy-tale beauty. Crystal chandeliers—each one containing over a thousand individual crystals—cast warm, golden light over round tables draped in ivory silk linens imported from Italy. The centerpieces were architectural marvels of floral design: towering arrangements of white roses and baby's breath that seemed to float like clouds above the tables, interspersed with trailing ivy and delicate white orchids that Garrett had flown in from Atlanta that morning.

The same delicate French lace that had adorned the church pews now graced the backs of mahogany Chiavari chairs, each one tied with silk ribbons that caught the light like captured moonbeams. Soft jazz music floated through the air from a seven-piece orchestra positioned on a stage decorated with more white roses and twinkling fairy lights that created the illusion of stars fallen to earth.

The room itself was a testament to old Southern elegance—marble columns soared toward a coffered ceiling painted with cherubs and gold leaf, while French doors opened onto a terrace overlooking the country club's championship golf course. The floors were polished to mirror perfection, reflecting the candlelight from hundreds of ivory tapers placed throughout the room in crystal holders that sparkled like diamonds.

Rose and Garrett stood at the entrance, still glowing from their ceremony, working their way through the receiving line with grace and patience. Each guest received a warm handshake from Garrett and a radiant smile from Rose, who seemed to sparkle even more brightly than the beading on her gown. The joy was infectious, spreading through the crowd like ripples on a pond.

"Congratulations, sweetheart," murmured Mrs. Patterson, one of Rose's regular customers from the store where she used to work. "You look absolutely radiant."

"Thank you so much for coming," Rose replied, her voice warm with genuine affection. "It means the world to us that you're here."

Garrett's hand never left the small of Rose's back, a gesture that appeared protective and loving to the guests but sent a small shiver through Rose—not entirely unpleasant, but somehow more intense than she expected. His touch was constant, claiming, as if he needed to maintain physical contact to assure himself she was really his.

The cocktail hour was in full swing, with white-gloved servers circulating silver trays of champagne in crystal flutes that sang like tiny bells when they touched. The hors d'oeuvres were works of art—delicate canapés topped with caviar and crème fraiche, phyllo cups filled with lobster salad, and tiny tartlets crowned with exotic fruits that looked like jewels.

A champagne fountain had been erected in the center of the room, its multiple tiers creating a cascade of golden bubbles that captured the light and sent it dancing across the walls. Guests gathered around it with their glasses, marveling at the extravagance while a professional photographer captured every moment with the skill of a master artist.

"Mr. and Mrs. Sinclair, if we could have you over here for the cake cutting," called the photographer, a jovial man who had been capturing every moment with professional enthusiasm.

The wedding cake was nothing short of a masterpiece—four tiers of ivory fondant decorated with cascading sugar roses so realistic they seemed to have been plucked from a garden that morning. Each tier was adorned with delicate pearl details that glowed like tiny stars, and between the layers, ribbons of spun sugar created the illusion of flowing silk. The cake stood on a crystal pedestal that had been specially commissioned for the occasion, surrounded by white roses and baby's breath that seemed to grow from the table itself.

Rose and Garrett positioned themselves behind it, their hands joined on the silver knife handle—an antique piece that had belonged to Garrett's grandmother. The blade was engraved with their initials and wedding date, another detail that Garrett had arranged without telling Rose, another surprise that showed the depth of his planning, his attention to every detail of their life together.

Camera flashes popped like small fireworks around them, and the guests pressed closer, their faces bright with anticipation and joy.

"Make a wish," Rose whispered to Garrett, her eyes twinkling with mischief.

"I already have everything I could ever wish for," he replied, his voice low and intimate despite the crowd gathered around them. His eyes held hers with an intensity that made her breath catch, and for a moment, the rest of the world disappeared.

They cut through the bottom tier together, the knife sliding smoothly through the layers of vanilla cake and raspberry filling—Rose's favorite combination, though she had never told Garrett that. Somehow, he had known. He seemed to know everything about her, sometimes before she knew it herself.

When it came time to feed each other, they were gentle and playful, Garrett carefully placing a small bite on Rose's lips while she laughed, her head tilted back in pure delight.

The gesture was tender, loving, but Lucy noticed how Garrett's thumb lingered on Rose's lips afterward, how his eyes darkened with something that looked almost like hunger.

"Ladies and gentlemen," Lucy announced as she approached the microphone near the small stage where the orchestra was set up, her rose-colored dress flowing around her like a captured sunset, "it's time for our happy couple's first dance as husband and wife."

The opening notes of "Nobody Loves Me Like You Do" filled the ballroom, and Lucy's voice, clear and sweet, wrapped around the melody like silk. The song choice had been Garrett's—another surprise for Rose, who had mentioned once, months ago, that she had always imagined dancing to that song at her wedding. He remembered everything, filed away every casual comment, every passing preference.

Garrett led Rose to the center of the dance floor, which had been polished to mirror perfection and surrounded by hundreds of white rose petals that seemed to glow in the candlelight. He pulled her into his arms with the confidence of a man who had found his missing piece, and they moved together as if they had been dancing for years.

Rose's train swirled around them like a cloud as they swayed to the music, the beading on her gown catching the light from the chandeliers above. The guests formed a circle around them, but Rose was aware of nothing but Garrett's strong arms holding her, his eyes locked on hers as if she were the only person in the world.

"Do you know how much I love you, Mrs. Sinclair?" he murmured against her ear, the words sending shivers down her spine.

Rose smiled up at him, her earlier worries about Bonnie feeling like a distant memory, burned away by the magic of this perfect moment. "As much as the bill for this wedding is, I hope a lot."

Garrett's laugh was rich and warm, echoing off the marble columns. "It doesn't matter. Nothing is too good for you, Rose. I swear I will love you for all my life. I am going to do everything I know how to make you very happy."

"You already have," she whispered back, meaning every word.

As Lucy's voice soared over the final notes of the song, the guests burst into applause, and other couples began to join them on the dance floor. The reception was in full swing now—waiters in white jackets circulated with trays of hors d'oeuvres that looked like small sculptures, the bar was busy with orders for champagne cocktails and single-malt whiskey neat, and laughter echoed off the ornate ceiling like music.

The orchestra transitioned seamlessly into a medley of romantic standards, and the dance floor filled with swaying couples. Rose's parents' friends moved with the practiced grace of their generation, while younger guests brought contemporary energy to the classic tunes. The mixture of ages and styles created a beautiful tapestry of celebration.

Rose and Garrett eventually slipped away to change into their going-away outfits, leaving their guests to continue the celebration. The dance floor was filled with swaying couples, and the energy in the room was electric with joy and good wishes.

Jack approached Lucy as she stepped down from the stage, straightening his tie with one hand while extending the other to her. In the golden light of the chandeliers, he looked every inch the successful businessman—tall, well-dressed, with the kind of confident bearing that came from years of being a bank executive. But there was something in his eyes tonight that seemed different, a shadow that hadn't been there during the ceremony.

"May I have this dance, ma'am?" he asked, his voice carrying a hint of his Southern upbringing.

Lucy pretended to consider, tapping her chin thoughtfully. "Well, let me check my dance card. Yes, I think I can fit you in. Show me what you've got."

"About all I can promise is not to step on your feet. I'll try not to embarrass you too badly," Jack said with a self-deprecating grin as he led her onto the dance floor.

They moved together easily, and Lucy found herself relaxing for the first time all day. Jack was a better dancer than he claimed, leading her through the steps with confidence and grace. The music wrapped around them like a warm embrace, and for a moment, Lucy allowed herself to simply enjoy the evening.

"This day has been so emotional," she said, her voice soft as they swayed together. "I don't think I have ever had a day like this."

"When two people are in love and get married, it should be," Jack replied, spinning her gently under his arm. The movement was smooth, practiced, and Lucy wondered fleetingly how many women he had danced with at weddings like this.

"Yes, well… that and the excitement before the wedding with Garrett's ex showing up." Lucy felt Jack's body tense almost imperceptibly, a subtle shift in his posture that she might have missed if she weren't pressed so close to him.

Jack's steps faltered almost imperceptibly, but Lucy felt the change in his rhythm like a discordant note in a symphony. "Bonnie? She was here?"

The way he said the name—with recognition, with what sounded almost like dread—made Lucy's stomach flutter with unease. "Yeah. You obviously remember her?" Lucy studied his face, noting the way his jaw had tightened, how his hand had unconsciously gripped hers more firmly. "She wanted to talk to Rose before the wedding and obviously cause trouble. What a classless thing to do."

"Did she talk to Rose? What did she say?" There was an urgency in Jack's voice that made Lucy's pulse quicken. This wasn't the casual curiosity of a friend; this was something else entirely, something that felt dangerous.

"Just trying to convince Rose not to go through with the wedding, and how Garrett wasn't the guy she thought he was. Apparently, a bad 'get back at your ex' move on his wedding day." Lucy watched Jack's face carefully, noting how the color had drained from his features despite the warm lighting.

Jack's grip on Lucy's hand tightened unconsciously. She could feel the tension radiating from him like heat from a furnace, and suddenly the beautiful ballroom felt too warm, too close.

"What's wrong?" Lucy asked, her voice dropping to a whisper. Around them, other couples continued to dance, oblivious to the tension that had suddenly sprung up between them. "She is just a crazy lady, right? There's nothing to it, right?"

Jack seemed to shake himself, forcing his features back into a mask of casual concern, but Lucy could see the effort it cost him. "Of course not. Garrett and Bonnie had a bad breakup. Does… he know she was here?"

"I don't think so. Eileen threw her out, and we started the wedding." Lucy's eyes searched his face, looking for answers he seemed reluctant to give. "Is there something you're not telling me, Jack?" The music continued around them, but she felt as though they were dancing in a bubble of silence. "You are his best friend, and Rose is mine. I care about her."

"No. No. No. There is nothing." But his voice lacked conviction, and he couldn't quite meet her eyes. When he did look at her, Lucy saw something that made her blood run cold—fear. "As I said, they had a bad breakup, as couples sometimes do. We've all been there. Rose and Garrett love each other a lot, and that's all that matters now. As you said, just a crazy ex trying to cause trouble."

They continued to dance, but the easy rhythm was gone now, replaced by a stilted awkwardness that neither could quite shake. Lucy's mind raced with questions she didn't know how to ask, while Jack wrestled with knowledge he couldn't bring himself to share.

The music swelled around them, but both were lost in their own troubled thoughts, each wondering if they had just glimpsed the first crack in what had seemed like a perfect day. Lucy found herself studying the other guests, watching how they moved together, how they laughed and celebrated, and wondering if she was the only one who suddenly felt like she was watching a performance rather than a celebration.

A commotion near the entrance drew their attention, and they turned to see Rose and Garrett making their grand reappearance. Rose had changed into a powder blue going-away suit that had been tailored to perfection, the color complementing her complexion and making her eyes seem to glow like emeralds. The jacket was adorned with tiny pearl buttons that caught the light, and she wore a matching pillbox hat with a small veil that gave her the look of a 1950s movie star.

Garrett looked dapper in a charcoal gray suit that had been custom-made on Savile Row, his tie a perfect match for Rose's ensemble. They moved through the crowd like royalty, accepting congratulations and well-wishes with grace, but Lucy noticed how Garrett's hand never left Rose's elbow, how he guided her through the crowd with the subtle but unmistakable control of a man who knew exactly where he wanted her to go.

"Ladies, gather round!" Rose called out, holding her bridal bouquet high above her head. The bouquet was even more beautiful now than it had been during the ceremony—the roses had opened slightly in the warm air, and the crystals hidden among the flowers sparkled like captured stars. "It's time!"

A group of single women clustered behind her, their faces bright with anticipation and laughter. Lucy found herself pulled into the group despite her lingering unease, positioning herself in the back row where she thought she'd be safe from the flying flowers.

Rose turned her back to the crowd, counted to three, and sent the bouquet sailing through the air in a perfect arc. It seemed to hang suspended for a moment, white roses and baby's breath tumbling slowly through the golden light, before landing squarely in Lucy's surprised hands.

The crowd erupted in cheers and applause, and Lucy found herself blushing as friends and family members called out teasing predictions about her own wedding day. She caught Jack's eye across the room and saw something flicker across his face—concern, perhaps, or maybe something deeper. Something that looked almost like a warning.

Rose rushed over to embrace her best friend, her face radiant with joy. "Oh, Lucy! This is perfect! You'll be next, I just know it!"

"We'll see about that," Lucy laughed, but her eyes were still on Jack, who had moved to stand beside Garrett. The two men were talking quietly, their heads bent together, and Lucy couldn't shake the feeling that they were discussing something far more serious than wedding pleasantries.

As the guests began to gather their things and prepare for the couple's departure, Lucy clutched the bouquet to her chest and tried to push away the nagging feeling that something wasn't quite right. Rose was glowing with happiness, Garrett was the picture of a devoted husband, and the day had been everything they had dreamed of. So why did she feel like she was watching the opening act of a tragedy instead of the happy ending of a love story?

The crowd followed Rose and Garrett outside, where a white limousine waited at the curb—a Rolls-Royce that gleamed like a pearl in the evening light. Its windows were tinted dark as midnight, and a chauffeur in full livery stood beside the open door, his white gloves pristine despite the warm Georgia evening.

Rice and confetti filled the air like snow as the newlyweds made their way to the car, laughing and ducking under the shower of good wishes. The rice had been specially chosen—white and pink grains that sparkled in the evening light, creating a magical atmosphere that seemed to lift Rose and Garrett above the ordinary world.

Garrett helped Rose into the back seat, his hand protective on her elbow, and for just a moment, as he looked back at the crowd, Lucy saw something in his expression that made her breath catch. It was gone in an instant, replaced by his usual charming smile and a wave to the cheering guests, but for that brief second, she had seen something else entirely.

Possession. Pure, unadulterated possession.

The look wasn't directed at the crowd, or even at the moment itself. It was focused entirely on Rose, sitting in the back seat of the limousine, her powder blue suit a splash of color against the white leather interior. The expression on Garrett's face was the look of a man who had just acquired something precious, something that belonged to him completely and utterly.

The limousine pulled away from the curb, carrying Mr. and Mrs. Garrett Jackson Sinclair toward their honeymoon and their new life together. The guests waved and cheered, calling out final congratulations and well-wishes, but Lucy noticed that Rose's hand was pressed against the tinted window, her pale face barely visible through the dark glass.

For just a moment, as the car turned the corner and disappeared from view, Lucy could have sworn she saw Rose's expression change—the radiant smile faltering, replaced by something that looked almost like uncertainty, but then knew it was just her mind overworking itself.

Lucy stood on the steps of the country club, the bridal bouquet still in her hands, and watched the taillights disappear into the gathering dusk. The evening air was warm and sweet, filled with the scent of roses and the distant sound of crickets beginning their nightly chorus. Around her, the other guests were beginning to drift away, chattering happily about what a beautiful wedding it had been, what a perfect couple Rose and Garrett made, how romantic it all was.

Beside her, Jack remained silent, his hands shoved deep in his pockets, his face troubled. The easy charm that had carried him through the day was gone now, replaced by something darker, more complex.

"Beautiful wedding," said Mrs. Patterson as she passed, her voice warm with satisfaction. "Those two are going to be so happy together."

Lucy nodded and smiled, but the words felt hollow. She found herself thinking about Bonnie, about the desperation in her voice, the fear in her eyes. Whatever had happened between Bonnie and Garrett, it had been serious enough to drive her to risk everything to warn Rose.

"Jack," Lucy said quietly, her voice barely audible over the sounds of the departing guests. "What aren't you telling me?"

Jack turned to look at her, and in the soft light from the country club's entrance, she could see the weight of whatever knowledge he carried. "Some things are better left alone, Lucy. Some secrets are meant to stay buried."

"But what if they're not?" Lucy clutched the bouquet tighter, the stems pressing into her palms. "What if Rose is walking into something she doesn't understand?"

Jack was quiet for a long moment, watching the last of the guests disappear into the night. When he spoke, his voice was so low she had to lean closer to hear him.

"All we can do is hope that their love is enough," he said finally. "Hope that whatever Garrett feels for Rose, it's strong enough to overcome... everything else."

Neither of them spoke about what they had seen, what they had felt, or what they feared might be coming. But as the other guests began to drift away, chattering happily about what a beautiful wedding it had been, Lucy and Jack exchanged one last look—a look that acknowledged the unspoken worry they both carried.

Rose was gone now, swept away in a cloud of powder blue silk and promises of forever. The fairy tale was complete, the dream wedding had ended, and the real story was just beginning.

All they could do was hope that when the credits rolled on this particular love story, it would be Rose who got to write the ending.

The Honeymoon

The suite at the Grand Ocean Resort was everything Rose had dreamed of—elegant without being ostentatious, romantic without being cliché. Soft candlelight flickered across cream-colored walls, casting dancing shadows that seemed to move in rhythm with the gentle ocean breeze flowing through the open French doors. The sound of waves lapping against the shore below provided nature's own symphony, punctuated by the distant cry of seagulls settling in for the night.

Rose stood at the threshold of the bedroom, her heart racing as she took in the scene Garrett had arranged. Every detail was perfect—too perfect, perhaps, as if choreographed from some elaborate romantic fantasy. Champagne chilled in a silver bucket that caught the candlelight like liquid mercury, rose petals scattered across crisp white linens in a pattern that seemed almost mathematical in its precision. And there was Garrett, the man she had just promised to love forever, waiting for her with an intensity in his eyes that made her breath catch.

There was something in that intensity that gave her pause—not fear exactly, but a flutter of something she couldn't quite name. The way he watched her, as if she were a work of art he'd just acquired, beautiful and precious and... his. Completely his.

"Mrs. Sinclair," he said softly, testing out her new name like a prayer, like an incantation.

The name felt foreign, even as it sent a thrill through her. Rose Sinclair. She was no longer Rose Nichols, the girl who worked at the department store at the mall. She was Mrs. Garrett Sinclair now, wife to one of Macon's most successful men. The transformation felt surreal, like stepping into someone else's life.

"I like the sound of that," she whispered back, stepping toward him, her bare feet silent on the plush carpet.

Garrett moved with deliberate slowness, as if he wanted to memorize every second of this moment. His fingers traced the delicate fabric of her negligee, the off-white silk feeling like gossamer against her skin. When he slipped the thin straps from her shoulders, his touch was reverent, worshipful—but also possessive, claiming.

"I've waited so long for this," he murmured against her neck, his voice rough with emotion. "For you. For us. You're mine now, Rose. Completely mine."

The words should have thrilled her, and they did—but there was something in the way he said "mine" that made her skin prickle with more than just desire. It was the way someone might speak of a treasured possession, something to be protected and cherished, yes, but also controlled.

But then his lips found the sensitive spot just below her ear, and all coherent thought fled. Rose had never felt so desired, so completely wanted. Every kiss sent electricity through her veins, every touch ignited something deeper than physical attraction. This was love in its purest form—two souls finally becoming one.

Garrett's lips found hers; she tasted champagne and promises, passion and forever. His kiss was consuming, possessive in a way that made her feel like the most precious thing in his world. She surrendered completely to the moment, to him, to the overwhelming rush of being truly, deeply loved.

Yet even as she melted into his embrace, some small part of her mind registered how his hands seemed to map every inch of her skin, as if memorizing her, cataloguing her. When she tried to pull back for air, his grip tightened just slightly, just enough to keep her close. "Don't go anywhere," he whispered, and though his tone was loving, there was something underneath it—a need that went beyond desire, beyond love. "Promise me you'll never leave me, Rose."

"I'm not going anywhere," she assured him, though the urgency in his voice surprised her. "I'm your wife now, Garrett. I'm yours."

The word seemed to satisfy something deep within him, and his kiss gentled, became tender again. The ocean breeze continued to stir the curtains as the candles burned lower, casting their glow over two people lost in each other, finally able to express the depth of their love without reservation or restraint.

In that perfect bubble of candlelight and sea air, nothing existed beyond the two of them and the sacred intimacy they were sharing as husband and wife. Garrett's hands never stopped moving, never stopped touching her, as if he needed constant physical confirmation that she was real, that she was there, that she was his.

Hours later, as Rose lay curled against Garrett's chest, listening to his heartbeat slow to match the rhythm of the waves, she had never felt more complete. This was exactly how a wedding night should be—passionate, tender, and filled with the promise of all the nights to come.

But even in her contentment, she was aware of how tightly Garrett held her, how his arm across her waist felt almost like a beautiful chain. When she shifted slightly, trying to find a more comfortable position, his grip tightened reflexively, even in sleep.

"I love you, Mrs. Sinclair," Garrett whispered into her hair, and she could feel his lips moving against her scalp, could feel the way his breathing quickened when she said the name back.

"I love you too," she replied, already drifting toward sleep, secure in his arms and in the certainty that she had married exactly the right man.

Outside, the ocean continued its eternal dance with the shore, and the stars wheeled overhead, bearing witness to what felt like the perfect beginning to their forever. The waves crashed with hypnotic regularity, and somewhere in the distance, a night bird called out—a lonely sound that seemed to echo through the darkness long after the call had ended.

In her dreams, Rose found herself in a garden where roses bloomed in impossible profusion, their beauty breathtaking but their thorns sharp enough to draw blood. She was walking through this garden, trying to find her way out, but every path seemed to lead deeper into the maze of flowers. And somewhere behind her, she could hear footsteps, following, always following, never quite catching up but never falling behind either.

She woke startled, her heart racing, but Garrett's arms were around her, solid and warm and real. Just a dream, she told herself. Just wedding night nerves. This was her honeymoon, her perfect beginning, her fairy tale come true.

Garrett did not stir, perhaps trusting that no shadow could reach her so long as she lay within his arms.

But as she settled back into sleep, she couldn't shake the feeling that somewhere in the perfection of this moment, something was watching, waiting, keeping track of every breath she took. It was a nagging feeling that things were too good to be true.

She rested her mind again, dismissing the feelings as nerves, and fell back to sleep in the arms of the man she loved.

Starting a New Life Together

Three weeks later, Rose stood in the grand foyer of what was now her home, watching movers navigate antique furniture through doorways that seemed designed for a different era. The Sinclair mansion perched on the highest hill in Magnolia Springs like a crown jewel, its white columns and wraparound porches speaking of old Southern money and established traditions. Even after three weeks, Rose still felt like she was playing dress-up in someone else's life.

The house was magnificent, certainly—fourteen rooms, each one larger than her mother's entire apartment. But something about its grandeur made her feel smaller, as if she were shrinking to fit into spaces that had been built for someone else entirely. The ceilings soared twenty feet high, making normal conversation seem to echo and fade into the vastness above.

"I still can't believe this house," Lucy said, craning her neck to look up at the crystal chandelier suspended two stories above them. "It's huge. I could get lost in this thing. If you happen to need someone to roam around in the west wing, just let me know."

Rose laughed, though she noticed how the sound seemed to get swallowed by the marble floors and Persian rugs. "You might actually get lost. I'm still learning my way around. Yesterday I went looking for the kitchen and ended up in the library." She pursed her lips. "Twice."

"That's a good problem to have," Lucy said, but her eyes were taking in the formal portraits lining the walls—generations of Sinclair ancestors whose stern faces seemed to watch their every move. "These people look like they could buy and sell half of Georgia."

"Probably could," Rose murmured, following Lucy's gaze. She'd been trying not to think too hard about those portraits, about the weight of history and expectation they represented. Garrett had told her stories about each one—great-grandfather Sinclair, who'd built a banking empire, grandmother Sinclair, who'd been the social queen of Macon for forty years—but Rose couldn't shake the feeling that she was an intruder in their legacy.

Eileen laughed, though Rose noticed it ended in a slight cough she tried to cover. "I think I would have the first choice on that one as her mother. My baby and her new husband need their space. I just hope she doesn't forget her way home once in a while."

The comment stung more than her mother probably intended. Rose had been so busy with the move, with learning to be Mrs. Garrett Sinclair, that she hadn't visited her mother as much as she'd planned. The guilt sat heavily in her stomach, another weight to carry along with the strange isolation of this beautiful house.

"Now you know better than that," Rose protested, directing a mover toward the formal dining room. "You two are still going to see me all the time, and we'll have you over for every party and cookout. I just wish you would take it easy, Mama. Did you go to the doctor like I wanted you to?"

Eileen waved her hand dismissively. "I did, but they want to run tests like doctors always do. I think they just want to milk the insurance, if you ask me."

"You should really let them, though. You need to know what's wrong." Rose's voice carried the concern that had been growing stronger each day since the wedding. Her mother seemed more tired, more fragile somehow, and Rose had been trying to convince herself it was just the stress of the wedding and all the changes.

"Hello, ladies." Garrett's voice echoed through the foyer as he appeared in the doorway, still wearing his banker's suit but with his tie loosened and sleeves rolled up. Even disheveled, he looked like he belonged in this house in a way that Rose wasn't sure she ever would.

"That sounds like my wonderful husband, and just in time," Rose said, her face lighting up the way it always did when he walked into a room. It was automatic now, that brightening, that quickening of her pulse when he appeared. "We all need a break."

"Looks like you've all been at it all day. I think I came just in time." Garrett surveyed the organized chaos around them with an amused smile, and Rose noticed how his eyes lingered on her, cataloguing her appearance, her mood, the way she stood.

"Sorry, but we have been at it, and I haven't even started dinner," Rose apologized, automatically falling into the rhythm of domestic concern. The words felt foreign in her mouth—when had she become the type of person who apologized for not having dinner ready?

"No worries. That way, I can take all you wonderful ladies to dinner."

"Wow, that's great! Thank you, Garrett," Lucy said with genuine enthusiasm. Then, with her trademark teasing tone, she added, "Just make sure he doesn't make you pay for it out of your paycheck, Rose."

"Rose doesn't have a paycheck anymore," Garret said matter-of-factly as he adjusted his cufflinks.

The words floated in the air for a moment, and Rose felt heat rise in her cheeks. She'd been meaning to tell Lucy about leaving the store, but somehow the right moment had never come up. Now it sounded abrupt, almost harsh.

Lucy's eyebrows rose slightly. "Really? Did you quit the store?"

"Garrett thought it would be better if I didn't work, since I have this huge house to take care of now, and hopefully soon, all these gardens." Rose's voice carried a note of explanation, as if she had suggested the idea herself. And she was—some mornings she woke up and reached for her work clothes before remembering she had nowhere to go, no schedule to keep except the one that revolved around Garrett's comings and goings.

"Well, that must be nice," Eileen said, though something in her tone suggested she wasn't entirely sure. Her mother had worked two jobs for most of Rose's childhood, and the idea of a woman not working seemed to sit uneasily with her.

"It is," Rose said quickly, though she wasn't entirely sure herself. The days stretched long and empty sometimes, filled with household tasks that seemed to invent themselves to fill the available time. She'd found herself reorganizing the linen closet three times last week, simply because she needed something to do.

"I agree," Lucy said, though her expression remained thoughtful. "You don't happen to need a maid, do you? They've cut my hours again at the store."

"Well, why don't you apply at the bank?" Garrett suggested smoothly. "It's more of a career position—much better pay and hours."

Lucy's face brightened immediately. "Are you serious? That would be great! Thank you. I'll do that tomorrow."

"I'll let them know you're coming when I get to work tomorrow." Garrett's smile was warm and generous, and Rose felt another surge of pride in her husband. This was the man she'd fallen in love with—thoughtful, generous, always looking out for the people she cared about.

"What a wonderful thing to do," Eileen said as Garrett headed upstairs.

Rose watched him go, her heart swelling with pride and love. "I told you. I'm the luckiest woman in Georgia."

But as the three women stood in the vast foyer, surrounded by furniture that spoke of money and tradition and permanence, Lucy couldn't shake the feeling that something had shifted. Rose seemed smaller somehow in this grand house, more dependent, more... contained. The Rose she'd known for so long had been vibrant and independent, full of plans and dreams. This Rose apologized for not having dinner ready and explained her choices as if she needed permission to make them.

***

The next afternoon, Rose was arranging fresh flowers in the front parlor when the phone rang, its shrill tone echoing through the high-ceilinged rooms. She'd been experimenting with different arrangements, trying to make the formal spaces feel more like home, but everything she did seemed to get swallowed by the grandeur of the house.

"I got the job!" Lucy's voice practically burst through the receiver.

"That's wonderful! I knew you would," Rose said, genuinely delighted for her friend. The pleasure in her voice was real—it felt good to focus on someone else's happiness instead of the vague restlessness that had been following her around all morning.

"We need to celebrate. I'll pick you up in fifteen minutes and take you to lunch."

Rose felt a flutter of excitement that surprised her with its intensity. When had a simple lunch invitation become something to get excited about? "Okay, I'll see you in a few."

She barely had time to grab her purse and check her appearance in the hallway mirror before Lucy's car horn was honking outside. As she locked the front door—a habit Garrett had insisted on, even though they lived in the safest neighborhood in town—Rose realized she hadn't been spontaneous in weeks. Everything had been planned, scheduled, and discussed with Garrett first.

They spent a blissful afternoon at their favorite café, then wandered through the boutiques on Main Street, Lucy trying on clothes she could now afford and Rose offering opinions on everything from blouses to earrings. It felt like old times—just two friends enjoying each other's company without any complications or responsibilities weighing them down.

"You seem different," Lucy said as they shared a piece of chocolate cake at their old favorite table by the window.

"Different how?" Rose asked, though she could guess what Lucy meant. She felt different, too, though she couldn't quite put her finger on how.

"I don't know. Quieter, maybe? More..." Lucy searched for the right word. "Careful. Like you're thinking twice before you say things."

Rose laughed, but it came out a little forced. "I'm just adjusting to being married, I guess. To being a wife. It's a big change."

"Good change, though, right?" Lucy's eyes were concerned, studying Rose's face.

"Of course," Rose said quickly. "Garrett's wonderful. The house is beautiful. I'm living a fairy tale most women can only dream about."

But even as she said it, Rose had almost forgotten how good it felt to be spontaneous, to not think about meal planning or household schedules or whether the pool man would need access to the back gate. For three hours, she'd been Rose Nichols again instead of Mrs. Garrett Sinclair, and the freedom had been intoxicating.

When they pulled back into the circular drive, however, Rose's carefree mood evaporated. Garrett's black Cadillac was parked at an angle near the front steps, and he was emerging from the house with quick, purposeful strides. Even from a distance, Rose could see the tension in his shoulders, the set of his jaw.

"He's home early," Rose said, a flutter of anxiety replacing her earlier contentment. "I hope nothing's wrong."

"Rose, where have you been?" Garrett's voice carried across the drive as he approached the car, and Rose noticed how Lucy's grip tightened on the steering wheel. "I've been calling and calling with no answer."

Before she could fully respond, he had pulled her from the passenger seat into a tight embrace that felt more desperate than welcoming. His hands pressed against her back, holding her against him as if she might disappear if he let go.

"I'm sorry, I didn't mean to worry you," Rose said quickly, the words tumbling out in her haste to explain. The apology came automatically, though she wasn't entirely sure what she was apologizing for. "Lucy was excited about getting the job, so we went to lunch to celebrate and then ran out to some shops. I figured I'd get home before you, so I didn't leave a note. I'm sorry. I didn't mean to worry you."

"It's my fault," Lucy interjected, though her expression had grown guarded as she watched Garrett's hands remain possessively on Rose's shoulders. "I was just happy about the job. Thank you again, Garrett."

"It's fine. I'm glad I could help." His smile returned, though it didn't quite reach his eyes, and Rose noticed how he seemed to be studying Lucy, noticing her expression, her body language. "Did you two have a good time?"

"We always have a good time. We're like sisters," Rose said, her voice still carrying that apologetic note. She could feel the tension radiating from Garrett's body, the way his grip on her shoulders tightened just slightly when she mentioned how much fun they'd had.

"I need to run," Lucy said, clearly sensing the tension. "I'm sorry we worried you."

"It's fine, Lucy. Call me tomorrow."

As Lucy drove away, Garrett's arms remained around Rose, holding her perhaps a moment longer than necessary. She could feel his heart beating against her chest, fast and hard, as if he'd been running.

"I had no idea you would be so worried," Rose said softly, looking up at his face. There was something in his eyes she couldn't quite read—relief, certainly, but something else too. Something that made her stomach flutter with an emotion she couldn't name.

"I just love you so much, and I worry. Too much, I guess, but with us being wealthy and all..." He paused, running a hand through his hair. "I just worry, is all."

"I'm fine. Besides, nobody would want to mess with Lucy—she'd give them a swift kick." Rose managed a laugh, trying to lighten the mood. "I'll be more careful. Thanks for caring so much."

"More than you could possibly know."

As they walked toward the house together, Garrett's arm remained around her waist, and Rose tried to ignore the way his grip felt less like affection and more like possession. She was probably just imagining things, she told herself. This was what it meant to be loved completely, to be cherished and protected.

But as they climbed the front steps, Rose couldn't shake the memory of those three hours with Lucy, of how free she'd felt, how much like herself. And she couldn't stop thinking about the way Garrett had been waiting for her, watching for her car, calling the house over and over again.

She was probably just imagining things, she told herself again. This was love, pure and simple. This was what she'd always wanted. To have a man who purely worshipped her and put her feelings first was what every woman dreamed about, so why did she feel this way?

Why did it feel like the walls of the beautiful house were closing in around her?

A Beautiful Surprise

The very next day, Rose was inside arranging some new pieces they'd purchased for the morning room when she heard a car horn outside. The sound was different from their usual vehicles—sharper, more musical somehow. She set down the crystal vase she'd been positioning and walked toward the front door, curiosity prickling at her.

Through the beveled glass panels, she could see a figure standing beside something sleek and dark. When she opened the door, she found Garrett standing beside a gleaming black Cadillac Allante convertible, keys dangling from his finger and a boyish grin on his face that made him look ten years younger.

"Did we get a new car?" she asked, stepping out onto the porch. The afternoon sun caught the car's paint, making it shimmer like liquid night.

"Not we. You. It's yours."

Rose's scream of delight echoed off the mansion's columns as she jumped up and down like a teenager. "Oh my God, it's beautiful! I love it!" The excitement was genuine and overwhelming—she'd never owned anything so beautiful, so expensive, so completely luxurious.

"You really like it?" Garrett's voice carried a note of deep satisfaction, as if her joy was exactly what he'd been hoping for.

"I can't believe it! I love, love, love it! You are too good to me." She threw her arms around his neck, and he pulled her close, breathing in the scent of her hair.

"I told you—nothing is too good for you, Rose. You needed a new car anyway. How about we take it for a spin?"

Rose practically flew to the driver's seat, her hands caressing the leather steering wheel as if it were made of silk. The interior smelled of expensive leather and new car luxury, and when she turned the key, the engine purged with a satisfaction that seemed to vibrate through her entire body.

"This is incredible," she breathed, adjusting the mirrors, the seat, and familiarizing herself with the dashboard. "I feel like I'm in a movie."

"You look like you belong in one," Garrett said, sliding into the passenger seat. "Beautiful woman, beautiful car. Perfect combination."

As they sped down the winding road that led away from the mansion, the wind whipping through her hair, Rose felt a freedom she hadn't experienced in weeks. The convertible responded to her touch like a dream, hugging the curves of the road with precision and grace. She laughed with pure joy, pressing the accelerator just a little harder, feeling the car surge forward with barely contained power.

Garrett watched her with an expression of deep satisfaction, his eyes never leaving her face. She was so happy, so grateful for everything he provided. And now, with this beautiful car, she would always remember who had given it to her, who took care of her, who made sure she had everything her heart desired.

"This is the most amazing gift anyone has ever given me," Rose called over the rush of wind. "I don't know how to thank you."

"Your happiness is thanks enough," he replied, but something in his tone suggested he was storing away her gratitude like a precious commodity. "I love seeing you smile like that."

The convertible purred like a contented cat as they drove toward town, Rose laughing with pure joy, completely unaware of the way Garrett's eyes never left her face, cataloging every expression of pleasure and gratitude like precious gems to be stored away for future reference.

"We should drive up to the lake sometime," Rose said, downshifting as they approached a stop sign. "Or maybe take a trip to Savannah. This car was made for road trips."

"Whatever you want," Garrett said, though something flickered across his face—a brief shadow that Rose, focused on the road ahead, didn't notice. "As long as we're together."

When they returned to the mansion, Rose spent another twenty minutes just sitting in the car, running her hands over the dashboard, adjusting the radio, reveling in the possession of something so beautiful. But as she finally climbed out and walked toward the house, she couldn't shake the feeling that the gift was almost too generous, too perfect. Like everything else in her new life, it seemed designed to overwhelm her with its magnificence.

"Thank you," she said again as they reached the front door. "Really, Garrett. This is incredible."

"You deserve incredible things," he replied, his hand settling on the small of her back as he guided her into the house. "You deserve everything."

***

A few days later, Rose stood beside the gleaming Cadillac in the parking lot of her mother's apartment complex, the afternoon sun making the black paint shine like obsidian. Even parked among the modest cars of the other residents, the convertible looked like it belonged in a different world—a world of wealth and privilege that Rose was still learning to navigate.

"Is this the most beautiful car you have ever seen or what?" Rose asked, running her hand along the smooth hood. The metal was warm from the sun, and she could see her reflection distorted in its perfect surface.

Eileen walked slowly around the convertible, her expression thoughtful. Her movements were more careful than usual, Rose noticed, as if each step required extra consideration. "It is very nice, dear... and very expensive. Your Garrett must really love you a lot to give you a surprise like this."

"He does." Rose's smile faltered just slightly, and she found herself looking away from her mother's perceptive eyes. "Sometimes a little too much, I think."

"What do you mean, too much? I didn't know you could love anyone too much." Rose leaned against the car, suddenly looking uncertain. The words had slipped out before she could stop them, and now she wasn't sure how to explain the feeling that had been growing inside her—a sense that Garrett's love was becoming something that wrapped around her like beautiful silk that was just a little too tight.

"I don't know. It's just sometimes he tends to go overboard to show me how much or gets too excited and upset if I'm out longer than he thinks I should be." She paused, then added quietly, "Like yesterday, when I stopped at the grocery store on my way home from running errands. When I got home, he said he'd been worried sick because I was gone longer than usual. He'd actually driven around looking for me."

Eileen's maternal radar sharpened. "Are the two of you having some problems?"

"Oh no, nothing like that," Rose said quickly, as if the very suggestion were dangerous. The denial came automatically, forcefully, as if she were trying to convince herself as much as her mother. "I'm sure it's just me. I know for a fact, Garrett loves me, and I love him. I just sometimes feel he worries too much."

"That's probably the first time I've ever heard a woman complain that her man worries about her or cares too much." Eileen's tone was light, but her eyes remained watchful. She'd raised Rose through two decades of ups and downs, and she knew when her daughter was trying to convince herself of something.

They both smiled, but Rose's didn't quite reach her eyes. "I know. I'm crazy, right?"

"You aren't crazy. I'm just saying many women would love to have your problem." Eileen paused, studying her daughter's face. Rose looked beautiful—her hair was perfectly styled, her clothes expensive and flattering, her skin glowing with the health that came from a life without financial stress. But there was something in her eyes that hadn't been there before the wedding, a shadow of uncertainty that made Eileen's chest tighten with worry.

"I suppose you're right," Rose said, though her voice lacked conviction. "I should be grateful. Look at this car—what woman wouldn't want a husband who surprises her with something like this?"

"Gratitude is important," Eileen said carefully. "But so is feeling free to be yourself."

Rose looked at her mother sharply. "What do you mean?"

"Nothing specific. Just... marriage is about partnership, not ownership. Even when someone loves you very much."

The words hung between them for a moment, and Rose felt something shift inside her chest—a recognition of something she'd been trying not to acknowledge.

"By the way, are you still able to drive me to the doctor tomorrow?" Eileen asked, changing the subject with practiced ease.

"Sure, I told you I would. I wish you would tell me what this is all about."

"It's just tests that you do as you get older. One day you'll understand. Trust me."

"You would tell me if something was wrong, wouldn't you?"

"Yes. I'll tell you everything when my tests come back." Eileen's voice carried a weariness that spoke of more than just age. "Now let's go inside. I have an apple pie I'm dying to get into."

Rose put her arm around her mother's shoulders, and they walked toward the apartment building together. As they climbed the stairs, Eileen couldn't help but notice how Rose kept glancing back at the expensive car, as if making sure it was still there—or perhaps wondering what the price of such generosity might ultimately be.

"Mama," Rose said suddenly, pausing on the landing. "Do you think it's possible to love someone so much that you... lose yourself?"

Eileen stopped climbing and turned to face her daughter. "What makes you ask that?"

"I don't know. Sometimes I feel like I'm disappearing a little bit each day. Like I'm becoming someone else—someone who needs to be taken care of instead of someone who can take care of herself."

"Honey, marriage changes people. That's normal. But it should make you more yourself, not less."

Rose nodded, but Eileen could see the confusion in her eyes. "I'm probably just adjusting. It's a big change, going from working and living alone to... all this."

"It is a big change," Eileen agreed. "But remember, you're allowed to keep being Rose Nichols, even if you're also Mrs. Garrett Sinclair now."

As they continued up the stairs, Rose found herself thinking about the car again—not about its beauty or its value, but about the way Garrett had watched her face when she'd first seen it, the way he'd seemed to be collecting her gratitude like evidence of something. She pushed the thought away, telling herself she was being ungrateful and paranoid.

But as they reached her mother's door, she couldn't shake the feeling that the beautiful car was more than just a gift. It was a golden chain, and she was only beginning to understand how tightly it was wrapped around her wrist.

A Hint of Concern

At the bank the following week, Lucy was deep in paperwork when a shadow fell across her desk. The familiar scent of expensive cologne reached her before she looked up to find Garrett standing there, his banker's smile warm but somehow calculating. He stood with the perfect posture of a man accustomed to command, his tailored suit impeccable despite the Georgia heat outside.

"Mr. Sinclair. How are you today?"

"I just wanted to see how our newest employee was doing." His voice carried that practiced smoothness that made clients trust him with their life savings. "How do you like it so far?"

Lucy set down her pen and looked up at him fully, noting how his presence seemed to fill the space around her cubicle. Other employees glanced over with the mixture of curiosity and deference that Garrett's visits always inspired. "It's a lot to learn, but I think I'm going to love it."

"I'm really glad to hear that." He leaned against the edge of her desk with casual familiarity, his gold wedding band catching the fluorescent light. "And what's with the 'Mr. Sinclair'? I'm your best friend's husband."

Lucy straightened in her chair, maintaining her professional composure despite the subtle pressure in his tone. She'd learned early in life that boundaries were important, especially with men who weren't used to hearing the word no. "Yes, you are, but at work you're the boss, and the boss deserves respect and professionalism."

"Well, I really admire your attitude." His smile broadened, but something in his eyes remained watchful, predatory even. "I think you're going to do really well here. Just don't forget about Rose. I'm sure you two can sneak in some lunches here and there."

The comment struck Lucy as odd—not the words themselves, but the way he said them, as if he were giving her permission for something that should have been naturally hers. "You don't have to worry about that. She's my confidant. I have to have my girl time with her."

"I'm really glad. I like it when Rose is spending time with you." There was something in his tone that made the hair on the back of Lucy's neck stand up, though she couldn't pinpoint why.

"Oh? Why is that?"

Garrett's smile never wavered, but his eyes sharpened with an intensity that made Lucy suddenly aware of how isolated her cubicle was from the rest of the office. "Well, if she's with you, then I know she's staying out of trouble."

The words caused a pause for a second between them, heavy with implication. Lucy forced a laugh, though the comment struck her as deeply wrong. Rose was the most trustworthy person she knew—what kind of trouble could she possibly get into? "If that's all you have to worry about, then you're good. Rose always stays out of trouble. She's the one who keeps me in line most of the time."

"I'm just glad she has a friend like you." His voice carried a note of finality, as if some unspoken agreement had been reached. "Someone I can trust to keep an eye on her."

Lucy felt a chill despite the warm office air. *Keep an eye on her? What did that mean?* "The feeling is mutual. Now, I better get back to work before I get in trouble for kissing up to the boss."

"You have a good day, Lucy." As Garrett walked away, his footsteps echoing confidently across the marble floor, Lucy stared after him, a frown creasing her brow. The conversation had felt like more than small talk — there had been an undercurrent she couldn't quite identify, as if he were testing her somehow or establishing some kind of understanding about her role in Rose's life.

She tried to shake off the feeling, telling herself she was reading too much into it. But something about the way he'd said "someone I can trust" made her stomach turn. Trust to do what, exactly?

That afternoon, Rose sat beside her mother on the faded couch in Eileen's apartment, both women's faces streaked with tears. The small living room felt even smaller now, crowded with the weight of unspoken fears and the medicine bottles that had begun to colonize the coffee table. Eileen's arm was wrapped protectively around her daughter's shoulders, her touch still strong despite the illness ravaging her body.

"Rose, please calm down. It's not over yet." Eileen's voice carried the same steady strength that had guided Rose through childhood scraped knees and teenage heartbreaks. "The doctor says he'll start treatment and see how it goes. Your tough old mom might just come through this just fine."

"I know," Rose sobbed, her voice muffled against her mother's shoulder. The fabric of Eileen's worn cardigan smelled like the lavender sachets she'd always kept in her dresser drawers, a scent that transported Rose back to safer times. "But I just can't stand the thought that something could go wrong, and I could lose you."

"Shh, now don't cry." Eileen's hand stroked Rose's hair with the same gentle rhythm she'd used when Rose was small and afraid of thunderstorms. "I'm still here now. Don't count me out yet."

"I'm just worried, Mom. I love you so very much." Rose pulled back to look at her mother's face, memorizing every line, every freckle, as if she could somehow preserve this moment forever.

"And I love you too, baby. I don't want to go away from you either, but dying is a part of living, and something we all have to do. Most of the time, we give up our parents first. I gave up mine, and it was hard, but I had you to think of. You'll understand that more when you have children of your own."

Rose's expression shifted, a shadow crossing her face like clouds over the sun. "It's just so hard. You're all I have left."

"Now, now. I'm not all you have left." Eileen's eyes held a mother's intuition, sensing the pain her daughter wasn't voicing. "You have Lucy and a wonderful husband who adores you and gives you big houses and buys you new convertibles. Besides, you need to start thinking about starting a family of your own. I'd like to be a grandmother while I can still enjoy it."

Rose's body tensed almost imperceptibly, her hands clasping together in her lap. "Now is just not the right time for that. There are too many other things going on."

"What's wrong?" Eileen's voice sharpened with maternal concern. After twenty-eight years of loving this child, she could read Rose's moods like her own heartbeat.

"Nothing's wrong. I just want to get this sickness behind us and you on the road to recovery, and then I can think of starting a family."

"Does Garrett want children?"

Rose's laugh held no humor, only a brittle edge that made Eileen's stomach clench with worry. "Oh, I'm sure he would love the idea. I could stay at home with it, and he would know where I was all the time." The words tumbled out before Rose could stop them, revealing more than she'd intended.

Eileen's maternal instincts, honed by years of protecting her daughter, immediately sharpened. "What does that mean? What's going on with you two?"

Rose's face flushed with the panic of someone who'd said too much. "Nothing. I shouldn't have said that. I'm just upset. You need to just concentrate on getting better."

"I will, but I'm still your mother." Eileen's voice carried the authority of someone who'd spent decades reading between the lines of her daughter's words. "I want to help you when you need me."

"I will always need you, Mom." Rose's voice broke on the words. They embraced fiercely, holding each other as if they could stop time itself, as if love alone could hold back the darkness that seemed to be closing in from all sides.

"I will always be here for you as long as there's breath in this old body." Eileen's promise filled the air like a prayer, though both women knew that some promises were beyond human power to keep.

***

Later that evening, Garrett held Rose on the large sofa in their mansion's living room, her head against his chest as the last traces of tears dried on her cheeks. The room around them spoke of wealth and taste—Persian rugs, original oil paintings, furniture that cost more than most people's cars—but it felt cold despite the warmth of the fire crackling in the marble fireplace. His face wore an expression of deep concern mixed with something else—a kind of satisfaction at being needed so completely.

"It hurts me to see you in so much pain." His voice was gentle, but his arms around her felt more like a cage than an embrace.

"I can't help it. She's the only family I have left in the world." Rose's voice was small, muffled against his chest.

"That's not true." His arms tightened around her, and she could feel the steady rhythm of his heartbeat against her cheek. "You have me. I am your family. I love you more than you could possibly imagine."

The words should have been comforting, but something in his tone made them feel like a claim being staked rather than comfort being offered. "I know that, Garrett, but you know what I mean. She's my blood, my mom. I love her so much, and we're so close. I just don't know what I'll do without her."

"I think you should spend as much time with her as you can while you still can." His hand stroked her hair, the gesture tender but possessive. "Do everything to make sure she's as happy and comfortable as she can possibly be and know I'm here to support you if you need it."

Rose felt a surge of gratitude despite her emotional exhaustion. "Thank you. It means a lot to me that you're so supportive in this."

"Your mother is a wonderful lady. I'm glad I had the chance to know her." His voice carried just the right note of sincerity, though his thoughts were already calculating how much things would change once Eileen was gone. "If there's anything financially that she needs, you spend whatever you need to."

Rose hugged him tighter, grateful for his generosity even as some part of her wondered why every act of kindness felt like it came with invisible strings attached. The thought was disloyal, ungrateful, and she pushed it away. "Thank you. I love you."

"I love you too, and I'll be here for you both right to the end and with you after." His words were a promise and a threat wrapped in the same breath.

"You really are good to me."

"I love you, Rose." As he held her in the dim light of their grand living room, Garrett's eyes held a gleam of something that wasn't quite love—it was possession, pure and simple. In the firelight, his face took on an almost sinister cast, though Rose couldn't see it from her position against his chest.

Soon, very soon, her mother would be gone, and Rose would have no one left but him. No one to run to, no one to confide in except the friend he was already managing through her job at his bank. Lucy would be his eyes and ears, whether she realized it or not. Every lunch, every conversation, every moment of Rose's life would be filtered through people who ultimately answered to him.

Everything was falling into place exactly as he'd wanted. The thought brought him a deep satisfaction that had nothing to do with love and everything to do with control. Rose was becoming more isolated by the day, more dependent on him, more trapped in the beautiful cage he'd built around her. And the most beautiful part was that she was doing it to herself, choosing to lean on him, choosing to trust him, choosing to love him even as he slowly, unintentionally, destroyed every other connection in her life.

The fire crackled in the hearth, casting dancing shadows across the room, and Garrett smiled in the darkness above Rose's head. Paradise of the all-consuming love was within his reach.

A Masterful Plan

The next morning, Garrett was adjusting his tie as he walked toward the front door when he heard the unmistakable sound of Rose's car failing to start. Through the window, he could see her behind the wheel, her face a mask of frustration as the engine made nothing but clicking sounds. The black convertible that had once been her pride and joy now sat lifeless in their circular drive.

He stepped outside, his expression the picture of a concerned husband, though beneath the surface, he felt a thrill of satisfaction. The car not starting caused Rose to depend on him completely. "Has it done this before?"

"No. I don't understand. It's never done this." Rose's voice carried a note of panic—she had promised to drive her mother to another doctor's appointment, and Eileen was depending on her. The car had been running perfectly just yesterday when she'd driven to the grocery store.

"Pop the hood and let me see if I can do anything."

Rose released the hood latch, and Garrett made a show of examining the engine, moving a few wires around without really doing anything useful. He'd already removed the fuel relay the night before to ensure the car would never start again, but Rose didn't need to know that. His fingers traced over the pristine engine components, putting on a performance of masculine competence.

"Okay, try it again."

The clicking continued, but the engine remained stubbornly silent. Rose turned the key again and again, each failed attempt increasing the desperation in her movements. "What am I going to do? I have to get Mom to the doctor's office in a bit." Rose's hands gripped the steering wheel tighter, her knuckles white with stress. This appointment was crucial; they were supposed to discuss treatment options, and she couldn't bear the thought of disappointing her mother again.

"Here." Garrett produced his keys with practiced efficiency, as if this solution had just occurred to him rather than being carefully orchestrated. "You take my car, drop me off at the bank, and I'll call the dealer to take care of this. You don't need this worry. You concentrate on your mom."

Rose felt a rush of gratitude despite her frustration. This was the Garrett she'd fallen in love with, the one who swooped in to solve problems, who anticipated her needs before she even voiced them. "Thanks. I'll pick you up tonight after work. We should be finished by then."

"No worries. Take care of your mom, and we'll work it out. Let me have your keys, and we'll leave so you'll have plenty of time to drop me off and get to the doctor."

"It must be the battery or something. It's always started right up." Rose handed over her keys reluctantly, already missing the familiar weight of them in her palm.

As they drove toward town in his Cadillac, Garrett allowed himself a small, satisfied smile. Phase one was complete. Soon, Rose would be completely dependent on him for transportation, and he would know exactly where she was at all times. The black convertible had been a symbol of independence; now it would become a symbol of his control.

Three days later, Rose and Garrett emerged from the mansion's front door to find a long black Cadillac sedan parked in their circular drive. The vehicle was so dark it seemed to absorb the morning sunlight, its chrome gleaming like polished obsidian. Beside it stood a man in his thirties, impeccably dressed in a chauffeur's uniform, his posture military straight and his eyes hidden behind dark sunglasses.

Rose stopped dead, her face a picture of confusion. The sight of the imposing vehicle made her stomach clench with unease, though she couldn't explain why. "What is this? Are we going somewhere formal?"

"This is your car and driver. Meet Mark. He'll assist you and take you anywhere you need to go." Garrett's voice carried the pride of a man presenting his wife with the perfect gift.

Mark stepped forward with practiced precision and removed his cap. "Good morning, Mrs. Sinclair. It's my honor to serve you." His voice was courteous but impersonal, the tone of someone who'd been trained to be invisible.

"Where is my car? I love my car. I want my car back." Rose's voice wavered between confusion and something approaching panic. The black convertible had been hers—the first car she'd ever loved, the first new car of her own she had ever had. It represented independence, freedom, and the ability to go wherever she wanted, whenever she wanted.

Garrett's expression grew grave, as if he were delivering terrible news. "Well, unfortunately, the computer brain in the car was bad. It's a problem with those particular models that I had no idea about when I bought it for you. I started thinking—what if the car broke down on you while you were alone, or out late like last week?" An explanation about the car he had read from an article in a car magazine that would sound logical if ever questioned.

"I told you I was late because I stayed with Mother." Rose's voice held a defensive edge that she immediately regretted. Why did she always sound like she was making excuses?

"I know, I know, but what if you needed to stay late with her again? As her condition deteriorates, you may need to be out late. What if you weren't close to a phone and got stranded? Now you have someone to help all the time. And you can just be with your mom and not have to worry about traffic or anything."

The logic was sound, Rose had to admit. And yet something about the whole situation felt wrong, like a beautifully wrapped present that contained something she didn't want. She let out a long sigh, her shoulders sagging with resignation. "I know it's a wonderful thing to do. I just really liked my car and the freedom of having my own vehicle."

"Where would you want to go that Mark can't take you?" Garrett's question was gentle, but there was something underneath it—a subtle challenge that made Rose feel foolish for wanting independence.

"It's not that I have somewhere to sneak away to." The words came out more defensively than she'd intended, and she saw Garrett's eyes sharpen slightly. "I just sometimes like to drive with no particular place to go."

"Well, you can still do that, and now you can just look out the window and not even have to worry about anything. You can just think." His smile was warm and reassuring, the smile that had first captured her heart that first day in the store.

"It's not exactly the same thing." Rose's voice was small, almost petulant, and she hated how she sounded. Here was her husband, spending what must be a fortune to make her life easier, and she was complaining about it.

"Just try it for a while. I promise, when you see how easy it is to have someone else do the driving for you, you'll wonder why you didn't have a driver the whole time." Garrett's confidence was absolute, as if he'd never doubted that she would eventually see things his way.

Rose looked unconvinced as she turned to go back into the house. Part of her wanted to argue further, to insist on getting her own car back, but another part—the part that had been trained since childhood to be grateful for what she was given—told her she was being ungrateful. After all, how many women had their own personal driver? This was luxury beyond most people's dreams.

The moment she was out of earshot, Garrett approached the chauffeur. His entire demeanor shifted, the loving husband mask dropping away to reveal something colder, more calculating.

"Remember—take her anywhere she wants to go, when she wants to go. Just remember who signs your paycheck, and make sure your memory is good. I expect to know everywhere you took her, who she talked to, how long she stayed, what she bought, everything. Nothing is too small to mention."

"Yes, Mr. Sinclair." Mark's voice was flat, professional. He'd done this kind of work before.

"Good man." Garrett handed him a business card. "My direct line. I want daily reports, and if *anything* unusual happens, you call me immediately."

As Garrett walked back toward the house, he felt the familiar thrill of control tightening around his chest. Rose might not appreciate it now, but she would learn to love her cage. After all, he was only trying to protect her—from the world, from other people, from her own poor judgment. It was what love looked like when it was pure and complete.

Later that afternoon, Rose and Eileen emerged from the apartment building to find the imposing black sedan waiting at the curb like a sleeping predator. Eileen stopped short, her eyes widening as she took in the vehicle that seemed to dominate the entire street.

"What's this? I'm not ready for a hearse yet." Despite her illness, Eileen's sense of humor remained intact, though there was an edge to her voice that Rose didn't miss.

"I forgot to tell you about this." Rose's laugh sounded forced even to her own ears.

"What is this? Where's your car?" Eileen's maternal instincts were immediately on high alert. She'd seen that black convertible make Rose happier than any material possession ever had.

"This is my car now. Mine wouldn't start the other day, and they told him it was a lemon, so he traded it for this." Rose tried to inject enthusiasm into her voice, but it fell flat.

"Ah, okay. I understand the car may have needed trading, but why not an Eldorado or something? Why the limo and driver?" Eileen's eyes narrowed as she studied the chauffeur, who stood at attention beside the rear door like a sentry.

"That was kind of my thought as well." Rose's admission slipped out before she could stop it, and she immediately felt guilty for the disloyalty.

Mark stepped forward and opened the rear door with practiced efficiency. "Good afternoon, Mrs. Sinclair. Ma'am." His nod to Eileen was respectful but impersonal.

Eileen glanced meaningfully at the chauffeur, then back at Rose. "Well, I mean, how do you have a private conversation with... him around?"

"You don't, but I think that might be the point." The words escaped before Rose could censor them, and she immediately regretted the admission.

"What do you mean?" Eileen's voice sharpened with concern.

Rose glanced at Mark, who stood motionless beside the open door, his face impassive. She lowered her voice, though she was certain he could still hear every word. "You know the other night when you weren't feeling well, and I was out late?"

"Yeah."

"Well, Garrett got worried and was pacing the floor when I got home."

"Why? He knew you were with me. He could have just called to check." Eileen's practicality cut straight to the heart of the matter.

"I said that too, but he said he didn't want me to think he was spying on me or checking up." Rose's voice grew smaller with each word, as if she were trying to convince herself as much as her mother.

Eileen's expression grew sharp with understanding, the look of a woman who'd lived long enough to recognize manipulation when she saw it. "But this isn't a form of checking up? Dear, you need to talk to him about this. How long has he been this way?"

Rose felt something inside her chest tighten, a mixture of defensiveness and the dawning realization that her mother was voicing concerns she'd been trying to suppress. "I guess in a way he's always been this way. It's not like he's jealous. He just worries too much, and sometimes he's overprotective. Maybe it's just me overreacting. I know he does love me. I just... I don't know."

The words tumbled out in a rush, and Rose realized she was trying to justify Garrett's behavior as much to herself as to her mother. He did love her—of that she was certain. The gifts, the house, the way he looked at her like she was the most precious thing in the world. But why did love have to feel so suffocating sometimes?

"I know he does seem to be a worrywart, and I truly believe he loves you too. Maybe you just need to have a good heart-to-heart. I wouldn't like this either." Eileen's voice was gentle but firm, the voice of a mother who'd spent decades protecting her daughter and wasn't about to stop now.

Rose managed a weak smile, though it didn't reach her eyes. "Speaking of which, we should get in the car before we're reported on as spying and plotting."

They looked at each other and laughed, but the humor felt forced, tinged with an underlying anxiety that neither woman wanted to acknowledge. As they settled into the plush leather seats, both women were acutely aware of the silent figure in the driver's seat, and the uncomfortable realization that even their most private conversations would now have an audience.

Rose stared out the window as they drove toward the doctor's office, watching the familiar streets of Macon pass by. Everything looked the same, but somehow different, as if she were seeing it through glass—beautiful but untouchable. The leather seats were luxurious, the ride smooth and quiet, but she found herself longing for the familiar rumble of her convertible's engine, the feeling of wind in her hair, the simple pleasure of choosing her own direction.

She told herself she was being ungrateful. This was what fairy tales looked like—the prince providing everything his princess could ever want. But why did it feel more like a beautiful prison than a happily ever after?

The thought was disloyal, and she pushed it away. Garrett loved her. He was protecting her. This was what love looked like when it was complete and unconditional.

But as the sedan glided silently through the streets, Rose couldn't shake the feeling that with each gift, each gesture of protection, each act of love, the walls of her world were slowly, inexorably closing in.

Crossing the Line

The afternoon sun cast long shadows across the marble floors of the bank as Garrett slammed the phone down with such force that the entire desk shuddered. His gold pen holder toppled over, scattering expensive writing instruments across the polished mahogany surface. He shot up from his chair like a man possessed, his usual composed demeanor cracking as he grabbed his jacket and headed for the door.

The call from Mark had been brief but devastating: "She dismissed me for the afternoon, sir. Said she wanted to walk around downtown alone. I followed at a distance as instructed, but she went into Mitchell's Department Store through the main entrance and never came out. I've been watching all the exits for two hours."

Two hours. Rose had been unaccounted for, unsupervised, free to do God knows what for two entire hours. The thought made Garrett's chest tighten with something between rage and panic.

"Hey buddy, where's the fire?" Jack's voice carried a note of concern as he stepped into the office, blocking Garrett's path. His friend's usually immaculate appearance was disheveled, his tie askew, and his hair mussed as if he'd been running his hands through it. "We're not being robbed, are we?"

"I need to go talk to Lucy. Excuse me." Garrett's words came out clipped, his jaw tight with barely contained anxiety. Lucy would know where Rose was—she had to. The two women were thick as thieves, and if Rose was planning something, Lucy would be involved.

"Lucy's not here today. She took a personal day."

Garrett stopped short, his eyes narrowing with suspicion. The timing was too convenient, too perfect. "A personal day? Why?"

Jack raised an eyebrow at his friend's intensity, noting the way Garrett's hands had clenched into fists at his sides. "I think that's why they call it 'a personal day.' She had stuff to take care of. Why are you so worked up? Is something wrong?"

"It's Rose." The words tumbled out of Garrett with an urgency that made Jack take a step back. "She hasn't been home all day. She's not at her mother's house, and now Lucy is missing."

Jack had known Garrett for many years, had seen him handle million-dollar deals and angry investors with unflappable calm. This version of his friend—wild-eyed and frantic— was usually foreign and now deeply unsettling.

"Whoa." Jack held up his hands in a calming gesture. "Missing is a little of an exaggeration. Maybe she and Rose are just having lunch and shopping."

"No. I would know that." Garrett's voice had taken on a hard edge that Jack had never heard before, something cold and possessive that made the hair on the back of his neck stand up. "Mark would have told me. Unless her mother is lying about her being there. I'm going to drive by and see if her mother's car is there."

Before Jack could respond, Garrett stormed past him toward the exit, his footsteps echoing off the marble floors with military precision. Other employees looked up from their desks, sensing the tension radiating from their normally composed boss.

"Garrett!" Jack called after him, but his friend had already disappeared around the corner, leaving only the faint scent of expensive cologne and an atmosphere of barely contained frustration.

Jack shook his head, a worried frown creasing his features as he watched the space where Garrett had been. Something was very wrong with his friend, and he had the sinking feeling that Rose was at the center of it. He was afraid that history had started to repeat itself once more.

The evening had settled into that particular kind of quiet that comes just before darkness fully claims the day. Rose stepped out of the black sedan, her heels clicking against the stone driveway as she made her way toward the imposing front entrance of the mansion. The familiar weight of the day's deceptions pressed against her chest—not lies, exactly, but the careful omissions that had become second nature.

She had spent the afternoon with Lucy, not shopping or having lunch as she'd told Mark, but talking. Really talking, for the first time in months. They'd found a quiet corner booth in a little café across town, far from the bank and the usual places where they might be seen. Lucy had listened with growing concern as Rose tried to explain the feeling of being watched, monitored, and controlled, all while receiving the kind of love and luxury most women only dreamed of.

"It's like living in a beautiful cage," Rose had whispered, stirring her coffee with nervous energy. "I know how ungrateful that sounds, but I can't shake the feeling that I'm disappearing somehow."

Lucy had reached across the table to squeeze her hand. "That doesn't sound ungrateful, Rose. That sounds like you're trying to tell me something important."

The conversation had given Rose a strange sense of relief, as if speaking the words aloud had somehow made them real and valid. But now, approaching the house she shared with Garrett, guilt crept in alongside the relief. He loved her. He provided for her. He worried about her. Maybe she was being paranoid, ungrateful, and selfish.

She pushed through the front door and headed upstairs to freshen up before Garrett came looking for her. The house felt too quiet, too still, in the way that large spaces do when they're mostly empty. The marble floors amplified every sound—the click of her heels, the whisper of her dress against her legs, the soft thud of her purse on the vanity table.

She had just started down the staircase when she heard the front door open with more force than usual, followed by footsteps that seemed to echo with barely contained energy.

"What were you doing outside? I was just looking for you." The words came out before she could think about them, genuine surprise coloring her voice. Something in his posture, in the way he held himself, made her instantly alert.

His answering smile was warm, genuine seeming, but it didn't quite match his eyes. "I heard the car drive up and went out to welcome you home."

"Sorry I'm so late. I hope you weren't worried. Mom isn't feeling well, so I wanted to sit with her for a while and make sure she was okay." The lie came easily now, practiced and smooth, though it left a bitter taste in her mouth.

"That was really kind of you to do. She's lucky to have you for a daughter." His voice carried all the warmth and approval she had once craved, but now it felt calculating, as if he were testing her response. "Is that all you did today?"

Rose felt a familiar knot forming in her stomach—the way he asked questions that seemed casual but somehow weren't. There was always an undercurrent of something she couldn't quite name, a sense that he already knew the answers and was simply seeing if she would tell the truth. "No. Actually, I had lunch with Lucy and ran a few errands, but that's nothing you couldn't find out on your own, is it?"

The words came out sharper than she intended, carrying months of accumulated resentment and frustration by the repetitive questions that seemed more like a test she had to pass. She saw something flicker across his face—surprise, perhaps, or calculation, or maybe something darker.

For a moment, the mask slipped, and she caught a glimpse of something in his eyes that made her stomach clench with an instinctive concern. Then it was gone, replaced by that familiar expression of loving concern.

"I was just curious. You know I'm concerned about your mom too. I just want to make sure you're having some personal time as well. It's unhealthy to be totally consumed, no matter how much we love someone. Sickness can do that. I just worry."

His voice was so reasonable, so caring, that Rose found herself relaxing slightly despite the voice in her head that screamed warnings. This was the Garrett she'd fallen in love with— thoughtful, considerate, protective. Maybe she was being too sensitive, reading malice where there was only love. "I know you do. I didn't mean to be cross with you. It's just... sometimes this whole driver thing gets to me. I feel, sometimes, like I'm being watched."

"If Mark is a problem or making you feel uncomfortable in any way, we'll get someone else." His response was immediate, solicitous, the perfect reaction of a caring husband. But there was something in his tone that suggested the problem wasn't with Mark specifically, but with her ungrateful attitude toward his generosity.

"No. It's just... I don't know. Mark is fine. He doesn't make me feel uncomfortable exactly. It just takes some time to get used to." Rose heard herself backtracking, apologizing for having feelings, minimizing her own discomfort in the face of his reasonableness.

"Many wealthy and celebrity types have drivers." The comment was casual, but it carried weight—a reminder of how fortunate she was, how many people would kill to have her problems.

Maybe I am creating this problem in my head, she thought. She wasn't entirely sure why she said it, but the words felt true enough, even as they tasted like betrayal of her own instincts. "I know. I'm sorry. I guess I was overreacting to it all. I just want you to feel you can trust me. I trust you."

Garrett's expression softened, and he reached out to cup her face in his hands with genuine tenderness. His touch was warm, familiar, and for a moment, she remembered why she'd fallen so hard for him. "Of course I do. You are my life. You are everything to me."

As he pulled her into his arms, Rose felt the familiar warmth of his embrace, the sense of being cherished and protected that had once made her feel so safe. But something small and uncertain continued to flutter in her chest—a feeling she couldn't quite name or dismiss, like a bird trapped in a cage, beating its wings against the bars.

She closed her eyes and tried to lose herself in the embrace, tried to recapture the fairy tale feeling that had once made everything seem perfect. But even as she held him close, part of her remained alert, aware, watching for the signs she was only beginning to recognize, or was it just all her feelings playing tricks with her?

In the gathering darkness of their beautiful home, surrounded by luxury and love, Rose felt more alone than she ever had in her life. And for the first time, she began to wonder if the cage she'd sensed was closing around her wasn't made of bars, but of kisses and promises and the kind of love that demanded everything in return.

Too Much Doubt

Garrett sat at his mahogany desk, his fingers drumming an anxious rhythm against the polished surface as he stared out the floor-to-ceiling windows of his corner office. The autumn light cast long shadows across the Persian rug beneath his feet, and the bustling street scene below— afternoon shoppers clutching coffee cups, business lunches spilling onto sidewalk tables, the ordinary flow of Macon life— might as well have been a foreign landscape. His mind was elsewhere, consumed by the growing certainty that Rose was keeping something from him.

The thought had been eating at him since yesterday, when she'd dismissed the driver and claimed she needed time alone at the house. The memory played on repeat in his mind: Rose's hand on the car door, her voice unusually firm as she told Mark he could leave early. The way she'd avoided Garrett's eyes when he'd called later, her answers coming just a beat too slowly, as if she were measuring each word.

Alone for what? The question had tormented him through a somewhat sleepless night, and now it sat in his chest like a stone, growing heavier with each passing hour. He'd built his entire life around control— controlling his investments, his business relationships, his environment. But Rose... Rose was proving impossible for him to contain, and the uncertainty was driving him to the edge of madness.

The soft knock on his door barely registered until Jack stepped into the office, his expression shifting from casual to concerned as he took in Garrett's disheveled appearance. Garrett's usually immaculate white shirt was wrinkled, his tie loosened, and dark circles shadowed his eyes like bruises.

"Is there something you wanted, Jack?"

Jack closed the door behind him and moved closer; his face creased with worry. At this point in his life, Jack had seen enough of life to recognize when a man was spiraling, and everything about Garrett's posture screamed trouble. "I wanted to see how you were doing. You were not in the best mood when you went tearing out of here yesterday."

Garrett's jaw tightened, the muscle jumping beneath his skin. The last thing he needed was Jack's well-meaning interference, especially when he could barely hold his own thoughts together. "It's personal."

"Rose?"

The single word felt like a physical blow, and Garrett felt his carefully constructed facade crack. *Of course, he knows.* Jack had been his friend for all these years, had seen him through the darkest period of his life after his first relationship had imploded spectacularly. Jack had watched him rebuild himself piece by piece, had been there during the long nights when Garrett had wrestled with his own demons. If anyone could read the warning signs, it was Jack.

"I really don't want to talk about it." But even as he said it, Garrett knew it was a lie. The pressure building inside him needed release, needed someone to either validate his fears or talk him down from the ledge.

Jack settled into the leather chair across from Garrett's desk, his movements deliberate and unhurried. He'd learned long ago that rushing Garrett only made him more defensive. "Well, buddy, you need to. I know you pretty well and I know how you get. You do not need to bottle up anything and let it get to be a larger problem than it needs to."

How do I get? The phrase stung because it was true, because it reduced his complex emotions to a simple, predictable pattern. Garrett had always been prone to obsession, to letting his fears spiral into something darker and more destructive. Even as a child, he'd been the type to check and recheck his homework, to count his baseball cards obsessively, to need everything in its proper place. That need for control had served him well in business, but in relationships... in relationships, it had been his downfall.

"What do you mean by that?"

Jack's eyes didn't waver, and his voice carried the weight of shared history. "You know exactly what I mean by that. Like last time."

The reference to his past—to Bonnie, to the relationship that had imploded under the weight of his paranoia and control—sent a chill through Garrett's chest. He'd sworn he wouldn't make the same mistakes again, had promised himself that with Rose, things would be different. But here he was, feeling the familiar claws of suspicion tearing at his peace of mind, the same patterns emerging like a virus in his blood.

Bonnie had been patient at first, had found his attention flattering, his devotion romantic. But slowly, gradually, his love had transformed into something suffocating. The constant phone calls, the need to know where she was every moment, the way he'd questioned her friendships—it had all been justified in his mind as protection, as caring. Until the day she'd packed her bags and told him she couldn't breathe anymore.

"I'm afraid it's happening again." The admission came out in a rush, as if saying it quickly might lessen its impact. "She lied to me and had her mom lie to me as well. Her sick mom!"

The words were sharp in the air between them, and Garrett could see his own desperation reflected in Jack's eyes. Here he was, a successful businessman, a pillar of the community, reduced to surveillance and suspicion of the woman he claimed to love more than life itself.

Jack leaned forward, his expression softening with understanding rather than judgment. "Maybe you are overreacting, and it is nothing. You have this driver spying on her now."

"He is not spying!" Garrett shot back, his voice rising despite himself. The accusation hit too close to home, exposing the ugly truth beneath his carefully constructed justifications. "He is driving her, so she doesn't have to worry about anyone but her mother." But even as he said it, he knew how it sounded, how it was. Mark wasn't just a driver; he was Garrett's eyes and ears, his way of maintaining control when he couldn't be there himself.

"OK, whatever." Jack's tone remained calm, steady, the voice of reason in Garrett's storm of paranoia. "The fact is, you know where she is most of the time. Why do you think she is lying? Plus, everyone needs a little privacy."

Privacy. The word ignited something volatile in Garrett's chest, a spark that caught fire and spread through his nervous system like wildfire. Privacy meant secrets, and secrets meant betrayal. In his world, there was no middle ground, no gray area where love and trust could coexist with independence.

"Privacy? For what? You know something, don't you? Has Lucy said something to you? I know you two talk. They were together. She is helping her, isn't she?"

The words tumbled out in a frantic rush, each accusation building on the last. In his mind, he could see it all clearly—Rose confiding in her best friend, Lucy whispering secrets to Jack, a conspiracy of silence designed to keep him in the dark. The logical part of his brain knew he was being irrational, but that voice was drowning beneath the roar of his fears.

Jack's eyes widened at the rapid-fire accusations, and for the first time, Garrett saw a flicker of genuine alarm in his friend's expression. "Helping her what? You need to relax and calm down."

But Garrett was already rising from his chair, pacing behind his desk like a caged animal. The spacious office suddenly felt too small, too confining, and he could feel his heart hammering against his ribs. The pieces were falling into place in his mind: Rose's recent evasiveness, her mother's convenient illnesses when he called, the way she'd dismissed the driver yesterday. It all fit together into a pattern that confirmed his worst fears.

"She sent the driver on an errand today so she could be alone at the house. Where's Lucy?"

"She's downstairs working. Buddy, I'm telling you that you need to relax and calm down. You are getting worked up for nothing."

"Nothing?!" Garrett spun around, his face flushed with mounting anger. The word exploded from him like a gunshot, carrying with it all his frustration and fear. "If she is lying to me, then there has to be a reason. I'm going to surprise her at the house and see what I might be walking in on."

The thought of catching Rose in whatever deception she was perpetrating sent a dark chill through him. Finally, he would have answers. Finally, he would know the truth, no matter how devastating it might be.

"Don't do that! Garrett stop! It's your birthday!"

The words hit Garrett like a physical blow, stopping his frantic pacing mid-stride. He spun around, confusion replacing rage like cold water thrown on a fire. "It's not my birthday. My birthday is not until the weekend."

Jack's expression shifted to something between relief and exasperation, and Garrett could see the pieces clicking together in his friend's mind. "Yes, and everyone has been trying to plan a surprise party for you. Rose wanted to do something special for your birthday. That is why she has been trying to get away from the driver."

The revelation hit Garrett like a freight train, derailing his carefully constructed paranoia in a single devastating moment. All the pieces of his suspicion—Rose's secretiveness, her mother's evasiveness, the dismissed driver—suddenly rearranged themselves into an entirely different picture. Not betrayal, but love. Not deception, but devotion.

What have I done? The question echoed in his mind as he stared at Jack, feeling the full weight of his own destructive suspicions. Rose hadn't been plotting against him—she'd been planning something beautiful for him. And he'd been so consumed with his own fears that he'd nearly destroyed it all.

"I don't know what to say."

Jack stood, his relief evident in the way his shoulders relaxed. "Well, first you need to chill down and stop acting like a crazy person. Next, you need to keep all this to yourself. If Lucy finds out I told you, she will tell Rose, and they will tar and feather me. Please don't say anything."

"I won't." The words came out as barely more than a whisper, and Garrett felt the shame wash over him in waves. How could he have been so blind? So willing to believe the worst of the woman who had shown him nothing but love? He felt ashamed of his feelings.

Jack moved toward the door, then paused, his hand on the brass handle. "Please act surprised at the party, and from now on start trusting a little. If you don't, you might end up losing the best thing that has ever happened to you."

Garrett nodded, unable to trust his voice. As Jack left, he sank back into his chair, his head in his hands. *The best thing that has ever happened to you.* The truth of those words cut deeper than any accusation could have. Rose was his salvation, his second chance at love, and he'd been so busy protecting himself from imagined threats that he'd nearly become the very thing he feared most—the destroyer of his own happiness.

Outside his window, the autumn afternoon was fading into evening, and the streetlamps were beginning to flicker on. Soon, he would go home to Rose, would hold her in his arms, and pretend to be surprised by whatever she had planned. But the real surprise was the revelation of his own capacity for self-destruction, and the terrifying realization that love and paranoia were more closely linked than he'd ever imagined.

For the first time in years, Garrett was having to wrestle with his own demons of jealousy and distrust that left a bitter taste in his mouth.

A Shoulder to Lean On

It had been three weeks now since Rose lost her mother, her confidant and only relative. The mansion felt different now—quieter, emptier, as if Rose's grief had settled into the very walls like dust. Even the grandfather clock in the hallway seemed to tick more slowly, its steady rhythm a metronome for sorrow. Garrett found her in the living room, curled into the corner of their wine-colored sofa, her knees drawn up to her chest. The late afternoon light streaming through the tall windows cast her in golden relief, but there was no warmth in her posture, no life in the way she sat motionless as a statue.

Even from across the room, he could see the tracks of tears on her cheeks, the way her shoulders curved inward as if she were trying to protect herself from the world. She wore one of his old college sweatshirts, the navy fabric dwarfing her small frame, and her auburn hair hung loose around her face like a curtain.

She's been crying again. He noticed as the sight sent a familiar ache through his chest, a helplessness that was almost physical in its intensity. In the three weeks since her mother's funeral, he'd watched Rose retreat into herself, becoming a ghost of the vibrant woman he'd fallen in love with. Her grief was so pure, so profound, that it made his own past paranoia seem petty and shameful by comparison.

The funeral had been everything Rose's mother would have wanted— elegant, dignified, filled with the white roses she'd loved. Garrett had spared no expense, had handled every detail so Rose wouldn't have to bear the additional burden of planning. It was the least he could do after the way he'd doubted her during her mother's final weeks, when Rose had been sneaking away not for secret meetings, but for extra time at the hospice, reading to her mother and holding her hand. His internal guilt was still nagging at his heart.

"Can I get you anything?" he asked softly, moving into the room with careful steps. The hardwood floors creaked beneath his feet, and he winced at the sound, afraid of disturbing whatever fragile peace she'd found. He could not stand seeing her in this state of mind when he was powerless to change it. He knew he had to do something to make this woman he cherished, his everything, whole again.

"No." Her voice was barely above a whisper, hoarse from crying. She didn't look up at him, didn't acknowledge his presence beyond that single word.

Garrett settled beside her on the sofa, the soft cushions sighing beneath his weight. He extended his arm, offering comfort without demanding it, and felt a surge of relief when she allowed him to encircle her shoulders. She felt so small against him, so fragile, like a bird with broken wings.

"I wish there was something I could do to make you feel better."

Rose leaned into his embrace, her head finding the familiar spot on his shoulder. Her hair smelled like the lavender shampoo she'd always used, but even that simple comfort felt muted now, as if her grief had dulled all her senses. "Just being here and holding me is enough. I want to thank you for everything you did for my mom and the beautiful service."

The gratitude in her voice made his chest tighten. He didn't deserve her thanks, not after the way his mind had questioned her devotion to her dying mother and to him during that time. "Anything for you and your mom."

Rose's breath hitched, and he felt her struggle against fresh tears. The sound was like a knife to his heart, and he found himself holding her tighter, as if he could somehow absorb her pain into himself. "I am just not sure what to do with myself now. She was the one I went to with problems, and I helped her through her sickness. I just feel lost now."

Lost. The word captured something Garrett recognized in himself—that feeling of being adrift without purpose, without direction. He'd felt it before Rose came into his life, during the dark years after Bonnie had left, when he'd thrown himself into work to avoid facing the emptiness inside. He couldn't bear the thought of Rose experiencing that same hollow despair, that sense of existing without truly living.

"Well, you still have me and Lucy, and maybe it would be good for you to do something you enjoy for a while just to take your mind off stuff until a little time passes."

Rose lifted her head to look at him, and for a moment, he saw a flicker of something—curiosity, perhaps, or the faint echo of interest. Her eyes were red-rimmed and puffy, but they were focusing on him with more clarity than he'd seen in weeks. "Like what?"

Garrett had been thinking about this for days, watching her stare out at the neglected gardens that stretched behind the mansion. The previous years had not been kind to the garden, and now it was a tangle of overgrown hedges and weeds, punctuated by the occasional flash of color from some hardy perennial that had survived the neglect. He'd brought her to the house partially for those gardens, imagining them restored to their former glory, but more than that, he remembered the way Rose's eyes had lit up when she'd seen them for the first time.

"You remember when you first saw this place?" he asked, his voice gentle. "You stood at the back window and talked about what the gardens could become. You said you could see it all—the flower beds, the walking paths, the way the light would play through the trees."

A ghost of a smile crossed Rose's face, the first he'd seen since the funeral. "I remember. It was like looking at a painting that someone had left unfinished."

"You always said that you would love to make that garden the showplace it should be. Why don't you do it? Make it everything you think it should be. Spend whatever you need to."

Rose's expression shifted, and he saw the spark of something—interest? Hope? —flickering in her eyes like a candle flame in the wind. But then reality seemed to settle back over her like a blanket, and she shook her head. "I don't know. It is a lot of work. I am not sure I am up to it. It would be fun to make that beautiful though. Mom loved pretty gardens, and I do too. We were just never able to have one."

Of course, they couldn't. The reality of Rose's past was something Garrett sometimes forgot in his comfortable bubble of wealth. She'd grown up in a small apartment above the bakery where her mother had worked, then moved to an even smaller one when she got out on her own, working at the store. The idea of having space for a garden would have been an impossible dream, as foreign as owning a yacht or a private jet.

But now... now he could give her that dream. He could watch her create something beautiful from the overgrown wilderness behind their home, could see her find purpose and joy in nurturing life from the earth. The thought filled him with a fierce satisfaction—this was what love should be, he told himself. Not surveillance and suspicion but enabling dreams and healing wounds.

"How about this? We get a gardener to come to do all the hauling and digging and hard manual labor stuff. Something the lady of the manor doesn't need to do." He smiled, trying to coax an answering smile from her. "You can arrange, plan and actually set the plants out. Something new to focus on for a while."

Rose straightened slightly, and for the first time in weeks, Garrett saw a glimmer of the woman he'd married. Her back straightened, her eyes cleared, and he could almost see the gears turning in her mind as she considered the possibility. "Are you sure? I mean, hiring someone new will cost, but it would be nice to have someone to do the stuff that may be a little more than I want to take on."

"I am sure. Anything to help you and make you happy. Nothing is too much for you, Rose. I love you."

She turned in his arms, her face tilted up to his, and for a moment, he saw the woman he'd fallen in love with shining through her grief. "I love you too."

And I almost threw this away, Garrett thought, remembering Jack's words about losing the best thing that had ever happened to him. The memory of his paranoid episode seemed like something from another lifetime, a cautionary tale about the dangers of letting fear override love. *Never again,* he promised himself. He would do better, be better. He would give Rose everything she deserved, including some trust and freedom he'd almost denied her.

As he held her close, feeling her body begin to relax against his for the first time in weeks, Garrett allowed himself to believe that they were turning a corner. Rose would heal, the gardens would bloom, and their marriage would grow stronger through adversity. He would be the husband she deserved, the man who lifted her up instead of tearing her down. Show her just how deeply her loved her and let her know there was nothing he would not do for her.

Outside their window, the neglected gardens waited in the gathering dusk, their potential hidden beneath layers of abandonment and neglect. Soon, they would bloom again—but what would grow there would be more than flowers and beauty. In the fertile soil of Rose's grief and Garrett's guilt, something else would take root, something that would change all their lives forever.

A Familiar Stranger

The afternoon sun cast dappled shadows across the overgrown garden as Rose stood among the untended beds, trying to envision what this space could become. The clear air carried the scent of dying leaves and the faint sweetness of late-blooming honeysuckle that had wound itself around the old garden gate. She had been out here for nearly an hour, walking the pathways and mentally cataloging what would need to be cleared, replanted, or completely redesigned.

The project felt overwhelming and therapeutic all at once—exactly what she needed, though she wasn't sure she was ready for the magnitude of it. Every few steps revealed another challenge: a section of fence that had collapsed under the weight of wild vines, flower beds choked with weeds that had grown taller than a garden such as this should allow, a stone fountain that had become home to a family of mourning doves who scattered at her approach.

Yet beneath the chaos, she could see the bones of something beautiful. The original designer had known what they were doing; the paths curved naturally with the landscape, the placement of trees created natural rooms and vistas, and here and there, a flash of color showed where something hardy had survived the neglect. It was like looking at a masterpiece that had been painted over with graffiti; the beauty was still there, waiting to be revealed.

She was kneeling beside a patch of struggling roses, their thorny canes reaching toward the light despite being nearly strangled by morning glory vines, when she heard footsteps on the flagstone path behind her. The sound was deliberate, measured—Garrett's footsteps, she realized, accompanied by a lighter tread she didn't recognize.

Turning, she saw Garrett approaching with a young man she didn't recognize—someone whose presence immediately shifted the quiet atmosphere of the garden. There was something about the stranger's bearing, a casual confidence that seemed to belong to the outdoors in a way that contrasted sharply with Garrett's perpetual air of indoor authority.

"Rose, can you come here for a moment and meet someone?" Garrett's voice carried that particular tone of pleasant authority he used when he had already made decisions but wanted to maintain the illusion of her choice. Rose had learned to recognize it over the time of their marriage— the way he would present foregone conclusions as collaborative decisions. "This is Kirk. He's been working as a gardener for the Clary family, but now they're selling out and moving, so he's looking for a new place. I thought you could talk to him and see if he would be the right person to assist you with building the garden."

Rose brushed the dirt from her hands and stood, taking in the young man before her. Kirk appeared to be in his late twenties or early thirties, with the kind of deep tan that came from working outdoors and a lean, athletic build that spoke of physical labor. His brown hair was slightly tousled by the breeze, and when he smiled, it reached his eyes in a way that seemed genuinely warm rather than calculated. He wore work clothes that had seen honest use—jeans with soil stains at the knees, a flannel shirt with the sleeves rolled up, sturdy boots that had walked through countless gardens.

"Hi, Kirk. How are you?" She found herself genuinely curious about this stranger who might become part of her daily routine. There was something refreshing about meeting someone who wasn't part of Garrett's business world, someone who looked like he belonged in a garden rather than a boardroom. "Let's chat about what you would be doing and see if this is something you might be interested in."

"Yes, ma'am." His voice was respectful but not servile, and there was something in his demeanor that suggested he was comfortable with himself in a way that Rose found immediately appealing. He didn't fidget under her gaze or try to fill the silence with nervous chatter.

"I'll leave you two to talk. I need to get to work anyway." Garrett glanced between them with what appeared to be satisfaction at a plan coming together. Rose caught the look—that particular expression he wore when he felt he had successfully managed a situation. "Rose, you can call me at the office later."

"Okay, bye." She watched him walk back toward the house, his polished shoes clicking against the flagstones, and felt a familiar mixture of gratitude and unease. Garrett meant well trying to show her the amount of love he possessed for her, she knew that, but sometimes his way of helping felt more like orchestrating than supporting.

Turning her attention back to Kirk, she was suddenly aware that this was the first time in months she had been alone with someone new, someone who wasn't part of Garrett's carefully curated circle. The realization was both liberating and slightly unsettling.

"So, Kirk, tell me what it is you like about gardening."

His face lit up with genuine enthusiasm, and Rose felt something inside her respond to that unguarded emotion. "A lot, actually. I enjoy working with my hands. I enjoy watching things grow and turn into something beautiful, and it gives me time to just clear my mind. There's something peaceful about it, even though a lot of the work can be dirty and hard."

There was something refreshing about his straightforwardness, the way he spoke about his work without trying to impress her or say what he thought she wanted to hear. In her world now, every conversation felt calculated, every interaction filtered through the lens of her husband's wealth and status. But Kirk spoke like someone who had never learned to perform for an audience.

"That's nice. I always wanted a garden to watch things grow. I love roses." She gestured toward the struggling bushes nearby, their blooms small and sparse but still trying to assert their beauty. "My mom and I were never able to have one. Now that she's gone, maybe I can do it for her and for me."

Kirk's expression softened with genuine sympathy, and Rose saw something in his eyes that she hadn't encountered in weeks—an authentic human connection, unmarked by pity or obligation. "I'm sorry for your loss. Mr. Sinclair told me about your mother passing recently."

The kindness in his voice caught her off guard. Most people had been offering condolences for weeks now, but something about the way Kirk said it felt different—less politically correct, more human. There was no awkward pause afterward, no desperate search for something else to talk about. He simply let the acknowledgment of her loss stand without trying to fix it or minimize it.

"Thanks. It's really been tough. I really miss her a lot." The words came easier than they had in days, and Rose realized she hadn't spoken about her mother with such simple honesty since the funeral. "I always wanted to make this garden a showplace, and Garrett thought this might be a good time to start. Maybe he's right."

"Well, if you decide I might be the one to help you with that, I would be honored, ma'am."

"I appreciate that, and please, call me Rose." The formality felt unnecessary and somehow created distance she found herself not wanting. "Can I ask you about the Clary place? I've driven by there—it's absolutely beautiful."

Kirk's smile broadened, and Rose could see the pride in his work shining through. "Mrs. Clary gave me pretty much free rein with the design. We started with just the front beds, but over three years, we transformed the whole property. She wanted cottage gardens, lots of color, something that would look like it had been there forever."

"And did you achieve that?"

"I think so. The trick is mixing in some natives with the showier stuff and making sure you have something blooming every season. Mrs. Clary used to say the garden should look like it was dressed for a party every day of the year."

Rose laughed, and the sound surprised her—light, genuine, the first real laugh she'd had since her mother's death. "I like that philosophy. What would you do here, if you were me?" As they continued to walk through the garden, Kirk's enthusiasm became infectious. He pointed out the good bones of the original design, showed her where previous owners had made unfortunate choices, and began to sketch out possibilities with his hands as he talked. His vision was both practical and beautiful; he understood the difference between what would thrive and what would merely survive.

"This fountain," he said, running his hand along the moss-covered stone, "this could be the centerpiece of the whole design. Clean it up, get the water flowing again, plant some shade perennials around the base. And see how this path curves? That's perfect sightlines—you want people to wonder what's around the bend."

Rose found herself seeing the garden through his eyes, imagining it not just restored but transformed into something better than it had ever been. For the first time since her mother's death, she felt a spark of genuine anticipation about something in her future.

"I have to ask," she said as they paused near the back gate, "why are you looking for a new position? It sounds like you and Mrs. Clary had a good thing going."

Kirk's expression grew wistful. "We did. But her husband passed last year, and she's moving to Florida to be closer to her daughter. She gave me the highest recommendation, but..." He shrugged. "Sometimes life takes you in directions you don't expect."

There was something in his voice that suggested he understood loss, that he'd faced his own share of unexpected turns. Rose felt a kinship with him that she hadn't experienced with anyone since her mother's death.

"Well," she said, surprised by her own decisiveness, "I think you're exactly what this garden needs. When could you start?"

Garrett's Good Idea

Meanwhile, across town in the bank's executive suite, Jack walked into Garrett's office to find his friend sitting behind his desk with an expression of unmistakable satisfaction, having just hung up the phone. The afternoon light streaming through the windows caught the gold frames of Garrett's diplomas and awards, creating a backdrop that seemed to emphasize his sense of accomplishment.

"That's nice to see. Good news?"

"That was Rose. She just hired a gardener to help her out." Garrett's voice carried the tone of a chess player who had just made a particularly strategic move.

Jack settled into the familiar chair across from Garrett's desk, noting the pleased expression on his friend's face. "I didn't know you were looking for one."

"We thought it would be good to help her get her mind off things. She's had a hard time since losing her mother." Garrett's voice carried the tone of a problem solver, someone who had identified an issue and found the perfect solution. "I found him through the Clarys—they've been clients for years. Top-notch references, good worker, and most importantly, he understands his place."

The last phrase caught Jack's attention, though he couldn't quite put his finger on why it bothered him. "His place?"

"You know what I mean. He's not going to get any ideas above his station. He's there to work, not to be Rose's friend." Garrett's satisfaction was evident in every word. "The last thing she needs right now is to be taken advantage of by someone who might see her grief as an opportunity."

Jack studied his friend's face, recognizing the familiar pattern of Garrett's protective instincts. "You've thought this through pretty thoroughly."

"Of course I have. Rose deserves only the best, and she deserves to feel safe. This Kirk fellow comes highly recommended, and he'll be perfect for what she needs—someone to do the heavy lifting while she focuses on the creative aspects."

"Yeah, Lucy said it had been rough for her." Something shifted almost imperceptibly in Garrett's expression, like a shadow passing across his face. "You seem to always know things from Lucy. Is there something you haven't told me?"

Jack raised an eyebrow at the subtle edge that had crept into his friend's voice. The question seemed to come from nowhere, but he recognized the undertone—the same jealous suspicion that had nearly derailed Garrett's relationship with Rose before their marriage and several times since. "No. Lucy and I are just friends. That's all. I think she's a really sweet and smart young woman. We just enjoy talking to each other. Plus, she helps me catch up on things related to you when you won't tell me anything."

"Like what?"

"Nothing. It was just a joke. I know you would tell me if there was anything to tell, but you seem okay right now."

Garrett leaned back in his chair, his satisfaction returning, but Jack caught the brief flash of calculation in his eyes. "I am. Everything is just as it should be."

But as Jack studied his friend's face, he couldn't shake the feeling that Garrett's version of "as it should be" might not align with everyone else's definition of normal. There was something in the way Garrett spoke about Rose's new project—not just as a loving husband supporting his grieving wife, but as someone who had successfully arranged the pieces of a puzzle to his liking.

"You know," Jack said carefully, "it might be good for Rose to have something that's entirely her own. Something where she can make all the decisions without worrying about what anyone else thinks."

Garrett's smile didn't waver, but something hardened in his eyes. "Of course. That's exactly what this is. Rose will have complete creative control over her garden project."

The way he said "her garden project" made it sound like a hobby rather than a passion, a way to keep her occupied rather than a genuine creative outlet. Jack felt a familiar unease settle in his stomach, the same feeling he'd had before Garrett's paranoid episode about the surprise party.

"And this Kirk fellow—he's local?"

"Lives in one of those apartments over on Riverside. Single, no family to speak of, moved here from Savannah about four years ago. Clean background, good work ethic." Garrett recited the information like a personnel file, and Jack realized his friend had done considerably more research than a simple reference check would require.

"You had him investigated?"

"I had him checked out. There's a difference." Garrett's tone suggested the distinction was important to him. "Rose is vulnerable right now. I have to protect her from any harm. I'm not taking any chances with her safety or well-being."

Or with her loyalty, Jack thought but didn't say. Instead, he nodded and changed the subject, but the seed of concern had been planted. He'd seen this pattern before—Garrett's love expressed through control, his protection implemented through surveillance. And now Rose, in her grief and isolation, would be spending her days with a young man who, by Garrett's own admission, was attractive, capable, and conveniently lacking in local connections.

Still, Jack said nothing. Some conversations, he had learned, were better left for another day. But as he left Garrett's office, he couldn't shake the feeling that his friend had just set in motion something that would test every promise he'd made about trust and freedom.

Back in the garden, Rose was shaking hands with Kirk, sealing an agreement that would change all their lives in ways none of them could yet imagine. The afternoon sun was beginning to sink toward the horizon, painting the overgrown paradise in shades of gold and amber, and for the first time in months, Rose felt something that might have been hope.

What she didn't know was that hope, like the roses struggling to bloom among the weeds, could be both beautiful and dangerous, capable of growing in unexpected directions and taking root in places where it was never meant to flourish.

That night, the bedroom was bathed in the soft glow of lamplight, casting gentle shadows across the silk wallpaper that Garrett had specially ordered from Paris. The heavy curtains were drawn tight against the world outside, creating their own private sanctuary within the mansion's walls. Rose and Garrett lay side by side on the king-sized bed, their bodies relaxed against the plush pillows, their conversation drifting lazily through the mundane topics of the day like smoke from a dying fire.

Rose felt more relaxed than she had in weeks, a lightness in her chest that she'd almost forgotten was possible. The garden project was giving her something to look forward to each morning—a purpose beyond the carefully orchestrated routine that had become her life. For the first time since her mother's death, she felt a spark of genuine excitement about tomorrow.

"So, you think he'll work out okay for you and do everything you need him to do?" Garrett's voice carried what seemed like genuine interest, though there was something else beneath it—a careful attention to her response, a subtle tension in the way he held his body that she didn't quite notice. His fingers traced absent patterns on the silk comforter, and his eyes never left her face as he waited for her answer.

"I do. He has experience with gardening, and I can use the knowledge, plus he can take a lot of the work off me." Rose turned on her side to face him, her expression animated in a way it hadn't been since her mother's death. The lamplight caught the auburn highlights in her hair, making it seem to glow against the ivory pillowcase. "Kirk seems to understand what I'm trying to create out there. He looked at the space and immediately started talking about soil composition and drainage patterns. I think he really gets my vision."

Garrett's jaw tightened almost imperceptibly at the way she said Kirk's name, but his voice remained steady and supportive. "You just make sure he does. He can dig the holes and haul the soil and fertilizer and manual stuff. That's what he's paid for. I don't want you straining and overworking yourself." The words were caring on the surface, but there was an undercurrent of something more possessive, more controlling.

Rose smiled, a hint of playfulness returning to her voice for the first time in months. "Unless we fire him and I make my dutiful husband do it after a long day at work." She reached out and playfully poked his chest, the gesture so natural and spontaneous that it surprised them both.

"If that's what you wanted, I would do that for you. I would do anything for you. You are my whole world." The intensity in his voice made her heart flutter the way it had when they were first together, back when his devotion felt romantic rather than suffocating. His hand came up to cup her cheek, thumb brushing across her skin with a tenderness that made her remember why she'd fallen in love with him in the first place.

"I know you would, but I don't want you too tired after work. I want you to be here to sit in the swing and hold me while we enjoy this beautiful new garden I'm building." Rose's voice grew dreamy as she spoke, already imagining the two of them in the evenings, surrounded by the roses and jasmine she planned to plant. "I want to create something beautiful, Garrett. Something that's ours."

"That sounds great to me." His response was immediate, but she caught something in his tone—a note of satisfaction that seemed to go beyond simple agreement, as if her desire to stay home and build something within the confines of their property was exactly what he'd hoped to hear.

Rose reached over and squeezed his hand, her fingers intertwining with his. "And Garrett, thank you for supporting me with this. I know hiring Kirk is an expense, and I appreciate you trusting me to make this decision."

"As I said before, anything for you, Rose. Anything." The words dissolved the space between them, weighted with meaning that went far beyond the simple conversation about gardening. In the soft lamplight, his eyes seemed to hold depths she couldn't quite read, and for just a moment, she felt a flutter of something that might have been unease. But then he smiled, and the feeling passed, replaced by the warmth of his hand in hers and the promise of tomorrow's work in the garden.

Outside their bedroom window, the night sounds of Georgia drifted through the glass—crickets and the distant hum of traffic, the world continuing its rhythm beyond the walls of their carefully constructed paradise. Rose closed her eyes and let herself imagine the garden in full bloom, not knowing that in Garrett's mind, he was already planning how to ensure that her new sanctuary would become just another beautiful cage.

The Confrontation

The next afternoon, the mall buzzed with its usual afternoon energy—teenagers clustered around the fountain, young mothers pushing strollers past shop windows, elderly couples sharing soft pretzels on benches. Rose wandered from shop to shop, enjoying the simple pleasure of browsing without any particular agenda, her footsteps lighter than they had been in months. She had dismissed Mark for the afternoon after he dropped her off at the mall, claiming she wanted to spend some time alone, and the freedom felt intoxicating after months of constant companionship. The weight of always being watched, always being accounted for, had lifted from her shoulders like a heavy coat finally shed.

She was examining a display of scarves in a boutique window—delicate silk squares in shades of coral and turquoise that reminded her of the flower beds she was planning—when something flickered in her peripheral vision. A movement that seemed too deliberate, too focused, cutting against the random flow of shoppers. Rose turned casually, scanning the crowd of people going about their business, carrying shopping bags and herding children, but saw nothing unusual. Just the ordinary chaos of suburban life continuing around her.

Shrugging off the feeling, she continued her leisurely exploration, moving in and out of several shops with the unhurried pace of someone who finally had nowhere urgent to be. But the sensation persisted—that prickly awareness of being watched that made the hair on the back of her neck stand up and her skin feel exposed. It was like having an itch she couldn't quite locate, a discomfort that followed her from store to store.

In the last shop she visited—a small jewelry boutique with classical music playing softly overhead—the feeling intensified. Instead of turning around immediately this time, she forced herself to continue browsing, moving slowly toward the back of the store where a display of pearls caught the light. Her reflection in the glass case showed a woman trying too hard to look casual, her shoulders tense despite her efforts to appear relaxed.

Then, in one swift motion, she spun around and walked quickly back toward the entrance, emerging into the main concourse with purpose. The afternoon crowd seemed to part before her as she moved with sudden determination. She knew someone was behind the large decorative planter in the center of the mall corridor—she could sense them trying to move around it, staying concealed as she approached like a child playing hide-and-seek.

"You!" The word exploded from her lips as she rounded the planter and came face to face with Mark, who looked like a deer caught in headlights.

His usual composed demeanor cracked completely, his face flushing red with embarrassment and something that might have been shame.

"What the hell are you doing? Why are you watching me?"

Mark's composure cracked completely under her fierce gaze. "I was just getting out of the heat from the car, ma'am," he stammered, his voice lacking any conviction. The lie floated in the air between them, transparent and insulting.

"Really?" Rose's voice dripped with incredulous anger, each word sharp enough to cut. "It's a new Cadillac. They have air conditioning." The absurdity of his excuse only fueled her fury. *Did he think she was stupid? Did they all think she was some naive little doll who wouldn't notice?* She thought with growing rage.

Her eyes dropped to his hands, where she caught sight of a small notebook he was trying to conceal against his leg. The binding was worn, as if it had been used frequently, and she could see writing on the open page. Before he could react, she lunged for it, her fingers closing around the paper as he tried to snatch it away. For a moment, they struggled, both pulling at the notebook like children fighting over a toy.

"What is this? Notes? You are taking notes on what I'm doing?" The words came out in a rush as she scanned the page, seeing her own life reduced to clinical observations: *2:15 PM - Subject entered jewelry store. Spent 12 minutes examining necklaces. Made no purchases. Seemed agitated.*

The betrayal hit her like a physical blow, stealing her breath and making her stomach lurch. Every kind word, every gesture of concern from Garrett suddenly took on a sinister cast. The way he always seemed to know exactly where she'd been, what she'd looked at, who she'd spoken to—it hadn't been intuition or devotion. It had been surveillance.

Without another word, she turned and walked away, her legs carrying her through the department store at the end of the concourse while her mind reeled. The familiar sights and sounds of the mall—the cologne samples, the muzak, the chatter of other shoppers—seemed to fade into background noise as the full scope of her situation became clear. She wasn't a wife. She was a subject. A specimen under observation.

In the back corner of the store, hidden among racks of winter coats that smelled of mothballs and artificial pine, she found a payphone and called for a taxi with shaking fingers. The plastic receiver felt slippery in her grip as she gave the dispatcher her location, her voice barely steady enough to be understood. She stayed hidden among the clothing racks until she saw the cab pull up outside, watching Mark search for her through the store windows with increasing panic.

His movements were frantic now, no longer the composed driver she'd known for months. He moved through the crowds like a man whose livelihood depended on finding her, which, she realized with bitter clarity, it probably did. But she slipped out unnoticed, the automatic doors closing behind her with a soft whoosh that felt like the sound of a chapter ending.

The ride home passed in a blur of anger and hurt, the Georgia landscape streaming past the taxi window like a movie she wasn't really watching. When the cab pulled into her driveway, and she saw Garrett's car already there—unusual for the middle of the afternoon—her fury crystallized into cold determination. The sight of his pristine Cadillac in the circular drive, so perfectly maintained and controlled, seemed to mock her.

She paid the driver, slammed the car door with enough force to rattle the windows, and marched toward the house. Her heels clicked against the marble steps like gunshots, each step echoing her mounting rage.

"Garrett! Garrett! Where are you?" Her voice echoed through the entrance hall with an edge that could cut glass, bouncing off the high ceilings and crystal chandelier that suddenly seemed less elegant and more like prison bars made of light.

Garrett appeared at the top of the staircase, his tie loosened, and his shirtsleeves rolled up as if he'd been working in his study. His face lit up with what appeared to be genuine pleasure at seeing her home early—the same expression she'd once found endearing but now seemed calculated. "Hi. I came home early—"

"You came home early because that damn spy you hired to drive me around and report everything I do to you called you!" Rose's words came out in a rush, her anger too big to contain. "I know he did. Don't even try to deny it. I caught him spying and taking notes!"

The confusion that crossed Garrett's face seemed utterly genuine. He descended a few steps, his brow furrowed as if he was trying to understand a foreign language. "Rose, please listen—"

"No, Garrett. You listen!" She advanced toward the bottom of the stairs, her entire body trembling with rage. "I love you and I think you love me, but this is going to stop and it's going to stop now! I have had it with the spying and watching my every move. If you love me, Mark goes, and he goes tonight."

"It's already done. If—" He started to speak, his hands raised in a gesture of surrender, but she cut him off with the force of her fury.

"I'm not finished." Her voice cut through his attempt to speak like a blade. "I want that car to be gone too. I want my own car to drive when I want and where I want. Do you understand?"

Garrett descended the stairs slowly, his face crumbling with each step. The confident banker who commanded respect in boardrooms looked suddenly small and lost, like a child who couldn't understand why his good intentions were being met with anger. "Rose, you know why I got you the car and driver. I—"

"You got it to keep an eye on me and that's stopping tonight! Do you understand? I have never given you any reason to distrust me. I have given you nothing but love, but this is too much. If you truly love me, you will do this and understand."

As her words filled and heated the air between them, Rose saw something that stopped her cold. Garrett's eyes had filled with tears, and his face held the expression of a lost child who couldn't understand why he was being punished. The transformation was so complete, so genuine, that for a moment she forgot her anger and saw only pain.

"If I love you?" His voice broke on the words, each syllable weighted with hurt and bewilderment. "How can you even question that? You are my life. I love you so much. I never want to hurt you. Never. Please don't be upset."

The tears were flowing freely now, streaking down his cheeks as he stood frozen on the staircase. Garrett looked so genuinely devastated that Rose felt her anger falter, replaced by something more complex and troubling. He wasn't the calculating manipulator she had imagined during the taxi ride home—he was a man who looked utterly broken by the realization that he had hurt the person he loved most. The tears weren't crocodile tears; they were the tears of someone whose world was collapsing.

"I don't mean this to be cruel or question your love for me. I know you love me, but sometimes you almost love me a little too much."

"There is no way I could love you too much." His voice was barely a whisper, hoarse with emotion. "Mark is gone. I fired him and there's someone picking up the car. I will trade it and get you one of your own. Anything to make you happy, Rose. Just please don't stop loving me or leave me."

The raw vulnerability in his voice undid her completely. This wasn't a man scheming to control her—this was someone terrified of losing her, someone whose love had twisted into something possessive and destructive without him even realizing it. In his mind, she could see now, the surveillance hadn't been about control. It had been about protection, about keeping her safe in a world that felt dangerous and unpredictable. The notebook, the reports, the constant monitoring—it had all been his misguided attempt to love her properly.

She walked slowly toward him and took his hands in hers, feeling how they trembled like those of an old man. "Garrett. I may want to slap the hell out of you right now, but I still love you. That is not a question, and even though I'm upset, leaving you has never been a thought in my head. I love you. Don't you know that?"

He pulled her against him so tightly she could barely breathe, his whole body shaking with sobs that seemed to come from somewhere deep and primal. "I'm sorry, Rose. I'm sorry I made you angry. I love you so much." His voice was muffled against her hair, and she could feel his tears dampening her scalp.

"I know you do. I'm sorry I came down on you so hard. I was just angry. Let's just get past this and forget it happened, okay?" Even as she said the words, she knew they were both lying. This couldn't be forgotten, couldn't be undone. But sometimes love meant pretending that forgiveness was possible, even when the damage had already been done.

"I will get the car traded tomorrow. I promise. No drivers or anything. I love you."

As they held each other in the entrance hall, neither of them noticed Kirk standing just around the corner in the shadow of the doorway that led to the garden. He had been coming in from the afternoon's work, his hands still dirty from planting the new rosebushes, when the confrontation began. Now he remained frozen in place, having heard every word of their exchange—the notebook in Mark's hands, Garrett's tears, Rose's anger and forgiveness. It all painted a picture that made Kirk's chest tighten with understanding and something deeper, something that felt dangerously like protective instinct.

He had seen men like Garrett before—men who loved so desperately that they destroyed what they claimed to cherish. The tears were real, the pain genuine, but that didn't make the behavior any less toxic. If anything, it made it worse, because how do you fight someone who hurts you out of love?

Quietly, he slipped back outside, but the echo of Rose's voice—strong and angry and utterly justified—stayed with him long after the garden gate closed behind him. And so did the memory of Garrett's broken sobs, the sound of a man who truly didn't understand that love without trust was just another form of prison.

Advice from a Friend

The Next day, the morning sun cast long shadows across the restaurant's outdoor patio, filtering through the canopy of live oaks that gave the small café its charm. Rose stirred her coffee absently, the spoon making soft circles against the porcelain cup as her mind still replayed the confrontation with Garrett from the night before. The memory of his tears, the way his voice had broken when he begged her not to leave him, felt like a weight pressing against her chest.

Lucy leaned forward across the wrought-iron table, her expression a mixture of concern and curiosity. She'd known Rose for some time now, had been her maid of honor, and she could read the subtle signs of distress that others might miss—the way Rose's shoulders held tension, the distant look in her eyes, the mechanical way she moved the spoon through coffee that had long since gone cold.

"So, do you really think the whole limo thing was just so he could keep tabs on you? Having that driver spy on everything you do?" Lucy's voice carried the careful tone of someone treading on sensitive ground, aware that she was discussing the marriage of her best friend to a man whose motives she had questioned from time to time.

Rose set down her cup with a soft clink against the saucer, the sound unnaturally loud in the quiet morning air. Around them, other patrons chatted softly over their breakfast, the normal rhythm of people starting their day, but Rose felt disconnected from it all, as if she were watching life through glass.

"He swore he didn't know Mark was taking notes, said he'd already fired him before I even got home. But Lucy..." She paused, searching for the right words to explain the confusion that had been eating at her since the night before. "I can never be completely sure anymore. I came down on him so hard last night, and he was genuinely devastated. The tears, the way he looked at me—it was like I'd broken something inside him. Something that might not heal."

The memory of Garrett's face crumpling, of his body shaking with sobs as he held her in the foyer, made her chest tighten. How could someone who loved her so desperately also make her feel so trapped? It was a puzzle she couldn't solve, a contradiction that kept her awake at night.

"Look, it's Garrett. We both know he can be overprotective." Lucy's tone was diplomatic, but Rose caught the underlying concern. "But having you watched? That crosses a line, Rose. It's not just protective— it's controlling. And honestly? A little creepy."

Rose felt the familiar knot of confusion tighten in her stomach, that constant companion that had become part of her daily experience. "I don't know what to think anymore. Most people would probably say I'm the crazy one here. He bought me a mansion, I don't have to work, and he gives me everything I could want. A lot of women would kill for a limo and driver. And now we have Kirk working on the garden..."

She trailed off, surprised by the way Kirk's name brought an unexpected warmth to her voice. Just thinking about him made something in her chest lighten—the way he'd looked at her garden plans with genuine interest, how he'd explained the difference between annual and perennial plantings without making her feel foolish, the easy way he moved through the world without the desperate intensity that seemed to follow Garrett everywhere.

"You can have all the material things in the world, but it doesn't mean anything if you're not happy," Lucy said gently, reaching across the table to squeeze Rose's hand. "Does Garrett still make you happy?"

The question was thrown out almost like a challenge, deceptively simple but loaded with implications that Rose wasn't sure she was ready to face. She found herself thinking not of Garrett, but of Kirk's easy laugh yesterday when she'd accidentally sprayed herself with the garden hose while trying to water the new plantings. The way he'd shown her the proper technique for pruning without making her feel incompetent, his hands guiding hers with a gentleness that felt natural rather than possessive.

"I love Garrett," she said finally, the words feeling both true and insufficient. "And yes, he makes me happy... most of the time. It's just that some things feel so over-the-top, so suffocating. Like I'm drowning in his love instead of being nourished by it."

Lucy smiled ruefully, her expression sympathetic but pragmatic. "Most people call that marriage, honey. At least he's not some deadbeat who beats you and leaves you wondering where your next meal is coming from. Half the women in this town would trade places with you in a heartbeat."

"I know. I shouldn't complain. All marriages have their issues." But even as she said it, Rose wondered if other wives felt this constant undercurrent of being watched, managed, and protected to the point of imprisonment. Did other husbands need to know where their wives were every moment of every day? Did other marriages feel like beautiful cages? "Even fairy tales have their problems," Lucy agreed, stirring sugar into her own coffee. "But Rose, fairy tales are supposed to have happy endings. The princess gets rescued, not locked in a tower by her prince."

The words hit closer to home than Rose wanted to admit. She glanced at her watch, suddenly needing to escape the weight of the conversation. "I should get back. I have seedlings coming from the nursery today, and I want to get them planted while Kirk is there to help." Again, that warmth in her voice when she mentioned Kirk. Lucy noticed it too, raising an eyebrow with the kind of knowing look that only best friends could give, but she had the wisdom to say nothing. Some things were too dangerous to voice, even between friends.

About thirty minutes later, as Lucy's car pulled into the circular drive of the estate, Rose felt the familiar mix of emotions that came with returning home—love and dread intertwined like the climbing roses on the garden trellis. A black Cadillac Eldorado gleamed in the afternoon sun like a predatory animal; its obsidian surface so perfectly polished it seemed to absorb light rather than reflect it.

Rose stepped out of Lucy's modest sedan, her breath catching at the sight of the luxury vehicle positioned perfectly in their circular drive. The car was beautiful—there was no denying that—but something about its presence felt ominous, like a beautiful spider waiting in the center of its web.

"Is that a new Cadillac Eldorado?" Lucy whistled low, her voice carrying both admiration and something that might have been concern.

Garrett emerged from the house as if he'd been waiting by the window, his face bright with the eager pleasure of a man presenting a gift he was certain would be adored. He moved with the energy of someone who hadn't slept, who had spent the night planning this moment, choreographing his redemption.

"Top of the line and fully loaded. It literally has everything you can get in a car." His voice carried the pride of someone who had spared no expense, who had called in favors and paid premiums to make this happen quickly.

"Garrett, you didn't have to buy me something this expensive," Rose said, though she couldn't deny the car was beautiful. The leather interior visible through the windows looked sumptuous, and she could see the gleam of real wood trim on the dashboard. "The Allante he previously purchased for her had been more than enough."

"Nothing is too good for you." His smile was radiant, but Rose caught something desperate beneath it—the smile of a man trying to buy forgiveness, trying to transform guilt into gratitude with the weight of his wallet. "I told you last night I'd get you a new car, and I meant it. This one's all yours, no strings attached."

Lucy circled the car appreciatively, running her hand along the smooth lines of the hood. "This is absolutely gorgeous. You know, if you need somewhere to park it to keep the driveway from looking cluttered, it could always stay at my place."

Despite everything—the confusion, the fear, the weight of the previous night's confrontation—Rose laughed. Lucy had always been able to do that, to find the lightness in heavy moments. "I can't do that, but I can take you for a ride in it."

"I have a better idea," Garrett said, practically bouncing on his feet with nervous energy. "Let's all go. I'll take you both for ice cream. We can test drive it together."

"You're terrible for my figure," Lucy grinned, patting her hip theatrically, "but I'm totally game."

Garrett handed Rose the keys with a flourish, and she felt the weight of them—heavy, expensive, another golden chain disguised as a gift. The key fob was substantial in her palm, loaded with buttons for features she didn't even understand. But when she looked up and saw Kirk in the distance, pruning the hedge near the garden gate, something shifted.

He glanced up from his work, their eyes meeting across the expanse of manicured lawn, and she felt a flutter of something she couldn't name. It wasn't just attraction—though she couldn't deny the way her pulse quickened when she looked at him. It was something deeper, more dangerous. It was the feeling of being seen without being watched, of being appreciated without being possessed.

Kirk lifted his hand in a small wave, and Rose found herself waving back, the gesture feeling both innocent and loaded with meaning. The new car keys felt heavier in her other hand, and she wondered if freedom could ever really be purchased, or if it was something that had to be claimed.

As they all got in Rose's new car, Rose could not help glancing back in the side mirror at Kirk working on the shrubs. A smile came across her face. Was it from this elaborate gift from Garrett, or the sight of Kirk?

Feeling a Closeness

The next day, the morning sun filtered through the oak trees in dappled patterns, casting a golden glow across the garden as Kirk maneuvered heavy bags of mulch closer to where Rose worked among the roses. The air was thick with the scent of jasmine and the earthy smell of fresh soil, creating an atmosphere that felt both intimate and peaceful. She was completely absorbed in her task, pruning with careful precision, and he found himself studying the graceful economy of her movements—the way she tilted her head to examine each branch, the gentle confidence with which she made each cut.

There was something almost meditative about watching her work, something that made Kirk forget, for moments at a time, why he was really there. The morning light caught the auburn highlights in her hair, and when she smiled at a particularly perfect bloom, he felt something shift in his chest that had nothing to do with his job.

"Those are really starting to take shape," he said, setting down a bag with a soft thud that seemed unnaturally loud in the garden's tranquility. "You might have a prize-winning garden here before you know it."

Rose looked up, a strand of hair escaping from beneath her wide-brimmed hat, and Kirk felt his breath catch at the unguarded joy in her expression. When she was out here, working with her hands in the earth, she looked different—younger, more alive, as if the garden had the power to strip away whatever weight she carried inside the mansion's walls.

"I'd love that, but I think we're getting ahead of ourselves. Besides, a lot of this success is because of the advice you've given me. That new rose fertilizer you suggested is working wonders." Her voice carried genuine gratitude, and Kirk felt the familiar stab of guilt that came with accepting praise for kindness when he was being paid to watch her.

"I'm glad I could help. That's what I'm here for." The words tasted bitter as he said them, heavy with the double meaning that only he understood. What was he here for, really? To tend the garden, or to be another set of eyes watching Rose's every move? The line between his official duties and his growing feelings had become so blurred he could barely see it anymore. "This garden seems to suit you. It makes you happy."

Rose's smile was soft, almost wistful. "It's an escape sometimes. It's nice to create something beautiful." She gestured to the emerging design around them—careful arrangements of color and texture that spoke of an artistic eye and a need for control over at least this small corner of her world. Every plant placement seemed deliberate, as if she was building not just a garden but a sanctuary.

"I agree," Kirk said simply, but his eyes weren't on the flowers. They were on her face, on the way the morning light made her skin glow, on the small smile that seemed to come so naturally when she was surrounded by growing things.

"Garrett was right when he suggested it as a way to help me get past my mother's death." Her voice caught slightly on the words, and Kirk saw the shadow that passed across her features—grief that was still fresh, still sharp enough to cut.

"And other problems that come up?" The question slipped out before Kirk could stop himself, loaded with the knowledge of what he'd witnessed, what he'd heard through the garden walls.

Rose turned to look at him, her cheeks flushing pink in a way that made her look even more beautiful. The air between them suddenly felt charged with unspoken understanding, heavy with the weight of secrets and the dangerous territory they were approaching.

"I didn't mean to upset you," Kirk said quickly, moving slightly closer without realizing it, "but I was here the other night finishing up and I heard the argument about the car. I didn't mean to listen, but it was hard to miss."

Rose's shoulders sagged slightly, and Kirk saw the mask of composure slip for just a moment. "I'm sorry you had to witness that. Not one of my finest moments, I'm sure. I completely overreacted to the whole situation."

"You didn't seem to think so at the time." Kirk's voice was gentle, without judgment, but filled with the kind of understanding that came from seeing someone's pain clearly.

"I never really know if it's me, or if..." She stopped herself, shaking her head as if trying to clear away dangerous thoughts. "I'm sorry. I don't mean to burden you with this."

"It's okay, really. Just you, me, and the roses." Kirk smiled, trying to lighten the mood while his heart ached for the confusion he could see in her eyes. "Though you might want to whisper around some of these roses. I hear they gossip."

Rose's laugh was like music—genuine and unguarded in a way that made Kirk's chest tighten with something that felt dangerously close to longing. "You're fun. Maybe I just miss having fun."

"You don't have fun?" The question seemed absurd. She was beautiful, wealthy, and had every advantage in the world. But as soon as he said it, Kirk realized how foolish the assumption was. Money couldn't buy joy, and all the luxury in the world couldn't fill the emptiness he could see lurking behind her eyes.

"I do and I don't." Rose's hands stilled on the pruning shears, and she seemed to be choosing her words carefully. "Garrett is really good to me, gives me everything a woman could ask for. But sometimes I feel like something's missing."

Kirk set down the bag of mulch and moved closer, drawn by the vulnerability in her voice like a moth to flame. He knew he was crossing lines, knew he was supposed to report back on conversations like this, but the thought of betraying her trust made his stomach turn.

"Things can't make you happy by themselves. You need experiences, passions. You have this now," he gestured to the garden, "and I think that's good. But you seem like someone who needs more than just staying home. Do you ever get out?"

"Getting out." Rose's laugh was bitter now, all the music gone out of it. "That's the question, isn't it? I'd love to travel, see the world. I used to dream about walking through the gardens at Versailles or seeing the cherry blossoms in Japan. But Garrett's always so busy with the bank, and when I do try to go anywhere..." She trailed off, and Kirk could see her retreating back into herself.

"What do you mean?"

Rose looked around as if checking to make sure they were alone, then spoke in a lower voice that made Kirk lean closer to hear her. "I feel terrible saying this because it sounds like complaining when I have so much, but sometimes I feel like Garrett wants me to be a prisoner in this mansion. Like he doesn't want me to have a life outside these walls."

Kirk felt something dangerous stir in his chest—a protectiveness that had nothing to do with his job and everything to do with the sadness in her eyes. The irony wasn't lost on him, that he was part of the very system that was trapping her, but in that moment, all he wanted was to see her smile again.

"You can't stay locked up here all the time. You need to have a life. Maybe you could try getting out more with him?"

"I've tried. It doesn't work." The resignation in her voice was heartbreaking, the sound of someone who had given up hope. Kirk made a decision that would change everything.

"Come on."

He reached out his hand to her, and the gesture felt loaded with possibility and danger in equal measure.

"What are you doing?" Rose stared at his outstretched palm as if it might bite her.

"Just come with me."

"I'm a mess." She gestured to her dirt-stained gardening clothes, her hair escaping from its pins, the smudge of earth on her cheek that only made her look more beautiful to him.

"That won't matter. Just come on."

When she placed her hand in his, Kirk felt electricity shoot up his arm. Her fingers were slender, still soft despite the gardening, and they fit perfectly in his calloused palm. He helped her to her feet, and for a moment they stood there, hands clasped, close enough that he could smell the faint scent of her perfume mixed with earth and roses. Close enough that he could see the flecks of gold in her green eyes, the way her lips parted slightly as she looked up at him.

For a heartbeat, the world narrowed to just the two of them, and Kirk felt the dangerous pull of possibility.

Kirk's truck bounced gently along the dirt road that led to his secret sanctuary, the suspension groaning softly over the ruts and stones. Rose sat beside him, the window down, her hair whipping around her face as she laughed at something he'd said about his early disasters in landscaping—the time he'd planted an entire bed of flower bulbs upside down, the client who'd asked him to create a "natural" garden that looked exactly like a magazine photo.

The sound of her laughter, so free and unguarded, made his heart race in a way that had nothing to do with the winding road. This was what she was supposed to sound like, he thought. This was who she was when she wasn't being watched, managed, protected into numbness.

"Where exactly are you taking me?" she asked, but there was no fear in her voice—only curiosity and a kind of giddy excitement that suggested it had been far too long since she'd done anything spontaneous.

"You'll see." Kirk pulled into a small clearing where ancient oaks created a natural cathedral overhead, their branches so thick and intertwined that they formed a green canopy that filtered the sunlight into dancing patterns. Through the trees, the sound of flowing water promised peace and solitude.

Rose stepped out of the truck and breathed deeply, her arms stretched wide as if she were trying to embrace the whole world. "This is beautiful, Kirk. How did you find this place?"

"I like to come here sometimes to think. To get away from crowds and complications." He studied her face as she took in the pristine beauty around them—the way her eyes lit up, the way her whole body seemed to relax for the first time since he'd known her. "I thought you could use a change of scenery."

"I can see why you love it here." She turned in a slow circle, arms outstretched like a child, and Kirk felt his chest tighten at the pure joy in her movement. "It feels good to be away from the house. These past few months, I was either at home, at Mom's apartment, or at the hospital. This is..." She paused, searching for words. "This is freedom."

Something in the way she said 'freedom'—like it was a foreign concept, something precious and rare—made Kirk's chest ache. How long had it been since she'd felt free? How long since she'd been able to move through the world without someone tracking her steps, recording her conversations, reporting back on her activities?

"Come on. There's a trail that leads to a dock on the river."

They walked in comfortable silence, but Kirk was hyperaware of every detail—the way Rose's hand occasionally brushed his arm when she stumbled on the uneven path, the soft sound of her breathing, the way she stopped to examine wildflowers with the same attention she gave her roses. She moved differently here, he noticed. Her shoulders were relaxed, her steps lighter, as if the weight of constant observation had been lifted from her shoulders.

The wooden dock stretched out over water so clear Kirk could see fish darting among the rocks below. Rose walked to the end and stood with her arms wrapped around herself, staring out at the gentle current. The breeze off the water caught her hair, and Kirk found himself memorizing the picture she made—a woman finally at peace, even if only for a moment.

"It's so peaceful," she said finally, her voice soft with wonder. "Thank you for bringing me here. This was really thoughtful."

"Sometimes I can do something nice, despite my bad reputation." The words slipped out before he could stop them, carrying more bitterness than he'd intended. The weight of his deception pressed down on him like a stone.

Rose turned to face him, her brow furrowed with genuine confusion. "How could you possibly have a bad reputation?"

Kirk found himself caught between truth and deception, between his growing feelings for this woman and the job he'd been hired to do. Every instinct told him to tell her the truth, to warn her, to explain why he was really there. But he also knew that would destroy whatever fragile trust was building between them.

"I guess it depends on who you ask."

"I'm still surprised you're not married." The observation seemed to come from nowhere, and Kirk saw color rise in her cheeks as soon as she'd said it, as if she'd revealed more than she intended.

"A lot of women want financial security. A gardener doesn't always impress." He kept his voice light, but the irony wasn't lost on him. Here he was, falling for a woman who had everything money could buy and seemed to value it least of all.

"It should be more about who makes you happy in the end." Rose's voice was soft, almost wistful, and Kirk heard layers of meaning beneath the simple words. "Security isn't all it's cracked up to be sometimes."

The weight of her words settled in the air like a challenge. Kirk wanted to ask what she meant, wanted to know if the sadness in her eyes had to do with more than just feeling trapped. But he also knew that way lay dangerous territory—for both of them.

"We should probably head back," he said reluctantly, though every fiber of his being wanted to stay here with her, to keep her in this place where she could be free, even if only for a few hours. "Don't want Mr. Sinclair wondering where we've gotten to."

Rose nodded, but she didn't move immediately. Instead, she took one last long look at the water, her expression wistful and sad. "It's nice to be somewhere nobody knows where I am. Thank you for this, Kirk. I needed it more than you know."

"Anytime." The word was out before he could consider its implications, loaded with promises he wasn't sure he could keep. "You didn't know you were getting a gardener and therapist all in one, did you?"

Her laughter followed them back up the path, and Kirk found himself memorizing the sound, storing it away like a treasure. As they drove back toward the mansion—back toward Garrett and complications and the job that was becoming more impossible by the day—Kirk made a decision.

Whatever Garrett was paying him to watch Rose, it wasn't enough to make him betray the trust he saw growing in her eyes. Some things, he was learning, were worth more than money. And Rose Sinclair's happiness was rapidly becoming one of them.

The truck pulled into the circular drive just as the afternoon shadows were beginning to lengthen, and Kirk saw the curtains in the upstairs window flutter closed. Garrett was home, and he'd been watching. But as Rose turned to thank him one more time, her face still glowing with the freedom she'd tasted, Kirk found he didn't care.

Let Garrett watch. Let him wonder. Some moments were worth the risk.

Making Decisions

The evening air was thick with humidity as Kirk loaded his tools into the back of his truck, the day's work finally complete. Each shovel and rake seemed heavier than usual, weighted down by the burden of secrets he carried. The Georgia heat clung to his shirt, but it was nothing compared to the heat that had flared between him and Rose earlier that afternoon when their hands had accidentally touched over the same gardening tool. He was looking forward to getting home, maybe grabbing a beer, and trying to forget the way Rose had looked at him when she'd said goodbye—like he was the only person in her world who understood her need for freedom.

The pristine garden around him seemed to mock his internal turmoil. Every perfectly trimmed hedge, every strategically placed stone, every bloom that Rose had coaxed from the earth with such tender care—it all existed within the golden cage that Garrett had built for her. Kirk had helped create this paradise, but he was beginning to understand that even the most beautiful prison was still a prison.

The sound of an expensive engine purring up the driveway made him pause, his hands stilling on the tailgate. The rumble was distinctly different from the working-class vehicles that usually visited the estate—this was the sound of money, of power, of a man who could afford to have everything he wanted. Garrett's midnight black Cadillac slid into view like a predator returning to its territory, and Kirk felt his stomach clench with something that might have been guilt if he'd actually been doing anything wrong.

But that was the problem, wasn't it? He was starting to wish he was doing something wrong. The thought of Rose trapped in that mansion, beautiful and withering like a cut flower in a crystal vase, made his chest tighten with a protective instinct he had no right to feel.

"Kirk!" Garrett called out, stepping from his car with the easy confidence of a man who owned everything around him—including, Kirk was beginning to realize, the people. The banker's suit was still crisp despite the late hour, his tie perfectly knotted, his shoes polished to a mirror shine. Everything about him screamed success, control, perfection. "How are things going?"

"Everything's good, Mr. Sinclair. We're really starting to see the garden take shape." Kirk kept his voice neutral, professional, but something about Garrett's demeanor set him on edge. There was a tension in the man's shoulders, a sharpness to his smile that hadn't been there in their earlier interactions. It was the look of a man who suspected his world wasn't as perfectly ordered as he'd believed.

"Excellent." Garrett moved closer, and Kirk caught the scent of expensive cologne mixed with something sharper—anxiety, maybe, or suspicion. The banker's eyes swept over the garden with the calculating gaze of someone conducting an inventory, checking to make sure all his possessions were still in their proper places. "Anything I should know about? Has Rose mentioned anything about me? About the situation with the car?"

The questions came rapid-fire, and Kirk felt the familiar twist of disgust in his gut. This wasn't a husband concerned about his wife's happiness—this was a man gathering intelligence, treating his own wife like a subject under surveillance. The irony wasn't lost on Kirk that he was supposed to be part of that surveillance system, the eyes and ears Garrett had planted in his own garden.

"She mentioned she had a new car. That was about it. We mainly just worked on the roses." The lie came easier than it should have, and Kirk realized he'd already made his choice about where his loyalties lay. He could still remember the way Rose's face had fallen when she'd told him about the "mechanical issues" with her previous car, the way she'd looked so defeated when she'd mentioned the new driver who would be taking her everywhere. She hadn't said it outright, but Kirk had read between the lines. The car hadn't broken down, it had been sabotaged, another link in the chain that bound Rose to this beautiful estate.

"I'm sure you two talk while you work." Garrett's smile was sharp around the edges, like a blade wrapped in silk. "Has she said anything about being unhappy? Anything else I should be aware of?"

The question stung as it floated in the air between them, loaded with implications. Kirk could feel Garrett's gaze boring into him, searching for any crack in his facade, any sign of betrayal. He thought of Rose's laugh that afternoon, the first genuine one he'd heard from her in weeks, and felt his resolve harden.

Kirk met his gaze steadily, feeling something shift inside him—a line being crossed that he couldn't uncross. "No, sir. She seems very happy working in the garden. Really appreciates that you're supporting her in it."

The words tasted like ash in his mouth, but they seemed to satisfy Garrett. The banker's posture relaxed slightly, though his eyes remained alert, watchful.

"Good." Garrett nodded, but his eyes remained calculating, already moving on to the next item on his mental checklist. "You keep doing a good job, Kirk. And keep your ears open." "Sure thing, Mr. Sinclair."

The dismissal was clear, but Kirk didn't move immediately. He watched Garrett walk toward the house, noting the way he moved like a man who expected the world to rearrange itself for his convenience. Every step was measured, controlled, purposeful. Even his love for Rose felt controlled, Kirk realized—not the wild, desperate thing that was growing in his own chest, but something carefully managed and maintained like the garden itself.

When the front door closed behind Garrett with a soft, expensive click, Kirk sat in his truck for a long moment, hands gripping the steering wheel until his knuckles went white. Through the mansion's windows, he could see the warm glow of lights being turned on, the shadow of Rose moving through the rooms like a ghost in her own home.

He was supposed to be watching Rose, reporting on her activities, her moods, her conversations. Instead, he found himself wanting to protect her from the very man who was paying his salary. The weighted feeling he had inside him—he was being paid to spy on the woman he was falling in love with. Every dollar Garrett handed him felt like thirty pieces of silver, payment for a betrayal he was determined not to commit.

The engine turned over with a rumble, but as Kirk drove away, he couldn't shake the feeling that he was driving toward something inevitable and probably disastrous. In his rearview mirror, the mansion glowed like a beacon in the gathering dusk, beautiful and isolated and utterly wrong.

Inside the mansion, Rose put the finishing touches on a meal she hoped would smooth over the tension from the past few days. Her hands moved with practiced efficiency, but her mind was elsewhere—on the afternoon she'd spent with Kirk, on the way he'd listened to her talk about her dreams of traveling, of seeing the world beyond these perfectly manicured grounds. Candles flickered on the dining room table, casting dancing shadows across the crystal and China, and she'd chosen Garrett's favorite wine—small gestures that felt simultaneously genuine and calculated.

The dining room was a masterpiece of understated elegance, from the mahogany table that could seat twelve to the original oil paintings that gazed down from the walls with disapproving eyes. Everything was perfect, carefully curated, museum-quality. Just like her life, Rose thought with a pang of something that might have been grief.

She paused at the mirror in the hallway, checking her appearance with the automatic precision of a woman who'd learned that her husband noticed everything. Her dress was one of his favorites—a deep emerald that brought out her eyes—and she'd styled her hair the way he liked it, soft and romantic. She looked like the perfect wife, the ideal companion for a successful man. The reflection staring back at her was everything Garrett had dreamed of when he'd first seen her in that store.

So why did she feel like she was disappearing a little more each day?

"Rose! I'm home!" Garrett's voice echoed through the entrance hall, carrying that particular note of pleased surprise that came when he found her waiting for him. There was something almost childlike about his delight in coming home to her, in finding her exactly where he expected her to be.

"Perfect timing," she called back, emerging from the dining room with a smile that felt only slightly forced. The smile came easier now, after months of practice, but sometimes she wondered if she was losing the ability to distinguish between genuine happiness and its carefully constructed imitation. "I have a special meal prepared for us."

Garrett's face lit up with the kind of boyish delight that reminded her why she'd fallen in love with him in the first place. When he smiled like that, she could see the man who'd courted her so sweetly, who'd made her feel like the most precious thing in the world. "Really? What's the special occasion?"

"Just wanted a nice dinner with my wonderful husband." The words came automatically, but as she said them, Rose realized she meant them. Despite everything—the watching, the questions, the suffocating protectiveness—she did love him. The problem was that love was becoming harder to breathe around, like being slowly strangled by silk scarves.

"You're in an amazing mood." Garrett pulled her close, his arms encircling her waist with possessive tenderness. His hands were soft, manicured, the hands of a man who'd never worked in a garden or built anything with his own strength. He studied her face with the intensity of a man reading a beloved but complicated text, searching for clues to her thoughts, her feelings, her intentions. "What happened today? Something special?"

The question was casual, but Rose could hear the undertone of need in it—the need to know everything, to control everything, to possess not just her body but her very thoughts. She'd learned to navigate these conversational minefields, to give him enough truth to satisfy his hunger for information while keeping the most important parts of herself hidden away.

"Nothing dramatic. I just worked in my garden all day." Rose slipped her arm through his, leading him toward the dining room. The word "my" felt strange on her tongue—was anything really hers anymore? Even the garden, which had started as her sanctuary, was becoming another stage for Garrett's surveillance. But even as she smiled and made conversation about the roses and the new fertilizer Kirk had recommended, she found herself thinking about the afternoon by the river, about the way Kirk had looked at her like she was a person rather than a prize to be protected.

"Tell me about the garden," Garrett said as they settled into their seats, and Rose could hear the careful interest in his voice. He was always careful now, always watching for signs of discontent, always ready to fix problems before they became threats to his perfectly ordered world. "How are the roses coming along?"

"Beautifully," Rose said, and for a moment, her smile was genuine. "Kirk says we should have blooms by next month. The soil is finally perfect—rich and dark and full of life." She paused, caught by her own words. When had she last felt full of life? "He's very knowledgeable about plants."

Something flickered in Garrett's eyes—so quickly that she might have imagined it. "Kirk seems like a good man. Hardworking." The words were carefully neutral, but Rose felt a chill run down her spine. She'd heard that tone before, usually right before someone disappeared from her life.

"He is," she said quietly, and realized she was holding her breath.

The dinner was wonderful, filled with casual small talk, but a lot of guarded words.

I've Had Enough!

The next afternoon brought one of those confrontations that feel inevitable in hindsight, though Rose didn't see it coming until she walked through her own front door and found Garrett waiting in the entrance hall like a prosecutor preparing his case. The marble floor beneath her feet suddenly felt cold, unforgiving, and the grand chandelier above cast sharp shadows that seemed to divide the space between them into territories of accusation and defense.

"You're home early," she said, setting down her purse with deliberate care on the antique console table. Her voice sounded too bright, too casual, even to her own ears. She tried to ignore the way his presence felt more like an interrogation than a welcome, the way he stood perfectly still with his hands clasped behind his back—a posture she'd learned to recognize as his preparation for battle. "I was trying to get back before you got home."

"Were you?" The question was sharp, loaded with implications that made Rose's stomach tighten. His voice echoed off the high ceilings, bouncing back at her with an accusatory edge that made her feel small and guilty for crimes she hadn't committed.

Rose felt the familiar flutter of panic in her chest, the same sensation she'd experienced as a child when caught in some minor transgression. But she was no longer a child, and she hadn't done anything wrong. The realization sparked something dangerous in her—a flicker of the woman she'd been before Garrett's love had begun to reshape her into someone more compliant, more manageable.

"I found some wonderful things for the garden today. There's this statue that would be perfect near the rose bed—" She was babbling, she realized, filling the silence with unnecessary details because something in Garrett's expression made her nervous. His eyes were too bright, too focused, like a man who'd been rehearsing this moment for hours. The late afternoon light streaming through the stained-glass windows cast colored patterns across his face, making him look almost stranger-like in his own home.

"You bought a statue?" His voice was carefully controlled, but Rose caught the edge beneath it—the same tone he used when reviewing loan applications from people he suspected of fraud. She'd heard him use it on phone calls, that precise, measuring cadence that meant he was gathering evidence for a case he'd already decided.

"Well, no. I didn't buy anything today. I wanted to get Kirk's opinion first, see if he thinks it would be too much or if it would work as a good accent piece." The explanation sounded reasonable to her own ears, logical even. Kirk had developed an eye for the garden's aesthetic, understanding how each element should work together to create the paradise they'd been building. But she watched Garrett's face darken, saw the muscle in his jaw tighten with barely controlled anger.

"He went with you?" Each word was precise, measured, delivered with the surgical precision of a man who knew exactly where he was cutting.

"No. I was alone." Rose felt anger beginning to kindle in her chest, a warmth that spread through her like wine on an empty stomach. The feeling was almost foreign after months of careful diplomacy and strategic submission. "What exactly are you insinuating, Garrett?"

The question exited her mouth like a challenge, and Rose saw something flickering in Garrett's eyes—surprise, maybe that she was pushing back instead of apologizing and explaining. For a moment, she glimpsed the man she'd fallen in love with, the one who'd been charmed by her spirit and independence. But that man was quickly swallowed by the stranger who stood before her now, the one who treated her like a possession that might be stolen if not properly guarded.

"You've been gone literally all day, telling me you found all this great stuff, but you didn't buy anything. Why not?" The questions came faster now, and Rose recognized the pattern—the same interrogation technique he probably used at the bank when he suspected someone of lying about their loan applications. His voice had taken on that professional distance, as if she were a client under investigation rather than the woman he claimed to love more than life itself.

"I didn't want to get the car dirty with plants and mulch. I figured Kirk could always take me back in his truck if I decided to buy anything." Her voice was rising despite her efforts to stay calm. The mention of Kirk's name seemed to ignite something dangerous in Garrett's expression, and Rose felt a chill of premonition. Kirk had become more than just a gardener to her—he'd become a confidant, a friend, someone who listened to her dreams of travel and freedom without trying to convince her they were dangerous or unnecessary.

"And that took all day? Since early this morning?" The questions kept coming, each one a small knife thrust designed to peel away her defenses layer by layer. Rose could see the calculation in his eyes, the way he was building his case against her brick by brick. The realization that her own husband was treating her like a criminal suspect was like a physical blow.

That's when something inside Rose snapped. The careful politeness, the patient explanations, the constant need to justify her every movement—it all collapsed under the weight of her frustration like a dam bursting after too many seasons of pressure.

"Garrett, this has got to stop. Right now." Her voice cut through the tension like a blade, clear and strong and carrying all the authority of a woman who'd finally reached her breaking point. The sound seemed to surprise them both—Rose couldn't remember the last time she'd spoken to him with such commanding certainty. Maybe it was not since the confrontation over Mark. "You constantly question my every move. The credit card receipts, calling when you know I can't answer, and interrogating me every time I leave this house. I can't take this anymore."

The words poured out of her like water from a broken dam, carrying with them months of suppressed resentment and suffocated independence. She could see Garrett flinch with each accusation, his face crumpling as if she were physically striking him. But she couldn't stop—the relief of finally saying the truth was intoxicating, dangerous, necessary.

Garrett's face crumpled with what looked like genuine anguish, and for a moment, Rose glimpsed the vulnerable man beneath the controlling exterior. His carefully constructed composure shattered, revealing something raw and desperate that might have been heartbreaking if it hadn't been so destructive. "Do you know why I question things? Why I worry?"

"Because you don't trust me." The words came out flat, final, carrying the weight of a diagnosis that couldn't be appealed or argued away.

"No!" His voice broke on the word, cracking like a teenager's. Tears were already gathering in his eyes, and Rose felt a familiar tug of sympathy—the same protective instinct that had made her fall in love with him in the first place. But she'd learned to recognize the pattern now: the tears, the vulnerability, the way he could make her feel guilty for having needs of her own. "It's because I love you and I worry about you. I worry that something might happen, that someone might try to hurt you—"

"You worry too much!" Rose felt a long train of suppressed frustration pouring out like poison from a lanced wound. The entrance hall seemed to amplify her voice, carrying it through the house like a declaration of war. "This might be a newsflash, Garrett, but I took care of myself for a long time before I met you. I'm a grown woman. I think I can handle going to a store or a restaurant without getting kidnapped or lost."

She could see him flinch at each word, but she pressed on, driven by a fury that felt both foreign and familiar—the ghost of the independent woman she'd been before love had taught her to make herself smaller, quieter, more manageable.

"You're my everything." Tears were streaming down his face now, cutting silver tracks through his carefully maintained composure. His voice carried the desperate edge of a man drowning, reaching for anything that might save him. "If something happened to you, I couldn't survive it."

The raw desperation in his voice should have melted her anger, but instead it only intensified it. She could see the love there, genuine and overwhelming, but she could also see how that love had twisted into something possessive and destructive—a force that demanded she sacrifice her identity on the altar of his need to feel secure. His tears, once so powerful in their ability to make her capitulate, now seemed like another form of manipulation, another way to make her responsible for his emotional well-being.

"Nothing is going to happen to me, Garrett. You've got to stop this. You're making me a prisoner in my own home. I can't breathe." The words came from somewhere deep inside her, a place she'd almost forgotten existed. "This trust issue, or control issue, or whatever you want to call it—it has to stop."

She could see the impact of her words in his face, the way his expression shifted from desperate pleading to something harder, more calculating. For a moment, she glimpsed the man who'd built a banking empire through careful control and strategic manipulation, the one who'd never met a problem he couldn't solve by applying the right pressure in the right place.

"I can't stop loving you. I can't stop caring—"

"I'm not asking you to!" Rose's voice echoed through the entrance hall, bouncing off the marble and crystal until it seemed to fill every corner of the house. "I'm glad you love me. But you've got to give me room to breathe. You're smothering me, and I can't take it anymore."

The admission powered out of her mouth like a bridge she'd burned, and Rose felt both terror and relief at having finally said it aloud. The truth was ugly and necessary, like surgery that had to cut through healthy tissue to reach the disease beneath.

"Rose—" Garrett reached for her with trembling hands, but she stepped back instinctively. The gesture was small, but it created a chasm between them that felt suddenly unbridgeable.

"Please. Just let me be alone for a while."

She turned and walked up the stairs, feeling his eyes on her back like a physical weight. Each step felt like a small act of rebellion, a reclaiming of space that had been slowly eroded over the length of their marriage. At the top, she paused and looked down at him—this man she loved who was slowly suffocating everything good between them with his need to control and protect.

Garrett stood there for a long moment, watching the space where she'd disappeared, his hands hanging useless at his sides. The entrance hall felt suddenly empty, cavernous, as if her absence had drained all the warmth from the carefully decorated space. The grandfather clock in the corner ticked steadily, marking the passage of time with mechanical indifference to the human drama playing out in its shadow.

Finally, he turned and walked toward the garden with the purposeful stride of a man who had decided something. His footsteps echoed off the marble with increasing urgency, and the sound carried a note of menace that would have made Rose's blood run cold if she'd heard it.

Some minutes later, Kirk was organizing tools in the garden shed when he heard footsteps on the gravel path. The sound was different from Rose's light tread—heavier, more aggressive, carrying the weight of a man with purpose. He'd been expecting this conversation ever since he'd seen Garrett's car pull up and heard the raised voices from the house, the sound carrying across the garden like distant thunder promising a storm.

Still, when he emerged from the shed to find Garrett bearing down on him with barely contained fury, his stomach clenched as he had tried to pull himself together after the confrontation with Rose. The banker's usually perfect composure was cracked, his tie askew, his hair disheveled as if he'd been running his hands through it. Most telling of all, his eyes held a wild light that Kirk had seen before in men who'd been pushed past their breaking point.

"Mr. Sinclair." Kirk kept his voice level, professional, though every instinct he'd developed in his rougher years was screaming at him to prepare for a fight.

"Where were you today?" Garrett's question came without preamble, sharp as a blade. His voice carried the authority of a man accustomed to having his questions answered immediately and completely.

"I was right here all day. Working." Kirk gestured to the evidence around them—the freshly turned soil, the pruned hedges, the irrigation system he'd been installing. The garden was taking shape beautifully, becoming the paradise that Rose had envisioned, but Kirk could see that Garrett wasn't interested in admiring their progress.

"And Rose wasn't here." It wasn't a question. Garrett's eyes swept the garden as if he might find evidence of some crime hidden among the flowering plants. "Do you know where she was?"

Kirk felt the weight of the moment, the crossroads he'd been approaching for weeks. He could lie, could claim ignorance, could protect Rose from whatever storm was gathering in her husband's eyes. But something in Garrett's demeanor suggested that lies would only make things worse.

"She said she was going to look for plants and maybe a statue for the garden. It's really coming along nicely—"

"Why didn't you go with her?" Garrett stepped closer, and Kirk caught the scent of expensive cologne mixed with sweat and something that might have been desperation. The banker's presence felt oppressive, like a storm cloud gathering overhead.

"She didn't ask, and I had work to do here." Kirk kept his hands loose at his sides, but every muscle in his body was tense. He'd been in enough confrontations to recognize the signs of a man looking for a fight—the slight forward lean, the clenched fists, the way Garrett's breathing had become shallow and quick.

"From now on," Garrett's voice dropped to a whisper that was somehow more threatening than shouting, "you find a reason to go with her. You're supposed to be making sure she's happy and safe. That's what I'm paying you for."

The words hit Kirk like a physical blow. There it was—the truth laid bare, ugly and undeniable. He wasn't just a gardener; he was a jailer. A spy. A man being paid to betray the trust of the woman he was falling in love with. The realization made him feel sick, not just because of what it meant for Rose, but because of what it made him—a collaborator in her imprisonment, a guard who'd been seduced by the very prisoner he was supposed to be watching.

"I'm sorry," he managed, though the words tasted like poison. The apology was for more than his failure to shadow Rose—it was for every moment he'd accepted Garrett's money while growing closer to his wife, for every smile he'd shared with Rose while knowing his true purpose, for the way he'd let himself believe he could be her friend while serving as her captor. "My mistake. It won't happen again."

"See that it doesn't." Garrett held his gaze for another moment, and Kirk saw something dangerous flicker in the banker's eyes—a calculation that made his skin crawl. Then Garrett turned and stalked back toward the house, his footsteps sharp and purposeful on the garden path.

Kirk watched him go, disgust rising in his throat like bile. The man's retreating figure looked smaller somehow, diminished by his own desperation, but no less dangerous for it. A desperate man with money and influence was like a wounded animal—unpredictable and capable of far more damage than anyone expected.

When Garrett disappeared through the patio doors, Kirk sank onto a nearby bench, his hands shaking with suppressed rage. The garden around him suddenly felt different—less like a sanctuary and more like a stage set for some elaborate performance. Every plant they'd chosen together, every pathway they'd designed, every small improvement they'd made—it all felt tainted now by the knowledge of what he really was.

He'd taken worse jobs for worse people, but somehow this felt different. This felt personal. Rose's laughter from yesterday echoed in his memory—free and genuine and absolutely trusting. She'd looked at him like he was someone she could count on, someone who understood her need for freedom. She'd confided in him about her dreams of travel, her longing to see the world beyond these perfectly manicured grounds, her growing sense that she was suffocating in her own life.

And all the while, he'd been paid to be her watchdog.

Kirk stared at the garden they'd been building together, seeing it now for what it really was—not a sanctuary, but a beautiful cage. The roses they'd planted with such care looked like bars now, the carefully planned pathways like the exercise yard of a prison. And he was one of the bars, complicit in her captivity, a trusted friend who was secretly reporting her every move to the man who was slowly strangling her with his love.

The question that would haunt him through the sleepless night ahead was simple: What was he going to do about it?

The evening air was growing cool, carrying the scent of jasmine and the distant sound of traffic from the world beyond the estate's gates. Kirk could hear the rumble of ordinary life continuing beyond these walls—people going home from work, families gathering for dinner, couples arguing and making up and living their messy, uncontrolled lives. Rose was trapped behind these gates like a character in a fairy tale, beautiful and doomed and waiting for someone to set her free.

The realization hit him like a physical blow: he was falling in love with her. Not just attracted to her beauty or charmed by her kindness, but genuinely, deeply in love with the woman who laughed at his stories and shared her dreams and looked at him like he was someone worth trusting. The knowledge should have filled him with joy, but instead, it made him feel like he was drowning.

Because loving Rose meant betraying Garrett, and betraying Garrett meant losing not just his job, but potentially his freedom if the banker decided to make trouble for him. Men like Garrett Sinclair didn't just fire employees who disappointed them—they destroyed them, systematically and thoroughly, with the same methodical precision they brought to everything else.

But continuing to spy on Rose meant betraying her trust, participating in her slow suffocation, watching the light die in her eyes day by day while he collected his thirty pieces of silver and pretended to be her friend.

Kirk stood up from the bench, his decision crystallizing with the sudden clarity that sometimes comes in moments of crisis. He couldn't save Rose; that was something she'd have to do herself. But he could stop being part of the machine that was grinding her down. He could stop being Garrett's eyes and ears in the garden where she'd found her only peace.

The question now was whether he could do it without getting them both killed in the process.

The Fairytale Unravels

Jack was heading back to his office when he noticed the boardroom door slightly ajar. The late afternoon sun slanted through the floor-to-ceiling windows, casting long shadows across the polished marble floor of the bank's executive level. He wouldn't have given it a second thought—the boardroom was used for private calls all the time—except he could hear Garrett's voice from within, low, urgent, and unmistakably tense.

"I want a report of everything she does, everywhere she goes, and who she is with. Do you understand? I want daily reports. I don't want to wait."

Jack's steps slowed involuntarily, his leather soles making no sound on the marble. The tone in his friend's voice sent a chill down his spine—it was the voice Garrett used when foreclosing on properties, when destroying business competitors, when wielding his power like a weapon. But this wasn't a business call—this was something else entirely.

Something that made his stomach turn with a sick recognition of what he was overhearing.

The words echoed in the high-ceilinged space, bouncing off the mahogany paneling and crystal chandelier with an almost physical weight. Jack had known Garrett for several years, had stood beside him as best man at his wedding, had watched him fall in love with Rose with the desperate intensity of a man who'd never expected to find happiness. But this voice—cold, calculating, threatening—belonged to a stranger.

"Money is no object," Garrett continued, and Jack could hear the rustle of papers, the scratch of a pen signing what sounded like a very lucrative contract. "I want to know everything. Who she talks to, what she buys, where she goes when she thinks no one is watching. Everything."

Jack felt his throat constrict. He should walk away, should pretend he'd never heard any of this. But his feet seemed rooted to the marble floor, held there by the terrible fascination of watching a friend cross a line that couldn't be uncrossed.

He heard the sharp click of the phone being placed back in its cradle, followed by silence that seemed to stretch and thicken until it became oppressive. Jack took a breath, steeling himself, then pushed the door open with what he hoped was casual friendliness.

"What's up buddy? Why are you in here all alone?"

Garrett looked up from where he sat at the head of the polished conference table, his face carefully composed but his eyes still holding traces of the intensity Jack had heard in his voice. The transformation was remarkable—in seconds, Garrett had shifted from the cold voice on the phone to the successful banker, the devoted husband, the man everyone in Macon respected and envied.

"I needed to make a private call." The words were very heavy, and Jack felt the weight of what he'd accidentally witnessed. There was something in Garrett's eyes—a challenge, maybe, or a plea for understanding—that made Jack's chest tighten with dread.

He settled into one of the leather chairs, trying to keep his expression neutral even as concern gnawed at him. The boardroom felt different now, charged with secrets and the lingering echo of that cold, threatening voice. The afternoon light streaming through the windows seemed harsher, more interrogating.

"Is anything the matter? Anything I can help you with?"

For a moment, Garrett's composure cracked, revealing something raw and desperate underneath. It was like watching a dam spring a leak, the carefully maintained facade beginning to crumble under the pressure of whatever was eating him alive from the inside.

"I don't know. Things are not going like I thought they would."

"At home?" Jack kept his voice gentle, non-threatening, the way he'd learned to speak to nervous loan applicants. But inside, he was bracing himself for whatever confession was about to spill out.

"Yeah." Garrett's shoulders sagged slightly, and for a moment, he looked older, more fragile, like a man carrying a weight too heavy for his frame. "Rose has not been the same since she lost her mother."

Jack leaned forward, his friend's pain evident despite his attempt to maintain control. He remembered Rose's mother—a warm, vibrant woman who'd treated Garrett like the son she'd never had. Her sickness and death had been very tough on Rose, leaving her devastated, with Garrett struggling to comfort a grief he couldn't fix or control.

"How so?"

"She has been more distant. She is gone a lot, where nobody knows where she is, and for long periods of time. I am afraid she might..." Garrett's voice trailed off, as if he couldn't bring himself to voice his fears. His hands were clenched on the table surface, knuckles white with tension.

"Might what?" Jack asked, though he was beginning to suspect where this conversation was heading, and the knowledge made him feel sick.

The silence stretched across the room, filled with the distant sounds of the bank's daily operations—phones ringing, printers humming, the muffled conversations of people going about their normal lives, unaware that in this boardroom, a man was confessing to having his wife followed like a criminal.

Finally, Garrett spoke, the words seeming to cost him. "I am afraid she may be seeing someone."

Jack felt his heart sink. Not Rose—not the woman he'd watched fall in love with his best friend, who'd seemed so devoted, so genuine in her affection. He'd seen them together at dinner parties, at social events, and had watched the way she looked at Garrett like he was the most important person in the world. The idea that she might be betraying that love felt like a personal blow.

"No. Not Rose. Garrett, she loves you. I know she does."

"Then why all the changes? Where is she going?" There was a pleading quality to Garrett's voice that Jack had never heard before, a vulnerability that made him want to reach out and reassure his friend that everything would be okay. But the memory of that phone call—the cold, calculating voice ordering surveillance—made comfort impossible.

"I don't know. Have you asked her about it?"

"When I do, she gets really defensive and screams and yells, saying it is all in my head."

Garrett's hands clenched into fists on the table surface, and Jack could see the frustration and hurt warring in his expression. "She acts like I'm crazy for being concerned about my own wife."

Jack studied his friend's face, seeing the doubt and fear written there, but also something else—a hardness that hadn't been there before, a calculating coldness that reminded him uncomfortably of the voice he'd overheard. "Well, is it all in your head?"

"No." The response was immediate, certain, and delivered with the conviction of a man who'd built his entire worldview around this single belief. "I call, and she is missing all day. She says she goes shopping but never has packages or credit card receipts. Nobody knows where she goes. She was very insistent on wanting her own car. I'm worried."

The pieces were falling into place, painting a picture that Jack desperately didn't want to see. The phone call he'd overheard suddenly made terrible sense—not the actions of a concerned husband, but the desperate measures of a man who'd lost control of the thing he valued most in the world.

"Garrett," Jack said carefully, "have you considered that maybe Rose just needs some space? Grief affects people differently. Maybe she's just trying to process her mother's death in her own way."

"By lying to me?" Garrett's voice rose slightly, and Jack could hear the edge of hysteria creeping in. "By disappearing for hours at a time? By refusing to tell me where she goes or who she's with?"

Jack wanted to point out that Rose didn't owe her husband a minute-by-minute account of her activities, that even married people were entitled to privacy, to time alone with their thoughts. But he could see that Garrett was beyond reasonable argument, trapped in a spiral of suspicion and fear that was feeding on itself. A trait Garrett had never realized he was consciously doing.

"I'm sorry, buddy." The words felt inadequate, but Jack didn't know what else to say. He was watching his friend destroy his marriage through his own paranoia, and there seemed to be no way to stop it.

"Thanks. I need to get to a meeting. We'll talk later."

Garrett stood abruptly, his movements sharp with suppressed emotion. Jack watched him leave, noting the tension in his friend's shoulders, the way he held himself like a man bracing for a blow. The transformation was complete—the vulnerable, hurting husband had been replaced by the cold, calculating businessman who'd ordered surveillance on his own wife.

After Garrett disappeared down the hallway, Jack sat alone in the boardroom for a moment, staring at the phone that had just been used to set some kind of surveillance in motion. The sick feeling in his stomach only grew stronger as he contemplated what he'd witnessed. This wasn't love—this was obsession, possession, the kind of destructive need that consumed everything it touched. It was part of who his friend was, even though, to Garrett, it was all just his mind being overprotective of someone he truly cared about.

Jack decided he needed to talk to Lucy.

He found Lucy at her desk in the lobby, efficiently sorting through a stack of documents with the focused precision that had made her one of the bank's most valued employees. The lobby buzzed with the usual afternoon activity—customers coming and going, tellers processing transactions, the comfortable hum of business as usual. It all felt surreal after what he'd just witnessed upstairs.

She looked up as he approached, and her expression immediately shifted from professional pleasantness to concern. Lucy had always been perceptive, able to read the subtleties of expression and tone that others missed.

"Hey. What's wrong? I can tell something is up."

Jack glanced around the busy lobby, then moved closer to her desk, lowering his voice. The marble columns and high ceilings made even whispered conversations carry farther than intended, and this wasn't something he wanted overheard by the wrong people. "I hate to pry. I feel really bad about it, but I need to ask you something."

Lucy set down her papers, giving him her full attention. Her dark eyes were alert, intelligent, missing nothing. "Sure. What's up?"

"Have you noticed anything different about Rose since her mother passed away?"

Lucy's brow furrowed thoughtfully, and Jack could see her mental wheels turning, reviewing recent interactions and conversations. "I mean she was upset. That is natural. She and her mom were very close, but she seems to be doing better now. Why do you ask?"

Jack hesitated, the weight of what he'd overheard pressing down on him like a physical burden. How could he explain what he'd witnessed without betraying Garrett's confidence? How could he protect Rose without destroying his oldest friendship?

"Garrett said she has been acting different since her mom died. He's a little worried about her."

"Well, it's Garrett. He's always a little worried. Maybe it's just his overactive imagination." Lucy's tone was light, but Jack caught the slight edge of exasperation, the voice of someone who'd watched a friend be overly protective one too many times. It was clear that Rose had confided in Lucy about Garrett's possessiveness, at least to some degree.

"I don't think so. Not this time." Jack's voice carried a gravity that made Lucy's expression grow more serious. He could see the shift in her demeanor, the way her casual dismissal gave way to genuine concern.

She studied his face for a moment, reading the worry and fear he was trying to hide. Lucy had always been good at seeing through facades, at understanding the subtext of conversations. "What aren't you telling me, Jack?"

"I can't... I overheard something. Something that made me think Rose might be in more trouble than any of us realizes."

Lucy's eyes widened slightly, and Jack could see her mind racing through possibilities. "What kind of trouble?"

"The kind where she might need friends who are looking out for her." Jack chose his words carefully, trying to convey the urgency without revealing too much. "I think Garrett's worry has crossed a line."

The silence that followed was heavy with implication. Lucy's face went through a series of expressions—surprise, concern, and finally, a grim understanding that suggested she'd suspected something like this might be coming.

"I have lunch with Rose on Friday. I will see if I can tell anything."

Relief flooded through Jack. If anyone could get to the truth without causing alarm, it would be Lucy. Rose trusted her, confided in her, and Lucy had the kind of intuitive understanding that could read between the lines of whatever careful facade Rose might be maintaining.

"Please, don't let her know I asked."

"Don't worry. We are just two people who care about our best friends." Lucy's smile was reassuring, but Jack could see the concern now flickering in her eyes, the way she was already planning her approach to the delicate conversation ahead.

As he walked away, Jack couldn't shake the feeling that they were all standing on the edge of something that would change everything. The bank's familiar surroundings—the marble floors, the polished brass, the comfortable routine of daily business—all felt suddenly fragile, like a stage set that could collapse at any moment.

And somewhere in the back of his mind, he wondered if Rose had any idea what was closing in around her. He thought of her laugh, her warmth, the way she'd lit up Garrett's world when they'd first met. Now that same light was being systematically extinguished by the very man who claimed to love her more than life itself.

The irony was bitter and complete: in trying to protect Rose from imaginary threats, Garrett was creating the very danger she needed protection from. And Jack was beginning to suspect that it might already be too late to save either of them from the disaster that was rapidly approaching.

A Place of Peace

Back at the house, Rose sat cross-legged in the garden, pruning shears balanced loosely in her lap as she stared at the rose bush before her. The morning sun filtered through the oak trees, casting dappled shadows across the carefully manicured beds, but she barely noticed the beauty around her. Her mind was elsewhere—caught in the suffocating web of her own life.

The irony wasn't lost on her that she was surrounded by beautiful roses. Garrett's obsession with giving her everything beautiful had extended even to calling their estate "Rose's Garden Manor." Every bloom seemed to mock her now—perfect, cultivated, controlled. Just like her life had become.

She lifted the shears, then let them fall back to her lap. Even this simple task felt overwhelming today. The weight of Garrett's morning interrogations still pressed against her chest like a stone. *Where are you going? Who will you see? What time will you be back?* The questions came disguised as caring concern, but Rose had learned to recognize the steel beneath the velvet.

Kirk approached from the direction of the tool shed, his boots crunching softly on the gravel path. Even without looking up, she could feel his presence, the way he seemed to bring a sense of calm to whatever space he occupied. It was dangerous, this feeling of peace he brought her. She'd been married long enough to know that peace was a luxury she couldn't afford.

"You seem really quiet today. Are you OK?"

She forced herself to look up, managing a weak smile. The effort felt enormous, like lifting a heavy curtain. "I'm sorry. Yeah, I'm fine. I guess I am not very into my work today."

Fine. The word tasted very bitter in her mouth. When had she become someone who lied so easily? The Rose from two years ago would have been horrified at how naturally deception came to her now. But the Rose from two years ago had believed in fairytales.

Kirk's expression was gentle, understanding. There was something in his eyes that made her want to tell him everything—the details of the driver who had reported her every movement, about the constant phone calls checking on her whereabouts, about the way Garrett made sure he checked every credit card receipt. "Everyone needs a break sometimes."

"More than you can imagine." The words slipped out before she could stop them, carrying more weight than she'd intended. Her heart hammered against her ribs. She was getting careless, letting her guard down. Garrett would be furious if he knew how much she'd revealed in those few words.

"I thought you found some things you liked to finish off the garden. Let's go see." Rose hesitated, the pruning shears suddenly feeling heavy in her hands. Another trip meant another report back to Garrett. It meant questions about timing, about what they discussed, about whether she'd seemed happy. The thought of facing that gauntlet again made her stomach clench. "I don't know."

But even as she said it, she found herself hungry for escape. The walls of the mansion felt like they were closing in more each day. The beautiful prison Garrett had built for her was still a prison, no matter how many roses bloomed within its borders.

"Come on. You said you needed a break, and the garden will not finish itself."

Despite everything, his easy manner coaxed a genuine smile from her. There was something about Kirk that made her feel lighter, more like herself or rather, like the self she used to be before she learned to measure every word, every gesture, every breath against Garrett's curious scrutiny. She set down the shears and followed him around the side of the house toward his truck.

The truck's engine hummed steadily as they pulled out of the driveway. Rose found herself studying Kirk's profile as he drove—the strong line of his jaw, the way his hands rested easily on the steering wheel. There was a quiet confidence about him that stood in stark contrast to Garrett's need to control everything around him.

These stolen moments in the truck had become precious to her. Here, for just a few minutes, she could pretend she was someone else. Someone who could go where she wanted, when she wanted. Someone who didn't have to account for every minute of her day.

"So, tell me what's really bothering you."

His directness caught her off guard, though she realized she shouldn't have been surprised. Kirk had a way of seeing through the facades she'd become so skilled at maintaining. It was both thrilling and terrifying to be truly seen after so long.

"Somehow I think you already know the answer to that."

She watched his hands on the steering wheel, noting the calluses from honest work. Garrett's hands were soft, manicured. They'd never known a day of real labor, just the kind of manipulation that came from moving money around on paper. When had she started making these comparisons? When had she started noticing the differences between her husband and this man who was supposed to be nothing more than hired help?

"Life is not always a rose garden, is it?" There was a gentle humor in his voice, but also genuine concern.

"If that's a play on words, the answer would be no." Rose stared out the passenger window at the passing scenery, watching the world blur past. Free people in free cars, going wherever they choose. "I just really never thought my life was going to be like it has turned out. I guess the fairytales we create in our minds are just that."

The admission came out of her mouth more like a religious confession. She'd never said it out loud like that before—that her marriage was nothing like the dream she'd imagined. Even thinking it felt like betrayal, though she couldn't say whether she was betraying Garrett or herself.

"Most of the time they are. You really just need some peace of mind, and the garden is not doing it for you anymore."

She turned to look at him, surprised by his perceptiveness. How had he seen what she was only just beginning to acknowledge herself? The garden had been her sanctuary at first, the one place where Garrett's control felt lighter. But even that had been corrupted. Even her refuge had become another stage for his surveillance.

"The garden was supposed to be mine," she said quietly. "The one thing that was just for me. But now..." She trailed off, unable to finish the thought. Even her refuge had become another stage where she felt watched, evaluated, never quite free to simply be herself.

As they turned into the nursery parking lot, Rose noticed a man in a dark sedan pull up to a payphone near the entrance. Something about his deliberate movements made her stomach tighten, but she pushed the feeling aside. She was becoming paranoid, seeing threats everywhere. This was what Garrett's love had done to her—turned her into someone who jumped at shadows.

The man spoke briefly into the phone, his eyes scanning the nursery entrance. "Mr. Sinclair. I just wanted to report that nothing has been going on. She was at the house all morning and is at a nursery now with the gardener. I will let you know if anything changes."

Inside the nursery, Rose moved through the aisles of plants without really seeing them. Her mind was churning, that familiar feeling of being watched settling over her like a shroud. The greenhouse was warm and humid, filled with the earthy scent of soil and growing things. In another life, she would have loved this place. She would have taken her time, examining each plant, planning where it might go in her garden.

But now she found herself calculating instead. How long had they been here? What would she tell Garrett when he asked about her choices?

Would he approve of the climbing roses she'd selected, or would he see them as some kind of symbol of escape?

When Kirk suggested they leave through the rear exit, she didn't question it. She'd learned not to question many things anymore. It was easier to follow, to let others make the decisions. When had she become so passive? The Rose, who had worked in the store, who had dreams and opinions and plans, felt like a stranger now.

But as they pulled back onto the road, she realized they weren't heading home. A flutter of panic rose in her chest. Garrett would want to know why they'd taken the long way. He would demand explanations, details, proof that nothing inappropriate had happened.

"This is not the way home. Are we going to another nursery?"

"No. I think we need a detour."

Kirk turned onto a familiar wooded road, and Rose felt her pulse quicken. The river. The place where she'd felt free, if only for a few stolen moments. But freedom came with a price, and she was already calculating the cost of this detour.

"I think you could use a break for a moment, and you seemed to like this spot."

"I do like it here."

Too much, she thought. She liked it too much, and that was dangerous. Garrett had radar for the things she liked, the things that brought her joy independent of him. He had a way of poisoning even her smallest pleasures with his array of questions.

They walked the familiar path in comfortable silence, the sound of their footsteps muffled by fallen leaves. The river came into view, its surface reflecting the afternoon sky like a mirror. Rose breathed deeply, feeling some of the tension leave her shoulders.

Here, for just a moment, she could pretend she was free. She could pretend she was the kind of woman who could walk beside this man without calculating the consequences. The kind of woman who could make her own choices about where to go and who to see.

"Thank you for taking me here. I needed to be out."

"I know you did. I have gotten to know you pretty well these past months." Kirk's voice was gentle but serious. "You are a wonderful woman, Rose, but you are not happy."

The statement was true and had a way of connecting their thoughts, simple and undeniable. Rose felt her defenses rising automatically. Happy was a luxury she couldn't afford to examine too closely. Happy was dangerous. "I'm OK, really."

"No, you are not. I see how upset you are and how miserable he makes you."

The words hit her like cold water. No one had ever said it so plainly before. Her mother worried but never pushed. Lucy made gentle suggestions but never confronted the truth directly. Even Rose herself had learned to couch her unhappiness in softer terms—adjustment difficulties, growing pains, the challenges of marriage.

"Garrett is not a bad person, he's just—"

"Too jealous, too overbearing, too controlling in every aspect of your life. That is not you, and I know it is not the kind of life you signed up to have."

Each word hit her like a physical blow, each one striking at truths she'd been trying to avoid. He was right. This wasn't the life she'd signed up for. The man who had courted her with such charm and romance had transformed into someone she barely recognized. Or maybe she was just finally seeing who he'd always been.

"Maybe in time we can work it out."

Even as she said it, she knew it was a lie. She'd been telling herself this same lie for months now, watching as Garrett's control tightened like a noose around her neck. But admitting the truth felt like stepping off a cliff.

"Do you really believe that? Do you think it is ever going to stop? How many times have you confronted him about his obsessive behavior? Does he change? Does he back off? No. He is getting worse."

Rose felt the tears swell in the corners of her eyes. Kirk was voicing every fear she'd been carrying, every doubt that kept her awake at night.

Each conversation with Garrett ended the same way—with his promises to change, his explanations about how much he loved her, his gifts to make up for his jealousy. But the promises were empty, the explanations were excuses, and the gifts felt more like chains with each passing day as things always reverted back to the way they were.

"I love him, and I think in his own way he really does love me too. It's just too much."

"How can you love someone and make their lives miserable?"

The question was really more like an accusation. Rose felt the familiar surge of guilt that came whenever she questioned Garrett's love. He told her constantly how much he adored her, how he couldn't live without her, how every concerning question and controlling demand came from a place of desperate devotion.

"I honestly don't think he is trying to do that. I don't think he realizes what he is doing. It is who he is."

"Yes. It is who he is. The question I am asking you is, can you live with who he is? Are you ready to spend the rest of your life being watched and followed? Being questioned every time you leave the house?"

The dam burst. All the pain and frustration and fear she'd been holding back came pouring out in tears that she couldn't stop. The sobs came from someplace deep inside her, from the part of herself she'd been trying to keep alive under layers of careful behavior and calculated responses.

Kirk was beside her in an instant, his arms wrapping around her, holding her as she sobbed against his chest. For the first time in months, she felt truly safe. Not the artificial safety of Garrett's protection, which she always felt came with strings and conditions and constant surveillance, but the real safety of being accepted exactly as she was.

"I'm sorry, Rose. I did not mean to upset you. I just felt like you needed to hear it. I care what happens to you. You are an extraordinary woman. You deserve better."

She looked up at him through her tears and found him looking back with such tenderness that it took her breath away. When had someone last looked at her like that? Not as a possession to be guarded or a prize to be won, but as a person worthy of love and respect? "I just don't know what to do. Why couldn't it just be like I thought it would turn out? Two people in love sharing a beautiful life together."

"That's what you need and deserve."

All the space between them seemed to disappear. Rose found herself drawn to him, to the safety and understanding she saw in his eyes. When their lips met, it was with all the passion and desperation of two people who had been drowning and finally found air.

For a moment, she allowed herself to fall into it—the kiss, the feeling of being truly wanted rather than possessed. His hands were gentle on her face, nothing like Garrett's desperate grasping. This was what she'd dreamed of when she'd imagined love—this feeling of being cherished rather than claimed.

But reality crashed back in, and she pulled away abruptly. The weight of her wedding ring felt enormous on her finger. The ghost of Garrett's voice echoed in her mind: *You and I belong together, Rose. Nothing will ever separate us.*

"I can't do this."

"I'm sorry. Forgive me for doing that."

"No. You don't have anything to be sorry for. I wanted it as much as you did, but I shouldn't. I am married, and I do still love him."

The words sounded more like duty rather than truth. Did she still love Garrett? Or did she love the memory of who he'd been during their courtship? The man who had swept her off her feet with his charm and generosity was so different from the man who now wanted to know every place she went and every person she saw.

Kirk's expression grew serious, almost painful. "I think you should know the rest of it."

Rose turned to face him fully, something in his tone sending alarm bells through her system. "The rest of what?"

"Garrett..." Kirk paused, visibly struggling with the words. "He wanted me to keep an eye on you. To watch you and report back to him on what you were doing and saying about him."

The world seemed to tilt sideways. "What?!"

The betrayal hit her like a physical blow, stealing her breath. Even this—even her one source of genuine companionship—had been orchestrated by Garrett. The man who claimed to love her so much had arranged for her to be spied on by someone she'd come to trust.

Kirk took a step back and looked toward the floor. He rubbed the back of his neck, struggling to look back up, to look her in the eye. "I have not told him anything except general stuff of us working in the garden and normal everyday things."

"You are another one of his spies?!" The words came out strangled, raw with pain.

Kirk threw up his hands as if trying to gauge—and brace for—the kind of violence a wounded animal might unleash. "No, Rose! I know it may sound that way. That is what he wanted me to be, but I told him nothing. I only kept up the charade to stay close to you because I thought you could use someone on your side."

Rose felt the ground shifting beneath her feet. How many others were there? How many people in her life were actually Garrett's employees, paid to watch her and report back? The driver had been, certainly. The housekeeper, probably. Maybe even Lucy—*God, please not Lucy.* She was now paranoid of everyone.

"If you were on my side, why didn't you tell me?"

Kirk put his hands on his chest. His eyes shone. "I'm telling you now. I am telling you because I care for you and want you to be happy."

Rose felt the world spinning around her. First the kiss, now this revelation. Everything she thought she knew was crumbling. The one person she'd felt safe with, the one relationship that had seemed honest and uncomplicated, had been built on deception from the beginning.

Rose looked at the ground, her lip quivering. "Kirk, I really can't deal with this right now. Can you please take me home?"

Home. The word felt like a joke. The mansion wasn't home—it was just a beautiful prison. But where else could she go? She had no money of her own, no job, no independence. Garrett had seen to that, systematically cutting away every tie that might have given her options.

Kirk stood up straight and looked her right in the eye. "Anything you say, but before I do. I want you to look at me and tell me you trust me. You believe what I am saying."

She studied his face, searching for any sign of deception. But all she saw was the same man who had listened to her, who had brought her to this place of peace, who had held her while she cried. Despite everything, despite the circumstances that had brought them together, she knew he was telling the truth.

His eyes held no calculation, no hidden agenda. Just genuine concern and something that looked like love. It was so different from the way Garrett looked at her—with possession and desperation and the kind of obsession that masqueraded as devotion. "I do, but please, right now, can you just take me back?"

"I will."

As they walked back toward the truck, Rose felt as though she was moving through a dream. The afternoon that had started with such promise had become another reminder of how thoroughly her life had been orchestrated by others. Even her moments of freedom had been shadowed by surveillance and deception.

But as she glanced at Kirk walking beside her, she realized that perhaps, for the first time in a very long time, she had found someone who was truly on her side. The knowledge was both terrifying and liberating. Because if someone was on her side, that meant she might have choices she hadn't considered before.

The drive back to the mansion was quiet, and both of them were lost in their own thoughts. Rose watched the familiar landmarks pass by—the same route she'd traveled dozens of times, but now everything looked different. The trees seemed less like scenery and more like bars on a cage. The beautiful houses they passed weren't homes but reminders of the life she'd thought she wanted.

When they pulled into the circular drive, Rose could see Garrett's car in the garage. He was home early, which meant questions. It always meant questions.

"Rose," Kirk said quietly as she reached for the door handle. "You don't have to live like this."

She turned to look at him, and for just a moment, she allowed herself to imagine a different life. A life where she could go where she wanted, see who she wanted, and be who she wanted. A life where love didn't come with conditions and surveillance.

"I know," she said finally. "But knowing and doing are two different things."

As she walked toward the house, Rose felt the weight of her wedding ring again. But for the first time in months, she also felt something else—a tiny spark of possibility. It was dangerous and terrifying and probably foolish.

It was hope. Real hope.

A Friend to Listen

The following day, the lunch crowd at Romano's was in full swing, the gentle clatter of silverware and murmur of conversation creating a familiar backdrop as Rose and Lucy settled into their usual corner table. But Rose's eyes kept darting around the restaurant, her hands fidgeting with the menu she'd barely glanced at.

The corner table had once been their sanctuary—a place where they'd shared secrets, laughed until their sides hurt, and planned their futures over endless cups of coffee. Now it felt exposed, as if Garrett's watchful eyes could follow her even here. Rose found herself scanning the other diners, looking for anyone who might seem out of place, anyone who might be watching.

Lucy studied her friend with growing concern. Rose looked exhausted, her usual vibrancy dimmed by something Lucy couldn't quite identify. Dark circles shadowed her eyes, and there was a tension in her shoulders that spoke of sleepless nights and constant worry. The Rose sitting across from her was a pale echo of the vibrant woman who had once lit up every room she entered.

"I am so glad we finally got together. This is long overdue."

Rose forced a smile that didn't quite feel as if it reached her eyes. Even this simple lunch had required careful orchestration—timing it for when Garrett would be in meetings, choosing a place close enough to home that she wouldn't be at a distance to get home late, preparing answers for the inevitable interrogation about who she'd seen and what they'd discussed.

"I know it has been a while, but with the gardens and all, I have been really busy."

The words felt hollow even as she spoke them. Busy. That was what her life had become—busy with the careful choreography of avoiding Garrett's displeasure, busy with the exhausting work of being the perfect wife, busy with the constant vigilance required to navigate his questions.

"You know I take offense to that?" Lucy's tone was playful, but she was watching Rose carefully. There was something different about her friend, something that made Lucy's chest tighten with worry.

"To what?"

"That a rose bush takes precedence over your best friend."

The jest fell flat. Rose's expression crumpled slightly, and Lucy immediately regretted the lighthearted comment. She'd meant it as their usual banter, but Rose looked as if she'd been struck.

"I'm sorry. It is not like that. A lot has been going on."

Lucy leaned forward, her voice gentling. She'd known Rose for many years, had stood beside her at her wedding, and had seen her through many major moments of her adult life. But the woman sitting across from her now seemed like a stranger—fragile, guarded, afraid.

"Oh? Like what?"

"Just stuff at home. It's complicated." Rose's fingers worried the edge of her napkin, folding and refolding it into precise creases. The motion was compulsive, desperate, as if keeping her hands busy might somehow keep her thoughts from spiraling.

Lucy watched the nervous gesture with growing alarm. Rose had always been composed, confident, the kind of person who handled stress with grace. This anxious fidgeting was completely unlike her.

"Are you and Garrett having trouble?"

The question seemed to break something loose in Rose. Her composure wavered, and for a moment Lucy caught a glimpse of genuine desperation in her friend's eyes—the kind of trapped, helpless look she'd seen in the eyes of wounded animals.

"I don't know what to do anymore. It is getting unbearable."

Lucy felt her heart sink. She'd hoped Jack was wrong about his concerns, that his ideas were overblown. Jack had mentioned that Garrett seemed possessive, that he'd made some comments about keeping Rose close, but Lucy had dismissed it as just male overprotectiveness. But looking at Rose now, she could see the strain written in every line of her body.

"What's going on? I thought it was better since you got your own car again."

The implication had been lost on Rose. The car that was supposed to represent freedom had become just another tool of surveillance. She had seen Garrett looking at her mileage, questioned her about every errand, and had recently covered things up by saying he wanted to make sure the mileage did not go past due of when the car needed to be serviced.

"He questions me when I am out late or gets home after he does and wants to know where I was and what I was doing." Rose's voice was barely above a whisper, as if she was afraid someone might overhear. Even here, in this public place with her best friend, she felt the weight of Garrett's presence.

Lucy tried to process this carefully. She knew Garrett could be protective—perhaps overly so—but Rose was making it sound almost sinister. Yet Lucy couldn't help thinking that Rose might be overreacting. After all, didn't married couples talk about their days? Didn't they share where they'd been and what they'd done?

"Well...it is Garrett. He is very protective of you and worries too much most of the time. I could see him being a little concerned if you were late and he did not know where. Is it a secret?"

Rose felt the familiar stab of frustration that came whenever she tried to explain her situation to others. How could she make Lucy understand that it wasn't just concern—it was interrogation? That Garrett's questions came with a subtext of suspicion, that his worry felt more like ownership than love?

"No! It is just none of his business if I want to go somewhere on my own and not tell him." Rose's voice rose slightly, drawing a few glances from nearby tables. She immediately looked embarrassed and lowered her voice again, the automatic response of someone who'd learned to monitor her own behavior constantly.

Lucy felt like she was walking through a minefield. She wanted to support her friend, but she also couldn't help thinking that Rose might be overreacting. Marriage requires compromise, communication, and consideration for your partner's feelings. Maybe Rose was just struggling with the normal adjustments that came with being a wife.

"OK. What else is he doing?"

"It's all the questions. Asking what I did all day. Wanting to know what I buy when I am out shopping."

Lucy struggled to understand the problem. These seemed like normal conversations between married couples—the kind of casual check-ins she and Jack had all the time. She'd ask Jack about his day, he'd ask about hers. They'd discuss purchases, share stories about their activities. It was what people did.

"I hate to sound like I am not sympathetic, but those seem like normal questions you may ask to discuss your day. I don't understand why that is so hard to answer."

Rose stared at her as if she'd been slapped. The betrayal in her eyes was immediate and devastating. Here was her best friend, the person she'd turned to in desperation, and Lucy was dismissing her pain as if it were nothing.

"What are you saying?"

Lucy realized she'd stepped wrong, but she pressed on, hoping to help Rose see things more clearly. Maybe if Rose could step back and look at the situation objectively, she'd realize that Garrett's behavior, while perhaps excessive, came from a place of love.

"I'm not saying anything. I just don't really understand why that upsets you so much for him to be concerned. He has always been that way. It's just Garrett. He loves you...a lot."

The hurt in Rose's eyes was immediate and devastating. Lucy's words felt like a physical blow, confirming Rose's worst fear—that no one would believe her, that no one would understand. Even her closest friend saw her as ungrateful, as someone who was complaining about being too loved.

"I really thought you might understand. You are my best friend."

Lucy felt a stab of guilt. She was Rose's best friend, and here Rose was clearly in pain, reaching out for support, and Lucy was failing her. But she also genuinely couldn't understand why Rose was so distressed by what seemed like normal marital dynamics.

"I am your best friend, and I really want to understand. Just help me see it from your point of view."

Rose felt tears prick at her eyes. How could she explain the suffocating weight of Garrett's attention? How could she make Lucy understand that love shouldn't feel like surveillance, that concern shouldn't feel like control? How could she put into words the way Garrett's questions made her feel like a child being monitored by a suspicious parent?

"Why can't you see it. Kirk sees it. He understands."

The words seemed to surprise Rose as much as they did Lucy. She hadn't meant to bring up Kirk, hadn't meant to reveal how much his understanding meant to her. But the contrast was so stark—Kirk, who listened without judgment, who saw her pain and validated it, versus Lucy, who was dismissing her concerns as if they were trivial.

"Kirk? Your gardener? He understands?"

Lucy watched as Rose's face flushed, a look of panic flickering across her features as if she'd revealed more than she intended. Suddenly, Lucy was seeing the situation from an entirely different angle. Was Rose confiding in her gardener? A man she barely knew was understanding her marriage better than her husband or her best friends?

"Well, all I am saying is I guess with him being there a lot, he can see it better." Rose's voice was defensive, and she wouldn't meet Lucy's eyes. She could feel the heat rising in her cheeks, could hear how her words sounded—like a wife who was growing too close to another man.

A dozen questions suddenly flooded Lucy's mind. How much time was Rose spending with this gardener? What exactly had he "seen"? And why was Rose turning to him for understanding instead of her husband or her closest friends? The dynamic Lucy was imagining made her stomach clench with worry.

Lucy studied her friend's face, noting the way Rose's expression had softened when she mentioned Kirk's name, the defensive way she was backtracking now. There was something here that went beyond employer and employee, beyond casual conversation about gardening. The realization hit Lucy like a cold wave—Rose wasn't just unhappy in her marriage. She was emotionally involved with someone else.

"Maybe so." Lucy kept her voice carefully neutral, but her mind was racing. Jack's concerns suddenly seemed far more legitimate. But now Lucy wasn't sure if the real danger was Garrett's overprotective behavior or Rose's apparent growing attachment to her gardener.

Rose seemed to sense the shift in the conversation and quickly changed the subject. "I look forward to you and Jack coming to dinner and to see the garden. I think you will be impressed with what we have done."

The phrase "what we have done" didn't escape Lucy's notice. Not "what I've done" or "what's been done," but "*we*." Rose and the gardener. Lucy felt a chill run down her spine. Her friend was in deeper trouble than she'd realized, and Lucy wasn't sure anyone could help her now.

Lucy managed a smile, though her head was spinning with implications. "I am looking forward to it too."

They finished their lunch with small talk about mutual friends and upcoming social events, but Lucy's mind kept circling back to Rose's mention of Kirk. The way her friend's face had changed when she spoke about him—a softness that Lucy hadn't seen in months. The defensive way Rose had tried to backtrack.

As they said their goodbyes in the parking lot, Lucy watched Rose drive away and couldn't shake the feeling that her best friend was walking into something dangerous. The question was whether the danger was coming from Garrett's pushing her away with too much concern or Rose's apparent growing attachment to her gardener, Kirk.

Either way, Lucy knew she needed to call Jack as soon as she got back to the office. Their friends' marriage was in far more trouble than any of them had realized.

Lucy sat in her car for a long moment after Rose had driven away, replaying the conversation in her mind. She'd failed her friend today—she could see that now. When Rose had reached out for support, Lucy had dismissed her concerns, had minimized her pain. But the alternative—believing that Garrett, charming and generous Garrett, was that controlling and manipulative—seemed almost impossible to accept.

Yet the evidence was there in Rose's hollow eyes, in her nervous fidgeting, in the way she'd jumped when the waiter had approached their table. This wasn't the Rose she'd known and loved for years. This was a woman who'd been systematically broken down, isolated, made to doubt her own perceptions.

And now, it seemed, Rose was turning to someone else for the understanding and support she couldn't find in her marriage or her friendships. Someone who saw what the rest of them had missed—or chosen not to see.

Lucy started her car with trembling hands, her mind already forming the words she'd say to Jack. They'd all failed Rose by not seeing what was happening. The question now was whether it was too late to help her—or whether their intervention would only make things worse.

As she pulled out of the parking lot, Lucy caught a glimpse of a man in a dark car who seemed to be watching the restaurant. For a moment, she wondered if she was becoming as paranoid as Rose seemed to be. But then she remembered the fear in her friend's eyes, the way Rose had scanned the restaurant as if looking for threats.

Maybe paranoia was just another word for finally seeing the truth.

Suspicions

Garrett sat rigid in his leather office chair, the phone pressed so tightly to his ear that his knuckles had gone white. The afternoon sun streaming through his office windows did nothing to warm the chill that had settled in his chest as he listened to the detective's report. Outside, the bustling sounds of downtown Macon carried on—cars honking, pedestrians chatting, life moving forward in its normal rhythm—but inside his mahogany paneled office, time seemed suspended in this moment of reckoning.

"...and they stayed around the lake for quite some time. I never could get close enough to see them without being noticed."

The detective's voice crackled through the receiver, each word landing like a physical blow. Garrett's eyes fixed on the silver-framed wedding photo on his desk—Rose in her flowing white gown, her radiant smile directed at the camera, at him. That smile had been his salvation once, the thing that made him believe he could possess something pure and beautiful. Now it seemed to mock him from behind the glass.

"Could you hear what they were saying?" Garrett's voice was carefully controlled, but his free hand had curled into a fist on his desk. The leather of his chair creaked under the tension in his body. His jaw worked silently, grinding back the words he really wanted to say, the accusations and demands that burned in his throat.

"No, sir. I could hear them talking, but it was too low at the distance I was at."

The inadequacy of the answer sent a surge of frustration through Garrett that made his vision blur momentarily. He was paying good money for surveillance—more money than most people made in a year—and all he was getting were vague reports about his wife spending intimate time by a lake with another man. His wife. His Rose. The woman he had plucked from that department store and transformed into a queen, only to watch her bloom under another man's attention.

The detective continued, oblivious to the storm building in his client. "They seemed... comfortable with each other. Relaxed. She was laughing at something he said, and when they walked back to the car, he helped her over some rocks near the water's edge."

Garrett's breath caught. Rose laughing. When was the last time she had laughed with him? When was the last time she had looked at him with anything other than that carefully composed expression she wore around the house, pleasant but distant, like a well-trained actress playing the role of a devoted wife?

"Next time, I want you to have a visual on them and hear what they talk about. Do you hear me?" The words came out harder than he intended, his carefully maintained composure cracking like ice under pressure.

"I'll do what I can."

The noncommittal response was the last straw. Garrett slammed the phone down with enough force to rattle the papers on his desk and send his Mont Blanc pen rolling across the polished surface. The sound echoed in the suddenly quiet office, followed by the soft tick of the antique clock on his bookshelf—a wedding gift from Rose's mother, who had been so grateful to see her daughter marry well.

He stared at the silent device; his face twisted with disgust and something that looked dangerously close to despair. His reflection stared back at him from the black screen of his computer monitor: a successful man in his prime, wearing a perfectly tailored suit and a silk tie that cost more than most people's weekly salary. On paper, he had everything—wealth, status, respect in the community. He was Garrett Sinclair, the man other men envied, and women admired from afar.

But his wife—his Rose—was slipping away from him, and he seemed powerless to stop it.

The irony wasn't lost on him. He who could orchestrate million-dollar deals with a phone call, who could influence city council decisions with a well-placed donation, who could make or break businesses with a word to the right people—he couldn't control the one thing that mattered most to him. The one person who should have been grateful for everything he had given her, everything he had made possible for her.

He pushed back from his desk and moved to the window, looking out at the city he had helped shape with his investments and influence. Somewhere out there, Rose was probably thinking about another man. Planning, perhaps, how to betray everything they had built together. The thought made his stomach turn with a mixture of rage and something that felt uncomfortably like heartbreak. He loved her so much. How could he make her understand that?

His hands pressed against the cool glass of the window, and he closed his eyes, trying to summon the memory of their early days together. Rose was trying on dresses he had bought for her, her eyes bright with surprise and delight. Rose at dinner, hanging on his every word as he told her about his business, his dreams, his vision for their future together. Rose in their bed, soft and yielding, whispering that she loved him in the darkness.

Had it all been a lie? Had she been playing a role even then, or had he somehow driven her away with his need to keep her close, to know where she was every moment, to ensure that no other man could steal what belonged to him?

The question tormented him because he knew the answer, even if he couldn't bring himself to acknowledge it. He had created this situation with his suffocating attention, his need to show her how deeply he loved her. But knowing it didn't make it any easier to stop. The thought of losing her was unbearable, but the thought of sharing her was worse.

Garrett opened his eyes and stared at his reflection in the window glass, superimposed over the city beyond. Somewhere out there, his gardener, Kirk, was probably thinking about his wife, remembering the feel of her hand in his, the sound of her laughter by the lake. The thought made Garrett's hands clench into fists against the glass.

He would not lose her. Not to some common laborer who worked with his hands and had nothing to offer her but stolen moments and empty promises. Rose was his wife, his forever, his reason for happiness. And he would do whatever it took to keep her, even if it meant destroying the very thing he was trying to preserve.

Getting Too Close

Later that afternoon, Rose emerged from the house into the garden, the afternoon air doing little to lift the heavy mood that had settled over her since lunch with Lucy yesterday. The magnolia blossoms hung heavy on their branches, their sweet fragrance almost cloying in the humid Georgia air. She paused on the flagstone path, taking in the paradise she and Kirk had created together—beds of perfectly arranged roses in every shade from deep crimson to pale pink, jasmine climbing the wrought-iron arbor, and the fountain they had refurbished last month, its gentle splash creating a soothing soundtrack to their work.

But today, even this sanctuary felt tainted. The conversation with Lucy kept replaying in her mind like a broken record, each word dissected and analyzed until she felt raw from the examination. The way Lucy had looked at her with such obvious confusion and concern when Rose had tried to explain how suffocating her life had become. Even her best friend, the person who had known her for so many years, thought she was overreacting, making mountains out of molehills. "But Rose, honey, he loves you so much," Lucy had said, her voice gentle but firm. "Maybe you're just not used to having someone care about you that deeply."

The words had stung because part of Rose wondered if Lucy was right. Was she being ungrateful? Was this what real love looked like, and she was too damaged by her past relationships to recognize it? Her father died when she was a teenager, and her mother had spent Rose's teenage years working hard to provide for them to be relatively comfortable in their lives. Maybe she simply didn't know how to accept devotion without feeling trapped by it. None of the other guys she ever dated made her the center of their attention like Garrett had. Except for her mother, nobody had ever loved her so much.

Kirk looked up from where he was adjusting the irrigation system near the rose beds, his weathered hands working efficiently with the copper fittings. The sight of him brought an immediate sense of calm to her chest—something she had stopped feeling when she looked at her husband. Kirk's presence was like cool water on a burn, soothing and healing in a way that made her realize how much pain she had been carrying.

"Did you have a nice lunch with Lucy?" His voice carried the easy warmth that had drawn her to him from the beginning. There was no hidden agenda in his question, no careful probing for information he could use later. Just genuine interest in her well-being.

Rose's expression immediately darkened, and she felt her shoulders tense. "I don't know.

No. Not really."

"Why not?" Kirk straightened, setting down his tools and giving her his full attention. The late afternoon sun caught the highlights in his dark hair, and she noticed the way his shirt clung to his shoulders, damp with honest sweat from his work. There was something about the way he listened—completely focused, without judgment—that made her want to tell him everything she felt. With Garrett, every conversation felt like a test she might fail. With Kirk, she could simply be herself.

"I don't know. It was not just lunch. It was almost like she was trying to pry into my life." The words tumbled out with more bitterness than she had intended. She began walking along the garden path, needing movement to contain her restless energy.

Kirk fell into step beside her, careful to maintain a respectful distance despite the electricity that seemed to crackle between them whenever they were close. "Being your best friend, I am sure she is just curious about things going on with you."

His tone remained gentle, understanding, but Rose could hear the unspoken question underneath. She knew he was wondering the same thing she was—if Lucy's concern was justified, whether Rose was losing perspective on her own life. The thought terrified her because it meant she truly was alone in this beautiful prison Garrett had built for her.

"I don't know. Maybe. Things are just so confusing right now." Rose sank onto the stone bench they'd placed near the fountain, suddenly feeling exhausted. The weight of pretending to be happy, of maintaining the facade of a perfect marriage, seemed to press down on her shoulders like a physical burden. She looked up at Kirk, taking in the genuine concern in his warm brown eyes, and felt something crack inside her chest.

"Like what?" Kirk moved closer, close enough that she could catch the scent of earth and sunshine that always clung to him. It was such a contrast to Garrett's expensive cologne and the sterile smell of his office building.

"Me. My life. Garrett..." She paused, looking at him with an expression that was equal parts longing and desperation. The words she really wanted to say hovered on her lips—that she thought about him constantly, that his presence in her life had awakened something she hadn't even known was sleeping, that the way he looked at her made her feel like a woman instead of a possession. Instead, she whispered, "You."

The single word filled the space between them, loaded with everything she couldn't say. Kirk's expression softened, and she saw her own longing reflected in his eyes. For a moment, the world seemed to narrow to just the two of them, sitting in the garden they had created together, surrounded by the beauty that had bloomed under their shared care.

Kirk moved closer, his voice soft but direct. "I don't think it is all that complicated. Your life with Garrett is not a happy one, and you need to find peace."

The simple truth of his words hit her like a blow from a fist. She had been drowning in complexity, in guilt and confusion, and the constant questioning of her own perceptions. But Kirk had a way of cutting through all of that to the heart of things. Her life with Garrett wasn't happy. It was beautiful on the surface, gilded with luxury and privilege, but underneath it was slowly killing something essential in her soul.

"I do love him. I really do." The words came out like a plea, as if she were trying to convince herself as much as Kirk. And maybe she was. There had been a time when Garrett's attention had felt like sunshine, when his gifts and devotion had made her feel cherished and special. But love without trust, without freedom, without the space to breathe and grow— was that really love at all?

"But you can't live with him." Kirk's words were gentle but uncompromising, and Rose felt something shift inside her at hearing her deepest fear spoken aloud.

The simple truth crossed the air between them like a bridge she was afraid to cross. Rose opened her mouth to respond, to protest or agree or ask him what he thought she should do, but Kirk suddenly stepped back, gently pushing her away from him. The loss of his presence felt like a physical shock, leaving her cold and confused.

"What—" she began, but then she turned and saw the reason for his retreat.

Garrett emerged through the patio doors, his expensive suit incongruous against the backdrop of earth and growing things. Even from a distance, she could see the tension in his shoulders, the way his eyes immediately swept the garden, cataloging every detail. He moved with the controlled precision of a man who was used to commanding every situation, but Rose had learned to read the subtle signs of his moods. The slight tightness around his eyes, the way his hands hung at his sides—he was angry, or at least deeply unsettled.

"Hello." His voice carried a forced casualness that didn't match the way his eyes were taking in every detail of the scene before him. Rose could practically see him calculating the distance between her and Kirk, noting the way they had been sitting close together on the bench, measuring the intimacy of their body language.

"What are you doing here?" Rose's question came out more sharply than she'd intended, but she couldn't help it. His unexpected presence felt like an invasion, a reminder that even in this one space that felt like hers, she was never truly alone or unwatched.

"I do live here, or at least that is the rumor." There was an edge to his attempt at humor, a brittleness that made Rose's stomach clench with familiar dread. She had learned to recognize the signs that preceded his darker moods, the way his charm could turn sharp and cutting when he felt threatened.

"I know that. I mean, why are you home so early? Were you trying to see if you could catch me doing something or not home when I should be?" The accusation spilled out before she could stop it, born from months of feeling constantly watched and questioned. She was tired of pretending not to notice the way he checked up on her, the way he always seemed to know exactly where she had been and with whom.

Garrett's expression softened, and for a moment, he looked genuinely hurt. The transformation was so complete that Rose felt a stab of guilt, wondering if she had misjudged him. This was the man she had fallen in love with—vulnerable, seeking her approval, wanting nothing more than to make her happy. But she had learned not to trust these moments of apparent sincerity. They were often followed by hours of subtle interrogation about her day, her thoughts, her feelings.

"No. Actually, I know you have the dinner tomorrow with Lucy and Jack coming and thought I would knock off early to come home and see if you needed any help with it."

Rose felt a stab of guilt sharper than before. He was trying to be thoughtful, and she'd immediately assumed the worst. The dinner party— she had mentioned it to him weeks ago, a simple evening with their closest friends. He had seemed pleased at the time, eager to play the role of the perfect host. Maybe she really was becoming paranoid, reading sinister motives into every gesture.

"Oh. Well, that is really nice of you. I am sure I can find something you can help with." The words felt stilted, but she forced a smile, trying to recapture some of the warmth that had once come so naturally between them.

Garrett crossed the garden with quick, purposeful strides, his expensive shoes clicking against the flagstone path. He wrapped his arms around her, and Rose allowed herself to be held, breathing in the familiar scent of his cologne and the crisp starch of his shirt. For a moment, she tried to remember what it had felt like in the beginning, when his embrace had been a sanctuary instead of a cage.

"I just want to help you any way I can and be a good husband to you." His voice was muffled against her hair, and she could hear the genuine emotion underneath the words. This was what made everything so confusing—the fact that his love for her was real, even if it was slowly suffocating her.

"Thanks, Garrett. That's sweet." The words felt hollow even as she said them, but she could see the hope in his eyes and didn't have the heart to crush it completely. Over his shoulder, she caught a glimpse of Kirk moving quietly toward the tool shed, and her heart clenched with loss. The moment of connection they had shared was broken, replaced by the familiar weight of her husband's attention.

Behind them, Kirk quietly made his way toward the tool shed, unnoticed by either of them. But Rose was aware of every step he took, every inch of distance he put between them. In the space of a few minutes, she had gone from feeling understood and cherished to feeling trapped and watched. The contrast was so sharp it made her want to weep.

As Garrett held her, murmuring plans for the next day's dinner party, Rose stared over his shoulder at Kirk's retreating figure and wondered how much longer she could live this way. How much longer could she pretend that love was enough when it came wrapped in golden chains? The garden around them bloomed with beauty, but Rose felt like something inside her was withering away, dying by degrees in the very paradise she had helped create.

The Betrayal

The morning sun was just beginning to warm the driveway when the sharp sound of a car door slamming echoed across the property like a gunshot. Rose stood beside her black Eldorado, fury radiating from every line of her body as Garrett emerged from the house, coffee mug in hand, his expression shifting from casual morning contentment to immediate concern. The humidity of the Georgia morning clung to the air, making her silk blouse stick uncomfortably to her skin, but her rage burned hotter than the rising temperature.

"What did you do to my car?"

The accusation stung as it divided the space between them, loaded with months of accumulated suspicion and resentment. Rose's hands were clenched at her sides, her knuckles white against the pale-yellow fabric of her dress—the same dress Garrett had bought her for their first anniversary, when such gifts had felt like tokens of love rather than gilded chains.

Garrett paused mid-step, his coffee mug suspended halfway to his lips, genuinely confused. His dark hair was perfectly styled despite the early hour, his crisp white shirt already pristine and pressed. Even at seven in the morning, he looked like he'd stepped out of a magazine—controlled, polished, unflappable. "What are you talking about?"

"It will not start. AGAIN?!" The accusation in her voice was unmistakable, colored by every previous incident where her independence had been systematically undermined. The car had mysteriously developed electrical problems just days after she'd driven alone to visit her mother. The flat tire that had appeared the morning after she'd mentioned wanting to take a weekend trip to Atlanta with Lucy. The pattern was too consistent to be a coincidence, too convenient to be a natural mechanical failure.

Rose's voice carried across the property, disturbing the morning peace and sending a mockingbird fleeing from its perch in the magnolia tree. Mrs. Henderson from next door would undoubtedly be peering through her curtains, adding this scene to her mental catalog of the Sinclair family drama. The thought only fueled Rose's anger—she had become a spectacle; a cautionary tale whispered about at the country club.

"Get in and we will see what is going on." Garrett's tone was reasonable, measured, the voice of a man accustomed to solving problems with calm logic. But Rose was beyond reason, beyond the careful politeness that had become the hallmark of their public interactions.

"No! I want to know what you did and fix it now!" Her voice cracked with frustration and something that sounded dangerously close to hysteria. She was tired of being reasonable, tired of accepting his solutions that always seemed to involve more control, more supervision, more restrictions on her freedom.

The shouting drew Kirk from around the side of the house, where he had been loading his truck with the day's tools. Concern etched deep lines around his eyes as he took in the scene—Rose vibrating with barely contained rage, Garrett standing frozen with his coffee mug like a man who'd stumbled into a minefield. Kirk's work shirt was already damp with sweat, his sleeves rolled up to reveal forearms bronzed by months of working in Rose's garden. The sight of him sent a confusing mix of relief and longing through Rose's chest.

"Rose, calm down. I have not done anything. I will call and have them pick the car up and look at it." Garrett's voice held the strained patience of someone who'd had this conversation before, who'd weathered these accusations and knew they would pass like summer storms. But there was something else in his tone—a weariness that suggested he was as tired of this pattern as she was.

"You are not taking my car again. I will not have it!" Rose's independence had become so precious, so fragile, that the thought of losing it again was unbearable. The car represented her last connection to the world beyond the gates of their property, her final thread of autonomy in a life that had become increasingly circumscribed.

"Can you please calm down?" It wasn't really a question, more of a plea wrapped in the tone of a confused husband who was trying to extinguish the situation. But Rose could hear the uncertainty underneath, the recognition that his usual methods of soothing her were no longer working.

Kirk stepped forward, his presence immediately changing the dynamic like a stone thrown into still water. "Can I look at it?"

"Please." Garrett's relief at having someone else intervene was obvious, and Rose caught the way his shoulders sagged slightly, as if he'd been holding his breath. He set his coffee mug down on the stone wall that bordered their driveway, his movements careful and deliberate.

"Try to start the car."

Rose slid behind the wheel, her hands trembling slightly as she turned the key. The engine made barely a whisper of sound—a weak, pathetic wheeze that died immediately. The familiar scent of leather and the vanilla air freshener Garrett preferred filled the car, but instead of comfort, it brought a wave of claustrophobia.

"Turn on your lights."

When Rose complied, the headlights glowed so dimly they were almost invisible, like candles flickering in daylight. She felt something shift in her chest—a small crack in the wall of suspicion she'd built around every mechanical failure.

"It looks like your battery." Kirk's diagnosis was matter-of-fact, professional, carrying the weight of someone who actually understood the mechanical world rather than just having enough money to make problems disappear.

"I will get someone out here immediately," Garrett said as he started walking in to use the phone, his body moving with practiced efficiency toward the house. Even in crisis, he moved with the confidence of a man who knew he could solve any problem with the right phone call and enough money.

"Those things just happen." Kirk's words were directed at Rose, and she caught the subtle message—this wasn't sabotage, just bad luck. The gentle understanding in his voice made her feel exposed, as if he could see through her paranoia to the frightened woman underneath.

Rose felt some of the fight go out of her, replaced by embarrassment that burned hot in her cheeks. "I'm sorry I blew up. I just have a lot to do with the dinner tonight."

The dinner party. In her rage, she'd almost forgotten about the evening that had been planned for weeks—Lucy and Jack coming over, the elaborate meal she'd spent days planning, the performance of domestic perfection she'd have to maintain for hours. The thought of it made her suddenly, desperately tired.

"Well, I am sure Kirk would not mind putting off whatever he was working on to help and drive you wherever you need to go." Garrett's suggestion seemed genuinely helpful, though Rose caught something in his tone—a satisfaction at having a solution that kept Rose under supervision while appearing generous and thoughtful.

"It would be my pleasure." Kirk's response was directed at Rose, his eyes meeting hers with an understanding that made her pulse quicken. There was something in his gaze that promised more than just a ride to the grocery store—a connection that transcended the mundane crisis of car trouble.

"See. All taken care of. I will call the dealer and have the car picked up and repaired for you immediately."

"Thanks, Garrett." Rose's gratitude was genuine, even if it was tinged with the complicated mix of appreciation and resentment that had come to characterize their relationship. He was solving her problem, being helpful and supportive, and she hated herself for being unable to simply accept his kindness without looking for ulterior motives.

Garrett moved closer and kissed her, a gesture that felt both loving and desperate. His lips were warm and familiar, tasting of coffee and the expensive toothpaste he special-ordered from Switzerland. But instead of comfort, Rose felt the familiar sensation of being claimed, marked as his territory in front of Kirk.

"I will come home a little early so I can help."

"You don't have to do that." The words came out automatically, but Rose realized she meant them. The thought of Garrett hovering over her preparations, offering suggestions and subtle corrections, made her feel trapped.

"I want to. I am really looking forward to tonight, so you can show off all the hard work the two of you have done."

After Garrett drove away in his pristine black Cadillac, the morning suddenly felt different—lighter, charged with possibility. Kirk approached Rose, his expression thoughtful, and she found herself noticing details she'd tried to ignore: the way his hair curled slightly at the nape of his neck, the calluses on his hands from honest work, the direct way he looked at her as if she were the only person in the world.

"If it is the battery, it is not something he could have done."

Rose nodded, feeling foolish for her immediate suspicion. "Flashbacks of the past, I guess."

The admission came out with understanding between them, acknowledgment of the paranoia that had become her constant companion. Kirk's expression softened with understanding, and Rose felt a dangerous urge to tell him everything—about her suspicions with the other mechanical failures, about how she always felt she was being watched, about the way Garrett's love had become a beautiful prison.

"Where is it you need to go?"

Rose looked at him for a long moment, seeing understanding and something deeper in his eyes. The grocery store, the florist, the wine shop—all the errands that would fill her morning with mundane tasks and careful interactions with people who knew her only as Garrett Sinclair's wife. The dinner party, the performance of domestic perfection, the careful choreography of maintaining appearances—none of it mattered in that moment.

"To our special place to be alone with you."

The words came out in a rush, surprising them both with their honesty. Rose felt her cheeks burn, but she didn't take them back. She was tired of pretending, tired of denying what had been building between them for months.

"I'll get the truck."

As they climbed into Kirk's pickup—a working vehicle that smelled of potting soil and honest sweat rather than leather and expensive cologne— Rose felt something shift inside her. The truck was freedom, escape, the promise of a few hours where she could simply be herself without weighing every word and gesture.

Neither of them noticed the dark sedan parked discreetly down the street, positioned behind the Hendersons' prized azalea bushes. The detective waited until they were nearly out of sight before starting his engine and following at a careful distance, his telephoto lens already mounted and ready on the passenger seat. The net was closing tighter around Rose, even as she reached desperately for the one thing that felt like freedom.

At the riverfront, the afternoon sun filtered through the canopy of trees, casting dappled light across the blanket where Rose and Kirk lay entwined beside the gentle murmur of the river. This hidden place had become their sanctuary—a bend in the Ocmulgee River where ancient oaks created a natural cathedral, where the sound of running water masked their whispered conversations and desperate kisses. Rose's hair fanned out across Kirk's chest like spun gold as he held her close, his arm wrapped protectively around her bare shoulders.

The world had narrowed to just this moment, this place, this feeling of being completely known and accepted. Rose could feel Kirk's heart beating steadily beneath her cheek, could smell the clean scent of his skin mixed with the earthy fragrance of the river. For the first time in months, she felt at peace—not the careful, controlled peace of her life with Garrett, but something deeper and more honest.

But even in the aftermath of their lovemaking, Rose couldn't quiet the voice in her head that whispered of consequences and betrayal. The sunlight filtering through the leaves seemed to pulse with accusation, and she found herself listening for the sound of footsteps, of voices, of discovery.

"I can't believe we are doing this. I am a married woman."

The words tasted bitter on her tongue, heavy with guilt and fear. She traced lazy patterns on Kirk's chest, memorizing the texture of his skin, the way his breathing changed when she touched him. Part of her wanted to lose herself in this moment, to forget everything else existed. But the other part, the part that had been trained to be Garrett's perfect wife, couldn't let go of the rules that had governed her life for so long.

Kirk's fingers traced lazy patterns on her shoulder, his touch gentle and reverent. "An unhappily married woman. A woman who needs to be free. You can't live like you have been."

His voice was gentle but certain, and Rose heard the weight of truth in his words. Kirk had seen her in ways that Garrett never had—had watched her wilt under the pressure of constant surveillance, had witnessed the slow erosion of her spirit. With Kirk, she didn't have to pretend to be grateful for a life that was slowly killing her.

Rose lifted her head to look at him, her eyes troubled. The late afternoon light caught the flecks of gold in his brown eyes, and she saw nothing but honesty and concern there. "I can't live like this either. I don't want to sneak around and have secret afternoons worried about getting caught."

The admission cost her something to make. This stolen time by the river was precious, but it was also poisoned by the constant fear of discovery. Every sound in the forest made her tense, every moment of happiness shadowed by the knowledge that they were living on borrowed time.

"Then don't. Get away." Kirk's words were simple, but Rose heard the weight of possibility behind them. He shifted to face her more fully, his expression earnest, and she saw her own longing reflected in his eyes.

"Kirk, it is not that simple."

But even as she said it, Rose felt something stir in her chest—a wild, desperate hope that maybe it could be that simple. Maybe she could just disappear, leave behind the beautiful prison of her marriage and start over somewhere else. The thought was terrifying and exhilarating at the same time.

"Because of the money? I am sure Garrett would give you a good enough settlement to start over somewhere else." Kirk's voice carried the practical certainty of someone who had never been trapped by wealth, who didn't understand that golden chains were still chains.

Rose sat up, pulling the blanket around herself as reality crashed back in like a cold wave. The movement dislodged a butterfly that had been resting on a nearby branch, and she watched it flutter away with something like envy. "Start over? Where? Besides, Garrett would never let me go. You see how he is when I am late. Can you imagine if I told him I was leaving?"

The thought sent a shiver of fear through her that had nothing to do with the afternoon breeze. She had seen glimpses of what lay beneath Garrett's polished exterior—the rage and fear that flickered in his eyes when he thought she might be pulling away, the way his hands would tighten with tension when he was displeased. He had never hit her or said anything cross to put her down, but she had learned to read the warning signs, to placate and soothe before his control slipped completely.

"Then don't tell him. Run away. I will help you and we can meet up later after you escape."

The word 'escape' was in the air between them like a bridge over an abyss, and Rose felt a shiver that had nothing to do with the cool breeze off the water. *Escape.* The word implied prison, captivity, and danger. Was that really what her life had become? Was she truly a prisoner who needed to escape rather than a wife who needed to work on her marriage?

"I can't believe we are even talking about this. I can't leave and no matter what I really do still love him."

The words came out in a rush, and Rose wasn't sure if she was trying to convince Kirk or herself. She did love Garrett—or she loved the man he had been when they met, the charming suitor who had swept her off her feet with his attention and devotion. But was love enough when it came wrapped in surveillance and control?

Kirk reached for her hand, his calloused fingers intertwining with hers. His eyes were intense with emotion, and Rose felt her heart skip at the depth of feeling she saw there. "I love you, Rose."

"Kirk—"

"No. I have got to say this." His voice was urgent, desperate, as if he'd been holding these words back for too long and they were burning him from the inside. "I love you. In the time we have spent together, I have got to know you and fell in love with the wonderful woman you are. I want to be with you, and I know I can make you happy."

The words struck Rose as hard as a physical blow, sending shockwaves through her entire body. She'd known this moment was coming, had felt it building between them like a storm on the horizon, but hearing it spoken aloud made everything impossibly real and impossibly complicated. Kirk loved her. Someone loved her for who she was, not for who they wanted her to be.

"Please stop! I can't think about this right now. We need to get back and get things ready for tonight." Rose began reaching for her scattered clothes, desperate to create some distance from the intensity of the moment. Her hands were shaking as she pulled on her blouse, fumbling with the buttons.

The dinner party. Lucy and Jack would be arriving in a few hours, expecting to find the perfect couple in their perfect home. She would have to smile and play hostess, would have to pretend that her world wasn't crumbling around her. The thought of it made her feel sick. After all, she had just made love to another man.

Kirk caught her shoulders, his hands gentle but urgent. "Please. Tell me you will think about everything I have said. You are unhappy and you feel trapped by a horrible man. I love you and I can help you get away."

Rose looked into his eyes and saw nothing but sincerity and love—a stark contrast to the suspicion and control that had become her daily reality. Kirk's love was different from Garrett's—it didn't seek to possess or control, but to cherish and protect. The difference was like comparing sunlight to fire—one gave life, the other burned.

"I will think about it, but for now, let's please just go home."

The word 'home' felt strange on her tongue. Was the mansion really her home, or was it just another beautiful house she dwelled under the roof of? Was home a place, or was it something you felt when you were with the right person?

They dressed in silence, the weight of Kirk's declaration and Rose's torn loyalties hanging heavy between them. As they walked down the familiar path toward the truck, Rose felt as though she was moving through a dream—or perhaps waking up from one. The forest around them seemed to pulse with secrets, every shadow hiding possibilities and dangers.

Halfway to the parking area, Kirk stopped and turned to her, pulling her into his arms. Rose melted into the embrace, allowing herself this moment of feeling truly wanted rather than possessed. His arms felt like sanctuary, like safety, like everything she had been searching for without knowing it. In the distance, hidden among the trees, a camera lens caught the intimate moment with a soft click that was lost in the rustle of leaves.

They continued walking, and Kirk stopped again, this time simply looking at her with such tenderness that Rose felt her heart might break. The late afternoon sun caught the highlights in her hair, and she knew she had never looked more beautiful or more alive than she did in this moment to him. They stood close, sharing a smile that spoke of secrets and possibilities and the kind of connection she'd always dreamed of having. Another soft click echoed through the trees, unheard over the sound of the flowing river and the distant call of a wood thrush.

When Kirk bent to kiss her, Rose didn't pull away. She kissed him back with all the passion and desperation of a woman who had finally found something real in a life built on beautiful lies. His lips were warm and demanding, tasting of possibility and freedom and everything she had been denied. The kiss deepened, and Rose felt herself drowning in sensation, in the knowledge that this might be the last time she could hold him like this.

The camera captured this moment too—the moment that would change everything. The detective, hidden behind a massive oak tree fifty yards away, adjusted his telephoto lens and smiled grimly. This was exactly what his client had been paying for.

As they finally reached the truck and drove away, neither of them noticed the figure moving through the trees behind them, or the telephoto lens being carefully packed away in its case. The detective had finally gotten the visual evidence Garrett had demanded—and more. The photographs would tell a story of betrayal and adultery, of a wife who had forgotten her vows and a marriage that was beyond saving.

The drive back to the mansion was quiet, both of them lost in their own thoughts. Rose stared out the window at the familiar landscape—the rolling hills and ancient oaks, the sprawling estates of Macon's elite—and wondered if she was seeing it all for the last time. Kirk's declaration had changed something fundamental between them, had forced her to confront the reality of her situation in a way she'd been avoiding.

"Rose," Kirk said softly as they turned into her driveway. "Whatever you decide, I want you to know that I meant what I said. I love you, and I'll do whatever it takes to help you find happiness."

Rose looked at him, this man who had shown her what love could be when it wasn't twisted by possessiveness and control. "I know," she whispered. "I love you too."

The words slipped out before she could stop them, and she saw the flash of joy in Kirk's eyes before the weight of what they meant settled over both of them. She did love him—had been falling in love with him for months without fully admitting it to herself. But loving him didn't make her situation any less complicated or dangerous.

Pictures Don't Lie

As Rose walked into the house to prepare for the dinner party, she didn't know that the photographs would be on Garrett's desk before she even had time to set the table. She didn't know that her husband was already planning his next move, or that the life she had been trying so desperately to escape was about to become a trap from which there might be no escape at all.

The mansion felt different as she moved through it, setting out china and crystal, arranging flowers and checking the menu one last time. It felt like a stage set for a performance that no longer mattered, a beautiful facade that was about to crumble. In a few hours, Lucy and Jack would arrive, and she would have to smile and play the perfect hostess while her heart was breaking, and her world was falling apart.

But for now, she had a few precious hours to hold Kirk's words close to her heart, to remember what it felt like to be truly loved, and to decide what she was willing to risk for the chance at real happiness. The photographs were already being developed, the evidence of her betrayal captured in stark black and white. But Rose didn't know that yet, and so she moved through her preparations with a lightness she hadn't felt in months, buoyed by the knowledge that someone loved her enough to offer her a way out of the beautiful prison her life had become.

The trap was closing around her, but for this moment, she felt freer than she had in years.

***

Back at the bank that afternoon, the late afternoon sun slanted through the tall windows of Garrett's corner office, casting geometric shadows across the Persian rug his grandfather had imported from Tehran decades ago. The familiar comfort of his domain—the mahogany bookshelves lined with leather-bound volumes, the crystal decanter of aged bourbon, the oil paintings of former bank presidents that watched over several generations of the SouthTrust banking empire—felt suddenly foreign, as if he were viewing it all through someone else's eyes.

When Margaret knocked and entered with the large manila envelope, her sensible heels clicking against the hardwood, Garrett was reviewing quarterly reports, his gold Mont Blanc pen moving in practiced strokes across the margins. "This just arrived for you, Mr. Sinclair," she said, her voice carrying that respectful deference she'd perfected over fifteen years of service. She placed the envelope on his desk with the same careful precision she applied to everything, then retreated with the quiet efficiency that had made her indispensable.

Garrett stared at the envelope; his pen suspended in mid-air. The detective agency's return address seemed to pulse with ominous promise. Patterson Investigations in neat, professional lettering. He'd hired them three weeks ago, telling himself it was just due diligence, just a husband's reasonable concern about his wife's new friendship. Nothing more than prudent oversight.

His pulse began to quicken as he set down the pen and reached for the envelope. The paper felt heavier than it should, weighted with implications he wasn't sure he was ready to face. His fingers, steady enough to sign million-dollar loans without a tremor, now shook almost imperceptibly as he tore open the seal.

The first photograph slipped out and landed face-up on his desk.

The world tilted.

Rose. His Rose. In Kirk's arms beside the old oak by the riverbank, her face turned up toward the gardener's with an expression that struck Garrett like physical blows to the solar plexus. It was adoration—pure, unguarded, luminous adoration. The same look she used to give him during their courtship, when he would surprise her with tickets to the symphony or a weekend in Savannah. The look that had convinced him she was the missing piece of his carefully constructed life.

When was the last time she'd looked at him that way?

His hands moved of their own accord, pulling out the remaining photographs. Each image was worse than the last, a progression of intimacy that documented the complete dissolution of his marriage. Rose laughed at something Kirk had said, her hand resting on his chest. The two of them were walking hand in hand through the canopy of oaks by the riverfront. Kirk's lips pressed to Rose's temple as she leaned into him with the easy comfort of long-standing lovers.

And then the final photos.

Garrett's vision blurred at the edges as he stared at the unmistakable evidence of their betrayal. Rose, beautiful even in her infidelity, her hair spilled across Kirk's chest as they lay entwined on the grass by the riverbank. The riverbank just down from where Garrett had proposed to her three years ago, where he'd gotten down on one knee and promised her the world.

The irony was so sharp it cut.

A sound escaped his throat—half laugh, half sob—and he pressed his fist to his mouth to muffle it. The rage building in his chest felt volcanic, white-hot, and threatening to erupt in ways that would destroy everything he'd spent a lifetime building. His other hand gripped the edge of his desk so tightly his knuckles went white, the wood creaking under the pressure.

How long? How long had they been playing him for a fool? How many times had he kissed Rose goodnight, tasting another man's lies on her lips? How many evenings had he sat across from her at dinner, making pleasant conversation while she mentally composed love letters to her gardener?

The photographs scattered as his hand swept across the desk, sending his quarterly reports and fountain pen flying. The crystal paperweight—a gift from the Macon Chamber of Commerce when he'd been named Businessman of the Year—hit the wall with a sharp crack that echoed through the office like a gunshot.

Garrett stood abruptly, his chair rolling backward to hit the window with a thud. He paced to the liquor cabinet, his stride uneven, and poured three fingers of bourbon with hands that shook visibly now. The liquid burned going down, but it did nothing to cool the fire in his chest.

Control yourself, he commanded silently, staring at his reflection in the mirror behind the bar. *You are a Sinclair. Sinclairs do not lose control.*

But the man staring back at him looked haggard, older than his forty-four years, with eyes that held a kind of desperate fury he'd never seen before. This wasn't the composed banker who commanded respect in every boardroom in Georgia. This wasn't the devoted husband who'd moved heaven and earth to give his wife everything her heart desired.

This was a man who'd been made a fool of.

I hired Kirk, he thought. *I brought him into our life!* The thought turned his stomach.

He drained the glass and poured another, forcing his breathing to slow, his heartbeat to steady. Think. Plan. React with precision, not emotion.

Tonight was the dinner party. Rose had been looking forward to it for weeks, their first real social gathering since her mother's funeral. Lucy and Jack would be there, along with all the images he just had to digest. Rose would wear the emerald dress he'd bought her in Atlanta, the one that brought out the green flecks in her eyes. She would smile and laugh and play the role of the devoted wife while knowing that tomorrow she planned to meet her lover in their secret hideaway.

The thought should have shattered him completely. Instead, something cold and calculating settled over him like a familiar coat. He could play a role too. He'd been playing one for months now—the unsuspecting husband, the trusting fool. What was one more evening?

He gathered the photographs carefully, studying each one with the same methodical attention he applied to loan applications. Details. Evidence. Ammunition for the reckoning that was coming.

A knock at his door made him look up. Jack's cheerful face appeared in the doorway; his tie loosened after a long day of meetings. "Hey there, still buried in paperwork?" his business partner called out with the easy familiarity of twenty years of friendship. "Don't forget about tonight—I've been looking forward to this all day, and you know how I love a good meal."

Garrett managed to summon a smile that felt like broken glass cutting the corners of his mouth. The muscles of his face protested the forced expression, but he held it steady. "I wouldn't miss this night for the world. Rose has been talking about nothing else."

"Great! See you at seven!" Jack's face disappeared around the corner, his footsteps echoing down the marble corridor.

Garrett waited until the sound faded completely before allowing his mask to slip. His reflection in the window showed a stranger—hollow-eyed, granite-jawed, dangerous in a way that would have surprised anyone who knew the mild-mannered banker.

He locked the photographs in his desk drawer, the key turning with a soft click that sounded like a death knell. Then he straightened his tie, smoothed his hair, and prepared to go home to his wife.

Yes, he thought as he gathered his briefcase and coat, *tonight would be very interesting indeed.*

The Dinner Party

The formal dining room glowed with warm candlelight, the flames dancing across the crystal stemware and casting shifting shadows on the burgundy wallpaper. Rose had spent the afternoon arranging everything to perfection—her grandmother's China gleaming against the ivory lace tablecloth, fresh roses from the garden creating centerpieces that filled the room with their sweet fragrance. Yet despite all her careful preparation, she'd barely touched her own plate, her stomach too knotted with anxiety to allow for much appetite.

Every time Garrett smiled at her across the table, she felt the weight of her guilt pressing down like a stone. His smiles tonight seemed different somehow—brighter, more intense, lingering just a beat too long. She told herself it was her own paranoia, her conscience making her see threats where none existed, but she couldn't shake the feeling that he was watching her with unusual scrutiny.

"That was absolutely delicious," Jack declared, pushing back from the table with satisfaction and patting his stomach theatrically. "Rose, you're a better cook than I ever knew. That beef Wellington was restaurant quality."

"The wine pairing was perfect too," Lucy added, raising her nearly empty glass. "How did you know to serve the Bordeaux with it?"

Rose felt heat creep up her neck. "Actually, Kirk suggested it. He said his former employer always paired red wine with beef, and when I mentioned what I was making..." She trailed off, realizing how easily Kirk's name had slipped from her lips.

Garrett's smile never wavered as he reached over to pat Rose's hand, his fingers cool against her warm skin. "Rose has many special talents," he said, his voice carrying that particular cadence he used in business meetings when he was about to make a decisive move. "One being the most wonderful wife I could ever hope for."

His fingers tightened almost imperceptibly on hers, not quite painful but firm enough to anchor her attention. Rose tried not to flinch at the possessive pressure.

Lucy beamed at them both, oblivious to the undercurrent of tension. "I think you're both very lucky to have each other. It's so rare to see a couple who still look at each other the way you two do."

Rose nearly choked on her wine. If Lucy only knew how Garrett had been looking at her lately—like a specimen under glass, cataloging her every movement, her every expression…

"I would have to agree with that," Garrett said, his thumb now tracing small circles on the back of Rose's hand. The gesture would have looked affectionate to their guests, but Rose could feel the controlled tension in his touch. "She's very good to me, and I want to be good to her and give her anything she could possibly desire."

The irony of his words hit Rose like a physical blow. If only he knew what she truly desired now—freedom, space to breathe, the simple joy of walking to the mailbox without wondering if he was timing her absence. And Kirk. God help her, she desired Kirk with an intensity that both thrilled and terrified her.

"Like the garden," Lucy continued enthusiastically, gesturing toward the French doors that led to the back terrace. "I can see it from here, even in this light, and it looks absolutely magical. I hear it's become quite the showpiece."

Garrett's eyes never left Rose's face as he responded. "Rose put a tremendous amount of work into it," he said, his voice carrying an odd undertone that made Rose glance at him nervously. "Hours and hours of... dedicated effort."

There was something in the way he said 'dedicated' that made Rose's skin crawl, though she couldn't pinpoint why.

"And Kirk," Rose said, unable to keep the warmth from her voice despite her growing unease. "I honestly don't know what I would have done without his help to guide me through everything."

Jack's eyebrows rose slightly at the fondness in her tone, and Rose caught him exchanging a quick glance with Lucy. "Kirk is...?"

"Our gardener," Garrett supplied smoothly, though his grip on Rose's hand tightened fractionally. "A very... hands-on sort of fellow."

Lucy leaned forward with interest, her instincts clearly piqued. "So, who did the actual work? You or him?"

Rose felt herself lighting up despite the tension in the room. "We both did. He and I spent hours working out the planning and digging together. I simply couldn't have done it without him." As she spoke, her voice took on that dreamy quality it always held when she thought of those precious afternoons with Kirk, the sun warm on their faces as they worked side by side, their hands occasionally brushing as they planted bulbs or adjusted stones.

She was so lost in the memory that she missed the way Garrett's jaw tightened almost imperceptibly, or how his free hand slowly curled into almost a fist on the white tablecloth.

"Hours together," Garrett repeated thoughtfully, as if he were filing away this information for future reference. "Don't forget all the hunting for just the right plants for the garden. All those trips to nurseries and garden centers."

Rose nodded eagerly, unconscious of the trap being laid. "That's true. We spent so much time finding plants, borders, statues—everything to make it as beautiful as it could possibly be." She was fully animated now, her earlier anxiety temporarily forgotten in the joy of describing her project. "Kirk has such an eye for design. He'd suggest something I never would have thought of, and it would be absolutely perfect."

Jack observed her transformation with growing interest, his businessman's instincts recognizing the signs of genuine passion—and something more. "Rose, you really light up when you talk about the garden. And this Kirk fellow."

Rose felt her cheeks warm. "It has brought me a lot of happiness," she admitted, the truth of it ringing in every word. More happiness than she'd felt in her marriage for longer than she cared to admit.

"Well, then let's go see it," Jack suggested, rising from his chair with the easy authority of a man accustomed to taking charge. "I'm wanting to see all this beauty you've been raving about."

Garrett stood as well, moving to Rose's chair to help her up in a gentlemanly manner. As they moved toward the French doors leading to the garden, Rose felt his hand settle possessively on the small of her back. The touch that had once comforted her now felt like a brand, marking his territory for their guests to see.

"After you, darling," he murmured in her ear, his breath warm against her neck. To anyone watching, it would have looked like an intimate gesture between loving spouses.

The garden was indeed spectacular in the evening light. Garrett had spared no expense on the lighting system—carefully placed fixtures illuminated the curved pathways and cast dramatic shadows among the plantings, creating pools of golden light that made the space feel like something from a fairy tale. The refurbished fountain Kirk had overseen the restoration of tinkled peacefully in the center, surrounded by the roses that had given the space—and Rose herself—their name.

"This is absolutely incredible!" Lucy exclaimed, turning in a slow circle to take it all in. Her hands were clasped in front of her chest like a child seeing Christmas morning. "It's like something out of Better Homes and Gardens."

"It certainly lives up to all the hype I've heard around town," Jack agreed, his businessman's eye cataloging the expense that had gone into creating this paradise. "You did a phenomenal job, Rose."

Rose felt a flutter of pride mixed with longing. "Thank you. It really has become my sanctuary."

Lucy moved closer to admire the carved stone fountain, running her fingers along the intricate detailing. "Look at this craftsmanship. This must have cost a fortune."

"Oh, that was Kirk's idea," Rose said without thinking, her voice taking on that telltale warmth again. "He has such a gift for planning things out and knowing what will work in a space."

Jack nodded appreciatively as he followed one of the winding paths deeper into the garden, noting how the curves created intimate spaces and hidden corners. "I like the way these paths curve and wind through everything. It makes you want to explore."

"Kirk thought that would be so much better than just straight lines," Rose said, following him with unconscious grace. "I wanted to do traditional rows at first, but he convinced me this would be more... romantic." The word slipped out before she could stop it, and she felt her face flame.

Jack and Lucy exchanged another meaningful glance; this one loaded with understanding. The pieces were falling into place with unmistakable clarity.

"It certainly is romantic," Lucy said carefully, her female instinct helping her navigate the suddenly charged atmosphere. "Very intimate."

Garrett's arm slipped around Rose's waist, pulling her closer against his side with just enough force to be possessive rather than affectionate. "This is her special place," he said, his voice carrying an odd emphasis on the word 'her.' "Designed just like she wanted it."

Rose looked up to see Kirk emerging from the tool shed at the far end of the garden, and her heart did that familiar skip that she could never quite control. Even in the dim light, she could make out his easy stride, the way he moved with casual confidence through the space they had created together.

"Kirk!" she called out, unable to suppress the joy in her voice. "Come say hello to our friends. They were just admiring our garden."

Jack leaned close to Lucy's ear, his voice barely audible. "Our?"

Lucy's slight nod confirmed she'd caught the slip as well.

Kirk approached with his characteristic smile, wiping his hands on a work cloth. In the soft garden lighting, he looked almost like a statue himself—tall with a lean, muscular stance, with those gentle eyes that always seemed to see straight through to Rose's soul. Rose made the introductions, acutely aware of Garrett's watchful presence beside her, the way his arm around her waist felt more like a restraint than an embrace.

"So, you're the famous Kirk," Lucy said warmly, though Rose caught the slight emphasis on 'famous.' "It sounds like you had quite a lot to do with creating this beautiful space."

"I need to steal you away to build one for me when I finally get around to buying a house," Jack added with a laugh that didn't quite match his eyes. "Though I'm not sure I could afford your level of artistry."

Kirk's gaze found Rose's naturally, instinctively, and she felt her heart skip a beat—it made her feel alive in ways she'd almost forgotten were possible. "I just took what Rose envisioned and helped make it a reality," he said, his voice carrying that gentle sincerity that had first drawn her to him. "She has such a beautiful imagination. And the passion to see things through."

The way he said it—'beautiful imagination,' 'passion'—the way his eyes lingered on her face as he spoke, made one thing clear to everyone present. They weren't just talking about gardening anymore.

Lucy caught it immediately, sharing another significant glance with Jack that spoke volumes about what they were witnessing.

"Well," Lucy said carefully, her voice taking on the diplomatic tone she used for delicate interview situations, "it was certainly nice meeting the man who helped Rose create something so... inspiring."

After Kirk excused himself and walked away, Rose's eyes followed his retreating figure longer than appropriate, and Jack checked his watch with obvious relief at having an excuse to leave. "I guess I should be getting you home, Lucy. Early day tomorrow."

"I do have that appointment first thing in the morning," Lucy agreed, though Rose noticed how both their guests seemed suddenly eager to depart. "Thank you so much for having us over. The dinner was wonderful, and the garden is truly beautiful."

"Anytime you want to cook another meal like that, I'm sure I could find time to come help you eat it," Jack said with his characteristic humor, though it felt forced now, like he was working to restore normalcy to an evening that had taken an unexpected turn.

Garrett chuckled, but Rose noticed it didn't match the look in his eyes. Those pale blue eyes that had once made her feel so safe now seemed to catalog every word, every expression, every revealing moment. "They certainly know the way to our hearts, don't they?"

As their friends walked around the house to their car, calling out final thanks and goodnights, Garrett and Rose stood waving in the garden. Rose kept her smile fixed in place until the sound of Jack's Mercedes faded into the distance, but the moment the taillights disappeared, she felt the atmosphere shift around them like a sudden change in barometric pressure.

Garrett's demeanor transformed subtly, the careful mask he'd worn all evening slipping just enough to reveal something harder underneath.

"Rose," he said, his voice taking on an unusual intensity that made her skin prickle with unease. "I've been thinking. Why don't we take a trip?"

"A trip?" Rose felt a flutter of panic rise in her throat. The suggestion felt less like an invitation and more like a summons, though she couldn't explain why.

Garrett moved closer, his hands finding her shoulders with that same controlled pressure he'd used at dinner. "Just you and me. We can make it a second honeymoon." His voice dropped to an intimate whisper, but there was something brittle in it, something that didn't match the romantic words. "A fresh start to everything. I think it would be good to have some time together—just you and me. Away from... distractions."

The way he said 'distractions' sent a chill down Rose's spine. Her mind raced, thinking of Kirk, of the plans that were slowly forming between them, the stolen moments that had become the only bright spots in her increasingly suffocating life.

"We have the people coming to do the interview for the garden piece from Southern Magazine," she said quickly, grasping for any excuse. "We can't leave now. They're coming next week, and I've been planning for this for months."

"We can leave right after," Garrett pressed, his grip on her shoulders tightening fractionally.

"What's a few more days? We could go to Paris, like we talked about during our engagement. Remember how your eyes lit up when I mentioned the Louvre?"

Rose remembered. She also remembered how those dreams had gradually been replaced by golden afternoons in the garden, sharing quiet conversations and gentle laughter with someone who saw her as more than a beautiful ornament to be displayed and protected. "Garrett, you don't even have my car back to me like you promised yet," she said, her voice taking on an edge of frustration she couldn't quite suppress. "How can we plan a trip when I can't even drive to the grocery store?"

His jaw tightened almost imperceptibly. "It's coming back. I promised you it would be here as soon as it was repaired." His voice carried a sharp edge now, the careful control beginning to fray at the edges. "These things take time, Rose. I want to make sure everything is repaired and it's completely safe for you to drive."

Rose felt trapped, cornered by his reasonableness that wasn't reasonable at all. Everything was always about her safety, her protection, her needs—as defined by him. "Well, let's get some of the other things finished and behind us first, and then we can think about it. I've worked so hard on this garden, I just need some time to enjoy it. To relax in it."

"That's exactly what the trip is for," Garrett said, stepping closer still, backing her subtly toward the fountain. "We can go anywhere you want to go. Tuscany to see the vineyards. The Greek islands. Anywhere on this planet you want to go, anything you want to do.

Anything."

His voice dropped to an almost desperate whisper, and for a moment, Rose glimpsed something raw and desperate in his eyes. "I love you, Rose. You are my world, my life, my everything. I don't know what I would do without you."

The intensity in his voice frightened her more than anger would have. This wasn't just love, it was passion and possession, pure and desperate and suffocating. "Who said anything about being without me?" she managed, trying to inject lightness into her voice. "Just give me some time, Garrett. I need some time for myself right now."

"Time for you," he repeated slowly, as if tasting the words and finding them foreign. "And what does 'time for you' involve, exactly?"

There was something in his tone that made Rose's blood run cold. A knowing quality that suggested her request wasn't as innocent as it sounded.

"I understand, Rose," he said finally, but the way he said it suggested he understood far more than she realized. Far more than she wanted him to understand.

Garrett dropped his head and started toward the house, his shoulders rigid with barely contained emotion. But at the French doors, he stopped and turned back, his silhouette dark against the warm light spilling from the dining room.

"Rose," he said, his voice carrying across the garden with an odd finality. "I hope you know that everything I do and have ever done was because I love you so much. You are the one thing in this life I cherish more than anything else. I can't live without knowing I can love you."

The words that flowed across the garden sounded more like a threat disguised as devotion, beautiful and terrible at once, to her suspicious state of mind. As he disappeared into the house, Rose felt a chill that had nothing to do with the evening breeze. In her mind, she knew Garrett was sincere, but in her heart, it no longer mattered.

She stood there for a long moment, her heart hammering against her ribs, before the sound of Kirk loading tools into his truck drew her attention. The sight of him—solid, real, uncomplicated—made her decision crystallize with startling clarity.

She walked toward the tool shed on unsteady legs, hoping to catch him before he left. She found him securing the last of his equipment in the bed of his battered pickup truck, and the sight of him made something inside her chest break open with relief.

"I'll go," she said breathlessly, the words tumbling out before she could second-guess herself.

Kirk looked up, confused, a coil of garden hose still in his hands. "What?"

"I'll leave. I'll go away with you." The words felt both terrifying and liberating. "We just need to figure out how and when."

Kirk set down the hose carefully, his expression shifting from surprise to hope to something that looked almost like fear. "Rose... what happened? What changed your mind?"

She looked back toward the house, where she could see Garrett's silhouette moving behind the sheer curtains of his study. "I realized I don't want to be a prisoner any longer," she said, the words coming out with such conviction that she surprised herself. "I can't live like this any longer. I just can't."

"We'll need to be careful," Kirk said, stepping closer, his voice dropping to an urgent whisper. "We will need money to start over somewhere. And we need to be smart about this."

"I can take care of that," Rose said quickly. "I know where there's some cash I can get my hands on immediately. It has to be soon, though. I don't think I can keep pretending with Garrett much longer."

Kirk's eyes lit up with possibility mixed with concern. "Tomorrow's my day off. I can get everything together on my end—pack what I need, make arrangements. Can you?" Rose nodded, her heart pounding with the magnitude of what they were planning. "Garrett's working late tomorrow night. He has that board meeting that always runs until at least ten. We could leave tomorrow evening before he gets home. When he arrives, we will be a long way down the road."

"Okay," Kirk said softly, reaching out to touch her face with gentle fingers. "I love you, Rose. This will be a great new start for both of us. You'll see. We'll be happy. All of what's happened here can be just bad memories."

He kissed her then, quick but tender, a kiss full of promise and hope for their future together. Rose clung to that promise, that hope, as if it were a lifeline.

Neither of them noticed the figure watching from the unused bedroom window upstairs or saw the way Garrett's hands gripped the window frame with such force that his knuckles turned almost white. Neither of them saw the expression on his face as he witnessed this final betrayal—the betrayal that would seal all their fates.

The Getaway

The next morning arrived with deceptive normalcy, sunlight streaming through the mansion's tall windows and casting geometric patterns across the polished marble floors. But beneath the surface tranquility, tension thrummed like a live wire. Rose had barely slept, her mind churning with plans and fears in equal measure. Every creak of the old house had made her start wondering if Garrett was awake, wondering if he somehow knew what she and Kirk had discussed in the garden.

She'd risen early, showering and dressing with mechanical precision, her hands trembling slightly as she applied her makeup. In the mirror, her reflection looked pale and hollow-eyed despite the concealer. She looked like a woman on the edge of running, and she prayed Garrett wouldn't notice.

Garrett descended the grand staircase with his usual measured pace, adjusting his silk tie with practiced precision. He looked immaculate as always—his dark hair perfectly styled, his charcoal suit pressed to perfection, his shoes gleaming. To anyone watching, he appeared to be the picture of a successful banker beginning another productive day. But Rose caught something different in his movements this morning, a deliberate quality that made her pulse quicken with unease. Did he know something or was this just her paranoia?

Rose hurried down behind him, her heels clicking urgently against the marble steps in a staccato rhythm that echoed through the two-story foyer.

"What time will my car be ready today?" she called out, trying to keep her voice light despite the knot of anxiety in her chest.

Garrett paused at the bottom of the stairs, his manicured hand resting on the mahogany newel post that had been carved by craftsmen his grandfather had imported from Italy. He turned slowly, his pale blue eyes studying her face with the same careful attention he gave to loan applications.

"I'll call and check as soon as I get to the office," he said, his voice carrying that measured tone he used when he was thinking several moves ahead. "The mechanic said it might be today, but you know how these things go."

"I really need it today, Garrett." The words came out more sharply than Rose intended, edged with a desperation she couldn't quite hide. She needed her freedom, her mobility, her escape route. Without her car, she was trapped in this beautiful prison with no way out.

Garrett's eyes narrowed slightly, and Rose realized her mistake. She was being too insistent, too urgent about something that should have been a casual request.

"If you need to go somewhere," he said carefully, "take me to the bank and use my car for the day. My Cadillac handles beautifully—you've always said you love the smooth ride of my car."

It was a reasonable offer. Too reasonable. And it would mean he'd know exactly when she left, exactly when she returned, exactly what condition the car was in when she brought it back.

"No," Rose said quickly, then forced herself to moderate her tone. "No, I need my car. Mine is... more comfortable for running errands."

Garrett stepped closer, and Rose fought the urge to back away. His movements were deliberate, controlled, like a cat stalking its prey. "If you need to go anywhere before your car arrives," he said, his voice taking on an almost conversational tone, "you could always have Kirk take you. I'm sure he wouldn't mind helping out."

Rose felt her cheeks burn with a combination of shame and panic. The suggestion felt like a trap, a test to see how she'd react to Kirk's name.

"He's off today," she managed, her voice sounding strained even to her own ears. "And I have some things that I absolutely must take care of today."

"Personal things?" Garrett asked, tilting his head slightly. "Anything I could help with?"

The offer was wrapped in concern, but Rose felt as if there was probing beneath it. He wanted to know what was so urgent, what was so private that she couldn't share it with her devoted husband. In hindsight, it was just a reasonable request, but she could not afford for anything to go wrong today, or it would destroy her escape.

"Just... errands. You know how it is." She tried to laugh, but it came out hollow. "A dozen little things that have been piling up."

"Just take me to work and use my car," Garrett repeated, but his tone had shifted slightly. There was something underneath now, a firmness that suggested this wasn't really a request. There was a question in his mind about why taking his car wasn't sufficient.

"Never mind," Rose said quickly, retreating toward the kitchen. "I'll manage somehow. Maybe Lucy can take me if I need to go anywhere."

She didn't see the way Garrett's jaw tightened at the mention of Lucy's name or catch the calculating look that flashed across his features.

Garrett followed her toward the front door, his footsteps eerily silent on the marble. When he reached for her, Rose forced herself not to flinch, but every muscle in her body went tense.

He kissed her with the same careful precision he applied to everything else in his life. His lips were warm and familiar, but Rose felt nothing but possessiveness in his touch, the way his hands framed her face as if he were holding something precious and fragile that might try to escape.

"I love you, Rose," he murmured against her lips, his breath warm on her skin. His pale eyes searched hers with an intensity that made her stomach clench with dread. "You know that, don't you? That everything I do is because I love you?"

Rose managed a smile that felt like it might crack her face. "Of course I know that."

But as he held her gaze, she had the unsettling feeling that he was looking for something—some sign, some tell that would confirm whatever suspicions were growing in his mind. After all, this time she actually was guilty of something.

"Have a wonderful day," he said finally, releasing her. "I'll call about your car." After the front door closed behind him, Rose stood frozen in the entrance hall, listening to the sound of his Cadillac's engine starting, then fading as he disappeared down the tree-lined drive. Only when she was absolutely certain he was gone did she allow herself to breathe fully, her shoulders sagging with relief.

But the relief was short-lived. She had so much to do today, and without her car, her options were severely limited. She moved to the telephone in the kitchen, her hands shaking as she dialed Lucy's familiar number.

Ring after ring echoed in her ear, each unanswered tone increasing her sense of isolation. Finally, the voicemail clicked on, Lucy's cheerful voice announcing that she couldn't come to the phone right now.

"Lucy," Rose said, her voice trembling despite her efforts to sound normal, "I was hoping to catch you before you left for your appointment. I really, really need to talk to you today. It's important." She paused, wondering how much she dared say on a recording. "Anyway, just please call me back as soon as you get this message. I love you."

She hung up feeling more alone than ever. The house seemed to echo around her, all fourteen rooms feeling simultaneously too large and too confining. She thought of Kirk, probably at his small apartment across town, making his own preparations for their escape. The thought should have comforted her, but instead it made her feel even more desperate.

Time was running out, and she was trapped.

***

Back across town at SouthTrust Bank of Macon, Lucy pushed through the employee breakroom door to find Jack standing by the industrial coffee machine, steam rising from his ceramic mug in the fluorescent light.

The room smelled of burnt coffee and the lingering scent of someone's microwaved breakfast sandwich.

"Hey," he said, looking up in surprise from the sports section of the morning paper. "I thought you had an appointment this morning."

"I did," Lucy said, pouring herself coffee from the perpetually brewing pot. Her movements seemed distracted, distant. "I got finished earlier than expected. Mrs. Patterson decided she didn't want to sell her house after all. Three months of loan work down the drain."

Jack studied Lucy's expression over the rim of his mug. Despite her casual words, there was something troubled in her eyes, a tension in her shoulders that had nothing to do with lost commissions.

"You seem preoccupied," he observed. "Everything all right?"

Lucy glanced toward the breakroom door, making sure they were alone. The morning shift was in full swing, but most of the tellers and loan officers were at their desks, dealing with the usual rush of customers.

"I have to say," she began carefully, "last night was a little... strange."

Jack nodded grimly, setting down his coffee with a decisive clink. "I was thinking the same thing. Like we discussed when I dropped you off—Rose seemed completely taken with that gardener."

"Kirk," Lucy supplied, then shook her head. "I mean, I've known Rose for several years. I've never seen her light up like that talking about anyone except Garrett, and even then, not for a long time."

Jack leaned against the counter, his expression thoughtful. "The way she kept crediting him for everything, calling it 'our garden'... and did you see how she looked at him when he came over to meet us?"

Lucy wrapped her hands around her coffee mug, seeking warmth. "As much as Garrett likes to know everything that's going on in Rose's life, I'm honestly surprised he didn't pick up on what we were seeing."

"Maybe he did," Jack said quietly. "Maybe he's just better at hiding his reactions than we thought."

Lucy's voice dropped to barely above a whisper. "You remember what you told me last month? About Garrett asking you those questions about Rose's behavior, whether you'd noticed any changes in her?"

"I remember." Jack's expression grew more serious. "He said he was worried about her, that she seemed different since her mother died. But now..."

"Now it makes more sense," Lucy finished. "He's been watching her. Maybe he's suspected something for a while."

They stood in silence for a moment, both grappling with the implications of what they'd witnessed the night before.

"She's your best friend," Jack said finally, choosing his words carefully. "Do you really think she would...?"

Lucy stared into her coffee, wrestling with many years of loyalty and friendship against the growing certainty of what she'd seen. "I don't want to think that," she said slowly. "I can't imagine Rose risking everything she has with Garrett. He absolutely worships the ground she walks on. He's given her everything a woman could want."

"Except maybe the freedom to breathe as much as she wants," Jack observed quietly.

Lucy looked up sharply. "What do you mean?"

"Come on, Lucy. You've seen how he is with her. The way he checks on her every move, calls constantly to check on her, hired that driver when her car mysteriously developed problems..." Jack paused. "I love Garrett like a brother, but even I can see that his devotion crosses some lines much of the time."

Lucy felt a chill run down her spine. She'd noticed these things too, but had always attributed them to Garrett's protective nature, his deep love for his wife. Now, viewed through the lens of what they'd witnessed last night, those behaviors took on a more sinister cast.

"You don't think he would..." she began, then stopped, unable to voice the thought.

"I don't know what to think anymore," Jack admitted. "But I do know that if Rose is involved with someone else, and if Garrett finds out..." He shook his head. "That's not going to end well for anyone."

"I should probably call her soon," she murmured, more to herself than to Jack.

"Maybe you should," Jack agreed. "And Lucy? If something is going on, if Rose is in some kind of trouble... she's going to need a friend she can trust."

As Jack gathered his things and headed toward his office, Lucy remained in the breakroom, her coffee growing cold as she grappled with the growing certainty that last night had revealed far more than anyone intended. The question now was what to do with that knowledge—and whether there was still time to prevent the disaster she could feel building on the horizon.

She thought about Rose's message when she checked her machine, the tremor in her voice, the desperate edge to her words. *I really, really need to talk to you. It's important.*

Lucy reached for the phone in the breakroom. Whatever was happening, Rose was going to need all the help she could get.

***

Back at the mansion, the grandfather clock in the foyer chimed eight times, each resonant note seeming to count down to Rose's freedom—or her doom. Upstairs in the master bedroom, Rose stood before her open closet like a woman at her own funeral, tears streaming down her face in steady rivulets that she no longer bothered to wipe away.

The suitcase lay open on the bed like a mouth waiting to swallow her old life whole. It was half-filled with carefully folded clothes, practical things, simple things that would help her build a new identity far from this gilded prison. But each item she selected felt like a small death, a piece of her soul being methodically carved away.

Her hands trembled as she reached for a simple cotton dress, one that Garrett had never seen her wear, never complimented, never commented on. The silk gowns and designer outfits he'd chosen for her remained untouched in the closet like abandoned dreams. She couldn't bear to take them; they felt tainted, marked with his possessive fingerprints, coupled with the guilt of leaving him.

The photograph of her mother watched her from the nightstand, the silver frame catching the lamplight. Rose's breath hitched as she picked it up, her fingertip tracing the familiar, beloved features through the glass. Her mother's warm eyes seemed to look right through her, questioning, worrying.

"Mom, am I doing the right thing?" Her voice broke on the words like waves against rocks. "I need you so much right now. I need you to tell me I'm not going crazy, that I'm not a terrible person for wanting to escape from paradise. That I am not imagining more about Garrett than what is really true. I know he loves me, but…."

She clutched the photograph to her chest, feeling the sharp corners of the frame press into her ribs. The silence of the house pressed back against her—no comforting voice from beyond, no mystical sign, just the oppressive weight of uncertainty.

The need to hear a friendly voice, any voice that might anchor her to sanity, overwhelmed her like a physical craving. Her hands shook as she reached for the bedside phone and dialed the familiar number of Garrett's bank.

"SouthTrust Bank main branch, how may I help you?" The receptionist's voice was professionally cheerful, blissfully unaware that Rose's world was imploding.

"Hi, this is Rose Sinclair. Is my husband available?"

"I'm sorry, Mrs. Sinclair, but Mr. Sinclair is out of the office this afternoon. Would you like me to take a message?"

Rose's heart clenched with an emotion she couldn't name—relief? Terror? "No, no message. Is Jack Morrison available?"

"One moment please."

The hold music played softly, with some innocuous melody that seemed to mock the chaos in her head. She stared at her reflection in the vanity mirror across the room—pale, hollow-eyed, a ghost of the vibrant woman who had worked in that store with a fairytale sweeping her off her feet so long ago.

"Hi, Rose. What can I do for you?" Jack's voice was warm, reassuring, like a lifeline thrown to a drowning woman.

"I'm trying to find Garrett, but they said he was out of the office." She tried to keep her voice level, casual, but heard the strain creeping in around the edges.

"I was in there earlier and he had some stuff on his desk from the Cadillac dealer. I think he's trying to get your car repaired."

The words hit her like a physical blow. Her car. It was needed for their carefully orchestrated plan that depended on the fact that her car was broken, that she needed Kirk to drive her places. If Garrett was actually dealing with the car repairs...

Rose's heart plummeted into her stomach. Her timeline was shifting, crumbling, their carefully laid plans potentially exposed. The walls felt like they were closing in. If her car was actually repaired, she wouldn't need to call Kirk to take her on errands because Lucy was busy at the bank.

"Oh, okay." Her voice sounded strange, distant, like it was coming from underwater. "I just needed to ask him about that."

"Is there anything you want me to tell him?"

"No!" The word exploded out of her before she could stop it, sharp and panicked. She could hear Jack's surprise in the silence that followed. Taking a shuddering breath, she tried again, forcing normalcy into her voice. "Ah, I'll catch up with him later. Jack, is Lucy around by any chance?"

Please, she thought desperately. *Please let me talk to Lucy. Let me hear one voice that might understand.*

"No, but I can have her call you first chance she gets. It's crazy busy today."

"Please do. Bye."

Rose hung up and collapsed onto the bed beside her suitcase, overwhelmed by the magnitude of what she was planning. The carefully folded clothes seemed to mock her—neat little piles of hope that might all be for nothing. Everything felt like it was spinning out of control, like she was trapped in a nightmare where every escape route led to a brick wall.

***

Down the hall from Jack's office, Lucy hurried past his open door, her arms full of files and quarterly reports, her mind racing with deadlines and the persistent unease that had been gnawing at her since their last conversation about Rose. Something had been wrong in her friend's voice, something desperate and frightened that Lucy couldn't shake.

"Lucy, hey!" Jack called out.

She paused in the doorway, balancing her heavy load, already mentally calculating how many hours until she could go home. "Yeah?"

"Rose just called and said to call her when you get a minute. She sounded... I don't know, upset maybe?"

Lucy's stomach twisted with foreboding. "Okay, when it slows down. It's been nuts today.

Got to run. Thanks."

She disappeared down the corridor, leaving Jack staring after her with a growing sense that something was terribly wrong. The phone call had felt off somehow, Rose's voice too controlled, too careful.

***

Back at the mansion, the phone rang insistently through the empty rooms, each shrill note echoing off the marble floors and crystal chandeliers like an alarm bell. Rose was in the master suite bathroom, the shower running at full blast, trying to wash away the guilt and fear that clung to her skin like smoke.

The hot water pounded against her shoulders, but she couldn't stop shaking. Soon, she told herself. Soon Kirk would arrive, and they would drive away from this beautiful prison forever. She would leave behind the woman who had been so foolishly grateful for Garrett's attention, so blind to the cage he was building around her.

255

The answering machine clicked on in the distance, and Lucy's voice filtered through the house like a ghost.

"Hey! It's me. Just got your message from Jack. It's been crazy busy here today, but something in your voice... Rose, I hope nothing's wrong. Call me back as soon as you get this. I'll try you again later."

Rose heard none of it. The shower had become a cocoon, the only place where the sound of rushing water could drown out the sound of her breaking heart.

The house fell quiet again, holding its secrets in the spaces between heartbeats, in the shadows between rooms. The grandfather clock ticked on relentlessly, counting down to the evening that would change everything forever.

In her suitcase, the photograph of her mother lay face-up among the folded clothes, seeming to watch over the remnants of a life about to be abandoned.

A Night to Remember

The fierce pounding on Kirk's apartment door shattered the evening quiet like gunshots, each thunderous blow reverberating through the thin walls and straight into his chest. Kirk froze mid-pace in his cramped living room, his heart hammering against his ribs as he stared at the door that seemed to buckle with each violent strike.

He had been wearing a path in the threadbare carpet for the past hour, checking his watch obsessively—7:23, 7:24, 7:25—counting down the minutes until he and Rose would finally escape this suffocating town and begin their new life together. His duffel bag sat by the door, packed with everything that mattered. In a few hours, they would be free.

The pounding came again, more insistent, more aggressive. The cheap wood trembled on its hinges.

"Just a minute," he called out, his voice catching slightly. He wiped his sweaty palms on his jeans and approached the door, assuming it was Rose arriving early, maybe panicked, maybe having second thoughts. His hand reached for the deadbolt, and for one brief moment, hope fluttered in his chest.

But when he opened the door, his blood turned to ice water in his veins.

Garrett Sinclair stood on his threshold like an executioner, his usually immaculate appearance somehow more menacing in its perfection. The hallway's harsh fluorescent light cast sharp shadows across his face, turning his features into something predatory. Flanked by two uniformed deputies whose hands rested casually on their weapons, he looked like a man who held all the cards and knew it.

Kirk's knees nearly buckled. The narrow hallway suddenly felt like a trap, the walls closing in. He gripped the doorframe to steady himself, his mouth going desert dry.

"May we come in?" Deputy Morrison asked, though the way he stepped forward made it clear this wasn't a request. The three men pushed past Kirk into his modest apartment like an invading army, their heavy boots echoing on the hardwood floor.

The small space that had felt cozy and safe moments before now seemed pathetically inadequate, exposed. Kirk's mind raced frantically, trying to process this nightmare scenario. How had Garrett found out? When? What did he know? His carefully laid plans crumbled to dust in his head as panic clawed at his throat.

"Mr. Sinclair," Kirk managed, his voice hoarse with terror, "what are you doing here? What is this about?"

Garrett prowled around the living room like a predator surveying his territory, picking up Kirk's books, examining his photographs, touching everything with a casual violation that made Kirk's skin crawl. The man's carefully controlled mask—the one Kirk had seen him wear at social gatherings, the perfect husband facade—finally began to slip, revealing the seething rage that had been building like pressure in a boiler since he'd first seen those photographs.

"I think we can dispense with the formalities," Garrett said, his voice deceptively calm, "since you're sleeping with my wife!"

The words hit Kirk like a physical blow. The blood drained from his face so fast he thought he might faint, but he fought to maintain his composure even as his world tilted sideways. "I really don't know what you're talking about. I know you seem to be an extremely jealous man, and you wanted me to report on Rose but—"

"Shut up!" Garrett's voice exploded through the small room like a bomb blast, causing one of the deputies to shift nervously. A vein pulsed visibly at Garrett's temple, his perfect composure finally cracking wide open. "I know about the two of you! I have proof! You and Rose alone at the river, kissing and making love like animals in heat! I have photos!"

Kirk watched in horror as Garrett slammed a thick manila envelope down on his coffee table with such force that his lamp jumped. Photographs spilled out across the surface like accusations made flesh—black and white evidence of their most intimate moments. There he was with Rose by the river, their bodies intertwined, their faces soft with love. Their private sanctuary by the old oak tree. Their stolen kisses in the garden.

The sight of their pure, desperate love exposed and violated, turned into something dirty and criminal, ignited a desperate fury in Kirk's chest. The injustice of it—that this controlling monster could spy on them, could twist their beautiful connection into something shameful—made him shake with rage.

"Fine!" Kirk heard himself saying, his voice cracking with emotion. "You want me to admit it? I will! I've fallen in love with Rose and we're going to be together! She's tired of living with your possessiveness, your constant watching, your need to control every breath she takes! We're leaving tonight and you can't stop us!"

Garrett's smile spread across his face like a crack in ice, cold and terrible. "Is that a fact?

We'll see about that."

"What are you planning to do?" Kirk's voice rose to near hysteria as the full weight of his situation crashed down on him. "It's not a crime to love someone! It's not even a crime to bed your wife when she comes to me willingly, when she's starving for real affection!"

The words were barely out of his mouth when Garrett lunged forward with animal fury, grabbing Kirk by the collar of his shirt and jerking him forward. Kirk could smell Garrett's expensive cologne mixed with sweat and rage, could see the murderous intent blazing in his eyes as his fist drew back.

"Mr. Sinclair! No! Don't hit him!" Deputy Morrison intervened, grabbing Garrett's arm just as his knuckles were about to connect with Kirk's jaw. "Let us take care of it like you wanted!"

Kirk felt ice forming in his stomach, spreading through his limbs like poison. The casual way the deputy spoke, the familiarity in his tone—this wasn't justice. This was a business transaction.

"Take care of it?" Kirk whispered, his voice barely audible. "What does that mean? Rose and I are leaving tonight. She's packing her things right now. She should be gone by the time you get there. I don't care how rich you are, you can't stop us from being together. I love her, and she loves me!"

Garrett straightened his expensive jacket with deliberate care, smoothing the wrinkles Kirk's desperate grip had left behind. His composure returned with terrifying swiftness, like a mask sliding back into place. When he spoke, his voice was silk over steel.

"I want you to escort him out of Macon. Way out of Macon." He turned to Kirk with the cold satisfaction of a man who owned everything and everyone around him. "If you ever come back around here again for any reason, I'll make sure you're picked up and arrested for felony theft."

"Theft?!" Kirk's voice cracked, rising to a near-shout that echoed off the walls. "Of what?! I haven't taken anything from you! I don't want your money, your house, any of it! I just want Rose!"

Garrett's eyes glittered with malicious triumph. "Money, and a lot of it, from the house.

Cash from my safe. Jewelry from Rose's collection. Trust me, there will be plenty of evidence planted, I mean, discovered—to make sure you're jailed, convicted, and put away for a very long time if you ever show your face around here again."

The casual way he corrected himself, the breathtaking corruption of it all, hit Kirk like a sledgehammer. The system, the law, the very concept of justice—it was all for sale, and Garrett owned it outright.

Garrett turned to the deputy with the confidence of a man who had bought and paid for his loyalty. "What do you say, Deputy? Think we could make a theft case stick?"

Deputy Morrison nodded with the grim satisfaction of a man earning his paycheck. "I'm quite sure we could come up with enough evidence to make sure he doesn't see the light of day for a very, very long time. Very long time indeed."

Kirk stared between them, watching his life, his future, his freedom being bartered away like livestock. The casual cruelty of it, the complete absence of justice or mercy, made him feel like he was drowning in ice water.

"You son of a bitch!" The words tore from Kirk's throat like a primal scream. "You think driving me out of town will keep us apart? It won't! She loves me, not you! In fact, I bet she's already gone—packed up and headed to somewhere you'll never find her!"

Even as he said it, Kirk prayed it was true. Rose, his beautiful Rose, please be smart. Please be gone. Please be safe.

Garrett's smile was triumphant and terrible, the expression of a man who had already won and knew it. "Get him out of my sight and make sure he never comes around Macon again.

Ever."

"We'll take care of it, Mr. Sinclair," the deputy assured him with professional courtesy. "Won't be a problem at all."

As the deputies moved to flank Kirk, their hands settling on his arms with practiced efficiency, he called out desperately, his voice breaking with anguish: "I will find Rose! I'll find her no matter what you do! Somehow, I'll find her, and she and I will be together!"

But his words echoed hollow and helpless in the small apartment as they began to drag him toward the door, toward exile, toward a future without the only woman he'd ever truly loved.

Garrett remained behind, standing alone among the scattered photographs of stolen moments, his victory complete but somehow hollow. The silence that followed was deafening.

Now for the final confrontation. Now he had to talk to Rose.

Garrett's Cadillac engine roared to life in the parking lot outside Kirk's apartment complex, its powerful purr masking the thunderous rage coursing through Garrett's veins. His knuckles were tight against the steering wheel as he navigated the darkening streets toward home, his mind replaying every word of the confrontation, every photograph scattered across Kirk's cheap coffee table.

The images burned in his memory—Rose's face soft with passion, her body intertwined with another man's, her hands touching Kirk with the tenderness she had once shown only to him. The betrayal cut deeper than any physical wound could have, slicing through his carefully constructed world like a blade through silk.

Twenty-three minutes. That's how long it took to drive from Kirk's apartment to the mansion, twenty-three minutes for his fury to build from a simmer to a rolling boil. The treelined streets of his exclusive neighborhood blurred past as he pressed harder on the accelerator, the speedometer climbing past safe limits.

The wrought-iron gates of his estate swung open automatically as he approached, their mechanical precision a stark contrast to the chaos in his head. The mansion's elegant facade was bathed in the golden glow of landscape lighting, every window gleaming, every line of architecture perfect. His sanctuary. His kingdom. The palace he had built for his queen—who had chosen to betray him with a common laborer.

Garrett burst through the front door like a man possessed, the heavy wood slamming against the marble wall with a sound like thunder. His footsteps echoed through the cavernous entrance hall, each step sharp and deliberate against the polished floor.

"ROSE!" His voice exploded through the house, bouncing off crystal chandeliers and oil paintings, reverberating through rooms that had once been filled with laughter and whispered endearments. "Rose, where are you?!"

The sound carried a mixture of rage and something that might have been panic—or perhaps desperate hope that she would appear, that somehow this nightmare could still be undone.

The house felt different as he stood in the foyer, chest heaving from more than just the rush upstairs. Too quiet. Too still. The very air seemed to hold its breath, as if the mansion itself was waiting for something terrible to happen.

Garrett loosened his tie with violent jerks, the silk sliding through his fingers like a noose being undone. His expensive suit jacket fell to the floor, abandoned like everything else that had once mattered to him.

"Rose!" he called again, but the only response was the hollow echo of his own voice bouncing back from the vaulted ceiling.

He took the grand staircase two steps at a time, his leather shoes slipping slightly on the polished marble. The portraits of family members watched his ascent with painted eyes that seemed to judge and find him wanting. At the top of the stairs, he paused, his hand gripping the banister until his knuckles showed white against the dark wood.

The master bedroom door stood closed at the end of the hallway, a barrier between him and whatever truth waited beyond. For a moment—just one moment, Garrett hesitated. Once he opened that door, once he saw what lay inside, there would be no going back. No more pretending that his perfect life hadn't crumbled to dust.

His hand reached for the crystal doorknob, then stopped. The silence from beyond the door was absolute, telling its own story without words.

Minutes passed—or perhaps hours. Time seemed to lose all meaning as Garrett stood frozen in that hallway, a man caught between the life he had built and the ruins of everything he thought he knew.

When he finally entered the room, his movements were different, slower, more deliberate. The rage had transformed into something else, something colder and more dangerous. His face was a mask of perfect composure, but his eyes held depths that would have terrified anyone who looked too closely.

The grandfather clock in the foyer chimed ten times as the house stood dark and quiet. Whatever he had found—or not found—in the master bedroom would remain his secret, locked away behind the same careful control that had defined his entire life.

The house settled around him, keeping its silence like a faithful servant, while somewhere in the distance, a siren wailed through the Georgia night.

Panic of Lost Love

Dawn broke over Macon like a reluctant witness, painting the sky in shades of pink and gold that seemed to mock the darkness that had settled over the Sinclair mansion. The morning brought a swarm of police activity that shattered the usual quiet of the exclusive neighborhood—squad cars with their red and blue lights flashing, uniformed officers with their notebooks and cameras, neighbors peering through curtains with the hungry curiosity of those who live for other people's tragedies.

Garrett sat in his leather armchair in the study like a man carved from stone, watching the organized chaos unfold around him with eyes that revealed nothing. He had managed to compose himself enough to play the role of the distraught husband, but the performance felt hollow even to him—a mask worn by an actor who no longer believed in the play.

The morning light streaming through the tall windows seemed to expose everything and nothing, casting long shadows across Persian rugs and highlighting the dust motes that danced in the air like tiny accusers.

Detective Williams entered the study with the careful steps of a man accustomed to walking through other people's nightmares. He was weathered and worn, with kind eyes that had seen too much and a manner that suggested he'd heard every lie and half-truth the human heart could conjure.

"Mr. Sinclair," he said, settling into the chair across from Garrett with a slight grunt. His notebook was already filled with observations, questions, and the kind of details that would matter later when the pieces started falling into place. "I know this is difficult, but I need to go over everything again."

Garrett nodded with the weary patience of a man whose world had collapsed overnight. "Of course. Whatever you need."

"You said your wife didn't come home at all last night?"

"I've already told you—she wasn't here when I got home from the office." Garrett's voice carried just the right note of worry and exhaustion, the perfect pitch of a husband clinging to hope while fearing the worst.

Detective Williams made a note, his pen scratching against paper in the quiet room. "What time was that?"

"Around nine-thirty, maybe ten. I had some business to take care of after work." The lie rolled off his tongue with practiced ease.

"And you waited until this morning to call us?"

"I thought... I hoped she might have gone to stay with her friend. Rose sometimes needs space when we've had a disagreement." Another lie, wrapped in just enough truth to be believable.

"We'll get out an APB on her car," the detective said, flipping to a new page in his notebook.

"She didn't take her car. It's still at Cadillac being repaired." Garrett had made sure of that detail long before this conversation, though he couldn't admit the real reason why.

At that moment, the sound of hurried footsteps echoed from the foyer, followed by Lucy's voice asking one of the officers if she could come in. She appeared in the doorway moments later; her face etched with concern and her hair slightly disheveled as if she'd rushed from her bed without taking time for her usual careful grooming.

"Garrett." Her voice broke slightly on his name as she hurried across the room. "I can't believe it. I came as soon as I got your message."

Detective Williams looked up sharply, his pen poised over his notebook. "Wait, who are you, ma'am?"

"This is Lucy Butler," Garrett explained, rising to accept her embrace with the weary gratitude of a man clinging to any anchor in the storm around him. "She's Rose's best friend in the world. I called her, thinking Rose might have stayed with her last night. When she had not heard from Rose, I thought she might be able to help."

Lucy's arms tightened around him, and for a moment, Garrett almost believed his own performance. Almost felt like the grieving husband rather than the man who seemed to hold all the secrets.

"Have you heard from Mrs. Sinclair in the last twenty-four hours?" Detective Williams asked, his pen ready to record every word.

Lucy pulled back from the embrace, her eyes bright with unshed tears that caught the morning light. "We played phone tag yesterday—back and forth all day—but it was extremely busy at the bank, and we never actually connected. She left a message on my answering machine at home, but I didn't get it until late."

"We may need to hear that message."

"Of course, anything to help find her." Lucy glanced around the grand study as if Rose might materialize from behind the leather-bound books or emerge from the shadows cast by the heavy drapes. "I still can't believe she's just... gone. Have you called all the hospitals? Is her car here?"

"It's still at Cadillac being serviced," Garrett repeated, the words becoming easier each time he said them.

Lucy's brow furrowed as she processed this information. "So, she would have had to take a cab or call someone or..." She trailed off, a thought forming behind her eyes like storm clouds gathering.

"Or what, ma'am?" Detective Williams prompted, leaning forward slightly.

"Or someone would have had to pick her up." The words came out slowly, as if Lucy was afraid of where the thought might lead.

"We've talked to all of the household staff," the detective assured her. "The housekeeper, the cook, the butler. Nobody saw Mrs. Sinclair leave or saw anyone come to pick her up before they went home for the evening."

Lucy's face went pale as realization dawned like a cold sunrise. Her eyes found Garrett's face, searching for something she seemed afraid to find. "What about Kirk?" The name filled the air between them like smoke from a gun barrel.

"Kirk?" Detective Williams looked between Lucy and Garrett with the sharp interest of a hunter who'd just caught a scent. "Who's Kirk?"

Garrett's jaw tightened almost imperceptibly, the only sign that the name meant anything to him at all. When he spoke, his voice was carefully controlled. "He's our gardener. Works on the grounds, maintains the landscaping. He didn't show up for work today."

The silence that followed was heavy with unspoken implications. Lucy stared at Garrett with dawning understanding, seeing something in his expression—or perhaps in his careful lack of expression—that made her stomach clench with dread.

"Is there something you'd like to add, ma'am?" Detective Williams asked, noting the sudden tension between them like a man who'd spent his career reading the spaces between words.

Lucy shook her head slowly, but her eyes never left Garrett's face. She was beginning to understand that there was far more to Rose's disappearance than anyone was saying, and the man she had come to comfort might have the clues to the very reason her best friend was gone.

"No," she said finally, though her voice carried doubt like a weight. "Nothing to add."

Garrett moved to stand beside her, and Lucy automatically put her arm around him in a gesture of support that felt increasingly false with each passing second. Her touch was gentle, but her mind was racing with terrible possibilities.

"We'll get every available man on this, Mr. Sinclair," Detective Williams promised, closing his notebook with a snap that sounded like a door shutting. "We'll find your wife."

"Thank you," Garrett replied, his voice carrying just the right note of grateful desperation. "That means everything to us."

As the detective prepared to leave, Lucy remained beside Garrett, her arm still around his shoulders but her heart growing colder with each breath. She was beginning to suspect that the man she was comforting might know more about Rose's disappearance—and that her best friend might be in far more danger than anyone realized. She knew Garrett's mind was probably forming the same conclusion that she had. Rose had left with Kirk.

The morning sun climbed higher in the Georgia sky, but the shadows in the Sinclair mansion seemed to grow deeper, as if the house itself was keeping secrets that daylight couldn't penetrate.

Looking for Answers

The late afternoon sun filtered through the heavy curtains of Garrett's office, casting long shadows across the mahogany desk that had once been his pride. The room felt different now—suffocating, as if the very air had grown thick with unspoken accusations and desperate hope. Three figures sat in the leather chairs that had hosted countless business meetings, but today they were united only by their shared bewilderment and grief and grasping for any hint of the mystery before them.

Lucy clutched a wadded tissue in her trembling hands; her usually perfect makeup streaked with tears that seemed to flow endlessly. She had barely slept in the three days since Rose had vanished, and it showed in the dark circles beneath her red-rimmed eyes. Every few minutes, she would glance toward the door as if expecting Rose to walk through it with that radiant smile, ready to explain away this horrible misunderstanding.

"I still can't believe this is happening," Lucy whispered, her voice hoarse from crying. "She was my best friend. How could I have missed it?" The words sounded more like an indictment against herself. She had replayed every conversation, every shared lunch, every phone call in the weeks leading up to Rose's disappearance, searching for clues she might have overlooked.

Jack shifted uncomfortably in his chair, his usually confident demeanor replaced by something far more vulnerable. As Garrett's oldest friend, he had watched this romance bloom from the very beginning, had seen the way Garrett's eyes lit up whenever he spoke Rose's name. But he had also noticed the gradual changes, the way Rose's laughter became more forced, the shadows that sometimes flickered across her face when she thought no one was looking.

"You didn't really miss anything," Jack said, his voice gentle but firm. "We all felt something was off." He paused, choosing his words carefully. The truth was, he had voiced his concerns to Garrett more than once, but his friend had been too blinded by his obsession to listen. Now wasn't the time for 'I told you so.'

Garrett sat behind his desk like a broken man, his normally pristine appearance disheveled and hollow. His expensive suit was wrinkled, his tie askew, and his hands shook slightly as he stared at the wedding photo on his desk—Rose's beautiful face beaming up at him from what now felt like another lifetime. The successful banker who had commanded respect throughout Macon was nowhere to be seen; in his place sat a man consumed by loss and disbelief.

"She is my everything," Garrett said, his voice barely above a whisper. "I tried to make her see that. I gave her everything—the house, the garden, all the beautiful things she deserved." His voice cracked with emotion. "How could she want to leave with... him?"

The name Kirk remained unspoken between them, a specter that haunted every conversation about Rose's disappearance. Garrett couldn't bring himself to say it aloud, as if speaking the gardener's name would make the betrayal more real.

Lucy looked up sharply, a flash of her old protective spirit breaking through her grief. "We still don't know for sure that she did." Even as she said the words, she could hear the doubt in her own voice. The timing was too convenient, too perfect, for it to be a mere coincidence.

Garrett let out a bitter laugh, but it held no humor. "They both come up missing at the same time. He said she would be gone when I got home, and she is, in fact, gone." The memory of that confrontation with Kirk burned in his mind—the way the gardener had looked at him with something that might have been pity, the casual way he had delivered what felt like a death sentence. "Plus, the money."

Lucy's head snapped up, confusion replacing some of her sorrow. "Money? What money?

Out of your account?"

Jack cleared his throat, looking uncomfortable with what he was about to reveal. As Garrett's partner in business and best friend, he had been privy to information that made the situation even more damning. "Apparently, some money from the wall safe is gone, too."

The words hit Lucy like a physical blow. Rose, her Rose, was many things, but a thief had never been one of them. Yet the evidence seemed to paint a picture that Lucy's heart refused to accept.

Garrett's voice was hollow, each word seeming to cost him tremendous effort. "I gave her the combination in case something ever happened to me. I wanted her to feel secure, to know she would always be taken care of." His words were bitter, self-recriminating. "It's gone. Fifty thousand dollars."

Jack nodded grimly, his business mind already calculating the implications. "Someone can get very lost with that kind of money. They could be anywhere by now—different state, maybe even different country."

The silence that followed was deafening. In that moment, the reality of their situation crystallized: Rose might truly be gone forever, and they might never know the truth of what had happened in that house, or in that garden where she had seemed to find her only happiness.

Garrett's composure finally cracked completely. Tears streamed down his face as he buried his head in his hands. "I would give anything to have her back," he choked out. "Everything I have, everything I am. I swear I will love her all my life, no matter what she's done, no matter where she's gone."

Lucy and Jack exchanged a glance of shared helplessness. They had no words of comfort to offer, no solutions to propose. They could only sit in witness to a man's complete devastation, in a room that felt more like a tomb than an office, while outside, Macon went about its business, unaware that one of its most beautiful roses had simply vanished into thin air.

The question that none of them dared voice aloud pressed against the walls of the room: Was Rose truly free by leaving with Kirk, or had something far more sinister claimed the woman they had all loved in their own way?

A Sign Twenty Years Later

The mansion had aged along with its owner, though its grandeur remained intact like a beautiful woman whose beauty had only grown more mysterious with time. Dust motes danced in the afternoon sunlight that streamed through the tall windows of the living room, creating patterns that shifted and swirled like ghosts of memories long past. Garrett sat motionless on the burgundy leather sofa that had once been one of Rose's favorite pieces of furniture, his body present but his mind wandering through corridors of the past.

At sixty-eight, he was still handsome in the way that some men are blessed to remain—silver-haired and distinguished, with the bearing of old money and older secrets. But the years had carved deep lines into his face like a map of sorrows, each wrinkle telling a story he had never shared with another living soul. His eyes, once sharp enough to spot every movement Rose made from across a crowded room, now held a distant quality as they remained fixed on some point beyond the glass that no one else could see.

The garden beyond the window had become a masterpiece over the decades, tended with an obsession that bordered on worship. Every bloom was perfect, every leaf precisely placed, every pathway maintained as if expecting a royal visitor. At the center of it all, one particular rose bush commanded attention—its blooms larger and more vibrant than nature should have allowed, the color of fresh blood in sunlight.

The soft sound of comfortable shoes on marble announced the maid's approach, her footsteps echoing through rooms that had grown too accustomed to silence.

"Mr. Sinclair," she said gently, her voice carefully modulated to avoid disturbing whatever reverie held him captive, "you have a visitor."

A young detective stood in the doorway, his notebook already in hand and his badge still shiny enough to catch the light. He had the eager look of someone new to the job, someone who still believed that all mysteries could be solved and all wrongs could be righted, someone who hadn't yet learned that some questions were better left unasked.

"Hi, Mr. Sinclair. My name is Detective Hawkins." His voice carried the professional courtesy of a man delivering what he hoped would be closure. "I had some information I wanted to make you aware of concerning the case with your wife."

Garrett never looked up from the window, his gaze still fixed on that single rose bush as if it held answers to questions he'd stopped asking long ago. His voice, when he finally spoke, was flat and emotionless as winter rain. "What is it?"

Detective Hawkins consulted his notes, clearly uncomfortable with the older man's lack of response. He'd expected curiosity, hope, maybe even relief. Instead, he found himself talking to a statue that breathed.

"A Kirk Davison was killed in a car accident in Indiana three weeks ago." The words filled the air like smoke. "He had been a suspect in your wife's disappearance, so the authorities there went through his apartment—the place he was living in currently—and found a photograph of him and your wife among his belongings."

Still no response from Garrett, though something almost imperceptible shifted in his posture.

"But the photo appears to be quite old," the detective continued, filling the silence with details that felt increasingly meaningless. "Maybe from years before she disappeared. If she had left with him that night, well... they clearly had not been together in quite some time. We just thought you might want to know that particular lead has been... resolved."

"Thanks, Detective," Garrett said quietly, his voice carrying no more emotion than if he'd been acknowledging a weather report.

The young man waited for a moment, perhaps expecting questions about Kirk's life in

Indiana, or some sign of relief that another piece of the puzzle had fallen into place. But

Garrett remained motionless, a figure carved from marble and regret. Eventually, Detective Hawkins shifted awkwardly, closed his notebook with a soft snap, and let himself out, leaving the old man alone with his thoughts and his memories and his garden.

Garrett continued to stare out at the rose bush, his eyes drawn to the single perfect flower that had opened in the morning sun. Its petals were a deep, rich red that seemed to glow with inner light, beautiful and perfect and somehow more alive than anything else in the carefully curated landscape.

The rose would bloom for a few days, perhaps a week, and then its petals would fall to nourish the soil beneath. But for now, in this moment, it was perfect—just as Rose had been perfect, just as their love had been perfect, before everything went wrong.

Kirk was dead. After twenty years of running, of looking over his shoulder, of building a life haunted by the woman he'd lost and the man who'd destroyed them both, Kirk was gone. Dead in some anonymous accident on some forgotten highway, carrying with him whatever truths he might have known about that terrible night.

But did it matter anymore? The photograph proved nothing except that Kirk had once loved Rose enough to carry her memory with him into exile. It didn't prove they had escaped together, or they didn't. It didn't prove they had ever seen each other again after that fateful evening when Garrett had discovered their affair. Maybe they parted ways after the escape.

Maybe their love did not work out.

It proved nothing at all.

Garrett closed his eyes and let the sunlight warm his face, carrying with it the ghost of a memory and the weight of twenty years of silence. Somewhere in the distance, a church bell tolled the hour, counting down the time that remained to him in a world that had never been the same since Rose disappeared.

Confessions of the Soul?

Time had not been kind to the Sinclair mansion, though perhaps kindness was not what it deserved. What had once been grand rooms filled with light and laughter now felt like a mausoleum, heavy with shadows and secrets that seemed to seep from the very walls like moisture from a tomb. The musty smell of age and neglect permeated everything, a testament to decades of solitude and the slow decay that comes when a house is no longer truly lived in, only inhabited by ghosts and memories.

The Persian rugs had faded to muted whispers of their former glory. The crystal chandeliers gathered dust like cobwebs in a forgotten attic. Even the marble floors, once polished to mirror brightness, now bore the reality of years and the weight of footsteps that had long since stopped caring about appearances.

But the garden—ah, the garden remained perfect. If anything, it had grown more magnificent with each passing year, as if fed by some secret source of life that defied explanation.

Garrett, now in his eighties, sat in his wheelchair by the familiar window overlooking the garden that had become his obsession, his religion, his reason for drawing each labored breath. His once-sharp mind had been claimed by Alzheimer's, that cruelest of thieves that steals the present while leaving the past to writhe in painful clarity. Most days, he didn't recognize the nurses who cared for him, calling them by names of people long dead or vanished. But the garden—the garden he always remembered. The garden and the rose bush at its heart, blooming with flowers the color of fresh blood.

Maria, his longtime caregiver, was adjusting his blanket against the afternoon chill when Garrett suddenly became agitated, his gnarled hands gripping the wheelchair's armrests with surprising strength for a man so frail.

"She's out there," he whispered, his voice thin and wavering like paper in the wind. "She's waiting for me. Rose is waiting."

"Mr. Sinclair," Maria said gently, following his gaze toward the garden where nothing moved except the gentle swaying of roses in the breeze, "there's no one out there."

But Garrett wasn't listening. His clouded eyes were fixed on that particular spot near the center of the garden, where the most magnificent rose bush bloomed year after year with an abundance that defied nature's usual constraints.

"I should have let her go," he began, his voice taking on the disconnected quality that meant he was traveling back through time, navigating the treacherous waters of memory where truth and delusion swirled together like oil and water. "She had been hiding upstairs with her suitcase when I got home that night... she was crying... said she couldn't live like a prisoner anymore."

Maria had heard fragments of this story before, but today something was different. Today, Garrett's voice carried the weight of a confession that had been buried for decades, rising from the depths of his fractured mind like something long drowned finally breaking the surface of dark water.

"She wanted to leave me. My Rose wanted to leave me." His hands trembled as he reached toward the window, as if he could touch the roses through the glass. "Said she didn't love me anymore. Said she loved... him. That gardener. That nobody! Who thought he could take *my* wife away from me!"

"Mr. Sinclair, would you like me to wheel you closer to the window?" Maria asked, but Garrett continued as if she hadn't spoken, lost in the labyrinth of his memories where every turn led back to that terrible night.

"She was trying to sneak out like a thief in the night. She had packed her mother's jewelry in that little blue jewelry case she always treasured." His voice grew stronger, more focused, as if the fog in his mind was clearing to reveal this one terrible moment with crystalline clarity. "I heard her on the stairs and told her she couldn't go. Told her I wouldn't let her destroy our love, everything we had built together, everything I had given her." Garrett's breathing became labored, his chest rising and falling rapidly as if he were reliving the physical exertion of that long-ago night. "She turned around at the top of those marble stairs... looked at me with such hatred... told me it was already destroyed. Said she'd rather die than spend another day pretending to love me."

Maria felt a chill run down her spine like ice water. In all her years caring for Alzheimer's patients, she'd learned that sometimes the deepest truths emerged when the mind's protective barriers crumbled, when the careful constructions of a lifetime fell away to reveal what lay beneath like bones in a desert.

"She tried to push past me," Garrett continued, his voice now barely above a whisper, each word seeming to cost him something precious. "I grabbed her arm... just to stop her from leaving me and going away... just to make her listen to reason. But she pulled away so hard... lost her balance..."

His voice broke completely, cracking like ice in spring. "She fell. My beautiful Rose fell down those marble stairs like a broken doll. The sound... God help me, I can still hear the sound her head made when it hit the bottom step. Like a melon dropping. Like the end of my world."

Tears began streaming down his weathered cheeks, carving silver paths through the landscape of age and regret. "She was so still afterward. So quiet. For the first time in months, she was quiet. No more arguments. No more talk of leaving. No more hateful looks."

Maria's hand flew to her mouth, her heart pounding as the implications of what she was hearing sank in like stones in dark water.

"I carried her out to the garden," Garrett continued, his voice taking on an almost dreamy quality, as if he were describing a romantic evening rather than... this. "To her favorite spot, under the rose bush she loved so much. The red one that bloomed just for her. I told her she could stay there forever, and I would visit her every day. She would never have to leave me again. We would be together always, just like I promised on our wedding day."

He turned his clouded eyes toward Maria, and for a moment, they seemed almost lucid, carrying the weight of decades of hidden truth. "I planted her there myself. Dug the hole with my own hands after all the servants were gone that night. She's been there all these years, waiting for me. My beautiful Rose, sleeping in her beautiful garden, under the roses that bloom so magnificently because they drink from her beauty."

Garrett's head lolled back against the wheelchair, exhausted by the effort of remembrance. "I take care of her still, you know. Make sure her roses are the most beautiful in all of Georgia. She always loved roses. Red roses. That's why I married her... or was it because her name was Rose? I can't remember anymore. The details get fuzzy, but the love... the love remains clear."

Maria stood frozen, unsure whether she had just heard the confused ramblings of a diseased mind or the long-buried confession of a horrible night. Outside the window, the rose bush in question swayed gently in the breeze, its crimson blooms nodding as if in acknowledgment of the terrible secret that had finally been spoken aloud after decades of silence.

But Maria had heard countless stories from Garrett over the years— tales of Rose coming to visit him in the garden at midnight, elaborate conversations with long-dead business partners, fantasies about trips to Europe that had never happened. His mind had been fractured for so long that distinguishing between memory and delusion had become as impossible as separating salt from the sea. Just last week, he'd insisted that Rose had called him on a telephone that hadn't worked in years, describing their conversation in vivid detail.

"Mr. Sinclair," she said gently, trying to ground him in the reality that still mattered, "You know Mrs. Rose left many years ago, don't you? Remember? The police searched for her. There was that detective who came to see you..."

But Garrett's eyes had already grown distant again, the moment of clarity—if that's what it had been—fading like morning mist. "She's in the garden," he mumbled, his voice becoming slurred with exhaustion. "My Rose... always in the garden... waiting for me to join her... soon now... very soon..."

His breathing grew shallow and labored. Maria recognized the signs—she'd seen them too many times before in her years of caring for the dying. She reached for the emergency button mounted on the wall, but Garrett's hand caught hers with surprising strength for someone so close to the end.

"Tell them," He whispered, his grip tightening with desperate urgency, his eyes suddenly blazing with an intensity that seemed to burn through the fog of his disease. "Tell them she never left me. She's there... under the roses... where she belongs... where we belong together... tell them I took care of her always... tell them how much I loved her..."

His eyes closed, and his grip loosened like autumn leaves falling. By the time the paramedics arrived twenty minutes later, Garrett Sinclair was gone, taking his secrets with him to whatever judgment awaited beyond the veil.

The Mystery Continues

Maria stood alone in the garden the next morning, the dew still clinging to the grass like tears that had crystallized overnight. The silence was profound—no birds sang, no insects buzzed, even the wind seemed to hold its breath in this place where beauty and death might be forever intertwined.

She stared at the magnificent rose bush that had always been Garrett's pride and obsession, the one he'd tended with religious devotion even as his mind crumbled around him. The crimson blooms seemed larger than life, more vibrant than any roses had a right to be, as if they drew their extraordinary vitality from some hidden source deep beneath the earth.

She thought about his words, his confession—if that's what it had been. The fall down the marble stairs. The midnight burial. The decades of lies told to police and friends and perhaps even to himself. It all sounded so real, so detailed, so weighted with the kind of specific grief that seemed impossible to fabricate.

But then she remembered all the other stories that had poured from his diseased mind over the years: Rose calling from Paris to say she was finally happy, Rose sending letters that the postal service kept losing, Rose planning to return for Christmas fifteen years running. The human mind, she had learned, could create such vivid lies when reality became too painful to bear, could construct entire alternative histories to protect itself from unbearable truth.

Had Rose Sinclair died on those marble stairs decades ago in a moment of rage and desperate struggle? Had she been buried beneath these very roses, her body nourishing their impossible beauty season after season, year after year? Or had she somehow escaped that night as planned, fleeing with Kirk or alone, leaving Garrett to construct an elaborate fantasy to cope with his abandonment?

The questions swirled in Maria's mind like leaves in a whirlwind. If Rose was truly buried here, the secret would remain with her forever, hidden beneath roots and soil and the magnificent blooms that had become her monument. If she had escaped to build a new life somewhere far from this place, she was probably an old woman now, perhaps reading about Garrett's death in some distant newspaper and finally—finally—feeling truly free.

Maria looked once more at the roses, their petals seeming to whisper secrets in a language only the dead could understand. She would never call the police with Garrett's confession. She would never suggest they dig beneath the rose bush. Some mysteries were meant to remain mysteries, some truths too terrible or too beautiful to disturb.

The wind stirred the roses, and for just a moment—just one impossible moment—Maria could have sworn she heard the sound of a woman laughing somewhere in the garden. Laughing with joy, or perhaps with the sweet relief of secrets finally told.

But when she turned to look, there was nothing there but roses blooming in the Georgia sun, keeping their silence as they had for many, many years, as they would for many more, as they would forever.

Garrett's Rose in Paradise. What really happened is now buried forever in the secrets of a lovely garden and the walls of a mansion on a hill, guarded by a beautiful, special, and perfect rose......

The End